The Chorito Hog Leg, Book 1

A Novel of Guam in Time of War

by
Pat Hickey

Bloomington, IN   authorHOUSE®   Milton Keynes, UK

AuthorHouse™
1663 Liberty Drive, Suite 200
Bloomington, IN 47403
www.authorhouse.com
Phone: 1-800-839-8640

AuthorHouse™ UK Ltd.
500 Avebury Boulevard
Central Milton Keynes, MK9 2BE
www.authorhouse.co.uk
Phone: 08001974150

First published by AuthorHouse 4/5/2007

ISBN: 978-1-4343-0202-1 (sc)

Printed in the United States of America
Bloomington, Indiana

This book is printed on acid-free paper.

CONTENTS

Part I

Coconut Grove on Guadalcanal

"The Marines I have seen around the world have the cleanest bodies, the filthiest minds, the highest morale, and the lowest morals of any group of animals I have ever seen. Thank God for the United States Marine Corps!"

-Eleanor Roosevelt, 1945

"There are only two kinds of people that understand Marines: Marines and the enemy. Everyone else has a second-hand opinion."

-Unknown-

Why do people behave in a particular way –in a manner that is unique to them and characterized by some code, life force or prejudice? People a lot smarter than your narrator can delve into the psyche and come up with all kinds of answers as to why a woman never marries and lives a life apart from the members of her family – sisters whom she slept in the very same room with, shared clothes with, sometimes lovers and crushes, jitterbugged to the same music, anguished over lost loves and shattered dreams of becoming a singer in Harry James's Orchestra and marrying John Agar after being received into the Poor Clares and told that though the cloister was solace for the dear girl and all of her religious sisters, that she could better serve God by propagating the faith and giving her self to a man, might never understand her estrangement from them and their brothers or attribute that distance she chose to picking up her older brother from an L station at 63rd & Loomis in late November 1945.

It happened to Joan Cullen. Her brother took an envelope from her that had a Giddings, Texas post mark from a family named Buck - Roper Buck.

That is only an action – an act that is cloaked in meaning for a small number of people but broadens. Joanie Cullen, seventeen in 1945 was as pretty as Audrey Hepburn would be to millions of movie goers in a few years and built the same way. Pious and Pretty – Joanie had not missed a Mass at St. Sabina Catholic Church from the time she was old enough to walk. Her sisters, Maeve, Adele and Frances often went with her, but Joanie went every day. Like the day that she would pick up Tim, who had been in the South Pacific since September 1943, was home; at least he was in Illinois, Joanie had gone to 6 A.M. Mass. PFC. Tim Cullen, USMCR was mustering out at Great Lakes Naval Station in a small town north of Chicago.

Joanie would meet Tim at the 63rd & Loomis Chicago Transit Station which ended the L line on the south side. Together they would walk to a Chicago Motor Coach street car stop on Ashland and take a street car south to the 81st Street stop and walk east to their parent's house at 82nd & Bishop. Tim would tell Joanie all about the war and the places he had been because his letters never said much.

Joanie seemed to change that day. What the hell that surly bastard said to her, or revealed to her, or explained to her about him or the 'precious' letter from Texas no one in the large Cullen family knew.

But this story is really not about Joanie at all. It is about Tim Cullen and a promise that he made to doomed but very much alive twenty four year old Marine 1st Lieutenant at a staging camp on the historical island of Guadalcanal, about a year after that historic and epic battle was fought – and continues to be re-fought by historians, novelists, film-makers (that sounds more high toned than movie –makers), bar-flies and teachers. Tim Cullen's epic battle – the one that really gave shape and dimension to the balance of his life and somehow linked the Battle of Gettysburg, the Little Big Horn, Myles Keogh, Wild Bill Longley, Gen. Buford , the Texas Rangers, capital punishment, abortion, Col. Colt, the New Deal in Texas, War Crimes, the Atomic Bomb and subsequent age, Paul Newman, Johnnie Carson, Race Riots, nightmares, fraternal contempt, Robert McNamara, Fire Bombings and heroic but ignored

Chamorros to the slaughter of his friends and comrades of Company A, Ist Battalion, Third Marines, Third Marine Division at Chorito Cliff/Bundeschu Ridge on the island of Guam in July of 1944.

Tim Cullen, now in his eighties, reads the *Chicago Tribune* at his kitchen table in south suburban Chicago Orland Park and witnesses the fact that he is still alive and the people attached to the names in the obituaries -very familiar to Tim Cullen, especially the ones with an American flag to the left of the name – are not.

Shrinks and behaviorists could have followed Tim Cullen around from the day that he got off the L-Car to meet his little sister Joanie and chalked up his attitude, mannerisms, speech, prejudices, humor, and decisions and rubber –stamped him as an example of survivor's guilt and they would be wrong. They would package everything neatly and clinically and say – 'Aha, this man survived the greatest war in human history and his friends did not and that is why his wife, children, co-workers, employees, doctors, dentists, acquaintances and passersby love , dislike, or intensely dislike Tim Cullen.' Survivor's guilt. Others might say that he is a racist and others that he is a Republican, or both.

But Tim Cullen never hit, slighted, hanged, bull-whipped, Jim Crow Legislated, gerrymandered, cheated, raped, slandered, or maligned any black man living or dead. He laughed out loud over Amos and Andy and the worst name that he ever called a black man was 'a strike-breaker.' In San Francisco, when the Liberty Ship *Adam Clay* brought Tim Cullen home from Guam, Tim took the side of a Montford Point Marine (a black hero) wounded at Okinawa and being bullied by a crowd of white Merchant Marines from another ship on the Pier. Tim did not want to pal up with Cpl. Tedord of Moulton, PA but would not allow any man in forest green take abuse from the bastards who ate steak and let Navy gun crews eat shit in their own galleys, while making about $15 an hour on hazardous duty pay.

Cullen and Tedord's hazardous duty pay amounted to $60 a month. No steaks and no overtime for Snuffies. They did get steaks –steak and eggs – before they landed at Red Beach 2 at Asan, Guam.

Racist? Arguable. Republican? Let's look on the card. Tim Cullen voted for Harry Truman, Adlai Stevenson, John F. Kennedy, Lyndon Johnson, George McGovern, Jimmy Carter, Walter Mondale, Mike Dukakis, Bill Clinton, Al Gore, and John Kerry from the time he left the Marine Corps; that's five wins and six losses but a Republican? No, he is anti-Abortion, Pro-Death Penalty, Pro-Union, and Anti- War – always. He hates anti-war protestors though. He admires pickets but only so long as they keep walking, dress like men, and fight for a living wage – all the rest is Commie Bullshit. He reads the *Chicago Tribune* and detests it as a scab-rag.

Tim Cullen is what smart people would call an un-extraordinary man. He is a successful business man (owns one of the first and largest refrigeration service companies in all Chicago), has three great kids and ten wonderful grandchildren, married a girl out of MGM's greatest dreams and never told anyone other than his sister Joanie – now dead ten years – what had happened to him from 1943 to 1945 and what the letter from Texas is all about.

Everyone else, your narrator included, can only guess what happened, make a play at explaining what happened, piece tiny fragments of the puzzle of history, analyze the man against the sweep and scope and violence of the historical events that embraced Tim Cullen in the greatest drama ever staged by Man, or ignore everything and just play life without another thought to the guy.

Here's my spin it. I'll lay the story out to you and you can accept what comes your way and consider the source. Like I said before, there's much smarter people out there telling you what history and fiction means; so, why not pause for a simple man's consideration of history and the fiction that rises from what we call history. I won't slander and if I bore you, toss the book and go watch Bill Maher.

Where do we get an understanding of history and the place of people we know in that history? I think that it comes from a story told by an uncle after about eight tall cans of Schlitz and a couple of pours of Canadian Club or VO about New Guinea or Bastogne or Inchon or Khe Sahn or Desert Storms I & II, or the Stockyard Strike of 1904, or Cardinal Mundelein's visit to St. Sabina's, or the Democratic Convention, or Super Bowl XV.

I also think that it might come from an artifact – a tooth stored for decades in a plastic capsule, a doll's arm wrapped in tissue paper in your mother's hat-box in a closet that 'you girls were told to never look into', or an X-ray of someone's lungs, the way your mother fell backward into the table full of expensive registered gifts when Mel Torme walked into Kitty's shower and stared right at her.

After all that, we seem to want to frame the talk or artifacts and try to make a nice 'something' out of it. I'll try and make something out this story that starts with a promise between two young men – actually things never start in the middle of things. That is just what we do to save time. I'll pop in and out of what happens in order to try and balance the things that are unfolding – I'll do my best not to be a pest or interfere too much. I can be a huge pain in the ass; bear with me.

Here's my story – history or fiction or fiction with history -scotch and soda. Which is the scotch and which the soda? You tell me. Maybe that is how we determine history.

CHAPTER 1
RAISIN JACK ON GUADALCANAL
APRIL 15, 1944

Tim Cullen lunged at the range stake and fell over, catching himself on one knee after nearly impaling himself on the stake itself. He had put away half a canteen of the raisin jack he'd gotten from the Seabees before the field problem took off over the last hour and the intense heat sapped the balance and the integrity of his movements. He was rip-roaring, shit-in – your – strides drunk.

It was over, well over, 100o in the shade and they were bivouac'd out in the open grass on the ridge-line near Mt. Austin. Sal and Wat Cranthorpe were drunk as well but no where near as drunk as their machine gunner Tim Cullen – on his circular disk 44345089, USMCR. C -O

The Seabees Tim had met on Bougainville back in November had a lister bag full of the potent bootleg hooch. Clyner Dahling of Mantauck South Carolina and Bollie Kant of Ridley, Louisiana and been in the CCC before their enlistment in the Navy and had been making potato jack, raisin jack, apple jack, and bread liquor all through the late 1930's and the South Pacific.

Clyner and Bollie took a liking to the kid recently taken off the line with a bad case of dengue fever and a worse case of dysentery. In fact they made the kid a hammock for which he gave the combat engineers several Jap battle flags with Jap writing all over them and a couple of soft cloth hats that they wore under their helmets . The kid had picked those items up when he had gone back up to the line to collect his 782 gear left behind when he had been ordered to the aid station by Lt. McWatt.

Clyner Dahling and Bollie Kant were Caterpillar operators and could also rig any apparatus imaginable. On Bougainville and before that on New Georgia they had cut airfields and roads out rainforests that had survived millions of years of evolution but not the tenacity or ingenuity of Depression bred American boys who knew how to fight or die.

Clyner met the young Marine, when Cullen was assigned to work details after being pulled off the line by his battalion commander. Cullen had come ashore on Nov. 1st with the first wave at Torokina. Cullen's LCP, the old ramp-less Higgins Boat model, had taken two hits from a Jap anti-boat gun, killing the two Coast Guard Lewis gunners and maiming the two most forward the bow of the landing party. Tim Cullen, a replacement pool shit-bird with no infantry training, had been folded into the Third Marines at Guadalcanal and shipped with the Division on October 14th, 1943.

Tim Cullen was assigned to carry the tripod as part of a seven man HMG squad detached from Weapons Platoon and put in 1st Platoon, A Company. Plt. Sgt. Rittenouer tapped Cullen to be Mike Honnel's asst. gunner in Cpl. Bob Foster's squad. When the 25 mm rounds hit the bow of their Higgins boat, Cullen froze for a second but Foster's shove on his pack signaled the boy's involuntary muscles to horse the tripod and his gear over the gun whale of the LCP.

Cullen belly-flopped into the surf eight feet from shore, but held onto the heavy tripod. Tim had no time to think but only struggle and with help of the powerful left hand of Bob Foster – another old China hand - managed to do what was expected by the Marine Corps Table of Organization –F Series. Foster's veteran hand horsed the prone submerged lamb up out of the surf and shoved the struggling feather-merchant onto the thin sand beach of Bougainville.

Jap fire was intense on this part of the beach and there was scant cover –'hope for the best, but kiss you balls for luck; those rounds ain't personal, Sonny, they can only kill you; move them fuckin' feet; there past them palms; don't look; move; he's fucked – fuck 'im; keep goin; throw down the 'pod – flat –out; find some belts; where's them fuckin' carriers? Dropped 'em! –Here, kid, receiver action is fouled – see if you can unjamb the action; I'm getting that ammo can –Honnel's fucked up bad 'n 'ain movin'none. Spare parts's'n the shoulder bag – here. Must'a took a hit when the Higgins was hit. Kay be back.'

Cpl. Bob Foster went two feet and fell face down with a five inch hole between his shoulders. Tim saw nothing of this but focused on the fouled mechanism of the weapon. Tim concentrated on the job he was given and that was how you conquered fear. He was shit in his pants scared but functioning. The breach block had been hit and a thick brown piece of metal wedged out of the receiver and the bolt coil was shattered.

In all of this Tim Cullen hadn't uttered a sound beyond the involuntary gasps and sobs and grunts incumbent upon being horsed out of the stricken Higgins boat, submerged and horsed back up by the now eternal Foster. While working the bolt housing open, Lt. McWatt shoved Tim's shoulder, 'You grab your rifle and come with me.' All Tim had was a .38 Smith and Wesson in a shoulder holster, but had been in the Corps since last May and responded. Leaving the crippled .30 Cal and the dead Foster on the beach, Tim followed Lt. Marvin McWatt into the green/black of Bougainville. He would stay pretty much there for the next three weeks and contract dengue fever, malaria, and dysentery.

McWatt gave him an old Thompson with a 50 round drum that had belonged to a runner now being evacuated to the *President Hayes.* The lieutenant knew that the kid had no infantry training and had only joined the Company two days before shoving off and was no doubt scared shitless. The Tommy was dependable and could take down whatever you pointed it at. Cullen was doing well. He had the .30 repaired by himself and pretty much man handled all ninety-eight pounds of it through the trail from the beach to its place on the exposed right flank of 1ˢᵗ platoon's line. That was a long day November 1ˢᵗ, 1943. The Company Commander set his own left flank position ten yards from Cullen's range stake and back a good five feet. The entire Able Company area was well positioned to take any threats from the jungle, but no organized assaults took place.

All of the skirmishing took place on the patrols to open the trails, at least for the first two weeks. In that time, Tim Cullen learned to walk noiselessly on the jungle carpet and use movement discipline in all of his time out of the slit trench back at the line. He never fired the .30 but had all of its mechanisms clean and open for business. The Japs were staying put. Rain.

From November 8ᵗʰ on it rained – sheets of rain that filled fighting holes and froze the nuts off of the Snuffies coiled inside them. The ponchos seemed to help fill the holes fast and only made the men colder. Tim and a horse-faced boy from West Virginia who had avoided the coal mines by enlisting in the Marines when he turned sixteen shared the hole on November 15ᵗʰ when Cullen didn't know if he was shitting or pissing or both, and since both boys' teeth chattered over the sound of the splashing sheets of rain, kept a squint-eye on the vegetation for flesh-forms in mustard wrapping like roly-poly dolls at the Carnivals both boys had gone to as Kids. One, in a *post office* designated by map as a community, and the other boy from an Irish village of bungalows and two-flats in the second largest city in America.

They knew kewpie-dolls and they knew that Japs would kill them without thought or compassion and that they would do the same to them -'fuck'em, Tim.' Tim had heard that word when he was growing up, as his father, a County Kerry farmer turned policeman and building janitor used the many confluences of the verb, but he could only remember saying it once before he had joined the Marines and that was in his sophomore year of high school and he had been asked to help

Mr. O'Donnell to convert his coal furnace to an oil –burning one and that was just before Pearl Harbor and Leo won its first City Championship over Tilden. Tim was on the Lights team and played behind Jimmy Arneberg on the Lights. He missed watching Babe Baranowski make Chicago sports history with his low to the ground running style. Babe was so short and would throw down an arm and pivot away from would-be tacklers, and Tim missed Babe's greatest game, because he had been 'contracted' to Edward 'Spike' O'Donnell to do the work with Mutt Torgeson the pipe fitter as his apprentice and go-fer. Tim did all of the pipe threading and cutting because the thirty-eight year old Swede was half- stiff with Aquavit or Glug – he new the play but couldn't execute. Tim was missing the game at Soldier Field that a crowd of more than 100,000 would watch on this late November day – the Catholic Leo Lions 46 and Public School Champs Tilden 14.

What sparked Tim to utter the 'Fuck!' was Mutt's inability to hold the pipe wrench causing Tim to take inches off of his knuckles. 'Cry-baby Irish I do that all day long!' commented the soaked Swede. ' Piss-off, souse!, Tim cut the dangling flesh off with his pocket knife, just as O'Donnell emerged from the back door on the alley side of the basement. 'What's all the hubbub? My wife's had a tough day listening to the clever language from you two. Not in my house you hear that?!!!!!!' Mr. O'Donnell was a wiry 6'4" dapperly dressed man in his late '40's. In 1922, he went to Joliet prison for his part in the bank robbery of the County Federal Savings Bank at 53rd & Ashland. He robbed the bank in 1917, but had stayed out on appeal because 'Spike' O'Donnell was heavier than whale-shit in this City; that is until the Capone mob started taking things way too serious about the cost of beer and Spike took a powder from the rackets.

Spike always got along with Capone but he had the devil's own time with that Polack Saltis and that Fat-Ass Nut-case McErlean. Spike had the dubious distinction of being the first man shot at with a Tommy gun and that was from the hand of Frankie McErlean – out of his mind altogether – killed his girlfriend and her dogs when he had a skin full of booze. McErlean hated O'Donnell with rummy's hate – go figure.

Spike and a copper from Brighton Park were talking on the west side of Western Ave. at 63rd Street – right in front of the drugstore – when a car pulled up and Butter-'N-Egg Faced McErlean gave out with a 'HIYA SPIKE!' and cut loose fifty rounds of .45 caliber slugs. Spike and the policeman had hit the pavement immediately and McErlean couldn't muscle the report of the Thompson and so most of the slugs went up the side of the building. True stuff.

Saltis and McErlean were doing needle beer in joints where Spike had good beer at low prices from his brewery in Joliet. While Spike sat in Joliet Federal Pen for the 1917 heist, Saltis and McErlean were working for Johnny Torrio who took Spike's absence as a green light to filter into O'Donnell territory. Twenty –two months from the start of sentence, Governor Len Small a pal to regular guys like Spike, even if he was a lousy Republican, sprang Spike from 'the Joint.'

Once out of the Joint, Spike learned that slugging a guy to make your point 'even with a black-jack' had gone the way of the 5 cent shave; now, guys were blastin' with heaters and tossing pineapples into an Egg's living room for Chrissakes.

In a few short years, Spike got shot at, indicted, stabbed, shot at, indicted, taken down town, taken for a Patsy, shot at some more, and even attacked when out with the wife and kids. More importantly, Spike buried his brothers Steve, Percy and Walter along side of Pop at Mr. Olivet Cemetery and Tommy the Baby went blind from bad hooch. In 1933, McErlean drank himself into a coffin in Beardstown, IL and got crated back to Chicago and buried in Holy Sepulcher Cemetery were he rots to this day – spiritual concerns notwithstanding.

Spike quit the rackets – the beer rackets – and made peace with the killing mutts and watched them fill holes in the ground with their own skins – Bucher, McErlean, Drucci, McGeoghan,

Saltis, Sheldon, and even Alphonse Capone – now screwy with syph and out of the picture in Florida.

Just a few weeks into the 3rd Marines, Tim Cullen read that Frank Nitti blew out his own brains one step ahead of a federal indictment, but Mr. O'Donnell – 'The O'Donnell' was flush with dough from political fixing for Mayor Ed Kelly and the New Deal –pushing heating oil for homes and giving the coal owners the night jitters all day long, and now while the Cullen kid is overseas, Spike is making Green with the Asphalt.

Tim Cullen now sitting in three feet of water with more pounding down, beside Watson Cranthorpe of West Virginia with his left hand covering the top pommel of the trigger grip and his right forefinger delicately on the trigger of the water-cooled Browning, Tim Cullen's teeth involuntarily chattered and his eyes tried to blink open an awareness of the jungle growth in front of him. Tim Cullen tried to make sense of his willingness to ignore every instinct within him to scream and run home to his mother.

The war with the world had absolutely nothing to do with his sense commitment to what he was trying to do at each moment. Tim felt that brushing the slate clean of everything that had been his life until this very moment was the only thing that would allow him to go home. If he saw an end to things or tried to will himself beyond this moment he would doom himself. His mother had cried loudly when he brought home the papers for his parents to sign and his father still argued that this was Britain's war and no son of his had anyplace in it; Tim's three older brothers Aloysius, Jack, and Martin were drafted in 1941: Al was still at Fort Sheridan, north of Chicago, Jack was on a destroyer/minesweeper in the Aleutians and Martin was in Africa with the Air Corps. Now, Tim had enlisted in the Marines with about twenty other boys from Leo High School hell-bent on avenging the deaths of Joe Auman Class of '40 and Larry Spillan Class of '41 killed on Guadalcanal last year. In fact, they were killed while Leo was winning its second Catholic League Championship and Chicago Title in a row.

'My cat had a pet mouse that kept coming into the kitchen and teasing Cole. Cole'd chase it paw it and let it go and damn if it come back afur more and you know what Tim ? That mouse'd sleep with Cole sometimes. Range card is all smeared we got new one in the parts bag? Anyway one day my brothers came home with a burlap bag of mice that they caught at the cook's tent near the shaft lift – by the mine? You know. 'llSir, Jeff throw open the sack an' all them mice about ten maybe start peelin' through the kitchen an 'Cole up's kills each and everyone of them. You know how cats lay pelts outside the door so's you can tell that they's doin' their job'n'all well, sir, Cole stacked every one of them mice about ten – all but the critter that Cole allowed to use our house. That's how I hope Jesus sees me. Here's the range card we got traverse right 80 'n then Poole's gun got it from there.'

Watson Cranthorpe was the ugliest human being Tim had ever met in his seventeen years on this earth. He had joined the Third after training in Fiji and New Caledonia before they formed up on Guadalcanal. Watson had been an ammunition carrier and Tim chose him to be assistant gunner. When Mike Honnel got clobbered coming ashore, Lt. McWatt made Tim Cullen the squad gunner under Cpl. Pat Holden who was taken from 2nd Platoon after Bob Foster was killed. It was Tim's God given aptitude with parts and gears that elevated him to the august position. Tim's two hands tremored on the gun grip and he shook uncontrollably. Watson reached over his dripping hand and felt Tim's head – he was burning up with fever.

'You a gotta bug boy – here better let me behind the .30'n keep watch.' Watson Cranthorpe moved like an eel in that slimy hole of mud and deepening water and soundlessly replaced the gunner and as quietly moved Tim further to the feeder position. Dengue Fever is what Tim had and good too. Nothing moved out front. It was still hours to darkness.

While turning the pages of his *Chicago Tribune* sixty years from then, Tim Cullen shivered because the rain greening his sodded lawn had awakened his afternoon on Bougainville with the ugliest and most thoughtful, and graceful man Tim would ever meet.

Reeling from the fever brought on by the raisin jack Tim Cullen had gotten from the Seabees he had met on Bougainville, the floor of the ridge-line near Mount Austin on Guadalcanal snapped up and met Tim Cullen's face. In falling forward, he had knocked the gun from its footing and spilled the cloth belt of 250 .30 caliber rounds to amusement of Sal and Watson and the quizzical attention of their new Platoon Commander, 1st Lieutenant John A. Buck – Notre Dame '4o and Northwestern Law School.

'Sgt. Rittenouer? Please, Sarn't take a look at Cullen and his crew? I'd say that boy's drunk, if I didn't know better. Try not to make a big ass deal of it?'

Lieutenant Jack Buck had a pleasing manner of asking a question and giving a command at the same time. It might have been a trick learned from his law classes at Northwestern, but more than likely it was quirk of character learned and practiced by past masters of the art – His father and his grandfather. The Buck's had all been Texas Rangers in the Austin/Giddings area going back to the War of Independence in 1837.

'Sarn't, get the three of them off and away from the field problem if they are in fact drunk? Have 'em load the gun on the cart and wheel their asses and that weapon back to camp and service the weapon without making their state known to the other men? And for God's sake, Karl, get them to avoid anyone on the trail back?'

'Aye, Aye, Sir!' quietly and without saluting Karl Rittenouer knelt down next to Cullen who was as fucked-up drunk as any man he had ever seen. As quietly and as soberingly threatening as he could he ordered Tim to square himself away secure the weapon on the pull cart load all of the ammunition cans onto the weapons cart and remove themselves from the field of men - and to do so without giving any further attention to themselves. 'You boys are well and truly fucked; I shit you not! Get!'

As loud as he could without doing a John Barrymore, Karl Rittenouer informed his commander, 'Lt., Sir, we got to send the heavy back and get it replaced. I told Cullen, Battaglia, and Cranthorpe to take carts and weapon back for service and folded the ammo carriers into Poole's squad. With Your permission, Sir'

Lt. Buck tried to look as interested as a man could be about a glitch in his table of organization and very understandingly replied, 'That is fine idea Sarn't. Let's get this Platoon up to that tree line and we'll loosen leggings for the day.'

'Aye, aye, sir!'

Cullen's surly smile faded as he knew that a young first lieutenant was not so much concerned with imposing his authority over the assholes commanded as he was with preserving the integrity of his platoon as an effect unit. This new platoon commander was a good man and Tim's sky-larking drunk could well put the man in the jack-pot with Captain Bundeschu. Cullen was shamed. Shamed, fucked up drunk, on verge of shitting himself, drenched in sweat, and now facing another court-martial and all since joining the United States Marines a little less than a year ago.

There were easier things to do than pull ammunition and weapons carts down a steep slope of tall grass exerting all of your strength to keep the carts from controlling that descent, but rip-roaring drunk as the three teenagers from West Virginia, Ohio, and Illinois were on Mount Austin in the Solomon Islands in 100 + degree heat was a journey for he-man. The three boys evading the slippery slope between childhood and manhood by warfare and focus to duty lost control of the ammunition cart once out of sight of their sober comrades thousands of yards up the mountain ridge. Sal was walking point and trying to will the raisin jack out through his pores.

Sal Battaglia never finished high school but worked in a Desoto plant in Elyria, Ohio when his father died in his sophomore year.

Sal was six foot, two inches tall and weighed 210 pounds – all defined and rock hard muscle. He could sing like Dick Haymes and made extra money for his mother and five sisters - money with the Chambers Motier Orchestra and played in the dance halls and union halls around Cleveland. He had trouble concentrating on the lyrics of many of the ballads and often flubbed the lines but made up for it with a self-effacing charm and menacing eyes that focused on the most simpering pup near the stage, 'Katie Went to Haiti' was a favorite of the girls from the Republic Tire Works in Elyria, especially almond eyed Katie Sobel the daughter of a Cantor. Sal took Katie out for Green Rivers and ice cream a few times after a show. The little Jewish girl was as Hep as any bobby-soxer on rampage and had it bad for the big handsome Guinea.

Sal took gentle liberties with Katie and never allowed his mythological strength and powerful allure to go where it was uninvited. That made the Cantor's daughter more than willing to press on her desire to complete her infatuation. 'Nix sister, your old man'd have the Hebe tough guys work me over.' Sal was hopelessly in love with the little Jewish bobby-soxer knock-out. The big Ginzo was a virgin.

Now on point with an M1 at the ready and his feet fighting the swirling alcohol in combat with his blood Sal Battaglia was Jap squinting. 'Micks always got guys jammed up. 'Hey, let's belt some down.' Great idea. Like, it's not hot enough already?'

Since coming to the Canal with the replacement pool from Efate, Sal had twice fired his weapon on Japs in the weeds – starving skeletons abandoned or shipwrecked on an island now festering with green and olive-drab killers intent on making the national vengeance their immediate task- to no mortal effect.

He was relieved – poor bastard. 'It's Tooooooooo darn Hot, It's TOOOOOOOOO darn hot. . .' No skylarking snap to.

Cranthorpe and the tough little Mick hoodlum were motherfucking each other in their struggles with the carts. Watson had ass ended Tim's weapon cart about every eight feet. Two little skinny guys - a stocky red-head with freckles and a human scarecrow with something like black hair and an endless wheeze to his Hollar Howl. Funny to listen to them. Tim, as smart as they come, and Wat, dumb as pig-shit, made the best team. Cullen didn't have book smarts though he went to a good school in Chicago – Fuckin'Noter Daym' to hear him tell it –but he had real brains and balls to match. Sal was the only one of the three of them not to see combat and Wat and Tim never mentioned it. Good guys.

The real Marines, guys who had sea school and the old campaign hats, really admired the way Cullen and Cranthorpe handled themselves on Bougainville. 'Lash fast to these shit-birds, Boots. This little brig rat and the hillbilly is cool under fire.' That was high praise. Sal had come to the Canal with the replacement pool that included Lieutenant Buck. Sal, Tim and Wat all liked the way the young officer carried himself. He was real Wild West with the Colt .45 Hog-Leg in the shoulder holster – it was his personal side arm and Lt. Buck never made a big show of it. He was easy in manner but very direct.

Their first night ashore and right after Buck spoke to the platoon seven twin engine Betty's broke through and bombed their camp. Most of the bombs fell in the grove and killed some trees and a late diving man cut his head getting into a skit trench, Through the raid, Lt. Buck calmly walked through the area until all of his men were in a secure cover and only then walked into his slit trench like he was easing into the shallow end of a pool.

Sal felt much of the fear evaporate after that raid. He felt that with Buck out front for his boys that maybe they would get through this war with all their skins on – he thought differently

– he knew better. This powder and steel had too much to say about what these teenagers wanted to do with their lives. " Just one look and then I knew/that all I longed for long ago was you/ . . . Jo Stafford homely with a honey voice 'Chills run up and down my spine/Aladdin's lamp was mine . . .' Tim's voice,' Get that out, Wat . Sal! A truck! Flag the Fuckers, SAL! Back to Grove like men! Army! Hey, Army Air Corps we got damaged weapons.'

The 2 ½ ton GM Truck hit the breaks and the three heroes loaded carts, weapons 482 gear and sorry assed hung over skins in the deuce and half. Love the flyboys!

On Mount Austin, Jack Buck put the three drunks out of his mind and conducted the field problem as if his center heavy gun had been eliminated in the engagement and sent two BAR teams to each flank and set up his two light .30s as the center of lines fire-power. The squads moved toward their objective using the enveloping fire of the light .30s and BAR teams taking advantage of defilade where available and sending the assault teams in a coordinated move on the ridge line.

Each of Able Company's three platoons took a level of the ridges assigned to them and linked up with an approving nod from Company Skipper Captain Geary Bundeschu. After a forty minute, ass-in-the-grass the platoons reformed a line of march for the five miles back to 3rd Division camp in the Lever Brothers Palm Grove. A light rain misted the sweating Marines, as they refitted their light marching packs and hit the trails back to their camps. They'd have company grab-ass and sack drill tomorrow after Company inspections and all officers would meet for a de-briefing and assessment.

Jack Buck was proud of his work today and the exercise of good judgment in not allowing the three stooges to impact on the unit's integrity. They 'may' be the first men killed in the impending action and he believed that his working of the problem had not gone unnoticed by Sgt. Rittenouer. He allowed himself the luxury of five minutes on his back before hitting the line of march.

Let's move away from this drama and clean up the 'clever' language, as Spike O'Donnell might say. To the more refined people enduring their second year of occupation – the heroic and largely ignored people of Guam the Chamorros.

CHAPTER 2
NOW SHOWING AT THE CORAL – APRIL 1944: ON JAPANESE OCCUPIED GUAM:

Betty Cruz's eyes were as dark and deep as her teenager's soul stuck, now, between sky and sand, soon to be sixteen, as she re-scanned the magazine. She shifted her weight to her right foot as she thumbed through a well thumbed and dog-eared three year old *Hollywood Star* that featured Marion Davis on the cover - she was old. Her newly emerged breasts were thick and rounded in the softness that exits a happy boy's anticipated invitation to nuzzle and caress them/ Betty liked them too and knew that they meant more than feeding greedy fat babies before falling away like old and empty wine-skins at thirty.

Betty had thick lustrous waves of ebony hair that fell in pouty defiance of her Father, when she was at home, and tightly bun-ed in defiance to twenty-six Jap sailors occupying the seats in her Poppi's Movie House - once the Coral Majestic and Now called *His Majesty's Smile* - no matter, the title was in Japanese on the Marquee and the People of Guam still referred to it as *The Coral*. No Chamorro asked for the sweet rice snack-cakes, but for the tiny bags of popcorn – its supply now almost depleted, after two years of Occupation. Small defiance is defiance and still rebellion and Betty was in rebellion – lovingly to her father's clucking and fearfully against the leers of the Imperial Naval Landing Force Team under Boson Otayama.

Mr. Cruz protected his beautiful daughter more than his depleted horde of American popcorn -stored in lined metal tanks - buried in the North of the island.

Betty was much more precious than two year old American maize - she was fruity and womanly at fifteen. The American Governor and his wife (now starving behind barbed wire and slaving their days away in Japan), Dr. Tanaka and his lovely red-headed American wife had all predicted that Betty would grow as the incarnation of Loretta Young in Chamorro subtitles.

Their joke was wasted because Betty was barely able to converse with villagers in Chamorro, once outside of Agana and should any pup-like little Chamorro like Bull-necked and toothy Hector Torres shyly make his way to Betty she would cast him into a corner of embarrassment with a haughty toss of her magically black hair - that seemed like the coal stored at Sumay when the sun hit it right and the purple of the Bay helped blend with its luster.

Poor Hector - Poor Mr. Cruz! He had ordered Betty to never leave their home down the street from the Coral without painfully twisting her hair into a bun the size of a fist and wearing loose fitting darker cottons as her skinny frame at 5'6 had evolved into a tight, firm and muscular vision of woman.

Betty at fifteen was stunning with fine large long lashed eyes that tried to hide the deep and intensely felt ripeness emerging in an intellect that understood the power in her body in constant combat with a spiritual devotion and moral goodness as fierce in its dominion over instinct as the desire in its own frustration to fulfill. Like her landscape Betty was at war and commands came from her soul as well as from the fear erupting from her Poppi's knowledge of the combat to come.

Mr. Cruz knew that Betty could withstand the shocks of handsome young Hector but the force behind the oafish Boson Otayama engendered greater defensive measures.

'Do *not*, young lady, lean on the candy counter when the Japs are in the theatre and do *not* speak when not answering their direct questions or commands. Otayama and his bastards will and can do as they please with us – All of Us. They are not the Americans and they answer to only their officers. Get more juice in the cooler and keep the counter clean. Betty! Keep that magazine hidden and at Home . . .No do as I say . . . Please!'

The poor girl understood only the fear *in* her father but not what that fear really meant. Father Duenas had explained sexual yearnings to the boys and girls in a frank and very open way that did not embarrass the already bewildered children. The changes in their bodies were frightening and also exciting and gave them some understanding of the intimate times their mothers and fathers shared alone and away from them. He equated those changes to the natural currents that changed the coral around Guam. He also developed a historical context for puberty.

The very old laughed at their parents who had become more Spanish than they had been. More devoted to Our Lady and the saints than to the coral and caribou had been to their lives.

Each wave brought new dimension to life around Guam as they learned from diving and swimming the reef that protected them. So too had the waves of time made the people more aware of the forces that mastered how they would live their lives - the Spanish, the Americans, and Now the Japanese.

Father Duenas explained the forces of change and the violence that made life terrible and beautiful -bloody and soothing. The boy would gently attack the soft and sensitive bodies until the love grown from trust and respect would grab hold and invite the forces of change within.

The sensitive priest was as handsome as any movie star and young enough to excite the passions of Betty and her friends. He was athletic and more given to wearing white, yellow, and pink polo shirts with his clerical black trousers than his white or black cassock.

He was tall and dark with thick wavy hair and had tight trim swimmers body that, out of the water, made him more impressive astride the back of the giant white stallion that the priest rode from church to church and village to village.

Father Jesus Duenas impressed people with God's power miles before he arrived to bless the *taro*, melons, roots, cane and fruits grown in the gardens of the far villagers and the cutters of sugar cane deep in the island of Guam.

Her father's theatre was stucco painted white with a curved glass ticket booth imposing itself out toward the street inviting Agana's citizens, occupiers, and all and sundry into its cool cavern. Since 1926, Cruz's family has owned and operated Guam's only movie theatre and largest auditorium. It was here that Gen. Takashima announced to the leading citizens his plans for the expected assault by the Americans. His plans would demand that the citizens of Agana continue to live in this Guam's largest city and force the American's to bomb their real enemies the free People of the Great Pacific Co-Prosperity Sphere. The people of Agana must stay in Agana, along with the Japanese civilian colonizers, the Saipanese, the Korean laborers, the Filipino opportunists and the heroic men of Imperial Japanese Army and Navy.

IJN troops *Kebeitai* under Boson Otayama would ensure businesses against looters and traitors. War criminals, like Tweed, would be caught and beheaded like the seven Navy cowards before him. Any Chamorro aiding the coward Rm 1sr Class George Tweed will be beheaded summarily. George Tweed was in the North and would soon be moving to the Asan area. He was living these last two years on the *lanchos and occasionally in caves.* He had Chamorro girls brought to him on more than one occasion and never really seemed too concerned about the people who were hiding them, but was just Mr. Cruz's opinion. Cruz felt that Tweed, unlike the five other sailors who were beheaded in last few months, did not give the War a second thought. He was Robinson Crusoe on holiday.

Classes will continue at the high school and the grammar schools under the direction of *Sensei's* and their Chamorro helpers.

Betty was in her third year at the high school and Mrs. Johnson for home economics. Mrs. Johnson's husband and sons had been shipped to Kobe, Japan long with the Spanish born Prelate of Guam, making Father Duenas the senior prelate for the whole island. Two Japanese priests had come to assist at St. Joseph's Church, but Fr. Duenas had no respect for them as priests and they proved themselves no more than stooges for the Jap military.

Betty and her friends went out to the villages and *lancheros* where Fr. Duenas would be for their instructions in the Holy Faith and in resisting the Japs. 'Never show any disrespect for them or their authority, *Ninas*, the Americans will be here in a short time. The war is turning against Japan and the suffering our people have endured is not unknown to Our Holy Mother and Jesus Her Son. You have a great responsibility, each of you, to obey these people and remember the Japanese people who are our *familia* , Dr. Tanaka and the good woman who runs the fabric store in Agana, Mrs. Iichii have helped to save many lives and the fortunes of our neighbors , like Don Romero.

29

Betty took Father aside after her catechism lesson and walked with the tall handsome Jesuit to his white horse. 'Otayama is taking money from my Popi every week to keep his sailors from bothering me, Father. I am afraid that when Adm. Halsey comes to save us that they might kill him. Momi has told me about rape and what I must do to 'clear my mind' and pray to Our Lady and allow things to pass; they are hideous boys, the Japs. I hate them so! How could they find pleasure in that?'

'It is not pleasure, Betty and it has nothing to do with passion which is God's gift to man and woman. The power of that passion brings the man and woman together in fulfillment of God's will. The pleasure that is revealing itself to you and Tonna, Jorge, Calvin, and Rita at your age is different but equally as blessed and good and holy sanctified in the bond of Holy Matrimony. Your Holy Mother, like your poor priest here sacrificed the fulfillment of those pleasures as part of God's great plan for us. And, *Nina*, there is pain great and terrible pain and suffering, as you have seen and heard when women give birth, but that suffering is eased by the joy of fulfillment in the birth of the baby – do you see?

Otayama's dogs just might kill your Poppi; that is not for us to say; they may well take their will on you – yes sexual assault – but in those horrible deeds there is no fulfillment. There is no end but only the act. The outcome will be vain. It will have no triumph. If that, and I pray with all my might that God watches all of you innocents, does happen Betty; find the strength to know that what is happening to you will end and that God will give you the joy of love and fulfillment. Faith is not to understand but accept and that is what we struggle with on this earth each day. Betty, I have chosen to be like Our Lady unfulfilled by the pleasures of the flesh with which I am blessed – Lord I am Too Blessed – and understand that my faith will have its end in Christ. I see that I have explained nothing. That too, child is knowledge in itself. Adios, I hope Pato has some good *lumpia* for this poor priest – He had no peppers in it last time.'

He was the most beautiful and sexy man alive. He looked like Robert Stack with horn-rimmed glass. Robert Stack was a polo player. They had a good story with lots of picture of Stack playing polo with Spencer Tracy. Tracy was ugly like that Irish Marine the Japs bayoneted because he had red hair. That man was so tough and brave, like Jimmy Cagney in *Roaring Twenties* and now all we get are those Jap movies that no one understands or likes – stupid musicals. Betty walked north - home to Agana.

Dr. Tetsuya Tanaka went to Gonzaga University in Washington State where his Dad had been a major shrimper; cannery owner; real estate genius; movie house chain operator in Spokane, St. Pierre and Sitka, Alaskan Territory. In 1926, Tanaka's father sent his son Tetsuya (Ted) a thoroughgoing Bing Crosby-like Joe College American. Ted Tanaka played on the Gonzaga Lightweight Basketball Team; President of the Knights of Blessed Sacrament, President of the Dance Committee; and the owner of the only Stutz Bearcat on campus.

After Gonzaga undergraduate, Ted entered the university's dental school – *Summa Cum Laude et Ad Majoram Dei Gloriam!* Ted was on fire. He pal-ed around with *Der Bingle*, smoked reefer with Cab Calloway, produced (ponied up dough) two records sung by the *Spokane Bearcats* actually opened for Bing and Bob Crosby in 1936.

The dentist with the most – Ted Tanaka was in Spokane's spotlight until he married the Redheaded Beauty who appeared in three shorts with Robert Benchley and one feature film with George Brent: Kara 'Cookie' Vanecko. Kara had gone from doing radio dramas on CBS affiliates in California and Washington to catching the break to Hollywood. Cookie was trained in ballet, but inclined toward burlesque with a wonderful and open personality, salted with a ribald sense of humor. She and Ted Tanaka began dating and then announced their wedding engagement – great ring and no rice.

The problem was that the two American kids were madly in love. They cracked each other up; trusted one another; devoted most of their thoughts to one another and were drawn to each other with a powerful sexual chemistry that seemed to ward off any other suitors. Cookie's Mom and Dad had died years ago in Minot, ND, but *Pater Familias* Tanaka, while a thoroughly American businessman, hated Occidentals with a cordial hatred – that included red-headed females and 'flesh-of-his-flesh who would lie with them.' Not only the Tanaka's but people who would hire Cookie or use Ted's money.

Immediately, Ted Tanaka was dropped from his Alumni duties, phone calls hung out in the ozone, and *Der Bingle's* people learned 'Ted Who?' Bing and Bob, both really great guys, were always just out of touch and well-out of range.

Ted's decision to marry for love did not put him in solid with the Family Tanaka either; in fact, his little brother Sonny became the heir to the canning, the real estate, and the movie houses: all but one in Agana, Guam. The owner of the movie house was Juan Cruz and the Tanaka's got 5% of all profits.

Ted and Kara took the Pan Am Honeymoon to the Orient – 1st stop Wake Island and then (last stop for the Tanakas anyway) Sumay, Guam. Chamorros had bum teeth too. In 1937, Dr. Tetsuya (Ted) Tanaka and his bride Mrs. Kara Vanecko-Tanaka took up residence as two of Agana's leading citizens. Seven year old Betty Cruz fell madly in love with Ted and worshiped at the altar of the red-headed beauty that at 5'7" towered over her molar-busting hubby's 5'5" especially when Red Kara wore the 3" man-killers. She had legs up to the clouds and every 'deck-ape and jar-head' garrisoned at Guam under the command of Lt.Commander McMillan drooled and ghouled over the knock-out who had been Hollywood. Every sheik in Khaki, pith helmet and leggings got a warm smile and a genuine conversation from this olive skinned red-head with legs to the clouds and a salty sense of humor that worked better than a Kitty-Nut-Cutter on the boys. They genuinely loved the Jap Jaw-breakers 'widow' – as the wishful thinkers referred to Kara Tanaka. She was 'the goods' and that was better than a Direct Order from the Old Man

Kara wore polka-dot cotton and broad-I mean Broad-brimmed –straw hat that waved and dipped fore and aft. She wore white pumps and pearls –neck and wrists and carried a white straw bag with a 12" white-leather handle when her playmate of seven years approached from the south. Kara had been allowed to stay in Agana, because her husband was one tough monkey and took no orders from Tokyo. Mrs. Anderson's sons(Chamorro boys) and her husband Bill and ex-Marine who came back to Guam in 1911 to marry his 'dear old gal' as he called the heroic woman in each letter to her, were sent to a civilian POW Camp in Kobe. Dr. Tanaka laid things out nicely to the Japanese Army Intelligence Officers – his wife stays with him or they could cut his head off right here and now. It was no bluff. Ted was one hard-boiled egg and the Siesii could like it or lump it. He would agree to ease transition and smooth operation of the schools and make the Japanese civilians and Saipanese welcome, but his wife stays put – 'Got it?' Got it. Kara Tanaka was off-limits to the sailors and soldiers occupying Guam and not one of them got so much as a nod from the courageous red-head. But she would cuddle close and publicly smooch the man who took her to bed each night and that really got the little toadstools as straight as Errol Flynn's pecker.

Kara was more concerned for the safety of her little pet Betty. Betty worshipped the ground that Kara walked on; she had been on the screen in her Poppi's theatre and the Cruz's had hidden the cans of Kara's shorts with Robert Benchley. All other Yankee movies got confiscated by the IJN the day after they took Guam.

Betty had gone to Tai for catechism and pep talks with Father Duenas. Kara loved the handsome and athletic priest – he could have been in the movies himself – but more so Kara felt that he was a saintly presence and that comforted her as much as the wonderful man she married.

'Hi Sweetie, get you holy card from Padre?' Kara was amused by the look of disappointment and guilelessness in this beautiful girl.

'No, we're too old now . . . Oh you're teasing me now. Thanks a bunch. Hey do you have the 1940 *Photoplay* with Robert Stack playing polo with Spencer Tracey? I think Father looks like Bob Stack; did you ever meet him, Mrs. Ted? He's dreamy – Bob not Father." If Betty could blush she did.

'Hey I think Father is dreamy too –it's OK I'm married I'm not going to cut-in on the Mother of God, Baby. Hey, Otis was palming your Dad again so stay with me until he oozes back to Piti Navy Yards. I hate that pig. He glares at Ted like he'd like to murder him and then comes kissing butt like the eel he is. The only honorable one is the new Navy Commander – I don't know his name but he is supposed to have dinner with all of us in July. Like it's some kind of national holiday."

"I've seen the man at the Mayor's Office and then he goes to the concrete pours up on Fonte ,' Betty chimed in, 'I hope that he keeps a leash on Otayama – I hate him. He always tries to finger my hair, but I pull back whenever it looks like he's gonna get fresh. He's the one who stabbed that red-headed Marine in the Plaza.

'That was Johnny McKenna – he was from Kankakee, IL. , I liked that boy. We used to kid that we used the same hair-dye. The Japanese believe that red-hair is a sign of bad-luck and trouble to come. The poor kid was so brave. Commander McMillan – God I Miss Karen! - told them that that would be remembered and they all laughed. Maybe my red-hair will bring them a little bad luck too. Don't forget, honey that so not all of them are like Otayama and maybe this new officer will tie the can to the creeps. We'll see. Let's get some juice – I'm parched,' Kara sang and waved away the 'miseries' like Scarlet O'Hara.

The two movie stars went into the theatre for a cool juice. Juan Cruz was waiting. 'The Beauty Queens of the Boulevard!' Betty get to the juice machine and make sure you have enough for night's movie. Expect about two hundred and get enough paper cups from stock. We're having the pilots from the field and the seaplane base to see another musical tonight. Your mother has a pot of the rice for you and your brother to start cooling and adding the syrup. Mrs. Tanaka you vision of loveliness, tell your land-lord –robber-baron hubby to expect more candidates for his torture chair – his kinsmen from *Dai Nippon* – *we have been over loading the rice cakes with sugar.* He can now be a war-profiteer as well as exploiter of poor honest working men. '

'Henry Fonda really did you in, Juan. Next you'll be making speeches 'wherever there's a movie-house louse salting the popcorn and jacking up the price of the fruit-juice – I'll be there; wherever there's a cockroach covered in carob and sold as an Almond Joy; I'll be there .. quit eyeing the talent, old man, and give us two working girls a tall one' , Kara left her white rimmed shades on in the dark theatre lobby on for full comic effect and did her best Garbo,

'I'm tired of men and their fawning attempts to please me – let me be alone.' Where's your wife, Tubby, you are throwing on the lard there Jackie-boy, me and the girls got dirt to dish now VaMOOSE!'

Juan Cruz never tired of the gorgeous and spirited girl who married his partner and friend Ted Tanaka. God blessed him the day the Pan AM Clipper brought the exiled couple to Guam. He filled tall chilled glasses with crushed ice and juice – pineapple. "Drink up, Ladies! And then you Miss Betty 86 the *pineapple juice* and give our guests tonight the papaya. Bolaguera delivered the syrup and it's out on the dock now. I'm shuffling off, Mrs. Tanaka – shuffling to get my better half.'

Juan Cruz was in this mid-40s and still had the body of the surf-swimmer and diver that he was when he courted Imelda. He listened to Americans and understood the opportunities that this beautiful island offered to a smart and aggressive young man. In 1926, Juan borrowed $ 300 dollars from *Don* Romero and contacted the Tanaka Canning Company of Spokane, WA for start-up funds in exchange for Cruz's business plan and prospectus that looked into the future of America's Imperialist Plans for the Pacific. Reading *The World's Work* and *National Geographic* that he found in the Carnegie Library in Agana, Juan Cruz followed the development of seaplanes and their impact on trade. Juan Cruz understood that more shipping and more trade would come through Guam and sailors and traders wanted entertainment and that entertainment was best and morally presented on a blank screen.

By 1927, *The Coral*, with capacity seating for 300 people - in electrically fanned comfort , enjoyed the latest (reasonably the latest) silver screen entertainment and helped keep marines and sailors sober for a few hours during their liberty. Along with the well manicured lawns, clean streets, prosperous 'main street' businesses moderate automobile and truck traffic, Agana was an American paradise known only to the very few who passed through this beautiful city on the way to Manila, Shanghai, Saigon, and Tokyo on Asian business. Movie stars rarely made a longer stay than was possible for the Pan Am Clipper to re-fuel and re-stock for its next leg on the Asian route. Ships and their crews were confined to Sumay and its low-life as Insular Police, Guam Militia, Naval and Marine Corps Shore Patrol maintained Agana's propriety and dignity.

The Tanaka Canning Company received its 5% of the operation every quarter without fail and through the economic Depression of the 1930's Juan Cruz was so successful that he not only repaid the $ 300 to *Don* Romero but made a no interest loan to the *Don* in 1936 to leverage his failing cane and fruit & nuts revenue: *Respetu- the reverence given to those who have done much for – the old ways. Ways before the Basilica Dulce Maria was built and before the Spanish. We knew! Our conquerors never really asked us. The way of the Chamorro.*

The boy who swam in the surf at Asan and collected coral samples for British, Japanese, German, and American scientists; caught crab and lobsters for officers mess; soaked Brasso in buckles for lazy Jar-heads; and courted the lovely Imelda, life on Guam was great.

Until the Japs came on December 8th, that morning Commander McMillan had tried to get some kind of defense on the island but it was more so to prevent any panic than really try to show teeth. His one hundred and forty eight marines had twelve heavy machine guns and no anti-aircraft .50 caliber weapons. His navy consisted of a few yard craft and an old gunboat from the Spanish American War that had been Spain's to begin with. The Japanese planes from Saipan bombed and strafed the Pan American building the beautiful Marine barracks and the Piti Navy Yards in a matter of minutes.

Chapter 3
Third Marine Division Camp
– Coconut Grove, Guadalcanal

Ist Platoon of Able Company met the trucks at the rendezvous point and like the three drunks who, hours before had returned to Third Marine Division tent city in the Coconut Grove of the old Lever Brothers plantation in a 2 1/2 Ton Truck, rode the bumpy trails after fourteen arduous hours of hiking in field packs and running up to the top of the designated ridge lines and simulated firing on enemy positions in greater comfort than they had begun the day.

Jack Buck rode in the back of the third truck with his communicators and Sgt. Rittenouer. Neither man spoke of the three machine gunners, nor of their sham condition getting the .30 caliber machine repaired. Buck knew that they had gotten into some home made alcohol and only assumed that the three Cullen, Battaglia and Cranthorpe had filled one of their two assigned canteens with raisin jack.

The trucks splashed into the company area of the grove camp and the marines dismounted and set to their individual tasks of cleaning weapons and securing webbing gear, prior to a general inspection. Lt. Buck gave the men until reveille for those tasks to get the work done, which would give them. Khakis and fore and aft covers for inspection, Sgt. Rittenouer, at 0700.

'Aye, Aye, Sir. I'll have the three report to your tent immediately, sir,' snapped the efficient career Marine.

'No, Please, Sergeant Rittenouer. I am going over to Weapons and talk to the three men myself and assess their conditions. The men did a fine job on the ridge lines today and performed well. I will tell them so at inspection, but please let each of squad leaders get the word back to the men. I am going to check on damaged heavy machine gun team.' Lt. Buck slowly clenched and unclenched both fists to fight off his fatigue as well as his anger and saw the three teenagers busily plotting out their work area at a long table under the palms. Jack drew a deep breath and slowly drew himself to command height and moved toward the drunks.

All three noticed the tall officer moving slowly toward them and they busily steeped coils, bolts, rods, breach locks in oil and brushed fouled works with the efficiency of terrified souses. Watson dropped the firing pin three or four times before Jack Buck reached them.

'Weapon under task, Marines? That's fine.' All three boys bolted to attention. 'At ease, but please keep working? Damn shame, it fouling as it did now what exactly was the foul-up on the weapon Private Cullen?

'Traversing mechanish jammed up bad, Sir,' slurred Tim Cullen, who had sweated most of the Jack horsing the weapon cart and stumbling down the ridges from Mt. Austin. Nevertheless the potent potable clung to his inner organs with enough vitality to keep the boy drunk for the waning hours of the day.

Lt. Buck ordered, 'Private Cullen, Sgt. Rittenouer will pick you up and bring you to my tent in thirty minutes – clean utilities and fore and aft. Finish fixing the traversing 'mechanish,

Private?' Buck pivoted around and slowly walked back to his tent.

Tim Cullen showered himself rather than the standard whore's bath and shaved this red stubble clean. He had well-pressed herring-bone twill dungarees and a clean khaki fore and aft piss-cutter. He buffed his boondockers and tightly laced up his leggings for his expected 'stand-tall' before Lt. Buck. Karl Rittenouer popped into the tent and told Cullen, 'Expect the syph and laugh when it's Clap! You are lucky the Old Man or the First Shirt didn't see you three shits. Bundeschu is a by the book San Francisco man – Mare's Island Marine. Maj. Opley would have shot you out of hand. You look good. Take your dose. Get!'

Together the two veterans of Bougainville walked down the immaculately policed company street that needed to be swept clear of rain-water every four hours or so. Guadalcanal it seemed was always under water – or at least the water was high enough to keep everyone miserable. Guadalcanal was paradise compared to Bougainville. All around the sergeant and the cleaned-up drunk, Marines were engaged in some form of clean-up, toweling off, wiping down rifle parts, scrubbing dungarees, pressing khakis, soaping webbing gear, mending netting, policing the grounds, emptying lister bags. In the Marine Corps, it was assholes and elbows from reveille to lights-out.

Sgt. Rittenouer called, 'Permission to enter.' Buck replied, 'Enter.' 'Private Cullen reporting as ordered, Sir!'

'Stand at Attention, Cullen, at ease Sarn't. Sarn't take your ease and try some candy from my Momma, please? Private, your weapon was not fouled, but you, and your crew, were drunk on duty in a forward area and on a field problem for up-coming Campaign in the Marianas. I sent you three back with the weapon so as not to break-down the integrity of my command. Where did you get the alcohol?'

'Sir, respectfully, I supplied the drink.' Buck feigned irritation, 'I am aware of that, Private, where did you obtain the liquor?'

'I had it, Sir and I did not share it with Privates Battaglia or Cranthorpe.'

'If you told that to a deaf mule, he would kick you to death Private. You and your crew were drunk. I see that you wish to stand for their charges?'

'Aye, Aye, Sir!'

'Very well, Private. You will assist Gunny Higgins over the next two weeks, when not performing your duties with the Platoon. You are going to Tulagi on Ammo runs and you will fit .30 magazines and belts. Sgt. Rittenouer tells me that a Marine has much to learn from Gunny Higgins and Cullen as my co-religionist you should have much to fear. It seems that Gunny Higgins and Holy Mother Church are at polar opposites and that the only two things lower in his order of esteem are brig rat Irishmen and Officers. Sarn't any thing to add?'

'No sir, I think that you have about covered the issue and that Gunny Higgins will make the finer points clear to Private Cullen. Sir, your Permission to retire?'

'Permission granted. How's that candy, Sarn't? Good caramel as you'll find in Giddings or Austin. Momma makes it for all the kids in the hospital each week. Helps with Daddy's electioneering and New Dealing. I am long on the sweet tooth and prefer good candy to hard liquor. Thank you Sarn't?'

With that the stocky red-fleshed and blond haired Platoon Sergeant put on his polished helmet liner and walked out of the tent's hatch and onto the company street. Marines still bustled with hygienic tasks with a limit of verbal banter on the outside.

Lt. Buck assessed the pressed squared away man before him still at needle-like attention. Chin-in, chest out, thumbs at the seams eyeballs locked. This was a combat veteran, afflicted by at least seven tropical diseases, a man fired upon and withstanding, a witness to butchery and participant in Death's dance. Eighteen years old. One year out of high school.

'Private Cullen, have you hit anything that you have fired at?'

'Sir, we were taught by the China Marines to take up the pavement in front of the attacking troops and that way we would cripple or knock down most of whoever is coming our way. Just before Piva Forks we were attacked by about fifty Japs and none of them got close to our position. I just traverse and adjust and kept the range cards close. I do what works best and that seems to be pretty good advice from the Salts. Sir, I appreciate your direction today with me. I made a very stupid mistake and one that is all on me. I consumed all the raisin jack. I got it from two Seabees that I met on Bougainville, Sir. They rigged up a hammock for me after I got sick with Dengue; they are both good men. I will not drink again under your Command. I was trying to be salty and I was stupid. Lt. Buck I will be squared away for you. I vow on my soul and on my oath as a Marine. Sir.'

'I read you papers, high school football. Where did you play in Chicago?'

'Leo High School, Sir, and City Champs the year before I shipped in.'

'That is something, Private, I saw Leo play in 1940 at Soldier Field, bigger crowd than Notre Dame gets. '

I was on the Freshman team then, Sir. I never got into the City Game myself, I played behind Jimmy Arneberg. He's here on the 'Canal, Sir, with the 4th.'

'Private, you swore on you soul and your oath that you would not indulge in any drinking under my command. Does that mean both on and off duty?'

'Sir, I will not so much as sniff a beer bottle cap, as long as you are my commander.'

'Well that's fine, Private. You take your soul and your oath pretty seriously? Are you a daily communicant?'

'I am weekly, Sir. I used to be daily. My sister Joanie goes every day and my Mom a couple of times a week. My Dad goes but gets out of it when he can. He was a copper and now he is an engineer.'

'A Designer?'

'No, Sir, a janitor really. He handles the boiler at the Highland Theatre and looks after most of the maintenance there. He quit being a copper after the Republic Steel massacre. Said that he would never work for any strikebreakers – cops or company. Mr. O'Donnell, a big shot, put him to work there. It also helps to have an ex-flat-foot to knock heads together when kids get out of line. Mr. O'Donnell has his offices there.'

'Private, I see that you have noticed my side-arm?'

'Sir, every man has; that is some hog-leg.'

'It's a family heirloom of sorts. It was given to my Grand Daddy by Wild Bill Longley; he is said to have killed almost forty men with it. Wild Bill only 'fessed up to eight before they hanged him. The real story is who gave the Colt to Wild Bill. Ever hear of Capt. Keogh?'

'No Sir,'

'He was an Irishman who fought in the War of Northern Aggression for the Union; after Gettysburg, Gen. John Buford presented this Colt to Keogh for his gallantry; Keogh gave the revolver to Wild Bill for saving his life against the Kiowa, just before Bill deserted. Well, Private, Capt. Keogh died with Gen. Custer at the Little Big Horn and his horse, Comanche was only living survivor of Custer's whole command. This Hog-leg has quite a pedigree.'

'It does that, Sir. Does have much of kick to it?'

'A strong man is knocked back by its report, Private. My Daddy sent it to me on Efate when we were in tropical training – you got yours on the job, I understand – the Colt must be forever in the hands of a Texan. I saw that you carry the .38 Smith and Wesson Victory over the .45 Auto – why is that, Private?'

'I am not a very good shot with the pistol and the .38 goes where you point it, Sir. Kind of like the heavy .30, puts down a lot fire fast and direct. Cpl. Foster taught me real quick on how to take care of the heavy .30 and how to lay down fire in front of attackers, because that was how he and his buddies did it in Shanghai and when he was in Haiti. We lost too many old timers on Boogan, Lt. they knew so much'

'Well, Cullen that is one reason why I am not stretching your drunken ass over an ant-hill right now; like or not you are a veteran and have seen combat and you will assume some responsibilities for getting us through the next big one coming up. In two weeks we ship out for Cape Esperance for ship-to-shore debarkation practice. It seems that we can expect more reefs to cross so the Higgins Boats will transfer us to LTVs and that will be a job of work.'

'Let me ask you why did you get so drunk? And on a field problem?'

'Stupid and scared, Sir or just scared stupid. I don't remember much from Boogan to tell you the truth; mostly I was sick and soaked. It seemed as if I was too busy to be scared, except for the Volcano eruption before we came back to the Canal. I thought that it was an air-raid and I could not get out of my hammock – the one the Seabees made for me and Watson had to cut me out of it. It was Christmas I think. Jesus, I am scared now, Lt.'

Buck started to clean his Colt but continued to talk with the still at attention young Cullen. 'Report to Gunny Higgins tomorrow after inspection. You are his until you are mine once again, Private. You fouled up an operation that may have repercussions in our next campaign. Keep that thought fixed. I do not want you sober –that goes without saying- I want you sharp and on the ball. Dismissed.'

Cullen walked into the Company street with a sense of balance that he had not had since coming overseas. Ever since his visit to his Mom after boots and the Santa Fe train was side-barred, Tim Cullen's experience in the Corps had been one nightmare after another. AWOL- Court-martialed; creepy four-eyed Navy Lt. Commander – 'Prison or Replacement Pool in the Solomons?' – Snapping in on the .30 caliber heavy with Cpl. Foster and Mike Honnel both face down on the thin beach at Bougainville – the boat getting hit twice while coming into the beach the dead Lewis gunners in the bow tubs, going over the side and nearly drowning in two feet of water. Then, the Campaign itself. Dengue, malaria, yellow jaundice, and what else? Attacking that Navy doctor, asshole. Getting backed up by Major Opley himself. Now, there is a real Marine.

Lieutenant Buck seemed much like the Major. Tall, wiry and dark and both spoke fluent Spanish. Tim's schoolboy Latin helped understand them when they *Habla'd* each other like two Mexicans at work. Opley was a mustang joined the Corps as a private fought in Nicaragua and served in China made a Captain before the War and made Major after Guadalcanal where he served with the 1st Raiders under Col. Red Mike Edson. Buck's Spanish came from his blood and his Momma's people. Interesting guy. He would write to Brother Finch about him. Cullen wondered about the Colt Hog-leg and it's place in his life; my reader my wonder as well – so here's a little back ground from the 19th Century American West. I'll call it Wild Bill Longley's Colt:

CHAPTER 4
WILD BILL LONGLEY'S COLT

A mouse had eaten through the last good pair of socks and also the ass bucket of his last clean union suit; as Bill rubbed off the last soapy water that would ever clean up his living frame and pulled on the union suit. The deputy had placed his good black suit, clean collarless shirt and shoes outside of the cell but within his reach.

In his last two hours he would eat a plate of beefsteak, rice and pintos with a side of peach pie and washed down with a tall glass of lemonade; meet and confess his sins to Father Pfetzheimer the new Swabian Catholic priest who replace old Father Metz down with fever and soon to follow Bill into eternal life; give his cash holdings and deeds – what they were to his brother Jim the lawman; and turn over claim to the Colt .45 thumb-buster that his been his since the day Capt. Keogh bestowed the gun given to the dashing Irish Papal guard by Gen. Buford after the Battle of Gettysburg.

Wild Bill hated every Yankee dick-eater and nigger lover that ever soiled or sullied the South, but Myles Keogh was man who gave Bill Longley the respect and recognition that escaped him most of his life. Capt. Myles Keogh pointed Bill into the arms of the Holy

47

Catholic Church in his final months on earth – after all of his article and letters had failed to move the Governor to grant him a reprieve. Rather the heroic and manly life led by Capt. Keogh, now rotting on a hill in the Dakotas had reminded Bill that outside of the Church there was no salvation.

Bill could have been a great soldier like Keogh, but after his patron had been given a greater command opportunity at Fort Riley, Longley could no longer depend upon Keogh's immediate interventions when Bill got into scrapes. Texas Bill Longley and the U, S. Army parted company on Bill's terms, just after Capt. Keogh's command of Company I became official. An Army deserter, he became a drifter in Oklahoma, Kansas, and Texas, sometimes going by the name of Tom Jones. But, at one moment in Wild Bill's life, he was a hero before God and Man. One man recognized that – Captain Myles Walter Keogh.

In Indian Territory one April day in 1871, Keogh and four troopers with no guerdon out of a punitive troop of fifteen, scouted after a murder party of Kiowa who had slaughtered five families in Oklahoma and Kansas in the lower Sand Hills and upper Cimarron River. Even after a particularly rainy winter this area of southwestern Kansas was remarkably dry and unseasonably hot. Keogh's four troopers would be enough to lure the Kiowa party of twenty into a chase North and east and back into the larger force of ten cavalry men. Five miles north of the Cimarron, Keogh's four troopers including Longley picked up their trail but were soon ambushed by the Kiowa between two ridge lines. The Kiowa numbered twenty and were armed with Army issue Springfields and revolvers. Their leader Ned Curtin had been an army scout tracker and a Confederate cavalryman under Gen. Joe Shelby in Arkansas. Ned Curtin knew cavalry tactics.

Three of Keogh's troopers were immediately wounded and Capt. Keogh was unhorsed. Bill Longley rode straight up the draw and killed three Kiowa's with his revolver turned his mount back down the incline and pulled his officer onto its back. The three wounded troopers had retrieved their mounts and organized a defensive position with their backs to the west and the setting sun and waited for Longley and Keogh in a gulley deep enough to provide ample cover for the five men and four mounts.

From the ridge on the left, the Kiowa sent seven mounted attackers leaving three to fire nuisance rounds at the wounded and unhorsed 'pony soldiers' in the gulley. Keogh took stock of the wounds of the three men only two had broken bones and all could return fire. They had enough biscuits and water for a siege of two days. Ammunition was the problem.

Longley had killed three Kiowa and the group from the right ridgeline could only send four mounted attackers. Lt.Brice and Sgt. Quackinbusch might get here to break the siege well before the ammunition ran low.

'Trooper Longley,' my compliments on your gallantry and marksmanship. For a man so new to military action your lack of hesitation and command of target opportunity indicates a genuine affinity for this work.'

Though filthy with sweat and dust – turned mud in the activity of the handsome and athletic Captain, Keogh exuded the essence of the beau sabeur. He looked like the very image of the 19th century cavalier and man of action, tested in Italy fighting for the Pope of Rome against Piedmontese, in the Shenandoah Valley (Keogh nearly captured Old Stonewall Himself while under Gen. Shields) and through the horrific carnage that followed Gettysburg to Appomattox. Myles Keogh was a gentleman but a bone – tough soldier who would attack Hell itself with a spoonful of water.

Longley pulled off his campaign hat and smiled, "I don't understand a word you just said, Captain, but I thank you. I have been shooting niggers and bad white men, mostly Yankees like you, since I was ten."

"I am an officer of the United States Army, Trooper, and you wear its blue as well and eat its salt!', replied the handsome killer of Kiowa and Confederates and Keogh smiled to himself in the sure knowledge that Longley had saved his life and that was a debt that

Keogh would repay with the gift of the Army Colt Buford bought for him after Gettysburg. But first, the Kiowa.

Two days before, Capt Myles Keogh had decided to take four men from the expedition and ride north as the trail south towards Texas had gone cold. The remaining column of fifteen under Lt. Brice and Sgt. Quackinbusch were to head north again today and meet at Wheaton Stokes ranch on the Upper Cimarron.

The Kiowa on horseback feinted to the left of the defensive gulley and split into two columns each firing a nuisance volley and then withdrawing out of effective range. They did this for the better part of an hour. No troopers were hit. Capt. Keogh and Trooper Gates a civil war veteran himself, though a Louisiana Warf Rat, covered the left flank and rear, while Longley and the other two took the extreme right and the ridges themselves. Dusk bested the fire discipline of the Kiowa as the setting sun gave them the most trouble – there would be a night action. The Troopers waited.

In the pink glow of the Kansas dusk dimming their backs, troopers took turns taking rest and water while the others watched the twin ridgelines. Capt. Keogh asked Longley, 'Why the intense hatred of people brought in chains to slave for their fellow man? Surely, you must have some sympathy for people crushed to ease another's time on earth. Longley that war was fight to make right the path for the Nation's best instincts. You were too young to shoulder arms in your prejudices; so why the passion against black men and those who sought to free the?'

'Capt. I was pupped in a shit-hole cotton field outside of Austin and after the War, Yankee carpet-baggers and their gaping apes took up patches of land that my family has bled for without a 'by-your –leave, Sir.' The niggers took up patches of land and had nigger blue coats from New Orleans to force their will on Texians. No sir. A nigger and those who help them steal what should be a man's birthright are my sworn enemies., Longley matter-of fact-lied his rosary of hates by rote, like a child spouting catechism for the bishop.

'As a soldier, Trooper, you did handsome work of the Kiowa and you have added years to my life. I am grateful, Longley.

I have soldiered since I left Ireland in the service of Pope Pius and not a stranger to shot and shell, but the moment my mount was killed under me I believed to be prelude to my eternal life.' I wish to make a gift to you of a Colt in my kit back at the post and hope that you will accept this from me as a comrade. Gen. Buford died of Typhus and I watched him breathe his last with his head cradled in my hands. He was a gallant and rough soldier —not unlike yourself and you favor him in many ways. After Gettysburg, Gen. Buford brevetted me to Major and gave me this fine weapon before he sent me on leave to Washington. Please, take the Colt and think of from whom it was handed. Buford stopped Lee and saved the nation.

Longley had never received anything but a kick or clout and contempt from his brother Jim. He had nothing in Texas and now had the admiration of a fine officer and gentleman. This Keogh had fought for the Pope and wore his medal. That must mean something. There were few Catholics in Longley's cotton patches and fewer people who tolerated them. Maybe this Pope had the Medicine after all.

Trooper Longley replied, "Capt. I will be proud to accept your gift and vow to you that once I possess it, the Colt will only be held by a Texian worthy of a gun from the man who stopped old Marse Robert – even if that allowed niggers to live like white men.'

As Wild Bill ate his beefsteak and rice and beans, he thought too of his vow. He had converted to the Catholic faith that had modeled such a man as Capt. Keogh – now buried in the Dakotas with Custer. Wild Bill had been paroled to Giddings for hanging by a Texas Ranger and Roman Catholic Chris't Buck. Their journey from Louisiana had been remarkable due to the exchanges between the men about the primacy of Pope and the intervention of saints in the lives of men. Chris't Buck was a convert to Catholicism having been a back-sliding Methodist who married a Catholic German girl. Texas was filling up with Germans and niggers.

White men, including his brother Jim were, gathered in throngs to watch Bill swing just days after his 27th Birthday. October 16th it was and today the 28th Year of Our Lord 1878. Well God Bless everyone, you'll not see me turn gopher. I'll kiss the padre and the sheriff!

Wish Chris't Buck would come by. He said won't stand to see a man hang – not this kind of show anyway. He already promised that Colt revolver would stay in his family's care. It would stay into Texas like the vow. Maybe that promise would atone for some of Bill's misdeeds. Perhaps not. God would take me for the miserable cur that I am; make good on his promise to the two thieves – but, they weren't murderers and Bill Longley was that and then some, he swore! May God and the Holy Virgin make clear the path for a wide sinner and give him the smallest scratch of dirt in eternity. Capt. Keogh would blast them bastards all for fools as well. He'd killed men and niggers but not near as many as laid claim he'd killed. The judge called up figure of near to forty. I'll swear to eight that I am sure and that man Anderson was a mistake and the Reverend in Louisiana was violator of young woman. Sawed off bastard rapist! Killed with Capt. Keogh's Colt. I mean Wild Bill –Texas Bill.

I'll shit myself and all this good food's for sure. Bill Longley heard the steps and spurs of the sheriff's men and the gates of Heaven. Bill was going there with shit in his drawers and holes in his britches – kind of like he did in life. Maybe he could, with the help of the Holy Mother herself, do someone some good from the other side. Naw, Fuck 'em.'

CHAPTER 5
A MONK AND A TOUGH GUY

Again, the colorful language needs to be candied up with a story of a saintly man. Irish Christian Brother Francis Rupert Finch wrote to Tim Cullen every week and was only matched by the number of letters written by his little sister Joanie. Tim's girlfriend Mae Funk gave him the gate before Boots was over and she did not exactly get writer's cramp. Mae was now dating some sheik in the Air Corps from Harper High School. 'Hope she gets a war trophy – seven pounds, six ounces of diaper soiling delight.' Joanie kept Tim up-to-date on pets, kids, dances, and Dad's official duties as an Air Raid Warden – 'Father, wears his Mass suit and clean brogans, gas mask bag and oversized white steel Kelly and shouts up and down Bishop Street and all around Foster Park for LOIGHTS OUT,LOIGHTS OUT YOU FECKINBASTARDS!SHUT THEM FECKINGLOIGHTS OUT CARNEY YOU FECKIN FARDOWN! – 'Pess OFF LAREE YE FECKIN"EEEJUHT!' from Mr. Carney the coal-hauler from

Derry and the two little guys Donal and Mossy go with father for the laughs and get lollipops from Capt. Hennessy.'

Brother Finch taught Tim Algebra, Geometry and Chemistry as well as Coached the Lights in basketball – Brother cut Tim from the squad which carried only ten boys and Tim was a fair but certainly not essential athlete. Brother Finch had been orphaned and sent to Iona House in Spokane, WA which was run by the Christian Brothers of Ireland and when he came of age joined the Congregation of Irish Christian Brothers. His first teaching post was Leo High School in Chicago and came to love and admire the people of this most Catholic of Chicago's neighborhoods. Even the Protestant and Jewish families identified with the Catholic culture along 79th Street – the son of the Lutheran minister told one of his friends at the local public high school to meet him at the soda fountain in his neighborhood so they could work on their Chemistry homework. When the other boy, a Jewish kid named Weiss, asked what neighborhood that was, the Lutheran Kid answered the Steinway Drugstore in 'St. Sabina's' Tim Cullen and his family were well known to Brother Finch.

In 1934, Brother Finch helped the Cullens get their oldest boy Aloysius into Leo after Al got in a beef with the Park District Police for stealing from the Field house at Foster Park. Al stole padding used to cover the walls of the gymnasium and a bunch of the Indian Clubs and sold them to members of Eagles S.A.C. on 47th & Ashland at the suggestion of Mr. Edward J. 'Spike' O'Donnell, retired from the rackets. Mr. O'Donnell, who had lost three brothers to Capone and the Saltis/McErlean gangs, got out of the beer business and into paving and asphalt. However, Mr. O'Donnell liked to encourage smart and tough young guys on their own paths to success and listened with delight to Aloysius Cullen's 14 year-old's scheme to make some real dough by snatching City of Chicago property (City always bought too much anyway) and selling it to the Polacks for their social athletic club.

Brother Finch, all 5'6" of him, not only helped ease Aloysius' matriculation process in spite of his record but physically confronted the 6'4" retired gangster in front of the Highland Theatre.

'Mr. O'Donnell may I speak with you for a moment? My name is Brother Finch and I teach at Leo – coach basketball, athletic director and admissions counselor.'

O'Donnell, in Brooks Brothers worsted wool (brown checked), fawn spats, highly polished brown Hickey& Freeman wing-tips, egg-shell silk shirt – and two inch blue field –red & tan polka dot Bow Tie, towered over the bespectacled close-cropped calm and scholarly head above the cassock wearing a letterman's jacket.

O'Donnell in his late thirties had been shot, stabbed, punched, threatened, indicted and subpoenaed many times. He was only imprisoned once – 'couple -a -years. He worried –not. 'Always time for one of the Church's men, Brother, always time for you. What's on your mind Brother Finch? Sure, I know you. I go to most of the football games and I have seen you out there with Ike Mahoney helping the lads. Great stuff. My boy Paddy is up in Wisconsin with the Jesuits, Brother. After the last egg tried to get tough with me and Paddy jumped in – it was in all the papers – I decided against his going to Leo and I sent him up to Campion Preparatory – get him out of the limelight so to speaks – hey flannel mouth me. Go Brother – sing it.'

'Mr. O'Donnell, I recently vouched for Aloysius Cullen and I would like to speak with you about any influence you might have on Al and any other boys attending Leo. I wish to ask you to lay off the kids. Try not to encourage any of them toward what they might mistake as an easy buck.'

'Brother, you mistake me for a man who actually gives a fat rat's ass what you or the Cardinal thinks of me and I'll tip you off to something – mind your own business –teaching, coaching, psalm-singing or what else. I am an asphalt paving consultant, Brother – I consult paving business and I do not write encyclicals or tell you how to run your basketball games.'

'Mr. O'Donnell, do not mistake me for a milquetoast or hypocrite. I came to speak with you man-to-man. I want you to not give any boys at Leo the impression that you care about or encourage their admiration for reputation as a tough guy and hard guy. I will make this a very personal matter between you and me and I will come to personally deal with each instance where you give any boy encouragement toward a life on the other side of the straight and narrow.' Brother Finch was irritated but controlled and exercised the very same winning judgment with this notorious gangster as he did will referees from the Public Schools.

O'Donnell looked down into the eyes behind the thick bi-focals and saw in their blueness the image of Our Lady or something like that. – nuts! O'Donnell did a comic shake-off! 'Brother I believe you! Put 'er there, Brother!' He extended his hand in a sincere gesture of admiration for physical and moral courage and also as means of conducting some of the genuine saintliness that he did, in fact see, in Brother Finch's eyes. This little guy had a set of grapes on him that any tough guy would buy.

'Brother Finch – I am a tough egg. I am frightened by no one. I don't take pushing around. I'm a hitter. But, I would break every bone in my body myself, if I welched on this promise to you. No kid at your school gets so much as wink from me for any larceny and if the kid does get in a jam – I'll reach out to who needs touching and give *you* the heads-up. I am a daily communicant and a weekly confession guy, Brother. I have a lot in my ledger against me, but let me assure you that I did a lot more than you're wise to – or will ever know about – that's for me and God. I'll help you and the kids when I can but only through you, Brother. I do not want Father Shewbridge taking me apart dime on top of dime – Father Steve McMahon's got his hooks pretty deep in me already over in Little Flower

Parish , where I got a bungalow – a man's wealth isn't limitless, Brother.'

'Mr. O'Donnell, Brother Curtis told me to stay clear of you and as far our conversation today, it goes only to Our Lord. You are a powerful man, Mr. O'Donnell, and the young men admire your toughness and resilience. You know that the straight path is the one to take – that is why your son is at Campion. Thank you for your friendship in this matter. Call me if I can be of help to you.'

The Hood and the monk parted company and ran into one another at Mass or at sports events. In 1937, Mr. Cullen was fired for insubordination from the Chicago Police Department when he refused to attack picnicking strikers on Memorial Day outside of the Republic Steel Plant in Hegewisch. Chicago cops were paid by the company to attack the picnickers and killed several. Larry Cullen, who had struck with Big Jim Larkin in Liverpool and come to America in 1912 and participated in the ill-fated Meatpackers Strike, refused to obey orders and was fired. Spike O'Donnell got Larry's card in Local 7 Firemen and Wipers Union and put him to work as the building engineer for the Highland Theatre. Larry also picked up a few bucks by carrying a beezer and sitting watch on O'Donnell's alleyway two nights a week.

Spike O'Donnell knew the Cullens to be great people (Al was a larcenous little sneak but OK, Martin was a choirboy, Jack a good athlete, but Tim was a Swiss watch. The kid could fix anything and pissed away more brains than his Dad had from the get-go. The girls were all pin-ups and sweet-hearts like their Ma especially little Joanie – Spike saw her at 6:00 Mass every day. Now Tim was in the South Pacific fighting Japs. Spike's own little girl was now working for the Streets Commissioner as a secretary. Age and good sense had taken *some* of the edge off of a tough guy like Spike, but there were still times when the union slugger and pioneer beer runner emerged from the impulses and nerves at the surface of his Celtic pelt.

Spike was embroiled in a court battle with one of the Boy Scout contractors who 'The O'Donnell' had helped secure a City contract to re-pave Ashland Avenue from 71st to 95th Streets – about $ 200,000 net for the mealy-mouthed slob. Spike had contacted all of the right boys from the anchor to the top-mast of Public Works Administration and the final sign off by Mayor Ed Kelly himself. Now the crumb welched on consultant's fee and went crying to the Cook County States Attorney that Spike was shaking him down. But, hey, only suckers beef. The Treasurer would help Spike brown the sugar from this lump of blubber.

Joanie Cullen always talked to Spike when the Biddies and the High hats avoided his gaze and immediate touch like Spike was a leper. 'Good morning Mister O'Donnell, Sister Malachy said to say hello to you when I saw you this morning and I told Sister that I you never missed Mass.'

O'Donnell was delighted by this skinny little chit in her veil and with rosary beads twined around her mitt like a knuckle-duster. Joanie Cullen had eyes the size of the hub-caps on O'Donnell's Chrysler parked at the steps of St. Sabina's. Father Gorey was taking his own good time in getting down from the sacristy in the hopes that Spike would disappear; Spike like to hang around just to tease the new guy taking Monsignor Egan's place.

'What'd 'Chin-Whiskers' have to say for herself, Joanie? She looking to take a few inches off my wallet for you fine young woman over at old Mercy High? That crone scares me back into Church, Honey. What'd she want any way?'

Joanie loved the gangster, like one her uncles. O'Donnell had been shot in the back the previous March when all the asphalt contracting hoopla had made it into the newspapers and became an issue in Mayor Kelly's re-election campaign – the greater issue was whether or not Spike would live, but the natural born tough guy recovered after a few weeks in Little Company of Mary Hospital and his standard walks around the neighborhood. Joanie – and everyone else in Chicago – had heard of his reputation as a bad man, but knew that tough dapper daily communicant who was so devoted to his wife, children, brothers and neighbors that he put out the glad hand and offer of help to anyone he met. He was as funny as Mr. Duffy the political boss and more at ease than Buck Weaver, the disgraced third-baseman from the Black Sox days who lived in a nice house over in Little Flower parish on Winchester Street. Those three men sat out in front of Hanley's House of Happiness and played pinochle almost every day or in front of the electrical appliance store near the White Castle hamburger stand at 79th & Loomis. Buck Weaver had a job as the Vice President of Standard State Bank – the safest Bank in Chicago – because Spike banked there – and had devoted most of his life to restoring his good name in baseball. Buck Weaver had known that his teammates were taking Arnold Rothstein's payoffs but refused to be a rat and that was the only reason that Kennesaw Mountain Landis banned Buck Weaver from Baseball for life. All the others, Shoeless Joe, Ciccote and the rest had snatched up the bribe and thrown the World Series – only Buck was pure.

Joanie Cullen added, 'Tim said hello to you too Mr. O'Donnell and asked how you were recovering. I'll bring the letter tomorrow and show you where he says so. He's training for another battle I guess and says that he is working with two nice boys, one an Italian kid from Ohio and the other a hillbilly from West Virginia. Tim said the Dago is a great singer and is with an orchestra around Cleveland, but works for Desoto and the hillbilly got his first pair of shoes in the Marines and had never been more than two miles from coal mines in his life. Tim says that he is a real sweet guy and the ugliest person he ever met and that includes Myron Muchinfuch, the usher at Notre Dame Games.'

'Uglier than Myron, come on that's Orson Welles stuff. Where is Tim, somewhere in the South Pacific again? Did he say where?'

'Mr. O'Donnell, Tim says nothing accept that he wants Mary Janes and Bullseyes from Morganelli's and he always asks about everyone else. Never know he's in a war, if it weren't for the V-Mail. Al, Jack and Martin talk about the War all the time and Al is up in Fort Sheridan – he's a cop, like Father was, an M.P. and keeps deserters in line.'

'Al, always had the right makings for the Chicago Police Department, unlike your Father who is too honest a man and a Union man to boot. When all of the rest of those apple robbing Micks in blue wool had no problem shooting at working men, your father, Joanie, had the steel to tell that louse Capt. Connelly to take a leap. That's why you old man ain't a cop any more. Too honest. Al will be a Captain with his own bagman someday. Joanie, here's a fin – load up on MaryJanes and Bullseyes for that brother of yours – best man with bag of tools I ever met in my life. Tell him I did a few laps around the rosary for him. Give my best to your mother and tell that Bog-man Father of yours that he had better keep his 'LOIGHTS OUTing' away from 82nd and Loomis if he wants to keep healthy and keep it on Bishop with the other bog-trotters like himself.'

Joanie laughed like she meant it and had no school-girl giggle which delighted the retired hoodlum more and she pocketed the five-spot for a trip to Morganelli's candy store on Ashland Ave. later that day.

Brother Finch goodmorning'd the hoodlum and the school girl with a smile and nod and picked up the folds of his cassock and genuflected the Holy Sacrament on his way out of St. Sabina's Church. He had picked up their talk about Tim Cullen, who happened to be a favorite of Brother Finch for some reason.

Brother Finch was a man that other men wanted to have a good opinion of their worth as men. Every boy who passed through Leo High School from 1934 until Brother Finch's death in 1999 – while teaching chemistry to the black students who now attend Leo High School wanted Brother Finch to have a good opinion of them. He did. He admired most, pitied some, prayed for more, loved all, but liked, genuinely liked a very few boys. Out of the thousands of boys who came into contact with Brother Francis Rupert Finch it might be safe to believe that he 'liked a couple of hundred.' Brother Finch had a light that glowed through his drab, quiet, bespectacled and humble mien.

On the train to New York and the Irish Christian Brother Novitiate in Iona, New York, seventeen year old Frank Finch wore a suit, shirt and collar, tie and carried a straw boater. He had thick wavy black hair, a thick chest, long muscle-corded arms and short powerful legs. His eyes were a blue that only seemed to appear in Byzantine Churches – if there is such a color let's say mosaic tile blue. Frank Finch decided to dedicate his life to Our Blessed Mother, Her Son and His Church in that order and that he would do so with the strong and powerfully hearted men that had raised Frank and his two little brothers in the Orphanage named for Edmund Rice.

In Iowa, Frank awoke in his eastward facing seat in coach to find a girl the very same age as himself but with green eyes, strawberry blond hair a heart shaped chin and cheek combination that cupped round thick lips a long Roman nose and those eyes that would appear to Frank on his death-bed in some memory charged electric moment before death.

'Hello, my name is Frank Finch. Do you have enough room for your valise and coat over there. I have plenty of room.' Frank was enchanted.

'Hello, Frank, I am Sylvia Schoenouer. My goodness it is cold in here. I thought that the train would be more crowded but there are many seats open. Did you get of the train in Clinton?' she cozied up inside of the arms of her good thick wool coat that she had taken off when taking her seat across from the handsome and scholarly young man.

'No, Miss Shoenouer, I did not as I have not slept too soundly since leaving Washington and the hour here in Iowa for water and passengers gave me a much needed nap.'

'You were snoring very softly, Mr. Finch, and I determined not to disturb you but, that in fact I did, did I not?' The girl's soft twang sweetened the question teasingly and siren-ed the traveling postulant into a dull stirring of his sexual appetites. Frank had yet in his life to be alone with a girl, even if it were on the Union Pacific eastbound Pullman. This was something.

'Where are you headed, Miss Shoenouer? Forgive my impertinence. I have not had occasion for social interplay with young ladies and my manners must be considered crude.' His manner was anything but crude and his smile and eyes belied the humility of his words and signaled a self-confidence and balanced ease that Sylvia had never encountered among the farm boys and shopkeepers sons in Clinton, Iowa.

'Not at all Mr. Finch, I am going to Oberlin College in Ohio, where I will study sociology. I have won a scholarship, I am happy to say, because my father is still reeling from drop in the grain market after the War. He borrowed heavily in the last year and bought more land for wheat fields. Things must pick up with Mr. Coolidge. I want to work in the big cities and help the poor overcome their horrible lives, through the science of social conditioning. I believe that if Mankind applies what he learns about how we steer human environments – neighborhoods –job opportunities we will be able to eliminate our problems that are rooted in that environment. Slums – if slums get cleared away – no more crime. If the saloon goes away as it will with the current movement afoot, so will gambling, prostitution, drug peddling, foot padding and suffering of all type and clime. Disease will be eradicated. Once we pass the laws that outlaw those things and that is where the sociologists will come into play to help the right thinking people to make laws to make the world a better place. My goodness, what a speech. Mr. Finch 'whither thou goest?'

'I will go; and where thou lodgest, I will lodge: thy people shall be my people, and thy God my God: Where thou diest, will I die, and there will I be buried: the Lord do so to me, and more also, if aught but death part thee and me.' . . . Sorry, I am showing off for a pretty girl. Ruth says this to Naomi, anyway, and that does not fit well in our conversation. I am after all, Frank.'

And the spout-er of holy writ blushed and gave forth his best and most open smile, duly pleased with himself for eliciting such awed quiet from an obviously talented and intelligent girl and one so extremely beautiful that Frank thought of forsaking his private vow to the Virgin Mary and offering a very public one to Miss Sylvia Schoenouer of Clinton Iowa as they crossed the Mississippi River at Bettendorf to Illinois.

A half- hour later, the beautiful world beater asked of her companion, 'Where are you headed Mr. Finch? To College yourself?'

'In a manner of speaking, yes. I am heading for Iona, New York. I intend to be a Christian Brother, Miss Shoenouer.'

'Is that some kind of fraternal order like the Odd Fellows? Or do you intend to be a lay missionary in China or the Philippines?'

'I am a Roman Catholic Miss Schoenouer and that order is a religious order – I intend to take the vow of a monk,' at this four letter word, the perky sociologist recoiled as if Franks had said he intended to pimp.

'You do not look like a Romish creature, Mr. Finch. You seem so American. '

Frank smiled, 'St. Louis born, Miss Schoenouer. You must have met some Catholics in Clinton? I was orphaned and my brothers and I were raised by the charity of the Christian Brothers of Ireland; they were the only parents we really knew. When I said monk, it seemed to have terrible effect upon you. Are you hungry? I have several wonderful Washington State apples in my bag. You must be famished.'

The girl accepted the apples from this devil of a boy – and there – her eyes popped open – 'the deceiver the minion of the Scarlet Whore of Babylon in the very seat in front of her!

'These are about the tastiest apples that I have ever had and I shall miss them where I am going. My horns stay safely tucked beneath my scalp, Miss Schoenouer, said the amused boy struggling with his own temptations – stop – on this moving train – the Via dolororosa! The Way! The path to Christ. Taking up the Cross. Frank Finch had fallen in love with a beautiful Protestant sociologist! He had until Ohio – two more states on this transcontinental pilgrimage to Iona. Frank wanted to pledge his love, but waited and watched the girl.

'This is hardly Eden to lose, Miss Schoenouer; this is the Union Pacific. Please, enjoy the apple.'

As the reluctant girl smiled at her own folly and ignorance she parted her red lip and dropped the lower jaw revealing the delicate tongue already moist in anticipation, Frank let loose, 'and they are not blessed or coated in chrism.'

'Mr. Finch!' The two teenagers laughed and softened to each other now. 'Mr. Finch, I have not met Catholics ever and from all that I have learned most of the vice and corruption that I have chosen to fight with my talents seems rooted in what Catholics have done in America. Forgive me if that offends you, but most of our jails and asylums seem to have been built for the sole occupation by followers of Church of Rome. '

'Miss Schoenouer, as that is your experience and prejudice; I will be the last man on earth to correct those sentiments of yours. I am not offended as I am too conscious of my own inadequacies. I hope that my talents might amend many of the powerful evils in my own small way as a teacher and maybe through sports promotion among the very poor you speak of. I go to Iona where I will be a postulant in the Fraters Scholorum Christianarum De Hibernia – the Irish Christian Brothers. I will live in a monastery with other Brothers and teach boys in poor areas of America. Not as grand or noble as what you set out to do, but then I do not have your charms or intelligence. I'll try and teach one or two boys to be good citizens and good Christians. I hope and pray.'

'That is wonderful, Mr. Finch. I think that a bigger broom is needed to sweep out the filth and corruption. There is a . . .'

Frank reached up his immaculate handkerchief and wiped apple juice and pulp from the progressive young girl ready to set torch to the world's rot. It went on like this until she detrained at Oberlin and Frank Finch took the memory of this beautiful young woman to his own Mass of Christian burial.

Now twenty years later, in 1944, Brother Finch walked to his classes at Leo High School six blocks to the east of St. Sabina's Church. He went in through the west side door near the office and greeted Mr. Doll the account keeper and Brother Rooster McCarthy, the Principal and climbed the stairs to his second floor Athletic Directors Office. Brother Finch was reminded of his train ride to Iona that morning and took out a fresh sheet of stationary to write a short letter to Tim Cullen – somewhere in the South Pacific.

However before I set the place for Tim Cullen again, I feel that it might be a good time to introduce the backgrounds of the two antagonists in this tale. One, Gunnery Sergeant Billy Higgins will test Tim's metal on Tulagi and present him with a minor struggle with his soul and the other Major Lucas Opley, a talented but intrinsically spoiled man, will do positive evil to a young man – and like all acts of evil do so out of a pretty small issue.

CHAPTER 6
A PAIR OF ANTAGONISTS

Northern Nicaragua in 1927 was bandit country for men of the 11th Marines designated as the Coco River Patrol. This group of Marines and their guides established the search and destroy principles as part of the Marine Corps presence in Central America. Two Marines from our story were pretty effective 'trail openers' who used Remington shot-guns, Tommy Guns, B.A.Rs and Colt .45 revolvers to, as Mr. Dooley once said about bringing American culture to our little Brown Brothers, 'civilize them stiff.' Lucas Opley was a Corporal and William Wheat Higgins was a Private First Class leading a squad of Capt. Merritt 'Red Mike Edson's Coco River patrol in northern Nicaragua.

Yanquis of the United States Marine Corps had returned to the Central American Democracy to ensure the safety of American Fruit and various mining interests getting rich outside of Managua. It was this 1927 build up of the Marine presence in that unhappy land of revolution and exploitation that the Marine Corps would first practice dive-bombing against General Sandino and his Sandinistas and effective jungle fighting tactics would be developed that would play out in the South Pacific Theatre fifteen years later –at Guadalcanal, Cape Gloucester, Bougainville and our focus –Guam.

Lucas Opley was thrown out of Purdue University in 1925, the year Tim Cullen was born, for having a French girl from St. George Illinois in his room over the Thanksgiving weekend. Lucas, a sophomore guard on the Purdue Boilermaker football team was the son of a wealthy limestone quarry owner in French Lick, Indiana. Lucas had been tapped to be one of the varsity starters for the next season and had asked permission to remain in the athletes dorm during the Thanksgiving break in order to 'bone up for his chemistry and geology finals; after all his family was celebrating the Holidays at Mackinac Island, Michigan. Lucas got permission and immediately hooked up with Orville Hodge and Oliver Duval –The Two Os – and set off for Glorydale in Momence Township along the Kankakee River in Illinois.

Glorydale was fishing and hunting retreat that also served as a get—away for Chicago bootleggers and sports with an array of shanty-retreats for assignations with the local talent. There, Lucas paid Fifty dollars for the Holiday favors of Rita Letourneaux who had given a child up to the Viatorian Brothers for adoption two years before and had become a sister of the fleshlier inclined congregation. Rita had worked off her shame with old Nell Clark in her nicely upholstered hooker shop on Station Street in Kankakee, Illinois and was now an independent contractor.

The Two Os had a similarly matched pair of Flappers and jazzed away the holiday season in Glorydale. Lucas wanted to show Rita the glories of college life over the State line and took the Ford back to Lafayette, IN. All was jake until, a Billy Sunday mooner from Kansas, also on campus, blew the whistle on the couple and the future Varsity John Boilermaker and his tramp were caught by school porters and dragged in disgrace before the Dean.

Shortly, thereafter, Lucas Opley drove the green Ford back to Glorydale to the delighted guffaws of the two Os and he drank and fornicated the balance of his days before *Mater et Pater* could return from the resort island in Michigan – 'might as well be killed for lion as a lamb!'

With that homely philosophy in mind, Lucas Opley boarded the train in Kankakee for Chicago, where he enlisted in the United States Marine Corps.

Hundreds of miles to the south, in Jefferson Parish's MacDonough Street of Gouldsboro across the Mississippi River from New Orleans lived the massive family of ferryman Billy and Marie Chiniquy –Higgins members of the First American Presbyterian Church founded by Marie's grandfather Pastor Charles Chiniquy, the only American Apostate: a French Canadian Catholic priest who led half of his congregation out of the Roman Catholic Church before the Civil War and who had become an avowed enemy of the Church of Rome and celebrated author and lecturer.

Billy Higgins was the grandson of a Louisiana Tiger of the same name who fought at Bull Run and was captured at Port Royal by the forces under the command of Gen. James J. Shields the only Yankee to defeat Stonewall Jackson. Billy Higgins went to Camp Douglas in Chicago and escaped in 1863 and became a footpad in Chicago under the alias of Mike Joyce.

After the war, Billy went south again as a carpetbagger and helped strong arm property from farmers in Tennessee and eventually Arkansas. From there he returned to New Orleans under his own name and bought a ferryboat and large shot-gun house on MacDonough Street. The Higgins Ferry took day workers back and forth across the Mississippi River. His son Billy was as tall muscular and larcenous as his father. He took money form the Italian Black Hand and tipped off the Italians who made out handsomely stealing from the Texas &

Pacific Railroad yards right here in the Gouldsboro District, to any and all police trouble as the officers of Yankee Law meant nothing to a man whose Daddy had witnessed the Death of Maj. Chatham Roberdeau Wheat at Gaines Mills in June, 1862 – 'Bury Me on the Field, Boys!'

Billy Wheat Higgins, the son of Billy Roberdeau Higgins, and grandson of Billy Mick Higgins –AKA Mike Joyce of Chicago was the last of eight sons of Billy Roberdeau Higgins and Marie Chamness-Chiniquy Higgins of MacDonough Street, Gouldsboro, Jefferson Parish, Louisiana. Born on June 12, 1904 – the sixty-second anniversary of the Death of Chatham Roberdeau Wheat – and is believed to have been the cause of his mothers death from heartbreak in 1916 when the twelve year old Billy Wheat burned three freight cars in the Texas Pacific yards and was taken into police custody by an Irish Papist Policeman for Jefferson County by the name of Quinlan, after thorough beating.

Billy was sentenced to six months in the Boys Penal Reform Farm outside of Metairie by Judge Paige Clavisheux a Knight of the Holy Sepulcher. The Church of Rome seemed to delight in heaping disgrace on the great-grandson of one of the Champions of American Protestantism. In Metairie, Billy apprenticed to Clyde Gault and his gang of young toughs and Knights of the Ku Klux Klan. The year before, D.W. Griffith's movie *Birth of Nation*, had sparked the rebirth of the Klan, dormant since being legislated out of existence at the state and Federal levels at the close of the 19th Century.

Billy Wheat Higgins was sworn in to the Klan and took every opportunity to link his larcenous inclinations to the tenets of 100% Americanism. Billy's mother admired his outwardly Protestant zeal, but despaired for his spiritual and moral ambivalence. Billy's soul needed a mast to cling to in the storm swept seas rocking his boat.

That mast was the Eagle and the Anchor dominating the Globe. Upon his release from Metairie, Billy Higgins worked for his father and helped bury his mother. On the ferry, Billy learned to steer, tie off, call commands and take fees. When the War with Kaiser Bill began Billy learned to never charge men in uniform and sailors and Marines coming back from Haiti, Cuba, and Vera Cruz appreciated the big happy kid who gave them the choice seats over the stay-at-homes, niggers, kikes, and greasers.

Billy fell madly in Love with the tall tanned and salty men home from protecting America's interests from the Pope's stooges and Kaiser Bill. Billy followed their exploits through the war in France – Chateau Thierry, The Marne, Belleau Wood, Amiens, and the Argonne. The Marines Billy came into contact with had no more of a role in those battles than he had, but that did not stop their sea stories from delighting the boy. In 1921, Billy Wheat Higgins enlisted in the Marine Corps and clung to the mast.

In 1926, the first year of his second five year enlistment Billy was sent from Beaufort South Carolina Barracks to Culebra Island where the special detachment of 11th Marines were forming for re-deployment to Nicaragua. In short, now bear with me here, American foreign policy in Central America and there were five Central American states in all, attempted to balance the political parties in each country with the tacit threat of American naval landings parties.

Nicaragua was a country with a small white (High Spanish Blood) population of huge land-owners, willing to allow American businessmen to exploit the natural resources of their country in name of free-trade and Democracy, and a massive mixed blood (Indian and Spanish – *mestizo) population of peasants, middle class clerks, and small land holders.* The smaller whiter population backed the Conservative Party and the more populous mixed breeds the Liberal Party. Both sides contended for political hegemony. The Conservatives held sway around the city of Granada on the west coast near the shores of Lake Nicaragua and the Liberals controlled the votes more to the northern region along the Coco River on the border of Honduras and in the mining areas near the Mosquito Coast on The Caribbean side to the east.

A mixed blood middle-class educated Liberal party leader by the name of Emiliano Sandino had taken stock of the situation and refused to sign the Tipitapa Agreement and privately armed and trained a band of soldiers and attacked and captured the mining towns in the North. Sandino defeated every Conservative and Liberal force sent out to subjugate his band and it was determined that American Marines were needed to bring this bandit, as the *Yanquis* called him to heel. Lucas Opley and Billy Higgins were up to the task.

On Culebra, Billy was assigned to Corporal Lucas Opley's squad in Captain Merritt "Red Mike' Edson's company. Edson was a jungle wise professional soldier who loved taking the odds away from his opponents by out-thinking them and moving faster than they could.

In December 1926, Boarding the U.S. Navy Cruiser *Denver CL-16* , Billy Higgins remembered that he had left a copy of the tract by his great Grandfather Pastor Chiniquy on shelf of the day room of his barracks along with pornographic photos he had bought in Culebra from the pock-marked greaser at Diego Jefferson's cantina. "Corp. those great frames of the chancre vendor! Shit, Mule, I'm fucked for pole waxing until we hit shore. How long this sea shoot we got? Day? Two?, Billy never tired of exercising his left hand and forearm and could often do his business quicker than it took to strip down.

Corporal Lucas Opley never tired of commanding Billy to 'present arms' for the amusement of the squad so long as officers did not get wind of Billy's manual of arms. 'Better leave it alone for the cruise anyway, Private. I have orders to keep you sea-horses at the ready for what's coming. No cantinas, whores, or set-tos for given and smart sharp Marines on the beach and in the boondocks. One hour to square away sea bags and hammocks and then fall in on the fan-tail for dry firing. Billy you get religion on this real quick. These boots we have are grave bait by the looks of them. You get the Jew, the Dutchman, and the four new fish smart on the Springfields. You'll drum major the Browning with the Jew carrying your ammo belts. The Dutchman gets the Thompson and the four dead men with Springfields. I'm drawing the other Thompson.

'Our squad goes straight to the trucks from the docks,' Lucas saluted the Officer of the Deck and turned to salute the flag aft., Hefting his canvass sea bag and hammock. Lucas loved being aboard ship again. This trip from Culebra to the Nicaraguan port of Puerto Cabezas would take three full days and in that time Lucas intended to sharpen his squad of seven men into a tight team. Calisthenics for two hours before chow tonight would get half of the aware that this was going to be no nap-cruise. 'Billy when we disembark in Puerto Cabezas we are going to be tight and trim. So get any thought of slipping off to fuck and get fucked. Captain Edson is a skipper who will be Commandant. We are going to shine like a baboon's ass for the Skipper.'

The skipper of the Marine Detachment, Captain Merritt Austin Edson, had seen duty with the Army in Mexico, transferred to The Marine Corps in 1916, served in France with the 11th Marines, who saw no combat. After the War, Red Mike became a Marine aviator and established the first air squadron on Guam in 1925. While on Guam Edson took trips in to the northern jungles outside of Agana and scouted trails and cut trails. The next war will be fought in these forward base islands and jungle fighting and use of the airplane will make all the difference in that war.

This action in Nicaragua will be laboratory for the Marine Corps. Red Mike intended to develop tactics and eventually doctrines in order to win the next war – and there will be a war. Maybe with the British or the Japs, but Red Mike was not counting the Germans out – he had seen Germany understood the depth of their hatred for the Allies and the Treaty. The Boche were not licked – not by a jug-full.

More than likely it would be a Pacific naval war against the Japs for control –maybe the British – of the oil production in Malaysia and the rubber in Indonesia. America had firm but not exclusive lock on steel production and those were the things folks fought over – the means of production and the rights to crow the loudest.

Edson's detachment of 160 Marines most of them raw recruits and few that had seen service in Haiti or China.

Master Sergeant Paul Pruchnicki had gone through World War I with the Sixth and was sparked to the 11th before they went into Germany and had helped Edson become a clear thinking Marine thanks to Pruchnicki's combat savvy. He never bested the young Lieutenant for having missed the slaughter in Belleau Wood or the fouled up coordination of artillery that ground college boys and street punks into offal all through the Argonne, but explained the necessity of officers to be able to read maps under every circumstance and with accuracy. 'That is coolness under fire Lieutenant not running ass-head into machineguns but calling down proper fire on those guns so that your boys have some chance of sticking in the steel. It is no good to march into fire or to have our own guns rain down TNT. A good leader reads maps knows where he is and knows what the hell he is supposed to do with the men that he has with him. All the rest, Lieutenant, is non-sense.'

Paul stopped the boys of the 11th from raping German girls and looting houses because he had the eyes of a killer and the soul of shepherd girl. He had the Legion of Merit and several French decorations that were bestowed upon him by the French Captain leading Moroccan troops in the Argonne. Paul went to Guam with Edson and also shipped out on *CSL -16 Denver*, when Edson got the call.

After Pruchnicki, there was Sgt. Jimmy Frogge, Sgt. Casper Miller, and Cpls. Gunt, Turner, Lightfoot, Somers, and Sanapple who were War veterans; China Marines and Haiti Marines who had been fired open in anger number a baker's dozen and the balance were untried in combat – that would change in the matter of days according to the orders and dispatches Edson had read.

Edson looked aft and saw Cpl. Opley. There was a James Montgomery Flagg Marine if ever there were one – Six foot, two inches; all neck and shoulders, powerful fat-thick thighs and the brains of a Purdue engineering student. Opley was destined for great things if he lived – he'd make a fine officer. Edson wondered only about the man's moral fiber. Sgt Major Pruchnicki seemed to damn him with faint praise – 'Gifted and brave – the boy was turned out of school –can't say much for his sense of honor – but that is not on the record, Captain. Everything from Boots on is – Outstanding.' Edson had to ask, 'Would you go into combat with him, Sgt. Major?'

The old salt never blinked, 'Into –any day including Sunday! He is a bear for balls and almost as tough as his Liberty playmate Higgins. Behind – the jury is still out on that one, Sir!'

Edson watched Opley talk to his men – he had a nice manner about him especially with the fresh meat from P.I... No bluster and no bullying, even that he-bull Higgins became more maternal around Opley. Both men were powerful boxers, but Higgins was a brawler too. He delighted in violence. Higgins always went for the windpipe when he could not flatten the nose –'Can't fight if you can't breathe, children! 'was his gospel and constitution.

The only man on earth who made Higgins crawl to Jesus was Sgt. Major Paul Pruchnicki and Higgins hated the man cordially for that very thing. Opley and Higgins were key men in one of Lieutenant Joe Murphy's platoon.

Joe Murphy viewed the Marine Corps as a notch in the San Francisco Society Page at the end of this, his second enlistment Murphy would return to California and play with his Daddy's railroad. Murphy did six months with the legation detachment in Haiti and wore the ice cream man suit and when he was supposed to into the brush to chase the Cacaos he took to his bed with malaria – how he got it is mystery for the ages. The man never slept in the brush once in his time in the Corps. That would change in a couple of days.

USS Denver anchor in the harbor off of Puerto Cabezas in northeast Nicaragua and the Marine shore party of 160 Leathernecks and their gear whale boated in shifts of twenty from the Light Cruiser and formed up on the wharves before being detailed into the Ford Trucks and drive fifty miles to steamboats on Rio Wawa and then on to the Coco River for the western interior of Nicaragua.

We will pick up on this story after returning to Tim Cullen on Guadalcanal.

CHAPTER 7
SHITBIRDS OF TULAGI

His eyes burned in front and throbbed in back, his tongue and throat never seemed satisfied with cool water and every nerve in his frame bugged up to perspiration, sensation, and irritation of every sort. In short, Tim had a hangover going on its second day without let-up and activity was what he needed most which worked out nicely with his place in the punishment detail forming up in front of 1st Battalion 'First Shirt' Gunny Higgins.

Gunny Higgins had no ears to speak of –rather, lumps of muscle that seemed to have been pegged aft of his temples. Wearing a pith helmet, impeccably pressed khakis, leggings and boondockers, Gunnery Sergeant Billy Wheat Higgins appeared to be standing on a platform above the two rows of ten green utility clad Marines wearing green fiber helmet liners as covers. He was standing on the same soil as the boys before him, but he was so much above each and every one of them in the eyes of men and boys.

'Side-Straddle –Hops until I am well pleased and I am never well pleased!' Throwing Arms to a point geometrically above his head and casting his legs out like colossus to His 'OW –un! And reversing the limbs at 'HOO!'

'Move MotherFuckers! I'm not doin this for my health!

'Ow-Un; HOO; OW-unHOO! & etc for fifteen minutes without let up.

'Fall out –You Box Me.' Fall out - Men Die. Fall out - Boys Might. Fall-out –Don't Try!'

After the full fifteen minutes Gunny Higgins' body snapped shut like and expensive switchblade to signal the end of calisthenics.

In the tropical heat with all of the physical snap and strain not a drop of sweat spotted his arm-pits or blemished the cleanliness of his khakis. Strapless his pith helmet never went askew, nor fell from his square muscled head. Gunny Higgins was Gorgon and Apollo wrapping the soul of Voltaire and the balls of Rabelais.

'I have served the flag in uniform from the time that you mewling tit-suckers tore out the snatches of some fine women. I do not ask who is my enemy or what his thoughts might be or if we had supped at the same table last night. I do not give a shit that the Pope locks up! Major Opley and men up the chain from him have determined who my enemy will be – Today –tomorrow- and until Jesus takes back the Aggies I stole from that Jew wood-butcher. '

Without looking into any man's face, Gunny Higgins pointed down from his majestic height and moved his long thick broken right fore-finger –slowly and judicially.

'Each and every swinging man-log on parade before my tired eyes is *my* enemy, because the very men up the august chain from whence all truth calls down have told me that *you are*. I have butchered greasers on the Coco River and Niggers in Haiti and Japs wherever I find them and traitors to the flag without so much as a thought because I was ordered to fight and kill them. But each and every one of you have made my enmity *boil* because you have pained your elders and betters up that august chain – You have soiled Duty and Honor as Fuck Ups! I will amend that before my next hard-on! LCM at the beach step lively – Now! '

And the twenty in green double-timed it to the awaiting landing craft. The coxswain ordered each of the twenty green fatigued men in the work detail to put on life-belts and made the port perch aft available to Gunny Higgins.

'Back ass in, dummies, to remember larboard and starboard and - larboard is port. Cullen – you wine-soaked Pope's pussy, stand tall down port of my shoes. You are my scratch pad till we sail for home, son. If I get the wind up down you go - hard. *Comprede, usted – cabronne?*'

'*Aye, Aye,* Gunny!' barked out Cullen.

'Cullen, fart me tune until I get tired of hearing you and crave to listen to Boson Bullshit! Tune up Yankee!'

'Ave Maria

Gratia plena

Maria, gratia plena

Maria, gratia plena

Ave, ave dominus

Dominus tecum

Benedicta tu in mulieribus

Et benedictus

Et benedictus fructus ventris

Ventris tuae, Jesus.

Ave Maria

Ave Maria

Mater Dei

Ora pro nobis peccatoribus

Ora pro nobis

Ora, ora pro nobis peccatoribus

Nunc et in hora mortis

Et in hora mortis nostrae

Et in hora mortis nostrae

Et in hora mortis nostrae

Ave Maria

'Cullen you ballsy tit-wringer! Give out some more from the Pope's bagpipes! Out with it boy and make these sea-hags happy - they ain't seen a man in hours!'

The Coxswain Let out a muted obscenity knowing Gunny Higgins as man of trim values – but laughed nevertheless.

Panis Angelicus

fit panis hominum

Dat panis coelicus figuris terminum

O res mirabilis!

Manducat Dominum

pauper pauper servus et humilis

pauper pauper servus et humilis

Louder, Motherfucker!

Panis Angelicus

fit panis hominum

Dat panis coelicus figuris terminum

O res mirabilis!

Manducat Dominum

Louder, Motherfucker!

pauper pauper servus et humilis

Louder, Motherfucker!

pauper pauper servus servus et humilis

'Now, shut the fuck up and let me think on what Romish curses and foulery you cast upon my noble brow in them songs. Got to get me a Jew to sing next. Niggers sing like me and fuck me! I see you laughin' Starboard stick three. I'll tell you oysters when to laugh and you ain't labored the privilege You are on fucking punishment tour with a man who knows pain's lexicon!'

'Tulagi beach master and step on it, Coxman! I might kill a handful of these pearls, before the task gets ripe, You a Louisiana Man Coxman?'

'Born and raised in Cribstone. . St Laurence parish . . .,' the warmed sailor began.

'Well, Fuck You then! Sail this craft without incident and I'll get beer call for you and your three sisters. Honor Bright!' and Gunny was as good as his word. He stepped down three of the steel rungs into the cockpit next to Cullen and put his steel portside arm around the boy's shoulders. 'I saw you on Boogan . . . in the aid station and later on the line. You handled that .30 like a salt with four hash marks; must be a gift, son. Stare ahead and don't eye-ball me son or I'll carve off your head and shit down your neck. Now, listen here, Major Opley remembers you from that scrap and saw your name down for my detail that is why I called you out. He liked your sand in taking that four-eyed Navy saw-bones by the stacking-swivel. Yes, Sir, that pleased him. He wants me to baptize you in the blood of lamb before our next walk on the beach. You need to step up into the shoes of the dead.'

The LCM beached at the Transport Cove on Tulagi and the twenty-one Marines disembarked and formed up. Gunny Higgins exchanged more obscenity laced compliments to the boat crew and informed them where they might pick up the cases of Drewery's beer in possession of 1st Battalion Gunnery Sergeant William Wheat Higgins.

The twenty man punishment detail stood at ease but alert to the coming commands of their overseer. Gunny Higgins had gone from the LCM to pick up the manifest from the Tulagi Beach Master's shack that would process the possession of 10 tons of .30 caliber ammunition for 1st Battalion, 3rd Marines.

All of the ammunition needed to be clipped and belted by the squads and gun crews in their company areas, but it would be the task of this detail to transport the ammunition back to Tetere Beach on Guadalcanal, check and clean the rounds before clipping and belting.

Gunny Higgins burst the propriety of the efficient beach master's shack with a hurricane of filthy language and imprecations against the Commander of the South Pacific Area, General Douglas Macarthur, whose domain included the ammunition stockpiles on Tulagi.

The designated stockpile had been bulldozed – 'to keep it safe from fire. Bullshit! Wacky Mac had decided to throw a screw into Gunny's Marines and that was the long and the short of it. His boys needed to bail through the mud and dig out their ammunition crates and could be assured that their tasks would be longer and more demeaning. Bougainville had been Admiral Halsey's show and Mrs. Roosevelt had come to the Canal to praise General Turnage's fine men who took that island from the Japs so handily. At this very moment dog-faces under Generalissimo Macarthur were slugging it out with the Japs and losing hundreds of men as well as real estate on Bougainville. The Third Division had handed the campaign over to General Patch on Christmas Day 1943 and now the U.S. Army was having a tough time sealing the deal. Macarthur hated the Marine Corps.

Standing legs spread and four-square before his detail, tall, tanned, khakied and commanding Gunny Higgins pointed over his port shoulder to the bull-dozed stock pile – his pith helmet squared.

'I have pissed rainbows of beer over taller mountains than God can lay bricks on full breakfast! From the rocky coast of Maine to sunny Frisco Bay, I have fucked them all – countesses, millionaires and movie stars! The sight of me makes proud men blush and maidens as wet as a New Orleans hooker shop in August. I have bested men and boys at cards, games and quick draw. I can eat the crotch out of a running Grizzly bear and ask for seconds on servings of mule shit, but I am four-eyed and fucked over this one, Girl Scouts!'

'*El Supremo* has determined that the men who snatched Boogan from Tojo need more work and so the Supreme Commander of South Pacific Forces ordered the Quartermaster Corps to have the .30 caliber ammunition earmarked for the 1ˢᵗ of the 3ʳᵈ Marines covered with Tulagi. Nothing to it, girls, but sweat and suet! Cullen get ammo carts from the beach master take four men - the other half of you get to digging, and relay passing all ammo to my feet. Move!'

Five peeled off in the direction of the Beach master's shack where he had already assembled ten ammunition carts and each man pulled two carts back to Gunny Higgins.

'That Yankee Momma's Boy has not seen the day where Men of the one True Corps can be set back a-heel by a candy-sucking cavalryman! Assholes and Elbows!'

With pride and anger, the punishment detail hefted and clawed and pulled and carted the heavy mud-caked and soaked ammunition crates. They loaded the ten ammunition carts and two man teams horsed them back to the beached LCM that would take these angry boys and their soiled ammo back Tetere Beach on Guadalcanal. For three hours this detail dug the prized rounds out of Tulagi soil and mud, gave the crates a perfunctory cleaning and stacked them on the carts and hauled them to LCM and restacked them.

As the job disintegrated like the caked soil on the crates, a knot of Army brass and journalists and photographers assembled on the knoll above the work detail. Centered in the group was the unmistakable Roman profile in crushed overseas cap with scrambled eggs, the foot long corn-cob pipe, the casually tailored khakis and slow sure gait of a Man of Destiny in his late sixties.

Gunny Higgins had his back to his enemy and like he had been in the jungle these last twenty years- well aware of his enemy's presence, their strength, and their deployment. His electric gaze targeting only the twenty individuals awed by Macarthur's apparition and enraged by his arrogance in slighting those beneath him. Tim Cullen pushed his loaded ammo cart with all the determination that he had legged on the football field for Leo High School and not unlike his playing days he was bested by a better man.

Gunny Higgins understood Cullen's intentions to howl, vent, threaten and *assault the Supreme Commander of the South Pacific* and with one casual step to his right, blocking any view of his subsequent actions from the gawkers and the patrician above and behind, Gunny Higgins telescoped his left arm to Cullen's throat, catching the boy's Adam's apple between his sandpaper thumb and his thick deadly forefinger with whispered, 'I love frying Papist Porgies for a Po'Boy but only in my own oil. Do not give that Army cunt one scintilla of reason to laugh at a Marine' and released the boy to cart the ammo to the LCM.

I love that boy, thought Gunny Higgins, Hell; I'd fuck all his sisters and the Pope's mule for that little display. That boy will do fine.

The work continued for another hour and without comment, the Marines took their contaminated ammunition away for cleaning. This incident spoke mountains for the small man on the hill and the giant hearts of those he thought he would abuse.

The LCM took proud and happy men back to Tetere Beach and none happier or more filled with pride than Gunny Sergeant William Wheat Higgins. Upon return, to 1st Battalion headquarters tent, Billy bubbled like a school-girl with new crush – he was dreamy in love with Tim Cullen! Major Opley was delighted as he had always been a great judge of character and this red-headed runt who had stayed on the line as sick as he was and found the strength to tear at the Battalion surgeon's throat for calling him a malingerer and now wanted to single-handedly assault a hill full of Army brass and reporters for fouling the Marines, no wonder Billy was in love.

For the next two weeks every man in the 1st Battalion had heard about Tim Cullen from 1st Platoon Able Company and how he tried to kill Douglas MacArthur and was saved by Gunny Higgins, while they cleaned and re-greased every round that they would fire during the up-coming Guam Campaign

PART II
LST 448

CHAPTER 8
BOSON OTIS

Boson Otayama was 27 years old and had been a Japanese Sailor since he was fifteen years. Born in the prefecture of Honshu, Otoyama's family had been fishermen from the time of the great flood.

The Imperial Navy was the proudest branch of the service and had punished the pride of the Czar and really brought about the collapse of that Empire more than the Bolsheviks.

Otayama was smart and efficient and in command of the Special Naval Landing Force 321st Kebeitai Agana. Lt. Komanura was over all commander of the Agana District and more concerned with finding Cruz's secret cache of American popcorn than with anything else. Komanura was a fearless leader and had fought bravely against the French and Dutch before coming to Guam. Otayama was a member of the original landing force on Guam and had bayoneted a red-headed Marine who was showing arrogance to Otayama. Otayama ran the red-headed fucker through the throat ensuring a long and painful death.

Since then Otayama had killed several Chamorros in order to make his point. These Indians were worthless and gutless, Komanura held Otoyama's arm these last two years – a brave man but too gentle with these dogs who ate American shit like it was a delicacy. The Dentist was an interesting man he had married a red-head American and still had her to fuck on this island. He was Japanese but so American – though loyal to Japan.

Otayama stopped at the bodega run by a Japanese/Japanese/American woman named Estherhausy. She had married an old time American Marine who died long before the war. 'Good Morning Mrs. Estherhausy let me have some of the candy and a packet of cigarettes, please.'

Otayama was always polite to the old woman who spoke in country Japanese very slowly, because she had spoken only English for so long.

'Good morning, Boson. Were any of your boys hurt last night? I hope not. The Bombers come too close to town these days.'

'Have no fear, Missus, our new squadrons will deal with them and they are flying the new Tony fighters that are so much faster than the Zero. They'll knock down those Clark Gables. I must check on the beach road later this morning and see if any one were caught out in the open; there are many new Koreans working up on Asan. This candy is wonderful! You make it nice and sticky like my Mommy did! Bye, Bye Mrs. Estherhausy

The Japanese Non-Com was now taking to wearing his dress blues every day and ordered his men to do the same as it gave them an air of assurance and warded off any thoughts by the Chamorros that invasion was imminent. That fucking priest was staying out of Agana anyway and was sticking to Tai or in the other Northern towns and so he could be the Army's problem. When he came down to Piti Navy Yard or any where near Orote people began to show arrogance against the Naval and Army troops – refused to bow and such. Fucker.

They should have chopped off his head or used him for bayonet practice immediately after the occupation.

In his dress blues and flat non-com's hat Otayama cut a powerful figure he was built for wrestling and his years at sea had given him powerful hands and fingers that could crush nuts and cans with ease. He often took walnuts or filberts in the shell and crushed them into dust for the Chamorro children and to scare their Daddies shitless. Today Otayama would check in on Cruz, a nice man with a ripe and fuckable daughter that he wanted to protect and made honor offerings to Otayama every week or so from the proceeds of the movie house and the candy concessions. For that Otayama kept his herd of forty-two sailors proper and respectful – in town. Out in the villages they could do as they pleased. Otayama was not interested in the Indians – he wanted that red-haired wife of the dentist. If anything happened to the tooth puller – Otayama intended to be there to 'protect' the movie star with the high legs and creamy skin. Otayama went stiff in the lumber just daydreaming about her.

He had a girlfriend, Hana, whom he would marry after he retired from the Navy in ten years, but in the mean time Kenta Otayama would take care of business like sailors before him did – by himself and with comfort women. He wanted to add the Dentist's 'widow' to his prayer cord.

The Day was beautiful, as every day on this island had been. There was no other posting that he had enjoyed as much as Guam. The waves hitting the reef a thousand yards out from the beach had a musical quality like a xylophone, due to the thin coral that protruded from the foamy surf and the sand was as fine as powder all the way up to the tree line. The palm trees were no longer filled with coconuts as a virus had infected the island's palm trees back in the 1920's, but the island abounded in wonderful fruits of all varieties, fish, crab, cane and rice.

The boson thought of retiring to Guam and he prayed that Japan would retain Guam in any peace settlement with the Americans who were already tiring of war. If they tried to take this little fortress they would get a bloody nose from the new guns emplaced with such skill and genius that every square inch of Asan was zeroed in. Orote was another matter – there the army would let them get ashore and then slaughter them with tanks. Here outside of Agana, Boson Otayama and his men would keep the Chamorros from panic and looting; fucking Indians and Mongrels.

Yeah, Boson Otayama would bring Hana back to Guam and maybe buy the Dentist's House. Kenta Otayama had a very sweet tooth indeed. Now, time to collect my sugar from Juan Cruz the movie spinner – fucking mongrel.

Two blocks from the theatre was the neat bungalow of Juan Cruz his wife Imelda and his two kids. Juan had the Craftsman lawnmower's blades sharpened the other day by Hector Torres who looked for any excuse to hang around the Cruz's home or the theatre because the kids was so pole-axed in love with Betty. Big husky kid and neat boxer. Hector offered to cut the lawn but that was Juan's domain and he jealously guarded the hour it took to cut, rake, weed, and fertilize the lawn and then sweep starry cuttings from the trim sidewalk along their street.

Juan remembered when the American sailors poured the street back in the 1920s and again in the 1930's and how proud every one felt that Guam had become main street America. Even the crabby old islanders out in the boondocks were happy. Every Year the Guam Carnivale brought islanders and Americans together in a collaborative festival of fun and pageantry. Now, the Nips were the top dogs and didn't give a fat-rats-ass as the Marines all say about the Chamorros or their traditions – the Americans the great hucksters and sellers – genuinely respected Chamorro traditions and customs and treated all of us like equals – no bowing or lording. We went to American schools and celebrated American holidays with them and they with us. When new sailors and Marines arrived from the Mainland it only took hours for the new ones to learn that this was their home and not place to wipe their feet. Please let them return soon.

From the kitchen window, Juan picked up the aroma of *Kadon Manok* and coconut eggplant – a real treat. It was getting hotter and the rain lasted longer these days. Soon – by July it would hit 100o on the average and this grass would need more cutting; maybe by then Juan would relent and allow Hector to cut his grass.

It looked fine! Dinner at 5P.M. Baked Coconut Eggplant and Kadon! Imelda's soup could always use more pepper but she was tired of hearing him beef about – add your own – the kids do not like it. Now, Juan would change and head up the street to the theatre and pay off that louse Otayama. His monthly *mordita* on top of the usual $ 5 a week. Bastard. $45 dollars in American. Had to have Ted convert for the bastard – he's going to beat America and keep American dollars in Jap bank.

Keeps the other drooling Japs from Betty. Time to go with Ted out to the jungle for more dollars. Ted must have $ 60,000 buried outside Tia and another $75,000 near Sumay. Who knows how much more that Ted and Kara have squirreled away. God Bless them! Both the new naval and army officers seemed like good men. Who knows what these people will do once Uncle Sam gets close.

Hector Torres on the verge of sixteen was a bull of boy who had been in love with Betty Cruz from the moment he first laid eyes on her in the movie theatre that his uncle took him to see his first Buck Jones western serial seven years before. Every Saturday afternoon at 2 P.M. Hector and the boys from his uncle's *lancho* two miles north of Fonte Ridge would walk to *The Coral Theatre* after his Uncle Ignacio would drive them into Agana in the back of his truck loaded with fruit, taro and eggplant for the groceries in the village. Hector would run to theatre to be first in line and always seemed to win the race. Betty was like none of the little girls because she seemed like she was a good two years ahead of everyone else. Betty could make change at eight, make popcorn, mix juice drinks and sing all of the newest hit songs – more importantly she was beautiful with huge black/brown eyes.

Red Rider with Buck Jones was kind of their date before the war started the were twelve and in 6th grade at Mrs. Johnson's preparatory school for George Washington High and had young Miss Bana who was killed when the Japs attacked – she walking to her apartment in Agana Heights that she had rented from Pastor Sablan of the 1st Guam Baptist Church who was now helping Father Duenas and Father Calvo get food and clothes to the Americans hiding in the jungle on the North of the island,

The Red Rider Serial lasted for six weeks of pure heaven for Hector with Betty's little hand gripping his already meaty hand when Ward Bond seemed to get the best of old Buck. Buck was short and stocky like Hector and also not much to look at but, Hell – Betty was gripping Hector's hand and Pamela Sue Young (Loretta's little sister) was smooching Buck – there you go smart guys.

Hector wanted to get at the Japs and especially protect Betty from that slob Otayama – he was Governor Homura's People's Dog with his other bayonet crazy sailor of the Kebeitai – they were just muscle. The real scary bastards were the Jap military police the *Minseibu* especially that new oily creep Lieutenant Ryugo Kato. Kato took over after the other one had failed to bring in the six Navy men who had eluded discovery. It did not seem that the Japanese put too much of an effort into the search and were more interested in getting Chamorro labor detailed for the airstrip to the south and cutting timber and hauling it up to Asan heights and Fonte ridge from the north west part of the island. This new man had purpose and young Hector wanted to stay clear of this man. Betty would be mixing juice at the theatre and that occupied Hector's thoughts entirely.

CHAPTER 9
ROPER BUCK

A world away – the vast deep island pocked ocean above the equator and half a continent to the east, near the State Capitol of Texas on wet but paved county highway, Roper Christian Buck squealed the balding tires of his Studebaker coupe but bounced the jack elope under the frame with the signal thud of a mortal strike –indicating some bumper and grill pelt, guts and maybe limb of the obnoxious freak rabbit. Damn his softer instincts; a full bore cruise over the damn thing would have been quicker for the critter and neater to the already dirty machine.

Lyndon had delivered on the PWA money for the electricity bill and also a few million in County improvement that would boost things for already firm lock Buck had on the Representative's seat in Austin. Rep. Johnson and Roper Buck had been friends from the time Lyndon headed the Texas Youth Administration that had helped to improve the education of the children in Lee and Williamson Counties and now called back from the Navy by FDR Lyndon was on the Truman Committee and a powerful voice about where Federal dollars were to be allocated in the State. Harv Bigley, the Republican County Chairman had put up to challenge Roper in this election year none other than Mr. Lawndale "My Voice" Sowery. Lawndale Sowery wasn't the biggest asshole in Texas but he would do. The husband of a wealthy woman from old cotton money in Dimebox east of Giddings, Sowery had a low wattage radio station that played old timey Gospel music and Lawn's rants against the New Deal and the evils of Negro suffrage and Mexican anything.

At 10 A.M., 1 P.M., 3 P.M. and 5 P.M. Sowery went on the radio for fifteens minutes of pure undiluted bile spewed upon Franklin Dela-nose Jewsevelt, The Jew Deal, Nig-rah Issues, the need for am electric fence along the Rio Grande to keep America for Americans and the Buck Family.

'The Buck people have stolen from every honest man woman and child in the three Counties that have allowed any Buck to occupy a seat in the Texas Legislature going back to when that outlaw with a badge; that friend of worst killer in Texas history Wild Bill Longley, Christ Buck helped the Pope's greasers of Spain blow up the USS Maine in Havana by secreting messages from his Mex wife to the Pope's emissaries in Vera Cruz and thence to Cuba! There's spit on microphone, Clel, now wipe it when you finish the crop forecast - & etc.'

Lawndale Sowery was a gift from God to any man holding or running for public office at any level – Road Marshall, County Honey-dipper, Deputy Superintendent of Public Morals all of which Sowery had run for and lost in landslides for some of the dumbest and most shameless crooks on the public teat, Democrat and Republican. His latest assaults on the Roper Buck family had to deal with a piece of legislation that consolidation eight grammar schools and four high schools in Lee and Williamson counties that would provide two large central high school districts with busing, meals, and books for all students regardless of race or economic state.

As 12% of the population was Negroes and another 36% Mexican, this latest outrage against the white, Protestant American citizen received full, loud and acidic treatment on the radio by Lawn Sowery. Today,' My Voice' quivered into the radio receivers in the Central Brazos –

"When the LORD, your God, removes the nations from your way as you advance to dispossess them, be on your guard! Otherwise, once they have been wiped out before you and you have replaced them and are settled in their land,

You will be lured into following them. Do not inquire regarding their gods, 'How did these nations worship their gods? I, too, would do the same.'

You shall not thus worship the LORD, your God, because they offered to their gods every abomination that the LORD detests, even burning their sons and daughters to their gods.

DOOTERNOMEE 12 29 U, Huh? through thirty Two, my friends – the Word of God and Not the Word of the Lying Ropers and their friends in Power over all of us! What Temples do they build? They do not they cast down God's Holy Temple Writ Large in the Words I just Let out for you. That crook and his Mexican wife want every American to think that any Child of Ham or Dan is kin to those of us who kneel under the Cross.

'You will be lured 'the Lord says right here?!! 'You will be lured into following them?!' Every Buck has from old Christ Buck to Young Christ to Roper and so Now to Jack – He sups with the Pope's Princes?! Schooled by his Priests!

Now, Harv Bigely – True America and Knight of the True Cross – has asked me to take on Rome and the Jews and be your candidate in November. ;

In the time between- your friend and Your Voice- "My voice' will be heard in these counties until the last ballot is counted fairly and truly and I shall be a sword in your hands and a cutting Vengeance on Buck and his forces.'

Now you come on down to the new Sowery Mattress and Bedding store on Fontana Street at Bonham for all of your bedding needs at prices no American can step over.'

Following that broadcast, Texas State Rep. Buck took out an advertisement in every penny saver paper in the two counties that read –

Nothing is New Here!   Only My Business !
– Will buy Used Mattresses and Pay Top Dollar
– No Offer Refused!

Lawndale Sowery (Triangle 4- 1296)
Sowery Mattress & Bedding
1067 Bonham Street
Dimebox, Texas

OPEN-Between the Hours of 8A.M. and 6 P.M. Monday thru Saturday.

Closed Sundays

For weeks, Lawndale Sowery and his hideous wife were showered with mattresses – pee stained, blood stained, dust stained, mildewed, decrepit, and smelly mattresses of every size and condition. Lawn needed to have every one of the piled cotton, down, goose or grass filled mattress haled out of the town limits and burned at no small expense to him.

As the advertising copy had arrived at the papers in the night slots and was prepaid by cashiers check from Sowery's own bank, he had a devil of time explaining and arm flapping.

Roper Buck smiled thinking of those moments enjoyed by hundreds of residents in Lee Williamson Counties. This would be a grand election season and old Harv Bigely would be sure of some fat patronage jobs for his folks.

That turd-faced coward had lit into Jack on that last broadcast – a boy fighting for his country. It carved the meat right out of Roper's heart – a Texas Ranger who had killed bootleggers in the 1920's and protected small farmers from Klan assaults to listen to this crap about his boy, Jack.

Jack was a bright penny as a little guys and could hunt, ride, shoot and make camp by the time he was seven. He was reading Latin by the time he was in junior high and translating Livy passages for Father Stehndahlgraff in 8th grade. Good basketball player, public speaking award all four years and a great help to his old crabby Daddy on the stump.

Now he was a 1st Lieutenant in command of the lead company of the U.S. Marines getting ready for something big – no doubt in the Central Pacific according to Lyndon. Roper sent Jack the Colt Hog-leg three months earlier and it had reached him on Efate before he went to Guadalcanal. Lyndon saw the boy in the New Hebrides before the President recalled him and the other Congressmen to Washington and said, that 'Jack would be great Congressional timber when we whipped these bastards around the world.'

I don't care much for politics and would much rather see my boy doing good as a judge or in the university life, thought the old campaigner. Roper Buck wiped the last of the jack elope from his Studebaker and headed to Dimebox to give Lawn Sowery's tits a twist on the street. Something about defrauding poor dirt farmers and hired men of what was rightful and just – just to corner the Brazos Region market for pissed on sleeping mats. Pissed stained mattresses must be like uranium, he'd wonder aloud. That is what Rope loved about politics – giving an asshole a good and thorough soaping.

Representative Roper Christian Buck started the Studebaker, damn it was a fine car, let out the clutch rolled slowly back onto the road toward Dimebox thinking about his little boy jack, now leading more than a hundred other father's sons into the battle to come and shuddered knowing that his boy would lead from the front. He'd write to Jack as soon as he had given Old Mattress King Sowery a public pants pull down – Texas fashion in front of a crowd of good people who'd get a dollar a piece just to witness this outrage. Yep, Jesus is a kind God. His Mama was making more caramel – God, that boy could eat candy.

CHAPTER 10
THE OLD CORPS

1st Battalion, 3rd Marines was commanded by Major Lucas Opley after appointment by General Barrett on New Caledonia in April of 1943. Lucas Opley was given the Battalion after his transfer to the newly formed 3rd Marine Division from the 1st Raider Battalion on the recommendation of Col. Merritt 'Red Mike' Edson.

Major Opley had been awarded the Navy Cross along with Gunnery Sergeant William W. Higgins for their two-man counter attack on the left flank of the Japanese at Bloody Ridge. Both armed with B.A.Rs, the then Capt. Opley and Sgt. Higgins swept the left flank of the Japanese attackers and helped save Henderson Field and thus the delicate American hold on Guadalcanal. Lucas Opley 38 years old was featured in photos with Edson in *Life Magazine* and the mentioned in the after action report that passed from General Vandergrift to Admiral Nimitz. This veteran Marine adventurer had the rugged good looks of Saturday Western Serial Star and the polish of a public relations man. Within that wrapping beat the heart of a killer who massacred the extended family of General Sandino in Nicaragua in 1931 on the Coco River Patrol.

Sergeant Lucas Opley and PFC. William Higgins led an eight man patrol west on the Coco river in two shallow draft motor boats after several mines in the Mosquito Coast had been raided by Camacho Ruiz the cousin of General Sandino, the Jeb Stuart of Nicaragua. Ruiz hated the *Yanqui* mine owners who had come down to exploit the wealth of his country's natural resources. Ruiz and Sandino had clerked for American Mine Owners in Honduras and in Mexico and knew the patterns of their payroll operations in Latin America. Ruiz robbed the offices of Canfield Zinc Operations in Tecaquita and killed four hired American guards Ruiz and his band of twenty men and four women burned the supply shed, warehouses, and closed the shafts with dynamite – in short Ruiz put Canfield out of business for four months.

In that time, intelligence had it that Camacho and his troop had cut northwest through the jungle and through the hills toward the Sandinista strong hold on the Coco River near Merizo in the North.

Capt. Edson sent a runner for Opley and Higgins in Cabo De Grazias de Diaz on the East Coast. ' Sergeant, I want you and Corporal, that's correct Private, you are now purple. Do not lose the stripes on liberty. Take ten men in two boats with supplies and ammo for three weeks. Take the Coco west to Nell Island off the village of Tuskru Tara about 60 miles west of Cabo. Leave two men with the boats. Leave the newer meat. Cross at the shallows and sandbar here on the southwest of Nell and cut trail to set an ambush for Camacho Ruiz, we figure that he will try to make Buena Vista and you should intercept his column to the east & west flowing creek between Keri, Tore Cinco and Campiamento Omega. He is taking mule and trail up fro the Mosquito Coast and you should intercept him - about here.' Edson pointed to map with his letter opener – mother of pearl handle with photo in-lay cameo – his wife.

'Gives you about eight square miles of patrol space to set up your ambush.'

'Do we need to worry about prisoners, Captain? Punitive expedition?'

'Purely.' Edson looked at Higgins and understood his eagerness to get started as he loved violence and exercise.

'Corporal, the United States of America is balancing the effectiveness of the Marine Corps in supporting Democratic Elections and not in creating an international incident. Prudent and effective termination of outlaw activity is paramount to that end. Exercise judgment. Lieutenant Murphy will want a complete report on your activities and you will maintain company records for this expedition as Sgt. Opley will have more than enough to do. I want an exact accounting for each round fired by whom and to what effect.'

With those orders, Lucas Opley and the skilled Corporal led the ten men into the boats – Opley and Higgins in the lead boat and PFC. Gunty with three men – the 60mm mortar and the Lewis Gun ands supplies. Two of the three would stay on at Nell Island to watch the boats and man the Lewis. Opley laid out the plan.

'Privates Sater and Dupuis, you will be charged with protecting the boats and ammo stockpile until the patrol returns. Gunty you will have charge of the .60 -mm. bring twenty rounds and take ten rounds on the trail and leave the rest with Sater and Dupuis. Pick your mortar team.'

Gunty pointed –'Essenhouse and Krieg. Draw shotguns and pistols. Geisser, Loew - Thompsons, Durkin, Flatt, and Pall take '03s and draw pistols all of you. Cpl. Higgins will take the Browning and Flatt –you will assist him. Each man will carry ten grenades and a hundred rounds. No mules so it will be all 'cut trail' about fifteen miles south of the Coco but all down hill. The bandits are coming to us. Each morning, Higgins or I will take one man with light pack and pistols for a look see. I expect to do three miles a day and no more. We want to stay fresh and sharp. When we spot the bandits we will have already staked out a solid ambush point and fleshed out any escape paths. We will not talk to natives on this one. We want to appear to be a standard patrol on the river. Equipment check in three hours – Corporal Higgins get the gear.'

Fourteen days later, after cutting trail and scouting the slopes south of the Coco, Sgt. Opley spotted the line of march of Ruiz and his Sandinistas. Half of the twenty four rode and the half guided the mules and traded every four hours. It was an arduous task moving the men and supplies up and out of contact with the Coalition Police patrols that only half-heartedly wanted to catch Ruiz. The *Yanquis* were another story, because they wanted to stay close to the *cantinas y putas* in Cabo.

How wrong they were. Opley set his ambush about sixteen miles south of the Coco River – midway between the towns of Torre Cinco to the east and Campamiento Omega to the west. Jungle country just west of the Wawa River where a shallow creek running southwest from the Coco curved away from the flow of the Wawa and the tired and confident Camacho column waded against its gently running waters between two sets of hills. No sounds but what God had placed there to give voice and echo – but that whistle?

Gunty's five nicely patterned .60 mm. mortar rounds wildly drove Camacho's column to meet the enfilading fire from Thompsons and Springfields and into the teeth of the powerful Browning automatic rifle in the hands of Billy Wheat Higgins. Every man and woman in the column was knocked *hors de combat* by the *Yanqui* lead and tried to fire back in panic and futility. Half of Ruiz's column was killed outright by mortar and the cross-fire. Camacho himself lay face up in mid- stream coughing up bits of lung and pints of blood while gulping in fresh cool water from the Coco River tributaries – purified through its course and now toxic with Nicaraguan blood.

Opley and Higgins emerged from their cover and signaled the other Marines to do likewise. They fired into the bodies of wounded and dead. One woman with her right knee shattered by a round from a Thompson found the strength to fire her revolver at Pvt. Flatt and hitting him square between the eyes before having her body shredded by Higgins. Billy picked up the woman's revolver - it was an Army Colt .45 but now useless as one of the rounds from the BAR had impacted on its cylinder. Billy tossed the gun. 'Meskita snatch out of business! Flatt's seen the end of days, Sergeant. 'Hollowed out the back of his melon for fair. The rest of you pollywogs make some holes in these greasers before one of 'em sends you on to the beyond.'

The firing continued tightly and efficiently. When every soul had been set free, Lucas Opley took a Kodak Rainbow Hawk-Eye No. 2A, Model C camera from his haversack and photographed every body where it lay including Private Lester Flatt, USMC age 17. He then took a picture of the seven survivors and Billy Higgins and then posed with Billy and handed the camera off to Gunty for his turn. The photographs would be developed and sent by Major Utley in Cabo to Gen. Augusto Cesar Sandino through his channels in Honduras. Copies of the photos would stay with the American charge d'affaires in Cabo. Opley kept duplicates for himself and his liberty mate Billy.

The patrol buried the bodies of the Camacho Ruiz column in shallow graves along the banks of the stream and returned to Nell Island in Coco River. In three days they were back in Cabo and Pvt. Flatt's body returned to the States. Sgt. Opley was commended for the success of his patrol and conducted three more such expeditions before the Marines were recalled to Culebra.

Capt. Edson recommended that Sgt. Opley be considered for an Officer's Commission and that recommendation went forward. Lucas Opley went to Quantico and completed the Officer's Training course and fleshed out his deficiencies in college credit at University of Virginia and received his commission in 1937. Billy Higgins went to China with the

6th Marines where he won the Asiatic Fleet Heavyweight Boxing Title in 1937 and murdered three Japanese soldiers who wandered into the International Settlement.

CHAPTER 11
LT. BUCK'S HOG-LEG

Seven years later Billy Higgins Gunnery Sergeant and 1st Battalion 'First Shirt' took a special interest in the Army Colt .45 Revolver worn by 1st Lt. Buck of Able Company.

'Lieutenant, where did you come by that Hog Leg? I shot an identical one out of the hand of *Meskita* before I sent her to judgment day south of the Coco River. Honor Bright, Sir.' Billy was watching the young man from Texas shoot out the bulls-eye on the pistol range outside of the Grove Camp.

'Gunny this fine weapon was used to kill Texians at Gettysburg and by Wild Bill Longley himself. My Grand Daddy and my Daddy carried it with the Texas Rangers and it caught up to me on Efate. It shoots well, Gunny?'

'As does the man who grips it. I was never much hand for side-arms – that is why I will die an enlisted man – that and the fact that I drink and fuck myself out of these stripes periodically.'

'Gunny, do not use familiarity in that tone and manner with me, please? I have the highest regard for your service and vital role as 'First Shirt,' but I feel it would undermine my authority if the men were to hear you taking that liberty with me. I mean no disrespect to your service, in saying this and ask it of you. I know that you are too fine a man to require an order of me.'

'My apologies Lieutenant Buck. I am so used to being the Major's shipmate and the bed of nails to the pollywogs that my salty side gets too familiar. You are a fine leader, Lieutenant and your skipper is only your better. You have a great command of those boys. Capt. Bundeschu has molded a fine combat company. The Major is making Able the tip of the spear. How you fixed for re-loads?'

'I make my own Gunny and I hope not to need too many. I would rather call down artillery than need to pull this in anger, to tell you the truth. Please, Gunny have a look at it.'

'Thank you no Lieutenant, but I am sure that Maj. Opley will want to get some play from it. The one I was going to give him is wrecked and at the bottom of a stream in Nicaragua.'

CHAPTER 12
ABLE COMPANY'S MIC-SIDE CROONERS

These were seventeen and eighteen year old kids with only months left to their lives and they were going to enjoy some music and songs. Most would be killed and maimed by the end of August in 1944. These enlisted men were:

1st Platoon – Guadalcanal & Guam April-August, 1944

Weapons Company –Attached to 1st Platoon

.30Cal water-cooled gun team

Pvt. (Later) PFC Tim Cullen

Pvt. Sal Battaglia

Pvt. Watson Cranthorpe

.30 Cal Light gun team

Pvt. Kurt Van Mill

Pvt. Louis Coe

.30 Cal light team

Pvt. Dick Raines

Pvt. Mitchell Vizier

1st Squad

Sgt. Jack Howard - Squad Leader
Pvt. Tadeuz Cynopkowitz
Cpl. Dan Miller
Pfc. Zeb Carrier
Pfc. Frank Dranago
Pfc. Lucius Whitely
PFC. Mike Cloud
Pfc. Norm Chad
Pfc. Neil Steinberg
Pvt. Lonnie Newman
Pvt. Henry Clay
Pvt. Cliff Pirie
Pfc. Leauregard Clavisill
Cpl. Ed Norris – Asst.Squad leader
PhM. 1C., Harry Brosnan, USNR

Neil Steinberg came from the same part of Ohio as Sal and the two of them often went off to sing and session with the stretcher bearers of the regimental band who were all hot musicians. Neil was a tenor who could sing great harmonies to Sal's Baritone. Today they would step into 'Juke Box Saturday Night' that they had rehearsed for hours and hours while Tim was on detail with Gunny Higgins. Neil was a rifleman in Sgt. Jack Howard's 1st Squad and buddied up with Ted C. Ted was a Polack from East Chicago, Indiana and B.A.R. Man for the squad. Neil carried his extra bandoliers and also helped him with his English as Neil's family members were Polish Jews.

But the bond formed in the unit did not preclude solid associations and confederacies of interests beyond the field problem, tent and foxhole. Tim Cullen, Sal, and Watson were welded together in their tasks on the heavy .30 and no others could breach their circle of comradeship, but each man sought out others who shared their hobbies, musical tastes, world view, baseball and football teams, girls, booze, and gangway to God.

Tim loved music – especially vocal arrangements like the Modern Aires and Tex Benecke and often accompanied Neil and Sal to the sessions at regimental band. But more so –Tim sought out the Seabees and especially the men working with generators and water purification machinery. He was nuts for working parts and he had God's own gift for learning and adapting to the *arcana* of mechanics.

Watson went to the Baptist Chaplain for Bible study and played 5-string banjo with the guitarists and bassists with country and mountain backgrounds.

Mandolins appeared out of nowhere –fiddles squealed *deus ex machina.* It drove Tim *out of his mind,* because it reminded him so much of the Celtic session music he had endured in his home and his father's dominance of the inept circle of scratchers and howlers who were not allowed to play with quality Irish musicians. Poor Watson was with two Yankee sophisticates who preened over the latest and the greatest from the Big Bands - Artie Shaw, Bob Crosby, Joe Sullivan, Fletcher Henderson ('Go 'Long ,Mule!'), Harry James, Tommy Dorsey, and Glenn Miller.

Watson was a fair banjo slapper who frailed through the singin' songs but couldn't 'pick-out on the kick-out' hot ones – he also used C - Tuning as opposed to standard G of most Blue Grass. He could wail out 'False Willie Duncan' and 'Whiskey Bill.' but gave way to real church trained singers on good numbers.

Gunny Higgins usually stopped by to listen and ask for songs about the size of a sailor's dick and such themed lyrics and generally 'FuckYEWED the boys good naturedly unless he caught a surly or disapproving look from a young mountain grown Marine, or moss back from Bum-Fuck, Florida.

Today, the 3rd Marines Band Section showcased 'Jukebox Saturday Night.' Neil and Sal took center pole in the big practice tent with the 3rd Marines Band Section of its Medical Detachment. The band was set up standard – Rhythm section,

Brass, Reeds and two good issue microphones were patched into the regimental sound system. Captain Rayler Meens commanded the band section of one hundred and twenty officers and enlisted men who doubled in combat as stretcher bearers dispatched to each company assault team in squads determined by Captain Meens and Lieutenants Puhl and Davidov, through Band Sergeant Major Karol Zgieb.

Tonight they would breakdown into sets for one March set, one classical brass set, and the open microphone for singers from each battalion. The massive tent swelled with lookers on from all over the Division and the audience would include Division Commander Hal Turnage, 3rd Marines Commander Carvel Hall, Major Opley and all of his Company commanders. Sal and Neil would go mic –side for two songs each: Neil would lead off with –

Just One Of Those Things
As Dorothy Parker once said
To her boyfriend, "fare thee well"
As Columbus announced
When he knew he was bounced,
"It was swell, Isabel, swell"

As Abelard said to Eloise,
"Don't forget to drop a line to me, please"
As Juliet cried, in her Romeo's ear,
"Romeo, why not face the fact, my dear"

It was just one of those things
Just one of those crazy flings
One of those bells that now and then rings
Just one of those things

It was just one of those nights
Just one of those fabulous flights
A trip to the moon on gossamer wings
Just one of those things

If we'd thought a bit, of the end of it
When we started painting the town
We'd have been aware that our love affair
Was too hot, not to cool down

So good-bye, dear, and amen
Here's hoping we meet now and then
It was great fun
But it was just one of those things

If we'd thought a bit, of the end of it
When we started painting the town
We'd have been aware that our love affair
Was too hot, not to cool down

So good-bye, dear, and amen
Here's hoping we meet now and then
It was great fun
But it was just one of those things

Just one of those things

Neil's comically calibrated tenor made special use of the punch and cleverness of lyrics unmatched by any singer but Ella Fitzgerald years after the Jewish kid from Shaker Heights sang to the regiment. Even Gunny Higgins quit yelling for more 'Hebe Tunes Hymie! Let's have 'Cohen Owes Me $97!'
And when Neil went into . . . .
My Heart Stood Still
I took one look at you,
That's all I meant to do
And then my heart stood still
My feet could step and walk
My lips could move and talk

And yet my heart stood still

Though not a single word was spoken, I could tell you knew
That unfelt clasp of hands told me so well you knew
I never lived at all until the thrill of that moment when
My heart stood still

Though not a single word was spoken, I could tell you knew
That unfelt clasp of hands told me very well you knew
I never lived at all until the thrill of that moment when
My heart stood still

Tough Guys teared up and Major Opley swayed to the music
and the lyrics like he meant it – *the girl he had some feelings
for in French Lick came back to him, briefly and humanely and
without his standard throb of blood gushing man-horse in his strides.*
Long buried softness emerged from the years of whores and
blood stewed on the Coco River and on the sandbags in the
International Settlement of Shanghai.

The applause was loud and only meant a greater set-up
for the only real vocal talent in the regiment – Big Ginzo Sal
Battaglia. Like he was straightening out a white diner jackets
sleeves Sal swept out his muscled forearms and delicately flicked
out four finger tips on his two hands as if dusting out stardust
magic to his yearning, needy boys - And Sal would give a Wow
Finish with . . .

You'd Be So Nice To Come Home To
You'd be so nice to come home to
You'd be so nice by the fire
While the breeze on high sang a lullaby
You'd be all that I could desire
Under stars chilled by the winter
Under an August moon burnin' above
You'd be so nice, you'd be paradise
To come home to and love

You'd be so nice to come home to
You'd be awful nice by the fire
While the breeze up on high sang a lullaby
You'd be all that I could desire
Under stars chilled by the winter
Under an August moon burnin' up there above
You'd be so nice, just like paradise
To come home to and love

Let's Get Lost
Let's get lost, lost in each other's arms
Let's get lost, let them send out alarms
And though they'll think us rather rude
Let's tell the world we're in that crazy mood

Let's defrost, in a romantic mist
Let's get crossed, off everybody's list
To celebrate this night we found each other
Darling, let's get lost

<instrumental>

Let's get lost in a romantic mist
Let's get crossed, off everybody's list
To celebrate this night we found each other
Darling, let's get lost
Not a man in that huge open air tent was lost on the lyrics
nor the special zip that Sal threw into Frank Loesser's lyrics and
the band crashed its Jimmy McHugh salute as two boys from
Able Company had the regiment, the Seabees, and the handful
for Red Cross women in this most forward of rear areas in the
South Pacific howling and hooting with approval. Vaughan
Monroe couldn't have done better and he thought that he had
when he brought that tune to the bobby-soxer public.

After the Championship game against Tilden Tech, Tim had felt elation and also embarrassment for having had so little to do with the victory for Leo High School. All of his sisters and his Mom and Dad were in the crowd, but he only was called to go in for three plays in the 3rd Quarter and the last four minutes of the 4th Quarter as Jimmy Arneberg was such a dominant player.

Jimmy knocked bigger men back with the ferocity of his coiled spring attack and tossed his body around like a weapon. Leo Coach Whitey Cronin loved Jimmy's style of play and open devotion to Our Lady. On top of being the most enthusiastic athlete in the whole school, Jimmy was the most devout. No contest.

Jimmy hated bad language but never was a hair-shirt about it; as Tony Kelly, Jimmy's best and oldest pal would say,' Jimmy wouldn't say 'shit' if he had a mouthful.' Along with Jimmy, Tony, Bob Walsh, Bob Baggott, Bob Kelly, Bob Hanlon and Don Broderick had made history as Chicago Catholic League football players and Tim Cullen was happy to have been part of that success. He was also embarrassed that he had contributed so little to the game – he was part of the team but the team all seemed so much bigger and that Tim, somehow, didn't merit the praise.

Tim went to Miner –Dunn Hamburgers on 79th and Crandon with Mae Funk the pretty blond with the longest eyelashes in Our Lady of Peace Parish, whose Dad owned the ice cream plant on 55th & Halsted and was President of South Shore Country Club and lived at 7742 S. Jeffery – a swell street for swell people. Mae went to St. Thomas Aquinas High School for Girls and was going to be presented in the Cardinals Cotillion this May. Mae was hot stuff.

' You should go into the Navy V-2 Program like so many of boys are doing and go to Notre Dame – Bob Kelly is going and so is Bob Hanlon; why don't you go Tim?'

'I'm not half the athlete that they are and my grades are not all that great either – a lot of Cs. I'm going in the Marines with Dick Prendergast and some of the other guys.'

'That is just stupid. You guys all want to play cowboy when you should be thinking about what's important. How are you going to rate after the war? '

'I just want to get through the war Mae, eat your cheeseburger; I gotta be at work at 6.'

'You are really sullen. The sullen Cullen.'

'Getting good grades in poetry Mae? Drop the junk Miss Funk.' And on and on the witty teenage banter played out but suspected that something was just not right about the pretty Miss Funk. She did not enjoy meeting Tim's mom it was clear from the last time Tim had had Mae over for dinner with his family after the Mercy Game against St. Rita and Tim had to take Mae home on the streetcar. Tim's Mom had come here in 1912 speaking only Irish from the Great Blasket Island off of County Kerry and worked as a cook at the Metropole Hotel and later the Washington Hotel on 22nd Street. In that time she learned English and had only a slight lilt as opposed to the indecipherable audio- roller coaster that is the Kerry Brogue of Tim's father – he needed two translators – one for literal meaning and one for the litany of profanities.

Tim's Mom was brilliant and as sharp in her read of a person's true nature as his father's was skewed. Larry Cullen had rock-ribbed integrity and loyalty but no sense for human guile and deceit – he needed to have his enemies immediately in front of him and told who they in fact were.

Tim had much of his father's integrity and only some of his mother's canny radar for deceit. Mae Funk had picked him out of the pack when she learned that Mr. O'Donnell who was silent partner in her father's ice cream works had singled out Tim Cullen as 'one sharp young guy;' which in the Funk household was akin to a canonization. Mae set her cap for the handsome red-head in their sophomore year and snared Tim at a St. Sabina Roller Skating Party at 79ˢᵗ & Racine.

Mae skated right up to Tim who was tooling around the rink with Dick Prendergast and Bud May. Bud had a brother who was killed on the Arizona two weeks before the party. America was getting hammered all over the Pacific – Guam had fallen and Wake was hours away from surrender. Gen. MacArthur had retreated to Corrigedor and Leo graduate Lt. Tom Gerrity, who had been wounded at Nichols Field near Manila while trying to take off in his obsolete B-18 was air liaison officer for General Wainwright on that island.

Mae cut between Dick and Bud and whirled away with Tim Cullen and they became a steady. She had met Tim at Bob Fitzgerald's Dance Band Parties at St. Sabina and when Bob Fitz landed a paying gig at South Shore Country Club and asked Tim and his pals to help carry the risers and the band stands. Mae liked Tim but really liked the fact that a big shot like Mr. O'Donnell liked Tim. She had never heard her Dad talk about a high school kid with such second hand enthusiasm.

When she got right down to it Tim was pretty darn cute on his own, but tended to be pretty much of 'gloomy Gus.' Cheer up Kiddio!

Tim thought long and hard and could not remember most of his first talk or any of his second, third or fourth conversations with Mae – they were all pretty much a pattern of her Gee Whiz! Thoughts on what everyone else should do for her – 'Mary Kay needs to ask her Brother for the car next week, so we can go shopping out in Lansing for the pattern Ida will need for my dress.'

Now, having learned that Mae had given him the heave –ho for an Army Air Corps Cadet from Harper High School – Tim was somewhat hurt but more so relieved – sort of like he felt about being on the Leo Football Team – Pride and embarrassment. Tim agreed with everyone – he was a strange

118

creature and he sang the third verse to a song he hated – the old man always screeched this out as well.

Paddy wrote a letter
To his Irish Molly O`,
Saying, "Should you not receive it,
Write and let me know!
If I make mistakes in "spelling",
Molly dear", said he,
"Remember it`s the pen, that`s bad,
Don`t lay the blame on me".
It`s a long way . . . .To Tipperary . . .
Remember it's the pen that's bad don't lay the blame on me.
Molly wrote a neat reply
To Irish Paddy O`,
Saying, "Mike Maloney wants
to marry me, and so
Leave the Strand and Piccadilly,
or you`ll be to blame,
for love har fairly drove me silly,
Hoping you`re the same!"
It`s a long way . . . .

Tim Cullen put all thoughts of that bitch and her fly-boy from Harper High out of his mind and merely appreciated the delicate power of his big friend's voice and soul. Tim walked out of the show and through the coconut grove's tall trees aligned like Grenadier Guards or the glass encased cigars in vertical humidor on Spike O'Donnell's desk in the Highland Theatre where he talked to Tim after the boy had practically installed the oil burning furnace in Spike's basement.

'Coal's out kid – as out as Prohibition and spats on a fat man. In the years to come every home in this city will be burning oil, because it's cheaper and it's cleaner. The air in these apartments and bungalows is thick with dust and we continue to send Aunt Mae and the Thin Kids to TB Asylums in Maywood – Christ!

The way folks live is get through until tonight and never a single thought to the consequence of what they did all day. What do you hope to do after high school, Tim?'

'I think that I'd like to go to Armour Tech and take up mechanical drawing or draftsmanship. My grades are not that great especially in Algebra but Brother Finch thinks that I might be able to get some good recommendations. I like to work with machinery, I would have been better off at Tilden than at Leo, because most of the guys who graduate go on to Loyola or DePaul and the better athletes go to Notre Dame or out to Loras College. That is - if we stay out of the War in Europe - but it looks like that might happen. My older brothers all like the service. Jack is taking engineering up at Great Lakes and will go out to the fleet soon.'

'The War's for saps and sheep, Kid. I stayed out of the last one by getting close to some smart guys and I was slugging for the Unions – that and some other things. You did a hell of a job for me and I know that the tank Swede barely held a wrench on the job. I'm not too hot with the tool bag but I'm not deaf. Here – take this and put it into an account at Standard. See Jack Duffy and no one else. I'm putting you on the payroll.'

Spike O'Donnell handed the boy a brown envelop with two one hundred dollar bills in it. And handed the boy a roll of 10 - ten dollar bills – 'This is your walking around money and to help your old man and the girls when it comes up; use half for yourself. Now, a smart guy will salt the other half with what's in the envelop that you give to Jack Duffy at Standard. This is to start bankrolling your plans. Now, what do you think of my converting this palace's furnace and what would you do?'

'I think that homes will need to be cooler in the summer and that will cut down on the expense of ice.'

'That's true, but think bigger. Everything in life connects, like the tools that you apply to machinery, so do people and relationships. I was a union slugger for the motion picture operators union and still consult with those fine friends of the working man and in my capacity as a consultant; I get to meet with the managers and owners of those businesses. There is a Greek who used to own a chain of ice cream stores by the name of Costanakides – Peter Costan. He took the refrigeration from his ice cream coolers and huge fans to cool his theatres. That, my friend Tim, is something to set in mind. Keep it there. You are a good boy. Stay in touch.'

That chat with Spike O'Donnell took place three years before Tim Cullen walked out of the 'Juke Box Saturday Night' show by the 3rd Band Section and his pals and took a long walk through the coconut grove on Guadalcanal. Watching him leave the show and following him - out at some distance was Lt. Jack Buck.

With the orchestra scatting for all it was worth, Jack Buck took the air and walked out to a Ford truck used by the Red Cross and put his left foot on the runner. He watched as that strange kid Tim Cullen walked down a lane of coconut trees seemingly in full concentration upon a huge issue. Ever since their confrontation on Mt Austin Jack was drawn to Cullen as person with a special glow he had seen this in people back home – his father had it and so did his mother and the Mexican horse breaker who worked for his Daddy on their get-away ranch, Ignacio.

'Boyfriend walk out on you, Lieutenant?' Her voice was clear, sharp and soft at the same time and Jack Buck had to take his foot from the runner in order to see from whom that voice broke his thoughts. It was a beautiful girl with no make-up with thick black hair pulled back into a tight bun abaft of a wide pink forehead that crowned huge blue eyes, a long Roman nose and perfect red lips accented by remarkable cheekbones.

'I was over him long ago. Too young for me and redheads make me nervous. Miss . . . .?

'Magdolyna Szabo – Maggie, Lieutenant?'

'Jack Buck, Maggie, I am pleased to meet you. Like the show?'

'That last boy – the Italian kid who looks like Mike Mazursky the Wrestler – what a voice! How did he not get a recording contract or at least get into the U.S.O.? He and the Jewish kid were unbelievable.'

'They are both mine – You could say that I am their manager/agent. Any rights that they have belong to me. So, if the Red Cross wants their services, You, my beautiful friend, will need to negotiate with me?'

'You make a command a question? Obviously you are from Texas. I am from the southeast side of Chicago.'

'So is the man who walked out on me. That kid taking in the coconut inventory for Lever Brothers is my heavy machine gunner and the Italian boy is one of his assistants. Tim Cullen is a south side Chicago Irish-er. You don't have Irish features?'

'I'm Hungarian. I'm a steelworker's daughter. I went to DePaul University and intend to go to law school. I want to study contract/labor law. Might have been one of that kid's relatives who killed my Pop – I have no use for the Irish. Pop was a steelworker's representative and he got shot and killed in the Republic Steel Massacre in '37. Shot down people at a union picnic just for a few lousy bucks. Capone's money is not enough for those pigs.'

'Some temper when touched Maggie. By the Way Tim's Dad was a policeman and he resigned for refusing to set on the strikers – true story. Now the old man is a movie theatre janitor or something.'

'Well I guess they can't all be on the pad. How about you Texas?'

'I'm Irish too – Notre Dame Class of '40! Actually I'm Scots-Irish/Welsh & Mexican. I was in my second year at Northwestern Law when my reserve status was called up Navy or Marines so I went with the Corps. Spent a great deal of time in Chicago and Evanston – great town, great parks. Never went down as far south as where you and my man Cullen live though passed through on the South Shore Line often enough.'

'It's called Hegewisch – the neighborhood – it's all steel mills and steel related factories. When I made my first Communion all our little white dresses were rust colored before we got into the church. Mostly, Hungarians, Polish, some Mexican and the damned Irish – cops, gangsters, and lay-about.'

'Would you care to take a walk? The Band will play until 20:00 hours. When do you need to report back –or can you let someone know that you are in the company of an Officer and Gentleman?'

'By act of Congress. . .'

'By act of Congress.'

The young couple walked the company streets avoiding the usual mud and canals of running water. Maggie was outfitted in utilities and boondockers – they only really put on the dog for formal visits by Eleanor Roosevelt or other dignitaries and big shots from the states and generally stayed in the useful and the drag as the Japs still had the capabilities of getting in air strikes. Maggie, wrote copy for Mrs. Cleanth the Back Bay Boston Boss of the Red Cross unit of twenty-five women and eight middle aged men who worked the canteen, operated the theatre, arranged USO shows – few and far between – only Bob Hope and Jerry Colona cared to tour this theatre – Oh,-and Chico Marx and his Orchestra!

Maggie got out press copy and prepared Mrs. Cleanth's schedule and interviews. In the words of Gunny Higgins – 'that old Bull Dyke is Heavier than Whale-shit - take the long trail around her.'

In fact, Mrs. Cleanth was a close personal friend of Mrs. Roosevelt and had made heavy contributions to Mrs. Roosevelt's 'causes' but not 'one dull penny to her gangster husband and his rabble machine.' Mrs. Cleanth had been fast-tracked to the Solomon Islands in January of 1944 and her unit had brightened the day of more than one service man on the 'Canal and now Lt. Jack Buck's dusk in May 1944 held onto the light a little longer.

Maggie liked the good-looking Marine Lieutenant immediately; he was as lean as a greyhound and had dancing bright black eyes that seemed to see horizons well over the globe's extent. He had humor – something can not be fabricated; it wells up only from a good heart – like her Pops. He could draw people to him by merely placing himself within sight and he was fearless in his love for his wife and children – demonstrative.

Jack Buck had that same look about him. Was this an Electra Complex – was Maggie searching for the Daddy taken from her by the Cop's bullets? Naw, this cowboy was sexy on his own. It oozed out of him – he had the goods. Jack noticed this striking girl's eyes gulping him down from the get-go. Kids, I met your Ma on Guadalcanal! How 'bout that?

'Maggie, I didn't see you at the formation for Mrs. Roosevelt. Major Opley would have been sure to try and scoop you up.'

'I was consigned to my typewriter and the teletype that whole week with time off for the cot and coffee. I must have written something the size of *Anne Karenina* and only nodded to the great woman herself. And your Major Opley has been in and out of my office more than Mrs. Cleanth herself with his - 'can I get my boys . . . my boys could use . . . Sweetheart can you see your way into getting my boys . . . and everything he asks is for his boys and readily available through Quartermaster and Navy Public Relations but he enjoys wowing me with tales of Nicaragua and the beauty of the beach at Culebra, P.R., or dawns and departures of his romantic insights. The man is a thug with clusters and about as interesting as a drunk out of town. I like you.'

'I've been to three State Fairs, eight hog-call contests, Maggie and that is the most impressed I have ever been and I was chased off the team by Frank Leahy himself! You are a direct girl. Might I add that I was pole axed by your voice – you had me hooked. I am not currently anyone's sweetheart; nor do intend to stray too far from your high opinion. May I walk you back to your quarters or would that cause you some distress from Mrs. Cleanth?'

'She may send me home on the next transport and break my heart. Lieutenant Buck, do you have prospects following the duration of hostilities?'

'Madam, I am propertied and nearly licensed to rob the poor with the Law's consent. My area of the Law will not conflict with yours as I am in property law and contracts. I intend to set up a real estate management and development company in Chicago and sell leases – My daddy always said' God ain't makin no more land and he's chargin' top dollar for that what's scratched already.' My Daddy is a Texas State Legislator and land holder, cotton, cattle and some oil. I hope to do on my own with what he has already endowed upon me and my Momma would like to see me out of the Brazos but visit often – she wants old Daddy to herself once he retires.'

The best looking couple on Guadalcanal, aside from the native couples walked and talked for a good two hours and found an out of the way place to embrace and softly bring lips, tongue, salt and fiber together and a sweet and fierce tangle of lonely and welcoming passion. For those of us familiar with the chemistry of the initial shock brought on by this loving contact, the electric surge not unlike the low voltage of small generator throbbed both young people and stirred the necessary chemical bondage. For those of us unfamiliar with love's lock on the lungs and the sweeping waves of energy incumbent upon emotion and physical cataclysm, my talents are sadly limited and true understanding can only be bested by your faith in understanding. Maggie Szabo and Jack Buck saw each other as often as possible for the remaining four weeks that they would have with one another.

Tim Cullen whose sulky walk away from the night of music; it was an escape from himself and an evaluation of his days.

CHAPTER 13
GOOD BYE 'CANAL

As May 1944 came to an end, there was very little time for swimming or visiting with pals in other regiments, taking an LVT –Alligator - out to fish with hand grenades, or trying to mooch a ride with a submarine patrolling TBM for a joy ride out to the Shortlands or Russell Islands and back. It was to paraphrase Gunny Higgins 'all assholes and elbows' -Work.

Once all of the .30 caliber ammunition from the Tulagi run had been cleaned, clipped and belted Tim Cullen and his two mates on the Browning .30 caliber Heavy, Sal and Watson had been humped out into the bush for field problems through the month of April and now were marching to Tetere Beach and onto LSTs for live rehearsals, four days a week through May.

The object was to be ready for any assignment on the D-day planned to take place. If Able Company were to go in the first wave as it had at Bougainville, they would go in on the alligators after transferring near the reef from Higgins boats; unless the LST would bring them in close and disgorge the Alligators from its womb. They would train for both contingencies – over the side, down the net as at Bougainville and into the Higgins boats and then up and over the gun whales in to the Alligators and then the LONG short ride over the reef and onto the beach; or straight out of the doors of the LST over the reef and into the steel and smoke.

Heavy packs and gear were donned and rifles and ammo checked for this morning's live rehearsal - the fourth of the week. Sal hefted the gun and Tim the Tripod, while Watson carried the condensation can hoses and ammo cans along with the near eighty pounds of personal equipment that bulked his knees.

'Spending hard dollars, this Navy is, for the trips we makin' and all to get ready for a couple of minutes on beach, Hell, I don't even remember getting on the beach at Bougainville. Seemed like the crowd carried me and not near as neat as our rehearsals beforehand, Tim. Hell, you only did one rehearsal before going in with us – that Jap gun was spittin'! I could see it from two hundred yards out and we got right up to the sand it musta hit seven times'n killed them Coast Guard Boys on the Lewis guns'n tore up the guys up front. Shoot we beached right in front of the damn bunker should a shot the damn coxswain. Hell, Tim you was there.' Watson always got chatty when he was nervous. When the men from the Quartermaster Company showed up and began lugging footlockers and marking tags – he shut up altogether. This was to be 'Goodbye to Guadalcanal!' They were going. None of the rear-echelon commandos said anything, but carefully tagged and marked each man's personal items and trunks as if it were their own. Some in their utilities and the new Raider caps nodded or winked to the men who would go in first under fire. Some of these men had done so themselves at Guadalcanal, or Bougainville, or Cape Gloucester and had been wounded badly enough to make them Quartermaster men for a few months and maybe miss this one.

The Trucks pulled up and Sgt. Rittenouer called out their names for each truck-the Heavy .30 crew would ride with 1st

Squad and Lt. Buck down to Tetere Beach. Lt. Buck was on
the other side of A Company Street watching each man and
approving a nod to each man in his platoon as he boarded a truck
– all business and no grab-ass. The men knew that time before
the attack was growing short and they had practiced and coiled
themselves into furious individual units of stern death-dealing
efficiency. They were going in – Theology students, high school
pretty-boys, boxers, CCC veterans, chain-gang graduates,
sharecroppers, coalminers, farm boys, rich college kids, soda
jerks, assembly line UAW union men, Dickens scholars, sneaks,
and Momma's boys sprinkled with China, Haiti, Nicaragua, and
Sea School Marines – all dead serious shock troops transformed
by the bonds of Marine Corps tradition and rote-repetition of
details. They were not fearless, they were Marines.

The trucks drove them the few miles to Tetere Beach where
they were met by the crewmen of LST 448 – blue dungareed
sailors who had been in more invasions than any Snuffy now
boarding their ship. Since being commissioned at Mare Island
last year – LST -448 had been part of the Aleutians, New
Guinea, Tarawa, Biak and Kwajelain invasions and battles. The
sailors had five Battle Stars and downed two Jap Planes and
been bombed and strafed eleven times. This was a solid, solid
crew of good men.

The tank deck crew and the beach party had already loaded
the fourteen LVT Alligators into the ship, taken on thousands
of gallons of fresh water, hundreds of tons of food, supplies and
ammunition, prepared bunks and officers billets for the 225
members of the 1st Battalion – A Company and Headquarters
company and staff/ the balance would board the next two LSTs,
which also carried aviation fuel and more ammunition. The
lush jungle odors were submerged in man-made synthetics
and mineral by-products of fuel, diesel, chemicals, corrosives,
explosives, and all manner of befouled food products. The
new fabricated steel world of welding and rivets; Cables and
capstans; hatches and overheads – confinement replaced the

open Tropical expanses of airy-roomy tents- Tight suffocating confinement. Sgt. Jack Howard lined up 1ˢᵗ Squad off to port of gaping maw of LST 448 for equipment check and Cpl. Danny Miller followed Howard as each man sounded off – Cynopkowicz B.A.R.; Steinberg, Rifleman; Carrier, Rifleman: Whitley, Rifleman; Chad, Rifleman; Dranago, Rifleman; . . . through to Newman, Cloud, Clay and last of all Leauregard Clavisill – an especially favorite target of Gunny Higgins LOW REGARD INDEED!" A fellow McDonough Plaza boy.

'You painstaking remembrance of mortal sin – you fucked out whore's sheets leavin's – your Momma should have drowned you in the soiled waters of the Old Man! At birth! MutherFucker! Clavisill! There is not a bullet calibrated for a fighting man's weapon that will have so much *Low Regard* as to penetrate that yellow skin of yours, boy! You are truly Blessed to be so fucked!' Gunny had boarded hours before with the staff officers of 1ˢᵗ Battalion. However, Gunny's omniscience had identified the approach of 1ˢᵗ Squad, A Company and the sad yellow jaundiced flesh of Pvt. Leauregard Clavisill. As the squad marched up the fat ramp of steel like a reptile's tongue, Sal started singing

' . . . I can't stand high posts and I can't stand fences – Don't fence me in! Let me ride through the wide open countryside that I love. .. and listen to the murmur of the cottonwood trees. . .'Til I see the Mountains rise , ,.

Gunny Higgins howled down from the Forty Millimeter Gun Mount high above them. 'Belay that Dago skylarking, Mutherfucker! Act like Marines, Vaginas!' And so they made a new home.

CHAPTER 14
'FOR ME TO KNOW . . .AND YOU CAN GO . . .FIND OUT'

Father Duenas had moved to the south of the island Inarajan but made trips north on his horse avoiding the main highways as much as possible because the Japs were moving men and material toward the invasion beaches at Orote and Asan. The new Kebeitai intelligence officer Kato was one frightening hombre – he had the sensitivity to American influences on Guam and the genuine affection people had for the Americans all the while attempting to completely undermine any confidence in America's willingness to 'let My People Go.' As a dedicated Communist, Kato had effectively submerged his radical socialist inclinations to the Imperial mindset in order to work for change within the military and as the Navy allowed for more original thought in its officer corps, the Imperial Japanese Navy afforded Ryugo Kato - the opportunity to influence his peers by acting as an overt Fascist.

Though new to Guam, Kato understood the love of the Guamanian people for its Church and its priests especially the young priest Duenas – Calvo was a fierce Catholic cleric but lacked the dynamic intelligence and aggressive antagonism of Duenas to the Japanese occupation. Duenas needed to die – for the cause of this war and one to come for world revolution. He needed to die fast and the yet unapprehended Radioman George Tweed would give Kato just that necessary outlet.

Father Duenas rode north to Tai taking the path on the edge of rice paddies that the Japanese had expanded in the south of Guam. More people were put to work in the seeding and harvesting from the *lanchos* and jungle villages during the last two years in order to help make Guam - the Imperial breadbasket.

Along with sugar cane production and refining, taro harvests, and fruit processing, rice production on Guam was vital to the Japanese war effort. In the last two months, since the arrival of new Army units from Manchuria, Admiral Homura, the island governor, had ordered the construction of a great camp – a concentration camp at Manengon in the south. All Chamorros who had displayed open hostility to the Japanese occupation were to be placed there until the American invasion attempt would be crushed The Chamorro moral code of *ina`fa`maolek* which demanded that the community come together to help neighbors in trouble kept Tweed alive and safe and in relative comfort.

Since his last visit to the north of island, Duenas had been allowed some peace and quiet from the Japanese, but now with Lt. Kato taking up the intelligence duties on the island and the Americans showing a greater naval and air presence in the Marianas it was clear that the holiday was over. Ever since his 'brotherly chat' with Monsignor Fukahori and Father Peter Komatzu – sent by the Japanese government to get Guam's Catholics to 'play ball' and his decision to stay as far from Agana and away from the Japanese as possible, Father Jesus had been allowed to minister as a priest and also to help the sailors scattered around the island. Father hummed the top tune among the people around the island – especially the hot-bloods of Inarajan – those crazy kids took shot-guns and old *pistols* that had belonged to their Spanish granddaddies and wanted to meet the Japs with hot lead on December 10, 1941 –when the invaders planned to move to their village, but Father had calmed them down and told them that the fight will come soon enough.

Eighth of December, 1941
People went crazy
right here in Guam.
Oh, Mr. Sam, Sam
My dear Uncle Sam,
won't you please
come back to Guam."

Goofy little song but it took Guam through this trial. On his last thirty-five mile trip north to Tamuning, Father had rejoiced in the intent to convert to Catholicism of Al Tyson and C.B. Johnston these two captive sailors had taken to the charity and courage of the island people and their simple but iron Faith and had asked Duenas to give them instruction in the Faith. It was not to be. Al and C.B. had been caught when a Saipanese girl had been witnessed taking blankets and medicine at one of the dispensaries in Agana Heights and followed by the men under Lt. Kato. Al and C.B. were tortured and executed. The last of the men, George Tweed, became an obsession with Kato. Father Duenas boarded his stallion Flashy for long ride north.

Father Duenas stopped at lanchos and villages on his journey and took in the love and legendary hospitality of the brave people who waited out the violence and terror of the world gone made with lust for possession and retention. The Americans who had wrested the dominion of Guam from Spain at the close of the last century proved to be odd but winning masters who brought much good to the land. The Japanese, newly powerful and majestic, controlled by force and contempt. In this vortex of steel and smoke whirled the people of Guam who clutched heroically to the island's bounty and the traditions of community and compassion that outlasted Spain, America and God willing Japan – let the days be short to that time.

CHAPTER 15
RENT ON A GUN TUB

While America now breathed easier with defeats on Japan piling up like copra and cane, Guadalcanal, New Georgia, Russell Islands, Bougainville, New Britain, Tarawa, Makin, Kwajelain, Eniwetok and all along the New Guinea coast, the young men packing into steel ships on the Solomon Islands and in Hawaii re-learned the shipboard life. They had made the great crossing to ever expanding Forward Areas and felt the heave and swale; the restriction and terror of being consigned to the role of passive attendant, while the skilled sailors whose daily attention to watch and mission eased the green dungareed and Khaki guests into their home for many weeks.

These sailors who welcomed the men of Company A, 1st Battalion, 3rd Marines were blooded and salty; they would take these Marines into the 5th Invasion of LST-448. They had de-electrified their ship; sailed its shakedown cruise; identified the expanding steel of its hull and beams; practiced loading cargo, landing craft, trucks, troops; landed those troops and supplies under fire; fought off air attacks from Japanese dive and torpedo bombers; and buried a few shipmates as well. Once, in the frozen waters and Williwaws of the Aleutian Campaign, LST-448 and her crew had carried another ship (an LCI) and successfully launched that ship. They were a seasoned crew of blue denimed fighting men. Like the Jarheads whom they now eased those first footsteps aboard on an LST, they were children of the Depression and sons of every State in the Great Forty-eight.

Tim Cullen hefted his sea bag after Gunny Higgins shouted down with Jovian power and even Sal went pale at the thought of many days and hundreds of nautical miles confined with the absolute most terrifying human being on earth. Along with his Transport pack, 782 gear, and his three and a half feet of khaki canvass private life, Tim Cullen, a feather-merchant at 124 lbs. was boarding ship with nearly his own weight. Tim, Sal and Watson would return to the deck ramp and load aboard their weapons cart, the tripod and the crated heavy machine gun once they had been given their berths on the tank deck's narrow quarters adjacent to the fourteen LVTs that would take A Company on to a hot beach in the Marianas.

Billy Higgins watched Cullen heft his sea bag and roll up the ramp to the LST like a salt with a score of 340 on the range and four service stripes. This little boy and thousands of others in the long snakes of sage green utilities had taken the bull by 'the boys' for the long tug. God! He was proud of these youngsters and whenever his colleagues of the Old Corps got womanly about 'the old days' Billy fingered these tough skinny little Man pups who had become Marines in so short a time and who had fought in tough climes against a vicious foe and beat him senseless. Fuck the Old Corps! These beardless virgins could out fight, out March, out soldier, out shoot and out service all of the Old Corps rate robbers combined – with himself being the exception.

No sir – not a one of the children had let him down – dying with Japs stabbing them when the ammo ran out on Edson's

Ridge. These kids held up the Globe and Anchor just fine and gave back as much misery to them yellow fuckers as they dished up in heaping servings every day on the Canal. And then at Bougainville, landing under fire for the first time, Marines, untested as a unit took out every Jap gun and emplacement and chased them out onto those miserable fucking trails. What a shithole that place was —ten times as rotten and miserable and disease ridden and rotting and shaking with that farting volcano.

Billy remembered the admiration that Lucas Opley had for the little red-headed brig rat that, sick with dengue and malaria refused to come off the line until McWatt nearly pulled his side-arm on the kid. Cullen goes back and nearly strangles the Doc for calling him a malingerer. Damn!

Cullen needed to stay close. Gunny headed down the ladder to the tank deck and watched the sailors berth the men of A Company. Lt. Buck was calling out the berths and setting the men in the four high racks and stowing their gear. All the sea bags had been tagged and set in the Company locker and the men kept their essentials and 782 gear hooked onto their racks. When 1st Platoon was set Lt. Buck and Lt. Gallo moved on to 2nd Platoon and Headquarters Platoon. Gunny approached.

'Lt. Buck, my apologies, Sir. Several of the rates on deck have asked Maj. Opley for volunteers to assist on Battle Watch and General Quarters on the secondary mounts, particularly the 20MM. mounts. They'd work managing the Magazines in the ready box and they'd have permission to berth in the gun tubs – stretch shelter halves over and boondock on the deck. Sir, I volunteered your Heavy thirty team to take # 4 gun starboard near the Officers Berthing. With your approval Sir.'

'Excellent idea, Gunny. Cranthorpe, Battaglia and Cullen – follow Gunny Higgins to the main deck and aft starboard. You will maintain 20MM action stations and assist that station at General Quarters.'

'You men, report to Ist Gunners Mate Chaffee at 20 Mount 4 Starboard. That is your new home for the cruise, Marines. You will name your first born for Gunny Higgins when you see the accommodations. You will sack under the stars and enjoy the sea-breeze, while the lesser blessed brethren sweat like whores in Church and come to believe that Coco Chanel invented diesel fuel. Follow me men!' Saluting Lieutenants Gallo and Buck, the three drunks from last April grabbed their gear and moved topside behind the khakied and squared away colossus.

Though still beached the relatively flat-bottomed LST-448 swayed and heaved, but the real beauty was the solid blast of fresh air that perfumed the three boys who had only been aboard the steel ship for twenty minutes. Already they were invigorated by the 100o cool and relatively free of the foul air below.

Ist Gunner's Mate Chaffee was the gun communicator for all starboard 20mm. Mounts and relayed orders from the Gunnery Officer who stood watch above the bridge. He introduced the three sailors from the black gang that manned this gun in combat – Machinist Mates, Tom Brown, Al Townsend, and Isaac Cohen. Cohen was the Pointer who would be strapped in to the gun itself and fire the weapon; Brown the trainer who elevated and traversed the weapon operating a series of wheels; and Townsend, with whom the three Marines would spend a great deal of time, the loader who manhandled the heavy magazines containing sixty rounds of 20 mm. contact ammunition. Each round needed to actually hit its target in order to explode, unlike the 5.5 inch gun and two 40mm. twin guns that fired proximity fused shells that exploded near its target. Thus, the 20mm. guns needed to throw out a lot of lead to hit the swift moving Jap dive and torpedo planes that they could be sure to arrive closer to the invasion target.

Ist Gunners Mate Chaffee made the introductions and walked off aft with Gunny Higgins to discuss control measures for the balance of LST 448's guests – Chaffee was also the Master at Arms – the ship's top cop. Chaffee had been a blue water sailor since 1937 and served on Cruisers *Astoria, Nashville, and Pensacola.* Chaffee was asked to take on the task of training gunners for the new LST fleet and enjoyed the Large Slow Target.

'We sleep in quarters behind the bakery and we get a breeze from the fans and take to the deck at times but our watch requires us in the engine room and that is one hot mother,' explained Ike Cohen of Pittsfield New Jersey.

'You birds will love the gun tub – plenty of room and air. All we ask is that you guys help us keep the 20 mags filled and coiled - the crank requires about 60lbs of tension – the first round is a sand round – it contains sand so if I forget to remove the plug at the end of the barrel the round will shoot off the plug without damage to the gun. Then, that blue painted round and every fifth round a red painted tracer round just like you guys do with the .30cal. Crank the rounds tightening the magazine is a bitch and a half – so don't let the crank slip or you'll crack a rib. ' Here . . .' Cohen pointed to two long vertical rectangular steel boxes welded to the walls of the gun tub. ' This box stores the spare barrel – we need to change the barrel after about four magazines of 60 are fired to keep it from warping – you guys can help on this under fire. We have extra asbestos gloves. Now, this box is to be kept filled with water – when we take the hot barrel out we put it in here and the water boils out like a volcano.'

Watson gushed, 'Hey, we saw a for real volcano on Boogan and it erupted before we shipped out back to the Canal and it made a earthquake that Tm and Me thought was a Jap air-raid and we was all fouled in our net hammocks that the CBs rigged for us . . .' Cohen held up his had to quiet the effusive West Virginian.

'Easy, pal , easy – this is work. When they sound GQ, open the ready box, have the weapon un – canvassed; check the water box that it's filled; stand aft of the gun. There is enough room in here for six but on action stations don't move until we tell you, OK? That's the rent boys.'

'Ike, want us to service the weapon after firing? Asked Tim eager to take something apart and grease it and divine its operating secrets.

'No, we had better not start that stuff. Brown here would be all over it but we need to clean and check our weapon, but thanks. You guys can bear a hand if you like. But basically don't screw around with it. This ship is pretty good and a fine feeder. You'll like it aboard her. The Skipper was a Chicago cop and reads Latin and Greek. He is a great sailor; in the Aleutians, we had to transport an LCI to Adak and Lt. Higgins got us there without incident and launched a ship almost as big as ours. That was the most amazing thing that I have ever seen in this war so far.'

Brown added, 'That and the white Russian women in Adak! Ike here chats the lingo with the Russkies'

'On the level, I'll bet I know him. My Dad was a cop.'

'Save it pal, Mo Higgins is all business, unless you have business on the bridge especially - no small chat. Good guy, but keeps his distance like a good officer should; it's always the friendly guys – buddy-buddies – that are the fuck-ups and get guys killed. Right before Tarawa, we had an ensign from the cargo deck watching some Marines who were doing target practice off the fan-tail – Chief Chaffee was there and this *Yutz* elbowed a guy doing his laundry into the drink and drown him – had no business being there in the first place and was supposed to be auditing the lash-down on all of the LVTs and fuel manifests. Turned it over to the Machinist Mate 1st Class on the watch and went up to watch the Sea-going Bellhops. What a asshole! He was always 'Jim, Ted, and Billing' us with what a great guy he was and always doping off. Lt. Higgins put him on the beach right after Tarawa and we got a good man, Ensign Kennedy, in his place. He's been with us since Tarawa.

Let's do a dry drill later after you guys get squared away, but before we anchor off the beach.'

Tim liked the three guys and he and Sal and Watson proceeded to make AA station # 4 starboard their home. Fifteen Marines from the Amphibious Tractor Battalion also made similar arrangements. They were the drivers and gunners aboard manning the fourteen LVTs packed tightly and lashed down below on the tank deck of the LST. Most of their crewmen sacked out in the vehicles themselves, while maintaining the vehicles engines operating systems. Three of the LVTs were designated armored Buffalos and carried a 37 mm. gun turret taken off an old Stuart tank and added to the craft for direct fire support of the landing force. Had these been available at Bougainville more Marines would still be with this veteran Regiment.

An LST, a three hundred and fifty – foot by fifty foot transport, was a marvel of invention and necessity – a work of genius. After the British got their pants pulled down at Dunkirk, Churchill put out a call for American designs that would help avoid the embarrassment of sending fishing boats and water taxis across the English Channel to take its troops away from a disaster. When Hitler's Panzers ate up Europe in a matter of weeks the British Expeditionary Force was nearly garroted on the French Coast. If not for the brave and haphazardly thrown together fleet of barges, colliers, trawlers, and freighters 'lending a hand' there might be German speaking troops occupying Northern Ireland today.

In 1941 the Admiralty and the American Navy's Bureau of ships called for the production of the Atlantic Tank Landing Ship which thanks to the design of Mr. John Neidermaier and the Bureau of Ships (BUSHIPS) The Landing Ship, Tank or LST was born. America industry responded and contracts went out and outfits like Kaiser built hundreds of this ship design. It was basically a 328 ft longs and fifty ft. wide ship made of steel with a basically flat bottom and wide doors at the bow with a tongue-like ramp that, when beached, and the doors opened would throw its reptilian tongue onto the shore and vehicles could be disgorged from its belly.

Its superstructure lofted aft of a long flat deck that would be crammed with more vehicles and equipment. From that ship's aft -castle, the Captain, usually of Lieutenant's rank – the equivalent of an Army or Marine Captain – guided the ship. Around this castle were positioned anti-aircraft guns and at the stern the only primary battery – 5.5 inch gun. These anti-aircraft gun positions were set inside an elevated steel tub in which a crew of three to five sailors operated a Swiss designed 20mm anti-aircraft rapid - fire cannon. This nest in Officer's country would be the home of three Marines from A Company.

CHAPTER 16
FLASHY & VICTORIA

While the stern anchor strained and pulled like sea-going Sisyphus, Father Duenas and his horse Flashy encountered the glass green paint job on the 1937 Packard Victoria 1507 of Dr. Ted Tanaka slowly making its way up from Agana to Agana Heights. In the last two years, the priest and the dentist had extracted as much of the pain and the suffering from the souls of the suffering Chamorros and balm-ed the fears of the Americans hiding from the occupiers as they could. Ted was taking more of his cache of American dollars hidden in the tire guards of the Packard out to Tai for burial on Don Rodriguez's *lancho* west of the village. Ted had buried thousand of dollars since the occupation leaving only ten thousand dollars in the Bank of Guam for the occupiers to assess and tax. He and Kara had suitcases of tens, twenties and fifties of the 'long green difference which the Doctor had slowly cashed out of the account on the recommendation of Governor McMillan.

Ted and Father Duenas found places to hide the money where it was believed that the Japanese would have no plans for setting up operations. This money had been used to bribe officials too friendly with the occupiers and there were not too many of them, reward policemen for tip-offs on Japanese sweeps in each of the districts, and set surety for the American liberation and aftermath. Dr. Ted Tanaka practically owned Guam would not call in his markers. He was loaded and happy and as American as the kids hiding out in the jungles; he was also necessary to the Japanese occupying forces.

The still elegant Packard was wax and buffed when the dentist left his home, but now with a good uphill spin under his white walls the great car was caked with mud and dust. "Get a Horse, Jawbreaker!' yelled the tall priest from his snow white stallion.

The Packard eased to a siding and Ted pulled off his aviator glasses. He was decked out in a pink polo shirt, egg-shell cotton slacks pink and brown argyle socks and white bucks – Yewow ZUH!

Father Jesus threw a muscled, long thigh over the horn of his saddle like Buck Jones himself, and thumbed up the brim of his straw hat and drawled, 'That Pretty Gal a Your'n dress you? My God, Man, you look like meat for the Dead End Kids.

'Age *Quod Agis, Sacerdotus* – You'll go ass end up off that hoofed hamburger. Balance, My Son, Balance. How's tricks by you, stiff collar; robbin' the poor boxes in the south? Where you get that straw Kelly? It's a Pip. Hey, have a sandwich Kara made the Tomato and cucumber relish with lots of minced onion and pepper. This island lacks garlic, Father, see if the Vatican can scare up some emergency cargo.'

'Father Calvo and I are pretty much on our own out here Ted, accept for the two stooges sent in from Dai Nippon – I understand that the two them could concelebrate in a phone booth with the crowd they get for Mass. My friend Pastor Sablan and I had a sweet and sunny meeting with *Ichi Ban* Homura a few months ago and wanted us to discontinue celebrating the feast days of the saints as it took the people's minds off of

The Divine Emperor. Pastor Sablan most loudly objected as he argued that the saints gave people comfort and I stepped in and said that when people are terrified they must call on the saints to intervene and Homura yanks out the samurai sword and starts screaming 'Why Fear Your Protectors?!' Lovely man – old world sensibilities.'

Dr. Ted wiped the mist and mud from his Kodak aviators, "Horseshit, Father! You were the fly in the old ointment on that one - remember I read all of the official transcripts, Don't try to gild the lily for Pastor Sablan – his martyr's crown is getting to be a pretty tight fit. We have stalled the census of all Baptists for Homura. He wants an old style purge of the Baptists and Sablan is at the top of his list. We are trying to stall until the American bombardments get heavier and they are. We are playing for time in this one. And you! Stay smart and stay south, for the love of God, Father.'

'Where'd Kara learn to throw food together like this? My son you are one blessed Jesuit cast-off. The woman has looks, legs, laughter, and longevity going for her and she's anchored to a fashion retard.'

'Try not to get your head separated, Father, its close very close. Here take these extra sammies there's a Fifty American under the lettuce on each – TAKE MONEY OUT BEFORE YOU swallow them. There's my patrol – two Saipanese bankers try to follow me whenever I leave town. I'm heading up to Yigo to bury some loot and make a drop to your pal Sablan.'

'Where you burying the dough?' asked the young priest as he righted himself in the saddle.

'Like I'd tell a Capuchin grave robbing priest who spent his seminary days in Manila rolling drunks. Be careful, Pal.' And the two men parted company one taking the rode up to Yigo in a Packard Victoria and the other on a pale horse to Tai.

CHAPTER 17
TAKE FROM THE SEA'S BOUNTY

'Now, here this! Now, here this all Marines topside starboard – utilities and fore and aft covers. Chart talks!'

Major Opley and A Company Skipper Geary Bundeschu and their platoon commanders stood around a blow-up aerial photo of the section of beach they were designated to hit on Guam, after the Saipan campaign set to go off on June 23rd and the Third Division would act as a floating reserve should they be needed.

Major Opley signaled Gunny Higgins to call the men to attention all 165 enlisted men in A Company snapped as a unit.

'At ease. The smoking lamp remains out for the next two hours. Grab some deck, Marines.' Two days aboard and no signs of losing any of the sharpness that Lucas Opley had witnessed in the hills and jungles on Guadalcanal and in the back-breaking tedium that was the live landings at Tassafangaro and Cape Russell. These kids were honed steel and there were enough veterans of Guadalcanal and Bougainville to paint over any dents in this landing force's skin.

'Col. Hall conveyed his warmest regard for A Company, the tip of this Division's spear at Cape Torokino on Boogan and now at Guam. We are liberating American soil, Marines. This isn't a sand shit-hole like Wake island and that everyone wants back, it is more. The people on Guam are more American than any of you tough guys from Philly, or hard cases from Florida chain-gangs, or CCC Camp foundlings, or coal miners like Cranthorpe here. They sure as hell are more American than this Irish brig-rat that can out fix any CB – when he's sober.'

The men punched and patted Tim and he smiled off the salty compliment. Tim welled with pride at having been singled out by the Battalion Commander – a real Marine of the old nature.

'That's right Cullen; Lt. Buck assured me that those lips will kiss Gunny's cheeks before they pass demon rum. Correct, LT. Buck?'

'Aye, Aye, Sir!' Smiled the man who had exacted a promise from Tim Cullen far more soul snaring than his sobriety vow.

Back on Guadalcanal, after showing Gunny Higgins his Colt revolver, Maj. Opley made a point of joining the young Texan on his next visit to the small arms range.

'That Colt is almost identical to one that *Meriza bandita* tried to kill me with, before Billy Higgins, First Shirt, put out of action with a Browning – the Colt and the *puta*. We were on the Coco River Patrol and ordered to intercept a Sandinista column that had robbed and dynamited a mining operation on the Mosquito Coast. I would a loved to have had that weapon. Where'd you get that fine hand gun Lt. Buck? '

'This is a family hand me down, Major; my grandfather was a young Texas Ranger and ordered to bring an outlaw by the name of Wild Bill Longley into Giddings for hanging. During' the trip from Louisiana to Giddings, Wild Bill and my Grand Dad hit things off. The Colt itself was given to Longley by

Capt. Myles Keogh who had himself been awarded the Colt by Gen. Buford after Gettysburg. Sir, Bill Longley had served in Cavalry for a brief time and had save Keogh during a Kiowa ambush in Kansas. Myles Keogh was later killed with Custer.'

'That is some pedigree. I remember an old G.A.R veteran who still wore his Colt in French Lick, Indiana – the old buzzard had to be seventy-five years old. I was a freshman football player at French Lock High School and used to watch the old guy watch our practices and hoop and holler when we scrimmaged and he always wore that hog-leg. So, I guess yours is the third one. Three's a charm as they say.'

'Yes, sir; would care to fire the piece?'

Opley thought -step out that hole, son, they're going right by you. 'No, thank you Lt. Buck, I'll stick with this old craftsman's tool. Nothing wrong with the Colt Automatic –stops 'em fast and they stay stopped.'

Shortly after that epiphany, Lt. Buck decided that should anything happen to him in combat, the good Major Opley had determined to add this 'charm' to his own webbed belt. Sgt. Rittenouer was old Corps and if ordered to turn over a fallen officer's side-arm he would do just that, but Cullen was another story altogether.

'We are going into Red Beach 2 with 3rd battalion going against Chorito Cliff and we will be under constant fire from the hills above the beach and these to land-out-croppings. The 2,500 yards of beaches used by the division lay between a pair of "devil's horns." Beaches RED 1 and RED 2, used by the 3d Marines, rested almost against the left horn, Adelup Point.

"A Company, Capt. Bundeschu will organize on the beach here cross these rice paddies and take the nose of hill you see insinuating itself toward the beach there are these woods to the right and gullies at the base of the hill line should provide good cover from whence to proceed – I recommend that two platoons Buck and Gallo make an enveloping assault and hold the third platoon in reserve. your fire-eaters should have the hills by noon chow. Once this objective is secured we will link up with the 21ˢᵗ Marines to the right and consolidate the beachhead.'

Every man on the deck of the LST could see that the elevation of that hill was sharp and a tough run. They would be climbing a 60o slope with packs and weapons under fire. The whole time. Tim raised his hand, 'Major Opley that hill is a sharp and long climb will we need to assault with the heavy .30 cal. or should we secure it on the beach?'

'I think that the water-cooled weapons can and should be left secure on the beach and brought up to effect night defenses once the crown of this hill is secured. Sharp eye to detail, Private. Captain Bundeschu, I have informed regiment and division that this objective shall be hence called Bundeschu Ridge – it's yours Captain, Take it! Officers in my cabin in five.'

Gunny Higgins stepped next to the C.O. to signal and end to the official round of this briefing. 'Platoon Sergeants and squad leaders with me. All hands bear a hand policing this deck of toe-nails, cigarette butts, and pogey-bait wrappers. Looks like Bonus marchers been here. From the Forty Mount to the 5 inch pop gun I want fifty yards of marines policing this deck at the slow and sure footed. Assholes and Elbows!'

After two hours the Marines were allowed to sun themselves, service weapons on the deck, belt up ammunition and can it, and smoke Lucky Strikes and for the few fortunate Chesterfields.

Tim Cullen was sunning his filmy Irish pallor into a robust red after days at sea. In the Gun Tub within haling distance of the bridge, Tim, Sal and Watson maintained the ready boxes and changed the water in the empty barrel tube with cold salt water. As there was a scarcity of fresh water on board the LST and limited to one shower every three days Tim and the other enlisted men had become used to oily feel of their skin and applied moisturizer to their faces immediately after shaving. Other than that and the BA PALM, BA PALM, BA PALM that the flat ship made as it coursed its way to the anchorage at Kwajelain, where the men would go ashore for running and conditioning, Tim and the others rested and prepared themselves for the invasion by reading and studying maps and hand-outs, but mostly by cleaning and re-cleaning their weapons. Into the sun's bright rays broke the towering majesty of Gunny Higgins whose shoulders eclipsed the late morning sun over Tim.

'Brig-rat, it is time that you learned to eat of the sea's bounty and as you are most mechanically aptituded fuck-up in this august body of fighting men under my mothering gaze - Get your side-arm and come with me.'

"Gunny we are not supposed to carry side arms on board but have them stowed,' replied Cullen with a cat's sense of scalding water to come.

'Pipe, down shit-bird, and lash on that Smitty Wesson, we going fishing.'

Cullen snapped to and donned the shoulder holster and the .38 revolver that he had carried since Bob Foster had handed it to him before Bougainville.

'Throw on your cover, Altar boy! We are in the shadow of our betters and they are in the Officer's Ward Room for the next three hours.' Tim put on his khaki fore and aft cap. 'Choirboy we are fishing for the fat-fucker who ate Jonah; 'Course being a Pope's Pussy you do not know or appreciate the beauty and majesty of the Bible – King James only. See the starboard davit? Aft of the LCVP is a small crane for lowering cargo and ammo. That is our fishing pole and this is our bait.'

Gunny Higgins produced a twenty pound slab of fat back bacon that he had commissioned from the Cook on condition that all galley rating got a cut of shark steak. Gunny Held the huge slab aloft as if he were a king and this was his first born male heir!

'We go fishing for the great fish – the Great White or his fat-assed lazy brother the Blue Shark. You will operate this crane and drag bacon until one of those torpedo-like chow-hounds gets more than he can swallow.'

Cullen almost wet his pants with excitement and took the gaffing hook from its lashing and pulled the large thick cargo hook over the gun-whale and Gunny Higgins speared the huge slab of bacon through the grain and then against it.

Tim operated the crane out and lowered way the chain slowly and carefully so as not to bring the line crashing into the thin hull of their transport.

'Kiss my heroic ass, if you don't handle mechanisms like you were born to them. Jesus, Brig-rat, you amaze me and I fucked humped back midget sluts in Shanghai before going to YMCA meetings. Makes you want to throw up; doesn't it Junior? Why, the taste of fine snatch in the Orient is only bettered by its nibble on a working man's wallet. You a Virgin, Candyass?'

Tim lied, 'No Gunny, I took pleasure in the whores of San Diego.'

'Don't lie to Gunny, Needle –dick, I have your service record and you went home to Mama after Boots, got tossed in the Brigs, took a Summary Courts, boarded *Bloemfontaigne* for New Caledonia, shipped to the 'Canal, surveyed on the .30 under Bob Foster, a better man never drew breath, crapped in your pants and everywhere else on Boogan, and you still got you cherry.'

Tim laughed to himself but tried to concentrate on the job at hand.

Between LST- 448 and the horizon were LCIs of every type- The Landing Craft Infantry was roughly half the size of the LST 128 feet in length with a beam of 23 feet and, like the LST, almost flat bottomed so every sailor and Marine aboard felt every wave. With crews of between 40 and 60 sailors the LCIs carried up to 200 Marines. There were also derivative models of the LCI modified to be gun ships, rocket ships, and mortar ships

The LCI(g), or gunboat carried 3" and 5" guns, extra 40 mm Gun mounts, and bristled with 20mm guns as well as .50 caliber machine guns. The LCI(r) carried rocket launchers and up to 600 4" rockets. LCI(m) was outfitted with heavy mortars to bombard hill-lines and take out bunkers on the defended beaches.

Destroyers of every Class and designation darted like ballroom dancers among the plodding transports. Like every day thus far aboard LST-448, Tim marveled at the vastness of the Pacific and imagined that he had traveled farther and to more historic impact than any other person in his bloodline. He did not need to imagine that he had in fact done so in his full year in the service of his country.

His mother and father had told their children of their individual odyssey's from County Kerry: his father working in Liverpool and Manchester and fighting the working man's fight with Big Jim Larkin and taking the passage to New York, boarding train for Chicago and the stockyards in time to work as a policeman during the Strike of 1912 and his mother, leaving a cabin on the Great Blasket Island and heading to Queenstown in County Cork for passage to New York and herself a train to Chicago to work in the kitchen of Metropole Hotel on 22nd Street. These were day trips in comparison. Tim had voyaged farther than anyone in his bloodline and that was fact.

Let's take this time to sweep out the attic of our imaginations and suspend the trinkets, tinsel, ticket stubs and teary-eyed treasures above the level of our thoughts-vision and look to port from Tim Cullen's thin steel housing. We have had, this narrator has at any rate, a clutter of junk that he imagines are the important mirrors of his experience on earth – a pretty good time most of us, despite the disappointments, deaths, diseases, distractions, and in some cases whole-sale de-railings of our journeys; but in the might and main we have had it pretty good.

The boss walks in and tells you that the McDonald's account will go to the guy who leaves at 3PM, spends the next three hours at a martini bar with the suits from the next level and 'big pictures' all the ideas that you have presented to the 'team' and that you should give this slug all of your notes and work-ups and keep him apprized. You have had it rough; you pay your own way; you meet the mortgage payments; you take the extra classes; you do the heavy lifting; you do not cheat on your husband; you do not make your wife do the lions share of the work with the kids and then beef about Andy's inability to master freshman algebra; you do not sleep-in when it's a twenty below zero wind-chill factor and Sacred Heart is five miles from the house; you do not reap the rewards for which you labor as a good woman or man – tough shit.

Your kids are not coughing up their little lungs and shivering under wet blankets in a tropical rain-forest after having had their cottages torched and pulled down and sent with all your belongings to Manengon on the other side of the island; you did not risk your life sneaking dried fish and fruit to an uncle named Blas who would walk thirty mile north through jungle and kunai grass, evading patrols of Japanese Naval Landing Force troops led by Boson Otayama, who was pissed off to have to take his twenty-seven sailors out of Agana to the wilderness on a wild-goose chase for the last of the Yankee sailors cowering in a cave; Otayama vowed that he slit open any gook that he found, from the dick to the lungs and leave him or her for the bugs and toads; You are disappointed. Take it and embrace it. Grow up.

Tim Cullen grew up fast, but he was still a kid even after Bougainville and he had a kid's sense of fairness and the arm of God and the protective cloak of the Blessed Virgin taking a direct part in his journey, like catechism books when he was a little guy at St. Sabina's Grammar School, do good and you will be taken care of – what about martyrs? – don't be a wise guy. Tim Cullen believed that Gunny Higgins was going to take care of the boys in the squad with a shark steak dinner.

Out there, strung out for miles, ships and smaller craft folded the waters into prayerful wakes like the hands of Virgins and saints in the statuaries of St. Sabina's a prayerful voyage and beneath the palms of foaming waters darted Tim's prey, who themselves sought out the weaker and the plaintive unfortunates who fell overboard – and they did with some frequency – American, British, Australian, Dutch, and Japanese combatants who were too clumsy, too trusting, to cocky, and too human and plunged to mercies of what they believed and what would be. Those sharks would eat them.

Tim had an American made Harrington Hoist built on Tchoupitoulas Street in downtown New Orleans by Standard Services Crane Company and a twenty pound slab of Iowa Landrace Hog in the palm of a very sharp hook. After an hour of slow and methodical trolling the bait hooked a sixteen 1/2 foot long Tiger Shark! The powerful monster threshed and thrashed and yawed in attempts to unhook itself from the baited trap, but the thick American steel cable and the Gary, Indiana forged hook help the trapped victimizer of overboard sailors and troops of all nations. Tim Cullen worked the controls slowly and eased the heavy dinner toward the starboard hoist aft of the rocking LCVP above Tim's khaki covered red-hair. Gunny Higgins watching from the starboard fly-bridge hooted and laughed aloud as his cloud-covered altar boy once again proved himself to be a boy of talent and steel.

'Cullen, you pie-eyed unregenerate brig-rat, you by God bested my take off of Cuba in 1932! That is a tiger and I snagged a damn thresher! Boy, you are a fire-tested pair of brass balls! Get that fucker aboard!'

Tim's heart pumped and he half-giggled but maintained his focus as scrums of sailors and Leathernecks jostled near the starboard crane when word of the feat spread through the Company. Sgt. Jack Howard's Jackie Coogan –face thrust through the scrum of faded blue denim and salt-bleached green herringbone – "YAYYYHOOO! Hook 'em Cullen! That's *my* gunner boys and girls!' Similar encomiums fell around Tim's shoulders and now the bridge above them was thick with pressed khakied officers who slept in well-ventilated berths in the ships castle while those below sweated and slumbered in the bowels of LST-448. The officers, especially Maj. Opley and Lt. Buck cheered their accomplished underling's feat of skill and luck.

After twenty minutes of coaxing and dexterous manipulation Cullen swung the huge gray fish over the gunwale and lowered the Tiger shark to the deck. The monster thrashed and snapped as if un-troubled by the snare of steel. Marines and sailors turned into mincing girls and danced toe-touchingly back from its razor sharp maw. Tim pulled the Smith and Wesson from his shoulder holster and put two bullets in the shark's brain and then the three last as the shark's last acts of will slowed to a violent and final snap.

'Now Hear This! Now Hear This! This is the Captain Speaking! Master-At – Arms! Disarm that Man and drag him to the brig!' Over the ship's loud-speaker, the voice explained the folly of Tim Cullen's trust in Gunny Higgins. Hoots and howls of laughter replaced the high Hozannas! 'The Brig-Rat's Return! Now, Playing 'The Man in the Iron Mask!' 'Piss and Punk Cullen!

'Aye, Aye, Sir!' Chief Chaffee replied to the call from the ship's Captain Lt. Mo Higgins.

Tim received three days on bread and water for firing an unauthorized weapon aboard a ship in a combat zone without the stated authority of the Master at Arms. Gunny Higgins took one arm while Chief Chaffee confiscated the machine gunner's side arm and marched the pawn to his steel screened dungeon behind the galley.

'You'll sweat off some chubby in here, Brig Rat,' opined Chief Chaffee.

'Hold on, there MAA this is a combat tested, fighting man only trying to feed the men who guide his life. Besides, he's all ribs and dick now as it is. He's a shell-back and won't miss kissing your disgusting paunch, Chief, any how! That's tomorrow we cross the equator – number twenty for me.'

Tim was stripped of his boondockers, shirt and trousers and in skivvies and socks laid down upon his bed of pain – again.

CHAPTER 18
DINING WITH A RED

The table was spread with some great Dresden China that Ted's mother had sent to Kara as a wedding present despite her husband's intolerant but final banishment of the young couple to America's outpost on the fringe of Asia. The China was bought through a flat wear and fine china merchant in Spokane and shipped to Ted and Kara upon their arrival in Agana along with a long and tender note to her little boy about forgiving her traditional husband, but Ted could care less and thrilled to the life in exile with his movie star.

Kara had Imelda help her untrunk the china and the glass settings and along with Betty spent a happy day in washing and drying and dishing the dirt about Betty Grable and Harry James who last were heard to be on the verge of divorce as well as Spencer Tracy's epic bender after making *They Gave Him A Gun* in 1936: 'I had a bit part in Bob Benchley's *How To Vote* with Ruth Lee and Jimmy Lydon. . 'Betty interrupted 'HenREE! – I can't stand him he's such a pest!'

Imelda gave her a loving crack on the back of her pretty head of hair; 'Don't interrupt! Go on Kara. .'

'Ruth Lee was a hoot and Bob Benchley is such a good guy and he likes to dip his beak as much as the next guy – but nobody tops Tracy. They say Errol; Flynn? Choirboy. Spencer Tracy on full boil is turbulent. Well, Tracy and Benchley had hit it off years before as drinking buddies and after Tracy wrapped *They Gave Him A Gun,* a real dog with Franchot Tone, he went on a toot that lasted for weeks. He drank his way off the Lot at MGM and made his way over to Paramount, because he LOOOOVED the two Bobs – Benchley and Montgomery. The three of them took off for Van Nuys and bottled up in a hotel there; well the two Bobs had had enough after three days of it –fun is fun, but Spencer got ugly when they wanted to go home to the collective Missuses – no problem for Mr. Tracy. He took off in hired taxi and drove up the coast to San Francisco and out of the State to Washington. My God he must be one unhappy man. MGM sent dicks to find him and bring him back in some kind of condition for his next three pictures. One of them was *Captains Courageous* – that man is brilliant – but troubled'

'Betty, honey, run over to Mrs. Esterhazey's bodega for some of those long matches tell her the taper matches. Here's sixty cents in Yen should be about Grand – Jap Funny Money.' When Betty had gone the two wives got to the nature of the chat and help – getting out of Agana. The new IJN intelligence officer Lt. Ryugo Kato was the guest of honor at the Tanaka's tonight along with the roast pig and the many rice sides and vegetables.

'Kara, you must get out of Agana and go south or somewhere, because . . .

As the woman set out the service for three on the white Irish linen table cloth, the whine and roar from the Naval Air Station increased as twelve torpedo bombers, eighteen dive bombers, and ten of the new fighters rev-ed engines for take off. Though ten miles to the south, the air ships sounded like they were in Kara's dining room. The whole house shook as the planes took off and roared to form up over the island.

'The Americans are getting near and there is more bombardments on the heights and south near Sumay and Piti every day. Ships are beginning to fire on the heights and are coming closer every day. Mrs. Esterhazy says that the baboon Otayama told her that most of his men are being taken north in the next two days, because they think they know where Tweed is hiding. Cookie this new Jap is smarter and more vicious than the other one.'

'Imelda, I will stay and so will Ted we'll get through this. Ted's burying money now out near Yigo – we'll all need that soon, either to bribe Otayama or this new rat and to buy food and medicine and if the Americans come we'll all be Ok. Look on the odd chance that Ted wants me to duck out I have my black dye ready and out goes this red mattress stuffing. I'll crook up like an old lady sneak out. But, Baby Doll, this is my place and I have been run-out before. We need o look out for Betty. She's the one I'm worried about – those bastards if they lay a drooling tooth near that baby I'll mow the fuckers down myself!' Kara knew that she was in danger of being raped and killed but even toothless Mr. Bina was too. The only thing keeping the Japs from any outrages was Governor Homura and he was a homicidal nutcase himself. Now, this new smart American educated naval Intelligence Officer Kato, a smooth and chilling character, had taken over control of the haphazard investigations into pro-American activities at the high school and had ordered that all Chamorros bow to Saipanese and Japanese civilians as well as all Japanese Naval and Army personnel. Two teenage boys had already been placed in the forced labor camps at Fonte for laughing while bowing.

Kara's husband Ted was being watched by two Japanese bankers in town and several Saipanese landlords out in the fruit country.

The dinner that night was an icy but civil affair and Kato was as Joe College charming as he could be – tales of beer guzzling escapades at Oberlin College and reefer smoking in graduate school at University of Chicago. Kato had two degrees in Social Work and had written his Masters thesis on racial red-lining practices in Chicago as the chief means of oppressing poor Negroes. He and Ted talked about jazz music and its ability to bring about real justice in America. Ted argued that dancing and finger popping was fun but hardly a revolutionary force, but Kato indicated that making America's nose rub in the shit for effectively expanding its Imperialism through race oppression would really bring about its economic as well as moral collapse. The Emperor was the sword and fire that would exact a just and rightful punishment for America's vanity.

Ted listened with patience of a dental professional who had listened to obscenities fired at him for ten years now and softly countered, 'However, Lieutenant, it was my honored and traditional father who exiled and disinherited me for marrying Kara. That was his greatest gift to me of all. Sending me here to this generous and lovely island of welcoming and happy people..'

Kato boiled over, 'These Niggers are like the Sambos shucking and Yawzuhing every slight and sneer and no different – these Niggers are beasts of burden and no more. Their priests have seen to that. Unlike the American Negro these niggers will never snap and fight back –they should all be locked in the caves up in the hills and have grenades tossed in after them, but who will do the work I suppose.'

'Lieutenant, for an Oberlin man to employ that low pejorative is surprising and frankly unnecessary especially as you are my guest here. These are lovely people and . . .'

'Boys, lay off the deep thoughts and let's get to the dirt.' Kara had instinctively diffused approaching disaster. 'Is there a Missus Kato? Or, are you, Lieutenant a marketable commodity. There are several sharp looking young girls from Saipan working at the Airstrip. I have helped a few of the girls with some fashion tips over the last few weeks. That Hiroki Susueni in Commander Bokoi office is a knock-out! Any hearts going to get broken here on Great Shrine Island?'

Kato burst out laughing at his own foolish display of his intellectual powers and revealing the chink in his armor as he noticed both Ted and Kara's glance to one another during his obviously Marxist rant. He'd need to kill these two as well as they foiled the purpose behind his work on Omiya Jima in the Emperor's name but for the World revolution to come.

'Mrs. Tanaka I intend to break all of their hearts!'

CHAPTER 19
THE BRIG RAT RESURGENT

After three days on wine and cake in a steel wire cage behind the ship's great galley the already skinny frame of Pvt. Tim Cullen, the now legendary A Company Brig Rat himself, was tossed his utilities and boondockers by Chief Chaffee and Gunny Higgins. Along with the clothes were four slices of toast covered in about two pints of creamed chip beef on toast, a ladle of peas and pearl onions, a beaker of cold frozen orange juice a pot of coffee and am individual sized deep dish peach pie. 'Eat your chow choir boy, we'll be back to take you to Capt. Higgins, Maj. Opley, Capt. Bundeschu and Lt. Buck.'

Tim shoveled in the beloved SOS as this delicacy was his favorite thing about joining the Corps. Never in his life had he eaten creamed chipped beef on toast as his mother, trained as a cook for years in the hotels and homes of rich Chicagoans, had yet to master this recipe invented by a Marine sergeant. Mary 'Hannah' Cullen served up roasts, steaks, chops, salads, chowders, stews, soups, and porridges of every variety (especially Welsh rarebit), but never mastered this quick and easy rib-sticker. Tim delighted every time he put away a mess-kit full of the grayish-brown topping for toast and barely had the strength to ease into the deep-dish peach pie that seemed to have been engineered by the soft hands of a mythological Mother figure, but, in fact, the pastry had been slapped pulled and stuffed by the Chesterfield chain-smoking ten-year Chief Cook of LST -448 – Marlon York of Shelbyville, Tennessee who sweated gallons of his human essence into morsel consumed by every man aboard.

On evening of the second day of Tim Cullen incarceration. Chief York served grilled shark steak to the founders of the feast Gunny Higgins and Chief Chaffee, Master – At – Arms, every man on galley watch, as well as every officer on LST-448, the staff of 1ˢᵗ Battalion, 3ʳᵈ Marines, and Capt. Bundeschu, and Lt's Buck and Gallo of Able Company. Capt Bundeschu asked Chief York to provide a special Bouillabaisse and French bread for the drivers and crews of the fourteen LTVs that would take Able Company on to the beach under fire.

The officers' feasted on shark steaks grilled over the open flames of Chief York's range and glazed with a citrus honey and peppercorn sauce, roasted peppers and rosemary potatoes, chilled tomato aspic salad, Waldorf salad, and iced tea. Each officer had a deep dish peach pie ala mode with scoop of vanilla ice cream. At the conclusion of the feast Capt. Maurice Higgins held aloft a tall glass of iced tea, 'Gentlemen, I give you Pvt. Timothy Cullen, USMCR! May God give him good health and long life!' The Naval Service Officers chorused 'To Cullen – Health and Long Life!'

Major Lucas Opley rose and added 'To Cullen's long life and short sentence; I add one stripe to his sleeve. Capt. Bundeschu have your clerk file the necessary paper work immediately moving Cullen up the pay-grade effective this night!'

Along with Capt. Bundeschu's 'Aye, Aye Sir' followed a round of 'Here, Here!'

With his shrunken stomach now bursting with good food, Tim Cullen donned his sage green utilities and smartly snugged up his leggings and carefully planted his khaki fore-and-aft cover for the trip to Officer Country. Gunny allowed the boy an emergency head call as the food coursed its way through Tim in a matter of minutes. While in the head, Tim heard the ship's loudspeakers, 'Now hear this, Now hear this! This is for all hands! Two days ago, American forces captured Rome and yesterday Allied forces landed on the beaches of Normandy, France opening the invasion of the continent of Europe. As of last reports, all beaches were secured and Allied forces have moved deep into the hedge country of France. God Bless America!'

The National Anthem was played and Tim rose in the head without any prompting or coercion, he was that moved. 'Square away, your stern Cullen! Sharply.' With all business personal and national attended to Tim joined the Master-at Arms and the Battalion First Shirt. Together the three enlisted men emerged from the darkness of the ships bowels and the two senior NCOs allowed the boy's eyes to adjust to the dazzling sun east of the Marshall Islands where 3rd Amphibious Group Task Force Transports and the slower LSTs and LCIs congregated along with the faster Attack transports and support ships and took on more fresh water, fuel and supplies for the long voyage and longer wait for the Marianas Operations (Forager for the Third – scheduled to follow the Saipan and Tinian Operations beginning on the 15th of June.).

Capt. Higgins, Maj. Opley, Capt Bundeschu and Lt. Buck smiled broadly as Tim Cullen uncovered through the hatch of the Captain's Office in the castle of LST-448. 'As Captain of this ship, I hold every man's life in my hands, a bit more importantly the mission of this ship's service to the broader Campaign ahead. The Master-At-Arms serves at my pleasure to enforce the safety and obedience to the laws of Maritime Justice. One of the most sacrosanct laws forbids the unwarranted use and firing of weapons without the express orders of the Captain through his MAA. You were summarily confined and punished according to my administration of this ship's mission and safety. MAA return the Private his side arm.'

'Aye, Captain! Secure and stow this weapon until such time as you disembark, Private!' Chief Chaffee returned the holstered weapon.

'Private Cullen. Your service record will not be affected by this infraction of Military and Maritime Law. This matter is Closed. Major Opley?'

'My apologies, Captain Higgins, but you are not addressing the man in accordance to his rank. 'Private First Class Timothy Cullen, take these stripes and have one sewn on to the sleeve of each item appropriate to the designation afforded you on June 6th 1944.'

'Aye, Aye, Sir!

; Nice shooting Cullen. Effective and efficient – the shark was magnificent! Return to your station at 20mm Mount Starboard # 4 and get your crew squared away for practice on the heavy thirty. Tomorrow you and Lt. Buck will demonstrate effective combat eminence of the water cooled thirty followed by a BAR cleaning and quick assembly lecture -Dismissed!'

PFC Cullen emerged from the brig a pay grade up when he exited Capt. Higgins' office he smiled with pride as the Gunny, Chaffee, and the Officers howled with laughter. Cullen had some twisted angels in his corner...

Chapter 20
First Alarm Orote Naval Air Station

Fernando Howard and Fidel Alupo pushed carts of crushed coral for the paving of the Orote Naval airfield as they had each morning for the last two years from dumpsite three hundred yards south of the airfield to the edge of the runway all day and every day along with two hundred other former Insular Guard members confined to the forced labor camp in the clearing created in 1942 by the Kebeitai.

On December 8th, 'Nando and Fidel had and their compadres of the Insular Guard had fought the Japs who landed near Piti and fell back as more and better armed Japanese Naval Landing Forces came ashore. The Marines at the Barracks at Orote had been ordered to lay down arms but the Insular Guards kept fighting until forcefully ordered to surrender and then they were marched into Sumay and abused by the Special Landing Force troops. They were beaten, summarily executed and starved for weeks and then impressed into forced labor companies around the island.

'Nando and Fidel had breakfasted on rice and over ripe mangos at 4:30 and arrived by truck at the airfield by 6AM they loaded their fourth burden of the day when the air-raid bells were hand clanged from the towers dotting the airfield. Hundreds of Japanese Navy troops bolted from their huts and dove into shelters, while scores of others operated the mechanisms of their dual-purpose guns mounted on elevated berms or clipped ammunition into smaller caliber machine guns in preparation for an American air strike on this field. Al; the Chamorro laborers and their guards headed for the pre-designated shelters on the edge of the airfield, giving the seating men a brief respite from their slavery.

Minutes after the first clang the roar of twenty six deep blue American Hellcats intensified as they began their dawn run on Orote peninsula and the Japanese airfield. The first four planes tore up the runway with heavy caliber machine gun fire that sent pine trees of coral chips and dust streaking to the skies – the lead plane banking left; then right; and then left and circling for the next pass. The following four fired on the Japanese Kates, Judys, Rufes, and Zekes parked in the protective revetment: Kates dropped torpedoes, Judys, were dive-bombers and the Rufes Seaplane fighters and Zekes fighter pursuit planes.

At the field to the North of Orote were the longer range Frances and Betty Bombers and at Sumay the Emily Seaplane bombers and more Rufes.

Here at Orote, the single engine craft were the targets of five groups of four roaring blue new Grumman Hellcat fighters from the heavy carrier *Essex*. These wildly versatile airplanes clawed up the airstrip with .50 caliber slugs from each of the six well maintained and fresh weapons. All of the back breaking hours of labor were dusted into useless dust and the once sturdy runway for Japan's heroic naval aviators pock-mocked like the faces of Guam's lepers colonized outside of Inarajan.

Shouts of *Kono yaro! Kuso yarou!* were fired up at the planes by pilots and ground crewmen along with the 25.7 mm and

7.7 mm ammunition from the gunners of 510th Naval Defense Battalion. All of the American Hellcats completed three passes without loss of a plane and they roared off to the southwest of Guam.

'Nando and Fidel climbed out of the dugout and witnessed the IJN airfield's damage and the rage of the occupying forces. Several revetments were aflame with the twisted wreckage of Judys, Nates. Kates, Rufes, and Zekes several Mitsubishi Type 8 Zeros were attempting to take off after the raiding Americans but were hampered by the torn up, bombed, strafed and rocketed runway that was a cratered mess of blasted coral. Six got into the air well after the American planes disappeared.

A Japanese Warrant Officer whose Rufe, still aloft on it's float, was burning one hundred feet from 'Nando and Fidel's dugout ran up to the two former Insular Guards and shot and killed them with his Nambu pistol.

In Agana, Boson Otayama and six of his sailors rampaged through the plaza beating and kicking every Chamorro that they encountered. Lt. Kato still hung over from the great wine and food at the Tanaka's dinner for him put on his mustard brown combat uniform, with sword and joined Otayama. 'Boson, make an example of the Cruz family – they are the most American of all people around here. Beat the old man in front of his daughter and slap the old lady around pretty good. Then tell him to get his ass up to Agana Heights at the 18th Infantry headquarters. Gen. Takashima wants to organize a civilian mixed brigade comprised of our people and the Saipanese. The 54th Kebeitai is under his direct command and Gen. Obata is in overall command. Governor Homura has moved his authority to Manengon camp. You and your twenty six men will be charged with directing the mixed brigade – use them to kill any Chamorro not actually doing anything to affect a good defense. Lt. Sensei is directing the killing of all dogs on the island and using the niggers from the villages. Bring Cruz to me – I want to kill a priest this week. Round up his nephews and meet me at the Butler lancheros at Agana Heights by 02000 tomorrow.' Otayama snapped to a robotically rigid form of attention and snap bowed, *HI!* He shouted and ran off.

The Southern Task Force of Operation Forager under command of Admiral Connolly at sea and General Roy Geiger in tactical command of all land forces on W-day closed south of the Marianas as D-Day on Saipan loomed. The 3rd Marine Division and the Ist Marine Provisional Brigade would act as floating reserve for the Saipan operations.

Chapter 21
That Goofy Kate

It was expected that the Japanese would affect a great naval and air opposition to the two forces poised to attack Saipan – a Japanese colony. More drills took place in expectation of those raids to come and the three men of Able Company occupying the starboard .20 MM # 4. Mount on LST-448 took special care of the anti-aircraft gun, its ammunition ready boxes and kept a solid supply of twenty millimeter ammunition loaded and tightened in the heavy re-load magazines. The Black Gang watch trio, Ike Cohen, Tom Brown and Al Townsend had relented under the persistent appeals of Tim Cullen and allowed the Jarhead machine gunners to help maintain the gun itself, after Ike came to appreciate Tim's gift with mechanisms and aptitude for working parts. In fact, while most other Marines aboard Cohen's ship were concocting pornographic epics of their tales ashore, losing money and possessions that many of them didn't have in the first place shooting craps and playing Byzantine variations of five-card poker, or picking fights with each other, Tim Cullen went below with Ike, Tom and Al on their watches and learned some of the wonders of the diesel generators, engines, and condensers, as well as the anatomy of the ship.

Sal and Watson generally stayed put in the gun mount and were often joined by hillbilly musicians and Neil Steinberg for songs under their shelter halves that served as a canopy over the walls of gun tub. As all of the bandsmen stayed afloat with the medical battalion aboard and APD attack transport, only the stringed geniuses of the Ozarks, the Great Smokies and the foothills of Appalachia provided accompaniment. In that time Neil and Sal covered some of the more popular Bob Wills, Sons of the Pioneers, and sage brush favorites/"Home in San Antone:" Low and Lonely /Miss Molly/No Letter Today and other such Gene Autry and Roy Rogers tunes supplanted the standard popular tunes much to the approval of the vast number of southern and farm boys marines and sailors. Starboard Tub #4 became a musical getaway and salve for the bored Marines and the overworked swabbies.

'General Quarters! General Quarters! All hands man your battle stations! Lash down all hatches! Seal all water tight doors! All Marines report to action station stations! Aircraft approaching Starboard! The guitars and fiddles dropped and stowed – Kapok life-jackets and helmets donned - every man to his station. In .20mm Gun Mount #4 Sal and Wat had shooed away all singers and guests, tore away the makeshift canopy, uncovered the .20mm Oerlikon Gun, removed the barrel plug, loaded in a sixty round magazine and stepped back.

In less than a minute Tim, Ike, Al, and Tom were topside and donning Kapok life jackets and helmets. Tim helped Ike strap into the weapon as he pointed the weapon at 40 degree angle starboard, Tom Brown stepped into the trainers spot and Big Al Townsend signaled the relay passing of ammo cans from the ready boxes with his right forefinger Sal to Wat to Tim to Me –all done wordlessly and efficiently.

After what seemed hours, *pa-pounds,pa-pounds,papounds, papounds*, of each rack of four .40 mm shells echoed from the starboard edge of the Task Force, the number and intensity of each quartet multiplied and now and the pa-pounds were highlighted by *crack-Ba-tows* of 5 inch guns on cruisers and destroyers. The sky was pock marked with orange flashes and black/blue/brown clouds, but still no visible sign of enemy aircraft. In that time not a word was spoken by the six men in the gun tub as they awaited word from the Gunnery Officer on the Bridge wearing the over sized helmet with the communications apparatti in place.

Fire was increasing from the picket ships on the horizon and the vast canopy of Pacific sky was smeared with war's oils. Here and there - clouds of black frowned down and were replaced in full fury by more chemical and electric fused combustion - scattering shards of steel in concentric circles while long comets of fiery tracers fingered their way into the atmosphere in search of prey. God's voice could have been shouted down by His earthy homicidal creatures, and was all over the planet, but to each man wearing a uniform this corporate noise was vital and God's voice could wait.

God's could but not that of the Gunnery officer's; His will be done!! 'All Guns commence firing starboard!" And they did!

Ike shook as the Swedish made gun rocked, recoiled and spit the once brightly colored rounds that Tim, Sal and Wat had so carefully placed in the steel can. 'Load!' commanded Tom as the indicator showed that sixty rounds were near expended and the next magazine was hefted in process and locked by Al Townsend and the firing continued. When six cans were expended, Tim would take out the cooled barrel and Al Townsend and Tom Brown with asbestos gloves would remove the white hot barrel now in use and dunk it into the cold water; and exchange the barrel in Tim's hand.

Finally Watson saw the old Nakajima torpedo plane and identified it according to Allied Code –'Kate!' 'Quiet!' commanded Ike who took aim on the torpedo plane that had picked out LST 448 and the nearly 400 men aboard for killing. The gooey green camouflage paint became visible at one thousand yards and the pilot of the bomber was adjusting his approach to the relative speed of Capt. Higgins's command. The bow .40mm and the stern 5.5" gun loudly reported on the approach of the plane. He had yet to drop his torpedo! What was that Nip doin? Every Marine on deck was shouting Get the Fucker! Splash him! Kick Him in the Nuts! And – the Jap plane released its torpedo right over the heads of the mass of troops on the deck and twenty feet from Gun Tub # 4 which continued to hose .20, mm rounds into and near the green speeding plane – every man a board could see the three Japanese heroes in the long cockpit – the gunner in the rear was mangled and dead, the torpedo/radioman bleeding from the eyes but calm and the pilot fixed and determined. As the plane and the loosed torpedo darted portside the bleeding man in the middle, the radioman, waved to everyone, like a homecoming queen!

The torpedo was not meant for LST 448 but the large Attack transport to port and three times the men aboard that ship would now die as the torpedo porpoised into the sea.

An LCI(G) witnessing the desperate attack weaved its path into the torpedo some two hundred yards abaft of LST 448. The six boys in starboard Gun Mount #4 never witnessed the impact of the torpedo on the LCI(G) but heard the horrific blast and rendered steel. The impact tore open the bow of the gunship and every man in every forward gun position on that ship was obviously dead. . . . Tim thought of the corner stone of Leo High School laid by Cardinal Mundelein in 1926 PRO DEO ET PATRIA. Those guys stayed at their stations; their skipper ran into that missile; those guys knew they were going to die. Tim said a prayer for the heroically maimed sailors – no one back home would know what they had done. Their Moms and Dads would read an antiseptic telegram.

The Jap pilot got away. Ike had hit the bastard for sure and he was smoking but he made to off to the horizon and back to Guam. 'Secure from General Quarters!'

Tim, Sal and Watson helped the sailors manning the .20mm secure the weapon and emptied the heavy canvas bags of hot smoking shell casings into the metal hopper for removal to the ordinance hands who would refit the shells with powder and cannon shot. Ike had removed his helmet and Kapok jacket and there was a four inch ring of heavy red bruising around his right eye from the gun sight tube. 'You look like Petey the mutt in the Rascals, Ike! Nice shooting, pal. One of them Japs ain't happy in that Kate anyway,' offered Sal as a means of snapping the sober silence out of his five friends in the little fort on the Starboard side. All six boys wanted to go portside to witness the damage to the LCI(G) that had so heroically imposed itself into the path of the torpedo meant for the APA stuffed with assault troops.

'The Skipper of that LCI sure killed a bunch of his boys but saved so many of our guys,' Watson belabored the obvious with such guileless insight that all five of the others smiled to one another.

'Here, Wat, bear a hand with this tub of shells,' commanded PFC Tim Cullen. Sal grabbed the whole thing and bear-hugged the heavy can himself. 'I'll heft this down to ordinance. Ike- nice shooting. Why don't you swabbies stretch out and let the audience clean up.' Ike was fighting the shakes and Tom and Al both were rigid with the after effects of close combat and they would need to re-adjust to their watch duties in the engine room shortly. 'Thanks, Sal, Tim when that barrel sits for about another twenty minutes shift the one in the gun and cool it down as well. Thanks, you guys, let's leg it to port guys.'

The three tired shipmates headed over to the crowded port side of the deck, already jammed with Marines who recounted the sail of the torpedo over their heads just minutes before and witnessed the seagoing drama of the smashed LCI and its twenty or more maimed sailors now being tendered by three minesweepers exacting evacuation of the wounded to the APA saved by their heroism. For the balance of their lives – those who would survive the next few months and those who would live beyond the World Series of 1944 – they would remember the faces of the two living Japanese aviators and the Japanese calligraphy written on the torpedo that flew over their heads and into another American ship.

Tim took up the asbestos gloves and worked the locking mechanisms of the .20mm and Watson poured cool salt water down its hissing barrel. Tim steadied the barrel and held it vertical to the deck and then horizontal while Watson added more cool water. Tim noticed the approach of Lt. Buck. He had the look of a man who had just watched his sons defeat the town bullies in a fair fight and also caught an intimation that his commander had a particular subject to broach with PFC Cullen.

'That was the most heroic thing that I have ever witnessed. The Captain of that LCI, so coolly and directly, speeding his ship as a sacrifice. Capt. Higgins is already filling out an after action report. I am proud of how well you men represented A Company in this brief action. I am going to depend on Veterans like you Pvt. Watson when we go in under fire? I feel confident that you will help me a great deal. PFC Cullen, when you have performed your chores here, please join me forward starboard side beneath the .40mm mount?'

The black clouds dissipated as LST-448 and the Southern Task Group plowed the Pacific south of the Marianas and Guam itself. The Third Marine Division would serve as floating reserve for the soldiers and Marines now dying on Saipan.

PART III
ASAN

CHAPTER 22
NO ONIONS FOR THE HASH

Three of Joanie's sisters worked at the new Ford Motor Aircraft Plant at 77th & Cicero and needed to take the street car and two more buses to the plant all of which took them about forty-five minutes. Maeve, Adele, and Frances had all graduated from Mercy High School and all were employed by Ford's Defense Work Plant at Clearing Industrial District just outside of the Chicago City limits and close to Metropolitan Field at 63rd & Cicero, making engines for the new B-29. Chicago had become an important war-production center and many of the City's local industries had been converted to War Production. Mayor Kelly stayed thick with FDR and never got thin. The right contractors met the right climate in the Windy City. Many Chicagoans, with sons off at war, became daffy with the new found prosperity linked so well to patriotic duty. Larry Cullen's girl's were making good money and not working anywhere near the hours that he put in himself. His wife Mary had plenty to do.

The Cullen girls dressed and readied for work at 5 in the morning and their Mother already prepared their breakfasts and lunches for them – usually Oatmeal and tea and toast and devilled ham sandwiches with pickle relish and an apple each. Joanie got up with the girls so all of the Cullen women could breakfast and pray for the boys in service each morning. Joanie went off to Mass at St. Sabina's while her older sisters boarded the trolley to Western Ave.

'In the name of the Father, The Son and The Holy Ghost Amen. Joan, say the Morning Offering. . , their mother began the usual morning's ritual.

O my God, in union with the Immaculate Heart of Mary, I offer Thee the Precious
Blood of Jesus from all the altars throughout the world, joining with It the offering of my every thought, word and action of this day.
O my Jesus, I desire to day to gain every indulgence and merit I can and I offer them, together with myself, to Mary Immaculate,
that she may best apply them in the interests of They Most Sacred Heart. Precious Blood of Jesus, save us!
Immaculate Heart of Mary, pray for us!
Sacred Heart of Jesus, have mercy on us!

All the Cullen women intoned 'Amen' and made the sign of the cross with slow and honest detail – none of the quick hand wizardry of present day Catholics or males contemporary to this story. Prayer was the food upon which tough women fed more so than the Barry's Tea and Quaker Oats.

'You father is working a double for Jim Montesano tonight so for God's sake pet him when he gets home and let him have the radio and none of your gob Maeve. Bring home a dozen of eggs from Sitoros when you get home tonight as well, girls. No, Joanie, you pick up the eggs, after Mass this morning and have Tommy chop some end cuts for hash as well. We'll have that tonight and tomorrow about two pounds, so. '

'Mom, Mr. O'Donnell wants me to pick up some candy to Tim at Morganelli's after school, if that is alright with you.'

'Sure, so; honey; when you get back from that take your father his tea for the second shift and bring back some popcorn from the counter. I like the show popcorn for Jack Benny so much better than my own here. Get enough for the little fellas too, so.'

With her girls out the door, her husband at the Highland Theatre for the next sixteen hours, and her three boys asleep up stairs until seven, Mary Cullen had twenty minutes to write a letter to her boy Tim.

Mrs. Mary Cullen
8134 S. Bishop Street
Chicago, Illinois Zone 20
Tadgheen (Tah -Jeen Irish for Little Tim)
A Cara,
Your recent letter tells me that you are aboard ship bound for some great thing. Know that your Mother loves you above the clouds themselves and that I remind you to keep Our Lady and Her Son ever in your thoughts and prayers. Your Lutheran chaplain sounds like a lovely man and give him the regard that you'd give to Father Gorey or Monsignor Egan himself, dear man.

I know how lonely and frightened you must be and know that your family keeps you in its prayers and thoughts each waking hour the girls and I just finished our stir-about and prayers for you and your brothers. Jack is still tied up in Sitka, Marty is at an airfield near Casablanca, and Al is selling silk stockings up at Fort Sheridan, talk a laugh, that boy is, so.

Here's a prayer to remember, Tadgheen: O My God, I adore Thee and I love Thee with all my heart. I thank Thee for having created me, for having made me a Catholic and for having watched over me this day. Pardon me for the evil I have done this day; and if I have done any good, deign to accept it. Watch over me while I take my rest and deliver me from danger. May Thy grace be always with me. Amen.

You are in my thoughts and prayers every minute of every day, love.

Mother

For a year now, Mary Cullen had prayed herself stiff with thoughts of Tim out there. Poor Joanie was blistered at the knees with her devotions to Our Lady and Novenas. Timmy was the one in the thick of it that boy Dick Burke, who had been so badly wounded in one of them strange places in the Pacific, told her when he had come home to Hines Hospital in Maywood and had sent Mary the note about Tim and all. And nothing about nothing from his letters the *shcut!* Ah me! What was I thinking and No onions for the hash.

CHAPTER 23
SEA-LEGS UNCOILED: ENIWETOK
ATOLL JULY, 1944

Eniwetok Atoll was a burning piece of sandpaper that still stunk to high heavens with dead, rotting, caved - in Japs, but it was dry land and every day was Easter Sunday to the water-logged men of the Third Division who had stayed aboard ship all through the Saipan Campaign, as the date for W-Day Guam was pushed back by the guys in the know.

Each Morning the shellbacks would jump to reveille for a half-hour of calisthenics and a mile run before chow. It was cool in the morning, at first until the Tropic sun stood tall as Gunny's manhood- meat.

'Move Girls! Time for one of you quim-crawlers to best me in a run or face me in the square ring; I swear to the Protestant God Above Me that I will box the last man in to Battalion CP on this dash and I am slower than Cullen is to a whore's snatch! LaughMutherfuckersanseewhodies! Move them Fucking Jew Legs like there's dollars out there Steinberg! You sing like Judy Garland – Hebe! Now rundown that Dago – beat him

185

Steinberg! Battaglia! Palestine's Naval Force is behind your Guinea Ass! Jack Howard is the Gold! Go for his back Jew Boy! That's runnin' Son! Cullen - you trunk stumped dwarf move your lazy ass even the Hillbilly is Catching you! Well, Bless My Soul the Yellow Menace! Ain't You Dead Yet MutherFucker? LOWREGARD CLAVISILL? I THOUGHT YOU DIED! You did and Bug Fucker Brosnan dug you up and breathed life into your sick and sorry soul! Fuck You, Clavisill! Chad you useless piece of shit don't help that corpse run! He's a dead man! Leave him on the beach! Brass! Shut the Fuck Up! Morning Gentlemen! Great day for the Corps and the Men Who Lead it! . . . Run Mutherfuckers or I'll taffy your asses and eat my way to your hearts!'

And on they ran . . . For the Entire Mile which grew hotter and bluer and the coral cut deeper into the leather soles of the boondockers. After three weeks in the twenty mile anchorage of the atoll crammed with every ship in the transport division of Admiral Close-In Connolly's Southern Task Force, punctuated every few days ashore here on this baking sheet of coral dust and shell-shattered shards of trees and bushes, their combat shoes were beginning to shred with the constant agitation of coral and the endless running and athletic sports competitions between companies, platoons, and squads. Every two days, LCVPs would be lowered from LST-448 and parties of marines and some sailors would get sand liberty. Then back to the steel deck roasting pan of the ship and always the fetid odors and suffocating heat of the South Pacific.

Today there would be warm cans of Drewery's beer and bottles of Coke and Bubble-Up or Ten Hi after the football game between 1st & 2nd Platoons of A Company. It would be the first taste of the exotic beverages for these Marines since they boarded ship at the end of May. Saipan had been a blood bath and the Third Division had sailed back forth at 180 degrees from Saipan for weeks, when the William Day for Guam was pushed back to July 21st, 1944 at 08:30 AM and the salted Marines sent to sit in Eniwetok Atoll's Lagoon.

Since taking Eniwetok, America had built up its three main islands with fuel farms, Quonset hut barracks airfields, supply warehouse, communications centers, dock facilities, piers, a 35,000 seat entertainment amphitheatre, and radar stations on the smaller islands in the chains. The twenty mile anchorage was home to an epic panorama of ships and flying boats that would make Homer gain back his sight.

Combat air patrols flew over the area and crisscrossed with outgoing sorties of bombers of every variety and capacity – B-25s, A-20s, A-24s, P-61s, P-38s, P-47s, B-17s, and B-24s. PBYs, TBMs, SOCs, & SBDs were sent off to bomb Guam, Tinian, Saipan, Truk, Ulithi, Leyte, Lingayan, Mindanao, and the Palaus, but mostly the by-passed atolls of the Marshalls and the Caroline Islands. Landing and refueling; landing and re-arming, landing and crashing and burning, and killing the kids who flew those missions; the planes became old hat to the sea-bound Marines running and pummeling the coral stretches of the islands. As Gunny Higgins' knot of runners – in green undershirts, running trunks, socks and boondockers, and piss cutter covers – slowed to double time on Gunny's command and again to a walk. They would do a cool down half mile from the dead-run. Gunny was proud; these boys were hard, he thought, and the Japs would be on the receiving end of some serious killers. He decided to treat them. Beer's on him before the touch football this afternoon.

'You man-bitches really tore up the coral today; so I will box – let's see – who's the smallest most inoffensive – likeable – almost pet-like one of you here? Cullen? No. I might get carried away and kill you, Brig Rat. Steinberg? Naw, Jews don't cry when you hit 'm – think that God'll be pissed at 'em. Clavisill? Already Dead. You – Bing Crosby – Battaglia. Let's go two rounds at two minutes each. First Blood stops the fight.'

Sal was hard muscle, sinew and strength; Gunny was his double. The squads of 1ˢᵗ Platoon made a ring and Cranthorpe was ordered to count time: 'You ignorant Holler Homer, count fingers – both hands; Toes – both feet and repeat six times that makes sixty times two that makes two minutes. Got it?'

'Aye, Gunny!' Watson was panicked and confused nevertheless and stood close to Tim Cullen. 'Give me a nudge ne're on two minutes – 'er Gunny'll kill me next.

Sal and Gunny both stripped bear chested and bare-knuckled took *en garde* as Watson yelled, 'Time!'

Gunny closed tight to Sal and Sal bounced on the balls of his feet to the right jerking his head left and caught Gunny's left jab flush on the nose. Sounding like an over-ripe Michigan plum splattered against the wall of a grocery store by bad little boys, Sal's nose exploded blood in a 360 degree circle, but the tough boy kept his feet and adjusted his guard. Tim Cullen yelled, 'First Blood!'

'Fuck You!' The Fight continued. Gunny took three good pops from Sal but to no effect and Sal had all that he could handle blocking the Gunny's jabs which were like sledge hammer hits. Both man backed away and both pumped punches into the other's frame to try and get at the opponent's short ribs – 'Time!' Watson yelled.

Tim pulled off and rushed his green shirt up to Sal's bleeding nose and held his head back for the thirty seconds Gunny gave as a breather. No one spoke. Corpsman Brosnan dumped his canteen full of water over Sal's head and ordered him to rinse out. Sal was pissed and ready to have at Gunny. Sal never boxed formally but was always a pretty tough kid – not a fighter but tough and he resented this obvious bullying by Gunny because Sal was so big. He knew Gunny meant to carve him up now and prayed that God or an officer would intervene – no chance. God stayed in Heaven and Officer's with their own - until they needed these guys.

'Time!' The two fighters closed, but Sal had lost the bounce and weaved less this time in order to study Gunny's approach – No good – Gunny popped three quick one to Sal's ribs and caught Sal under his right cheek bone – down! Sal posted his fall with his beam-like left arm and pivoted away from Gunny's attempt to finish him off. Gunny never changed his expression but his eyes twinkled with the delight of a killer having fun.

As Sal swung to his feet off his left arm, Gunny feinted with his right and mysteriously opened his guard enough to be obvious to Sal, who shot out a left like the firing pin in a Garand, catching Gunny square between the eyes.

Goliath went down and stayed out. 'Wat – the count quick before he stirs,' moused Cullen.

One, Two, Tharee, Oh Shit, and Sal you killed him! Fower, Doc look at him!'

Count! Shouted 1st Platoon as a man.

'Fave, Sex, Seven Ate, Nahn, Ten – Broz! look to Gunny!' whimpered Watson who truly loved the homicidal First Shirt.

As Navy Corpsman Brosnan approached the supine Sergeant, Gunny Higgins launched himself to his feet from a full stretch- flat back rest to his feet squared fists on hips and eyes as clear and mischievously deadly as always. 'Wanted to see if you could count to ten, Cranthorpe. I told Maj. Opley that you could. Stout Fellow! You hit like Judy Garland, Sal, but take a hit a like a Marine – names Billy – Gunny extended his hand – 'Proud to know you! Beers're on me Girls - Double time!' Sal, who's nose had not been broken, thanks be to God, was the happiest of the trotting green knot of young men. Sal had missed Bougainville and come aboard Able Company like so many of the faceless others, including Lt. Buck, but had been berthed and squaded with two of the most popular young guys – Cullen and Cranthorpe. They were not Old Corps like Jack Howard and Sgt. Rittenouer but they were blooded and tested and found worthy by standing up to the carnage at Torokina Beach on Bougainville and had cut trail in the island's sponge-like jungle to meet and turn an ambush on the Japanese and to do so with disease coursing through their blood. Gunny Higgins had run the Japanese off Bloody Ridge with Maj. Opley and had the papers for the Navy Cross in his sea bag. A sea bag that had been issued to Gunny after four others had worn out with salt, shot, sand, and semen. Now, because he had faced Goliath with his own powerful slings and gotten his Dago honker flattened in the bargain – he was Sal to Gunny Higgins.

This sweaty and bloody good feeling was keened out of the atmosphere by the slow groaning ArrrrrRrrrrrRRrrrrrRRRR of the emergency landing signal from the big new airstrip five hundred yards from the makeshift camp of the 3rd Marines beach parties. The rotating shifts of island liberty Marines from the many LSTs, LCIs, and APAs chained in Eniwetok's Lagoon scratched out shelter - half tent cities along the airstrips seaward sides wherever they could. Ist Battalion, 3rd hobo-ed near the A-20-G Bomber Squadrons attacking by-passed airstrips and military facilities on one of the many, many tiny islands in the Marshall Islands. A returning flight of eight bombers had taken fire and one bomber – a new A-20G with the new gun turrets – was returning with a wounded tunnel gunner/radioman and a dead gunner/engineer. The plane was smoking furiously as it could be seen begging its way back home. Gunny offered this commentary -

'Dead Fly-boys at three o'clock – Saw an old A-20D come back like that at Boogan; blew up when it stopped, Spread out thin and get ready to cover if that thing bounces. Go!'

Officers were also making ready to effect defilade where it could be found and eagerly prepared themselves for the inevitable destruction of a brave crew. All were amazed that the shot-up bomber could even stay in the air and wondered at the resolve of the man at the wheel and rudder – in praise of his determination. Major Opley commanded his officers for the return to the LST, cut short this beach party and get to business

with weapons and ammo for some more scorching days aboard
their host vessel

'Look at that heroic man, gentleman – he knows he's dead
and he is bringing that plane back by the book. My God –
Grant him quiet Lord. Bravest man I know is Col. Edson
and he has not flown since Nicaragua. Capt. Bundeschu, the
game is cancelled; have your men break camp immediately,
after we see if we can be of any assistance to Col. Goldstein and
his emergency crews. Geary, send a runner to Col. Goldstein.
Capt. Krieg – Padre, head to the field! Those boys will not
walk away from this one. Lt. Gallo – beach master. Take the
semaphores and wave in the LCVPs for the relays back to 448.'
I want us off this coral with enough time for salt showers before
chow – Move! Lt. Buck, join me while we break the news to
your boys.'

Maj. Opley still had the powerful build that would have
made him John Boilermaker 1925 had he not been asked to
leave Purdue. Though his hair was still a deep dark brown,
he was getting intrusions of gray above the ears. Lucas Opley
had flourished in this active life; in leading men by example;
in organizing an effective fighting battalion that understood
mission, method, and execution as much as his Purdue
Boilermaker linemen; his rough and tumble river patrols on
the Coco River; in the table of command programs he attended
after Nicaragua; in working out the basic platoon manual for
Tropical Warfare; in commanding a Company of Marine
Raiders under Red Mike, in leading a battalion ashore and
under fire at Bougainville and in orchestrating the campaign
that was sparked upon first seeing the Colt .45 revolver worn
by the 1st Lieutenant of the lead platoon of his lead company
in the invasion to come. He'd perk this Texas boy, just as he
had petted his alligator Billy Higgins, and exercise command
fraternity with him. A Brotherhood of trust; a confederacy of
mutual honor. Unlike, wading through the soup and salad on
the Coco River, or Guadalcanal, or even Bougainville for the

most part, these amphibious campaigns of recent days had been met with horrific fire before and on the beaches. At Tarawa, platoon leaders were wiped out in the initial waves, at Kwajelain – at Roi-Namur, at Eniwetok, and now at Saipan the lead elements were carved up wholesale before their feet got wet. Lucas Opley would survive – no problem – he'd be in the thick of the lead and smoke, but he'd survive; so would Billy – you can't kill a man born to hang – and Opley felt destined for higher command – regimental, brigade, division, Corps, Commandant. It was in the cards.

' Jack, when we get back to ship I'd like you do another weapons lecture – use the Brig Rat on the B.A.R. – I want every man in your company as hot on the Browning as his Garand or Carbine. We are going to take heavy fire getting ashore make no mistake. You remember the maps of our approach – Red Beach 2 is triangulated from Chorito Cliff, Fonte Plateau and that nose of ridge to the south. Fonte will be real problem; the Japs can yet fire down on each of the other two objectives, once seized. It will be vital that you men secure the next highest ground south of Fonte in order to affect good Fire Control and Air Support for the link up with the 21st Marines and the 9th are to the right of them. Remember, Jack, that field phone of yours kills more Japs than that carbine or that Colt of yours. 1860 is it not?'

'Yes, it is, sir. Went through Gettysburg and made it home to Texas. It should again. My Granddaddy took it to Cuba and never even fired it against the Spaniards. Colt Killed more Texians than any other species, in point of fact sir. I will use the phones and keep my communicator hard by sir.'

'Again, secure the heavy machinegun but come back for it once you have a defensible perimeter staked out on the ridge. They'll come hard on you to throw you off and nothing puts down fire like the heavy Browning. Until you have that weapon set up – and I told Gallo as well – make sure every man, Brosnan included, is hard with the Browning this one is going to be a bitch and a half; make no mistake Lieutenant Buck. We know that the Japs have heavily reinforced their Naval Landing Force – Jap Marines – with Army Units from China and they have been hard at this war from the time Gunny and I were on the Coco River. This is going to be rugged. Make sure that you ask a good man to care for that Colt, if anything happens to you. I'd have a good man like Sgt. Rittenouer hard by to see that it does not end up the trophy of some clown from Bolweeville, Alabama – anything can happen in combat.'

'Thank you sir!' I'll do just that. Will we have a JASCO team with our company?'

'No, but Col. Hall will link up a JASCO section with A Company once the objective is secure and their spotter can call in naval fire and air support. Until then, keep in touch with your company commander, wear him like skivvies and he'll stay linked in with me on the Beach – if it gets too thick; I'll send up Gunny to swat flies and kick lard.'

'Jack, take care of yourself on this one. Don't expose yourself just to make points. You are a good leader. If anything happens to Bundeschu, Able is yours.

'Thank you, sir! I'll try to live up to your confidence.'

'Make sure that you do just that – corpses make lousy leaders. Let's tell the men that it's back to the boat.'

In all of their talk, the Douglas A-20-G Havoc trailed oily smoke and flame banked to the field landed on its left wing and exploded. Lucas and Jack looked up and continued their conversation. 'Now, tonight, I want the B.A.R. show and pick out the dumbest and most fumble fingered to work out the kinks and have Cullen re-demonstrate the right way –that boy is a masterpiece of a mechanic – he gets almost hypnotic. During the cruise when he was not monkeying with that .20mm, he was following the black gang down into the engine room. Capt. Higgins and I ran into him –literally - below several times and it is like Pluto's playpen down there.'

'I am amazed by the man myself sir. He is a solid leader as well as a great operator. My God, that giant Battaglia and Cranthorpe worship him and other men look to him as much as Sgt. Howard. He should make Corporal.'

'If he stays out of the brig – not only is he mechanically aptituded, he is also plagued by a black cloud that he calls his own. Of course his latest, confinement was completely Gunny's doing. He's Gunny's pet – like a toy goat or monkey, I guess – and more fun to abuse and kick around, mind you. He's a good man under fire – all business. One night just before he was pulled off the line – his section was hit by a wave of about fifty Japs – he and Cranthorpe and a kid that took one through the eyes – can't remember his name - knocked down a lot of them. Just kept up at it like they were on a field problem. All mechanics. I'm more battle-charged myself. Whatever wins the fight, as the man said.'

'I want to thank you for your confidence in me, Major. We will help Capt. Bundeschu secure our objective and on time. I am very proud to be fighting alongside these boys who were schoolboys only months ago. They are a credit to our country, sir; I can't imagine better men to die with if needs be.'

'There is no one alive that I choose to die alongside, Lieutenant: alongside, before, ahead, above or below and that is the honest to God's truth. Unlike those flyboys smoking in that heap over there, I am going on to better things. You need to think that way. Don't you have a girl? Back home – on Guadalcanal?'

'I do that, Sir; she is the Red Cross publicist at Tetere beach near the Grove, Sir. She's from Cullen's town, but more south.'

'I believe that I met her. Pretty girl?'

'Indeed, Sir. Great fun to be around and a law student like myself. Plans to go into labor law.'

'Labor? She a Red?'

'I don't believe so, Sir, but her father was killed during a strike; she hates policemen.'

'Sounds Red to me. America can do without the Reds. Pretty Girl – yes, I believe that I met her.'

'Yes, sir.' Jack Buck remembered that Major Lucas Opley had frequently laid siege to Maggie's attentions and was repulsed on each advance; much to Maggie's amused disgust. She only once brought up Maj. Opley's *dangerouse* attempts to woo her, but her opinion of the Major seemed to be bearing fruit as his intentions opened during the course of their 'fraternal' conversation – especially when possession of the Colt Hog-leg surfaced in almost every encounter – punctuated with a 'anything can happen in combat' for one and all to hear. Together, the two Marines set about their tasks in getting their men back to LST-448.

Tim Cullen watched the flyers flaming deaths and thought of the guys who had gone to Leo High School. Before, and with him who went into aviation. Brother Finch had told him in a recent letter that the boys at the school were building wooden models of enemy aircraft for plane spotter courses given by the War Department and that Tom Gerrity, of the Charter Class of 1930 had been awarded the DFC and the Silver Star after leading squadrons against Jap's in the Bismarck Sea. Tom Gerrity had escaped from Bataan only hours before the Japs took it by repairing a shot-up amphibious plane and flying out to Mindanao with ten other pilots. From Mindanao they boarded a B-17 and on to Australia and then got back in the war. The *Chicago Sun Times* published the story of his escape through his letters to his young wife. Tim remembered thrilling to Tom Gerrity's account of his escape, after reading the sports pages.

Now, three guys were incinerated on a stretch of coral thousands of miles from Escanaba, California, Otis, North Dakota, and Taylor, New Mexico and their girl friends would be sipping cherry rickies, hot-leathering to Gene Krupa, dousing letters to them in eau de cologne bought by the quart at Steinways Drugs and flirting with sheiks at Miller's Terminal Merchandise on the corner of 4th and Main in each town. The three dead men flew hundreds of miles westerly only hours before armed with four two hundred pound bombs and eight five inch rockets. Streaked in over the Egapop Atoll and let loose on the island's remaining revetments packed with already shot-up and burned Japanese Naval and Army Tonys, Oscars, Rufes, Kates, Judys, Bettys and Zekes hit just days before – 'there might be a couple of serviceable craft left, men, and they could hit us with a sucker punch; so take 'em out again!' . It was one of the many redundant missions that they flew to goofy islands with goofy names that are not even listed on maps anymore – and just barely in their time As their silver Army bomber pulled up from its last run, the ship shook and rocked and then again as Toby Morgan screamed from the now rendered and bloody turret gunner's position 'Mugg upp shlaa!' which meant something else and from the dorsal tunnel Oh, No-ing Bob Landsman tried to staunch the bleeding from his inner thigh (Oh, No;No,No, Oh,No) with wadded maps and papers, while Pilot Terry McEldowney, twenty-one, tried to compensate his speed to the wild popping of his engines. Terry steadied the plane and reduced or flooded oil and aviation fuel mixtures as he had been instructed and followed the formation home over the vast blue seas.

Tim shook off this story and squeezed sweat and Sal's blood out of his green fatigue undershirt. Gunny called them all together when it was clear the crashing light bomber would not skid into his boys and had them sound off none the less. 'Sit tight! Take off your packs and loosen your leggings – I know Cranthorpe – we are in shorts and skivvies shirts- well aware of that you masterpiece! Sal how's the face dick? Good. Cullen take that fouled gear of yours to water, for God's sake, and rinse it out or the stains will set in if it dries and you'll loose that stripe. Doc Brosnan – just, how were you about to revive me, cupcake? Jack, where the fuck is Karl?'

'Lieutenant Buck had him getting movies from the Coast Guard APA – any more Gale Storm bullshit and that fag hoofer again and the boy's woulda gone Asiatic. Coast Guard has *Destination Tokyo, Oklahoma Kid, All Through the Night, and Porky Pigs.* He sent their skipper twenty pounds of that Texas Caramel his Momma makes and Capt. Higgins kicked in two cases of peaches. Karl is not looking too good Gunny. Better have a talk with him. He's all morbid and shit.'

'Karl's hard meat, Jack; leave him alone. He's a deep thinker; all them back-sliding Amish are; he's Ok. Your boys are hard and tight, Jack. You did a great job with them on the Canal. God dammit, I wish I was goin' in with these pukers just for the laughs they'd hand me, but I have to wet-nurse the brass. Capt. Crawford asked if we were taking the LCVP all the way in and he's the exec – pussy. Lucas wanted to toss him to the sharks, but he's so damn efficient in all things else. Transferring to the Alligators puts shit in his blood and we've done it about a hundred times. This reef off of Guam is a motherfucker; so, until every LTV is put out of action, no wade in. Third and fourth waves should wade in OK and by then the LCIs will be able to get in close. I miss the old Higgins boats – they were easier and safer to get out of – that's the Corps, Mac.'

'Can't wait to see that Bogey show it's got gangsters and Nazi spies – it was in *Stars and Stripes* and they said it's a corker.'

'I can't wait until we secure this objective. I was here with Lucas on Guam in 1940 doing jungle problems for a Naval War College paper and there was a great whorehouse in Agana just down the road from their movie house –*The Coral*. There is a Jap dentist, American born, that's married to a tall red-head piece of ass that makes grown men weep like boys with two dicks and no know-how, as I recall. Never saw her but I went to this whorehouse with Johnny McKenna and he mooned about the Jap's wife all night. He's probably dead or in some Jap wire shithole. I just hope that the red-head is a widow and horney. Fuck! I don't care if she is horney! Wait until she gets Billy's

197

tackle into a few openings and she'll go blond without peroxide, Praise Jesus! Officers skipping to us Jack – all hands right as the mail, Sirs!'

'At ease, Gunny! Games off, men. We are shoving off. Lt. Buck, carry on.'

'Sgt. Howard, set all men for embarkation. Steinberg and CZ collect all camp refuse and burn it prior to embarkation. Cullen – B.A.R. lecture with me tonight. Snap to it!' And they did.

CHAPTER 24
GETHSEMANE AT TAI

Ryugo Kato detested all religion, believed in no God, including the Emperor, and worked in the Japanese Naval Forces for the revolution to come. From his days as a Congregationalist seminary student at Oberlin College where he encountered the brilliant and charming Dr. Sylvia Schoenouer who introduced Ryugo to the world of social work and directed him on the path to real revolution, he had been a dedicated Red. Dr. Schoenouer was now Midwest Director of the American Civil Liberties Union. From Dr. Schoenouer Kato learned that Man's problems were rooted in the constant support given to the capitalists who controlled the ways and means of wealth through institutions that enslaved the proletariat. Only through the co-opting of social services could real revolution make its way into the temples of power. This work could only be achieved by destroying the pillars of those temples – trust in government, confidence in law enforcement, faith in religion, and devotion to bourgeoisie manners and customs.

The true revolution would not sweep a tide of change but gradually and evolutionarily rot out the pillars of the temple. Like the Parousia or the Millennium or the Messiah, the Revolution might not happen in Kato's lifetime or those of his children but it would come. Any means that would affect that end would justify and sanctify that mission. Kato received a Masters Degree from University of Chicago in Social Work in 1939 and returned to Japan and enlisted in the Imperial Navy. He became an investigator for the Keibeiti and served in Dutch Malaya where he rounded up Dutch, British and American military who escaped capture through a reign of Terror that pitted the Moslem Malays against their formers masters and allies. Likewise, he ingratiated himself to American missionaries won their trust siphoned information and murdered the fools for Christ. This devil knew the King James like Gunny Higgins. Now, with the advent of an American Invasion, Ryugo Kato had the most strident American lover bound in Butler's barn at Tia – Father Jesus Duenas was ordered to Butler's *lanchero* for a conference with Lt. Kato concerning the criminal Tweed and the dog-killing campaign ordered by Gov. Homura. The idea was to exterminate every dog on the island, as dogs were known to give away hiding places and signal human occupation. All over the island, Chamorros, Saipanese and Japanese civilians were marshaled against every living mutt on Guam. Stupid.

Nevertheless, a pretext to kill a priest, though not needed, was appreciated. Father Duenas and his nephew were brought to the Butler *lanchero* and immediately seized by twelve IJN sailors, bound and beaten with canes and dumped in the barn. Father Duenas's nephew never regained consciousness from the initial beating but gave forth a moan periodically. 'Let the boy go home, Kato. His mother is a widow and there are hard times coming. In God's Name, do this!'

'At Gethsemane the perfect Master made no demands, nor did he beseech his tormentors in any way. But then he was a full-blooded Jew of the House of David – by the way there is a House of David religious cult in Benton Harbor Michigan – all of the men wear long beards and are dedicated to the American sport baseball. I love baseball and was a pretty good third baseman for Oberlin College 1937. I was never a long ball hitter always a short choppy grounder – here let me show you, Jesus, 'The dedicated Red took a thirty-six & ¾ " tube of cane from a sailor and gave a few cuts in the air and one sharp cut to Father Duenas's right ear which stunned the priest and split the ear itself. . . .'Short, choppy grounders win the game. Where is that fucking Yank? He's a fucking deserter at best and has been hiding out to save his own worthless skin. Fuck, him! give him up and nephew legs it back to Mommy. No? Kato threw a check swing that missed the right ear by millimeters.

'See, I ain't such a bad guy; just doing my job. Where is the deserter? Give him up and nephew goes home. Here, let me sponge the ear with some warm water. No, fuck you. How's God looking to you? Here's a parable A Centurion orders 'one man come' and he comes; to another he says 'Go' and the man goes' I'm a Centurion – render to Caesar, priest. You are in violation of the Laws. You know where a felon is hiding and you refuse to give the legal authority assistance – You are a liar. Your God is Liar! The Meek are the chattel of the World, priest! These ignorant fucks who do not speak a lick of English, by the way, believe that the four eyes they worship is the Son of God as well. A Timid, near-sighted orchid cutting in-bred dummy and just like your Jew carpenter no more God than that creeping coward you are trying to hide. Fuck Him. Give Him Up. Where is he?'

The bleeding priest, so handsome two days ago, so confident and determined in his devotion to his people: yet, so at war with his own manhood and his priestly vows. That was the cross of every good priest to forsake the comfort and glory of a beautiful woman's kisses and the soft moist muscular direction of her passions to yours that would manifest itself in years of caressing affection supportive constancy. This was as nothing compared to that. One of the boys from Agana, pressed into killing dogs sneaked in a little tea and sugar to Jesus and his nephew and offered to cut his bonds and help them escape, but Jesus refused knowing that the now near frenzied Japs would slaughter more Chamorros. Enough Chamorros were dying for Tweed already – he should be on his way off the island by now anyway. Jesus never warmed to the guy. Too wrapped up in his own world and very unlike the other boys who were asking to be baptized more in thanks to their protectors than to any basic religious convictions. Kindness did not seem to matter Tweed, he could be wrong. But comradeship seemed to matter less as Tweed went off on his own.

Kato was tired and wanted some of that soup Mrs. Butler had added the rice to – taro root and lamb and spicy peppers and a good splash of lime. 'Okay Father Flanagan, Boys Town's burning! Last time – where is this deserter.'

Bound, bleeding and ready for more baseball, Father Jesus Duenas smiled at his tormentor 'That's for me to know and you to find out!'

Kato grinned, 'Some epitaph! Here's a thought to take with you, holy man - When we get back to Agana, Otayama, let your boys loose. Take them out and cut their heads off!'

CHAPTER 25
A HOMILY ON TARGETS

On March 15, 1943, just before Tim Cullen, Dick Prendergast and Jimmy Arneberg left for the Marines after early graduation, Spike O'Donnell walked south on Loomis and turned west on 83rd Street and right off the alley, between Loomis and Ada Streets, a guy creep-ed up and pumped a shot into Spike's back. The louse tried to put one in Spike's ear but the goof's beezer misfired and the skunk jumped into a car and Spike crawled home to his wife Elizabeth and daughter Rita.

All this had to do with Spike's 'consulting work' in the asphalt business. From the time that Spike quit the beer rackets, he had used his political clout to help asphalt paving contractors meet the right guy in Washington, when FDR started bringing the country back from the Depression with jobs. Mike Carrozza who ran the Laborers Union in Chicago was tapped as the paving czar for the PWA and he and Spike trusted and respected one another from the old days. One bright boy, a real clean good-government type, asked Spike's help in securing the low bid for a three million dollar paving job for which Spike's fee was

agreed to be $ 70,000 the Cook County States Attorney and
the Chicago Street Commissioner were already in the pocket
of another bidder and tried to freeze Spike's guy out; so the
do-gooder reneges on his fee to get back in the good graces of
the other pigs; so Spike gives the lying bastard a slap-around
in front of his employees and the States Attorney has Spike
pinched. Reason prevailed and the do-gooder louse woke up to
the fact that Spike saved his hard-earned cash and thousands of
dollars for Father Steve McMahon and Little Flower Parish by
walking into the failing bank on Ashland Ave. in October 1929
with a violin case and telling the Bank's President 'I want to
make a withdrawal – *all accounts* for Mr. Edward J. O'Donnell
and all accounts for Father Steve McMahon and *any and all*
for Little Flower Parish, please And I don't want to make two
trips, see?' Neither Mr. O'Donnell nor Little Flower Parish lost
a nickel in the great crash.

The reneging Asphalt mogul did not press a charge of assault
and battery against Spike O'Donnell. But neither did he pay the
tough-guy consultant the fee suggested. Mr. O'Donnell made
it known that the Streets Commissioner of the City of Chicago
was a crook and so was the States Attorney. From September
1942 to March 1943, while Marines fought to keep a foot - hold
on Guadalcanal, while Ike landed American forces in North
Africa, while millions of American boys were training to fight
and die all over the globe, Edward J. Spike O'Donnell of 8234
S. Loomis in Chicago, Illinois fought a jungle war against
the craven interests of crooked politicians (those not in Spike's
vest pocket) and two-faced louses who vote Republican - good
government phonies.

On the same day that Brutus stuck a shiv in Caesar's kidneys,
1900 years later; some louse popped a lead capsule just to the left
of 53 year old Spike's spine that lodged in his chest. Fortunately,
Spike's assassin was paid and not honorable and took to his heels
when his beezer gave out. Spike laid up in Little Company of
Mary Hospital for months with Capt. Dan' Tubbo' Gilbert and

his boys keeping visitors out on orders from the States Attorney. The Papers screamed bloody murder as most Chicagoans got a kick out of Spike who publicly gave politicians the miseries with his circular narratives, punctuated by jabs to the ribs, and always delivered out of the side of his mouth. Spike O'Donnell was a tough-guy who got tough with louses and crumbs that had it coming, or so the common man held.

When visitors were allowed, Joanie Cullen brought her Mom's homemade Chili sauce that was sweet and cinnamon zested and went great with pot roast and beef shoulder, a Mass Card from all the Cullens and a big box of candy from Steinberg's drugstore – now called Steinway Pharmacy. Tim dropped by to tell Spike that he had joined the Marines and Spike wanted to kiss and also clout the kid. 'Are you soft upstairs? You should be working on airplanes or in the Navy like your brother who wouldn't know a pipe wrench from a Mary Jane. You clowns are all gonna kill Tojo. Well, pal, let me tell you this. I been shot at – and hit because my back was turned – and it's no roller skate date at Foster Park. You make damn sure that you know how to operate what your shooting and you had better keep it oiled and chambered. Now listen – when you shoot at a mug you are shooting at a target and that is all. If you get all Shirley Temple and *human* he'll kill you – end of story. When you take off?'

'The end of April Mr. O'Donnell.' Tim was impressed by his friend's frank and forthright – though – unwitnessed, tutorial on weapons and their uses.

'Ten years ago, when Danny McGeoghan was trying to kill me everyday of the week – over beer sales – he had a nut-job Polack tough-guy jump ship to me. The guy killed about three guys, or so he said, and he wants to get close to me. One night, the guy comes into my house for the pad to old Capt. Somerville, and one of the kids, I forget who it was, comes out in diapers crying about the loud man. Anyway I picked her up and patted her back to sleep and put her to bed. The Polack is staring green at the baby the whole time. I'm not thinking clear, see, so I leave the him in the living – this was in my nice house over at 81st and Wolcott the one the G snatched from me for taxes last year –room and I go down to the basement for some money. I go round the front of the house for some reason and while I'm in the gangway I see him in my baby's bed room giving the baby a crack. She's bawling and by the time I come up the front porch he's back on the sofa - as nice as pie. "Hey Spike that Baby is really giving out since . . ." I hold up my hand and wave it off 'No sweat Pal.!'

Two weeks later we go down to Momence for some target practice. This guy Meehan has a shit farm south of the Kankakee River, see. We set up targets but the Polack sees these goats having lunch and decides to kill the poor things for no reason. "I tell him nice shooting and ask him to set up a target for me a couple hundred feet from where the dead goats are toes-up. Before he went two feet, four slugs ran into the back of the Polack's head – nice target. Get me?'

Tim nodded with deep appreciation and conviction as he fully understood the entire tone and temper of the parable, which Mr. O'Donnell offered without homily – take care of your weapons and hit what you aim at. The targets put themselves there.

CHAPTER 26
COOKIE TANAKA CRUMBLES

Kara and Ted fought – if you can call it that – after the dinner with Lieutenant Kato. Ted understood all too well the man's dangerous nature and was determined that his love would leave Agana for the less militarily populated western villages. Kara saw through the arguments 'Cookie, I need you to watch over the resources that we have buried; I want you to care for the people who have never lived out of town, you're from the Wild West – Minot!'

'Yeah, Teddy, and there's usually three foot of snow and ninety mile an hour winds – just like Guam! Look, Bub, we came here together and we stays together got it? Or, do you have plans to duck down to Annabelle's cat-house while Mommy is playing dress up in the sticks?'

It went on like that for about a half hour and Ted started crying and begged her to go. This was no ruse. The little Gonzaga sheik was a tough bird and could take every manner of abuse – he was a dentist for Chrissakes. Kara understood that her husband needed to stay in Agana as liaison to the Governor and Kato's Keibeiti and she also understood that Ted was a tough guy who would take no crap from anyone. He'd be in danger on his own abilities, but maybe Kara would put her husband in the jackpot by staying in Agana – she was the American and after all the only reason she was not now in a camp in Japan was Ted's resolve and stiff backbone with Homura. Maybe it was time to disappear – go to Manengon.

CHAPTER 27
JANE POWELL FOR NOW

The Class of 1944 had just graduated and nearly every boy went into the service, several became Novices to the Irish Christian Brothers and were already bound for Iona, New York; four boys entered the seminary at St. Mary of the Lake in Mundelein, Illinois; Tommy Driscoll received a full scholarship to DePaul University and was destined to become a great pediatrician, and Brother Finch wanted to see a movie in peace. Brother Daly always wanted to go to the Capitol Theater on Halsted where the bill of fare was always a diet of Buck Jones shoot 'em ups, gangster movies, and the Ritz Brothers - detestable, but Finch won out on the day – today, Jane Powell would dance away the blues or whatever ailed you. He and the courtly Brother Daly would be the guests of Larry Cullen who was working two shifts at the Highland Theatre on Ashland – a longer walk for Brother Daly, but a good one. The year had been very rewarding as Brother Finch's Lightweight Basketball squad had mirrored the fine season of Red Gleason's Heavies losing only to Mount Carmel and Joliet – Bart Murphy, Bucko

McGinnis, Jimmy Kilgariff, Dick Kloser, Bob Kozlowski and all the other boys and especially Art Zerega made Frank Finch a proud man and a very humble servant of God.

These boys were sacrificing so much for their pride in the school and Leo boys were now sacrificing themselves all over the globe to fight tyranny. Whitey Cronin continued to build upon the great success of his '41 and '42 Championship football season teams and this past fall had made a good run at the Kelly Bowl again. Frank remembered how frustrated Tim Cullen had been during the Kelly Bowl of '42 and only got in for a few plays. That is God's will – we do not always get what we desire – especially if one is playing behind a Jimmy Arneberg.

Today, after Mass at St. Sabina, and a nice breakfast at Gossage Grill, Brother Finch and Brother Daly would take in the nine o'clock shorts, news reels, cartoons, and a feature at ten o'clock and be back at the residence for after noon Divine Office, lunch and then a walk to Foster Park. Frank found a V-mail envelop with his name on it on the refectory –dining room – buffet table. It was letter from Tim Cullen – that would make his father happy.

PFC Timothy Cullen, USMCR
A Company, 1ᵗ Battalion, 3ʳᵈ Marines, 3ʳᵈ Marine Division
APO San Francisco
Dear Brother Finch,

I was promoted to Private First Class last month. I never thought that would happen, as I was in trouble the day before it was announced. Nothing real big. I was fishing and broke some rule. I feel great. I was sick a great deal of time on Bougainville and I still get malaria set-backs. Our outfit has been doing a great deal of PT Physical training and the ground that we run on is worse than Shewbridge field if you can believe it.

We spent about three weeks aboard ship and we had one air attack on our ship. My friends Sal, Wat and I were ordered to assist three great Navy guys at their battle stations – an anti-aircraft gun – we would help load and pass the ammunition – which my buddy Sal would sing every time we went to General Quarters until the Jewish Kid on the gun, Ike Cohen, threatened to evict us. We sleep in the gun station and considered to be very lucky to do so.

During the attack we were so busy that we didn't really notice the action, but our guy Ike hit the Jap plane several times and it was trailing smoke. This is very dull out here, but we try to stay sharp. My platoon commander, Lt. Buck, has me work with him giving lectures on how to maintain weapons. I am pretty good at that, but I would really like to learn more about boilers and generators. Mr. O'Donnell and I talked about my setting up a furnace and boiler repair service after the War.

I got a big box of Mary Janes from Joanie and couple of nice notes from my Mom and the girls. Please, send me the year end football and basketball scores, Brother Finch. I go to Mass with our Lutheran Chaplain every Sunday. Here's a story you will like and you can tell it to the Knights of the Blessed Sacrament – When I was on Guadalcanal back in April, I ran into Dick Prendergast, Dick Burke, and a another guy from St. Rita and they told me that Jimmy Arneberg was in Carlson's Raiders. The Raiders were deactivated and folded into the 4th Marines as part of the 1st Provisional Brigade. We went to their area and I ran into Jimmy coming out of the shower. We went back to his tent and met his bunkmates one guy was that great running back from Austin High School Izzy Kagan. Kagan told me that Jimmy makes him get up for Mass EVERY MORNING! He says, 'Jimmy I'm a Jew for God's Sake!' and if Izzy doesn't get up out of his rack Jimmy picks it up and dumps the whole thing into the air-raid slit trench along the sides of our tents. Jimmy says nothing is going to happen to Izzy as long as he keeps going to Mass! We got a great kick out of that. All Jimmy said was , I'm Serious!' we know, Jimmy, we know!

Well, Brother, thank you being a great teacher and coach. Give my love to everyone, especially my Mom and the girls. Give my warmest regards to Brother Daly – is he still taking jug bribes to pay for his

trips to the Capitol Theater ? They show lousy movies. Keep me in your prayers Brother things are going to heat up soon.
    Your Student,
    Tim

Tim never mentioned his father in the letter, but Brother Finch would pretend that he had when he sees Larry today. He and the boy never seemed to like one another and Larry always felt that Al and Martin and Jack were cat's whiskers. Tim was always missing. The old man didn't even go to the big game last November and Tim did play after all. Larry was still a mean old Kerry farmer at heart, but he was fiercely honest and forthright man. Unlike too many Irish, Larry never took a sup of booze, as far as Brother Finch knew and he remembered how brave and closed mouthed Larry had been when he was fired from the Police Department for refusing to act against the strikers at Republic in 1937. He was given a chance to cop a plea and get a position with the Park District Police but he told them all to 'go shit in your hats, so!' That's when Mr. O'Donnell took a hand in matters as he often did in this neighborhood, quietly and forcefully. He had offices for his consulting business on the Ashland side of the building and it was believed by many that he, in fact, owned the whole block of buildings including the theatre itself, but that was rumor. Last year, the Federal Government took away his house n Little Flower Parish and now he and his wife and three kids lived in a two flat next to his mother on Loomis Street.

Finch and O'Donnell liked each other because neither man ever called a chip on one another – they would do favors for prayers; exchange information for tickets –O'Donnell had sideline passes for all Leo games and O'Donnell got White Sox tickets for Leo boys. Both men thought the world of Tim Cullen. He was not an easy boy to get to know – he was clever, athletic, and social but never a plunger or stuck on himself.

He had a brooding nature that he tried desperately to kill with good cheer and laughter. He was always on a team but not the standout. He was bright but not a great scholar. Tim was tough but never a bully or a wise guy. In short, he was a walking metaphor for most of God's creatures.

Today, Brother Finch would clear his mind and concentrate on Jane Powell's beautiful legs – Francis Rupert Finch was devout, honest and chaste; not a corpse.

CHAPTER 28
A NIGHT AT THE OPERA

Kara, Betty, and Imelda were loading the back of Juan Cruz's truck with suitcases and boxes of clothes, picnic jugs full of water and fruit juice, and boxes of food, when three Chevy trucks with Otayama's sailors pulled up. Otayama jumped from the cab of the Chevy and directed his men to confiscate the suitcases, water and food. The three women stood off to the side while the sailors tossed, gulped and devoured everything that they had packed so carefully that morning. Otayama pointed to Betty and squeaked out a command that only Kara understood who immediately screamed – 'Do not touch that girl, or Lt. Kato will have your head!' in badly mangled Japanese. Otayama grinned broadly and struck Kara with his the same bamboo cane that Kato had cut across the ear of the now beheaded Father Jesus Duenas. 'Lieutenant Order Same, Shit Nose!' shouted Otayama in equally butchered English and directed the two older women be brought into Cruz's house, while banjo-eyed Betty was dragged into the back of the first of the three trucks.

Otayama told the two that his men 'Go to Groucho Show!' and giggled like he had gotten off a real corker.

Eight of youngest Kebeitai sailors drove Betty, to the movie house and looted the candy counter of what remained, slapped Betty until she had threaded the reels of the movie they wanted, turned out the house lights, started the projector and watched a copy of *A Night at the Opera* that Chico Marx had given to Juan Cruz in 1939 on a tour with his orchestra that included Guam, Manila, Hanoi, and Hong Kong. Fifteen year old Betty Cruz (whose lifelong protector and Buck Jones fan, Hector, was out in the jungle killing dogs for the last two weeks),   so in love with the movies and Hollywood, her family, Robert Stack, and Father Duenas was raped by eight laughing young Japanese sailors in turn until Capt. Spaulding set things comically right to the sounds of *Hello, I Must Be Going – Hurray for Captain Spaulding!* and *Baita! Mocca-Mocca Su Su !! Urusai gak!*

Nothing is more horrific to witness than the abuse of a child's innocence in the exercise of power and this narrative will not despoil the propriety of her mother's anguish and the ancillary pain of her friend's torment in the knowledge that a beautiful little girl would have her dreams and woman's treasure assaulted in this manner.   The bastards did what they willed as their comrades took similar delight in slaughtering, raping and robbing the heroic people who had endured so much and would carry more of Christ's cross in this Pacific Gethsemane – to use Lt. Kato's turn of phrase.

Kato was busy doing paper work on his execution of Father Duenas and his nephew.

Following Betty's rape, the ransacking of the Tanaka and Cruz homes and a horrific beating of Imelda and Kara themselves, the two friends made their way to *The Coral* and found the devastated teenager and gave her what maternal and womanly comfort that they could. 'Baby, you are alive and with us. We are going to Manengon. You will be alright. Daddy will join us there.'

At Dededo at Tia, at Piti, at Sumay, at Orote anywhere Japanese Army or Naval forces encountered the Chamorros similar exercises in power took place. At Fena, thirty teenagers were herded into a cave and Japanese soldiers tossed in grenades until no human sounds could be detected. On the roads, Chamorros rushing to get to the supposed safety of the Japanese built camps were similarly raped, bayoneted, robbed and left for dead. These horrors happened though sixty plus years now we try to pretend that they never took place. Intellectuals, with whom your narrator is proud not number himself, play at the reification of crimes as mere symbols and acts so insignificant in the totality of War's ledger as to be brushed off of memory. John Hersey's tiny *Hiroshima* has coated over the tortures and mutilations exacted upon the helpless occupied in the Greater Far Eastern Co-Prosperity Sphere in the name of Man's better angels by those so much smarter than all of the rest of us. We blotted out the memories of what happened to these courageous and valuable people –we should be ashamed of that. No such shame for Otayama, Kato, the eight young sailors who raped Betty, the soldiers who tossed teenagers in a Cave at Fena and switched off their lives, because they could. The smarter some of us get the less we choose to remember. God Bless us dummies.

CHAPTER 29
STARS AND MULES

No one seemed dumber than Watson Cranthorpe, except maybe Leauregard Clavisill and the jury stayed out on that one for the duration of the War, but no one had greater human wisdom. The night after the A-20G exploded a couple of hundred yards from the running Company A, when all had attended Cullen and Lt. Buck's BAR demonstration and Clavisill had almost matched the speed with which Tim Cullen could strip, clean reassemble, lock and load the weapon, Watson Cranthorpe commented on the canopy of stars in the Pacific sky.

In their home for last two months – or nearly two months, Starboard .20 mm Gun Mount #4. tub, Tim, Sal and Wat never ceased to be awed by the uncountable stars placed in the ceiling by the Prime Mover. 'Them stars a got things of their own to think about up there and they seem to have first say on what goes on down here. They'sa ol' girl back home that matches mules to the stars that she sees at night to folks that need them for to get groceries back to home from the AGA near the mines. Well, sir, that old gal says that she can fix on to one star and takes out a mule from her string of them until the mule nods up so to speak and sees the star that she fixes on and then sells the mule to folks where the star wanders over their home so to speak.'

'Wat, slow the fuck down,' Sal pleaded. Sal's nose was the color of the purple tuck-pointing cement that Tim's father had mixed for years and seemed to caulk and patch every crack in their bungalow on Bishop Street. 'Jesus, Sal, that's got to be killing you. I can't believe it's not broken,' Tim managed to wedge into Wat's homily and Sal's pleas for clarity. 'I says that theys'a old woman in my home town that sells a mule to folks after she gets a fix on the star that mule sees after she –herself –has seen the star and then she knows where the folks lives that reside under where the star fixes and takes the mule to the folks and sells them the mule because that is where the mule belongs. Is that clear enough for you? God, I lost what I was saying. Anyway – all I'm saying is that the stars and look up at 'em – are there for some purpose that is fixed here on earth or why else is they up there? Anyway this woman has sold mules for near on fifty year and she is a wealthy woman because none of her mules has ever fallen off a footing and died because it was not sure of its place in the Holler and there is many sharp takes up the trail to some folk's homes I warrant. Tim, you see stars in Chicago?' Tim thought about it and recalled that the street lights pretty much obliterated any and all star view, but for certain stretches of Foster Park. 'No, nothing like this. My Mother was from an island off of Ireland and told us kids about how the stars would 'blacken the dark with light, if you can imagine' she'd say. We were such punks that we'd take it as Greenhorn Blarney like all the *banshees* and *leprechauns*.' Tim could tell he was talking Turkish to Wat. 'The salt-water Irish, those that just come over, believe in ghosts and goblins and stuff. I had a baby sister, who died when she was two years old and my Mother believes it was the *banshee* who took her and not the fever.' Tim watched the rapt faces of his gun crew –they wanted more. 'I was about five when all this took place. There was a puppy that howled all night – a real loud and whinny howl and the puppy was only a little thing, Eileen, started bawling like all get out and the girls ran to Mom that the baby was hot and burning up with fever. My Dad was a cop then and my older brother Al called the station on Ashland and he got a ride home real quick. By the time he got home, Dr. Cusack had shown up and called for an ambulance to the baby to Englewood Hospital and all this time the puppy is howling and baby is screaming. I was standing next to my Mother and bawling with the girls for some one to do something and Mother picked up Eileen and the crib collapsed and the puppy quit howling and Eileen was dead and that's no bullshit.' 'Jesus!'   fired out both of the tough teenagers who shuddered at the story's finale that crashed down on them like the final note in some Straus symphony.

Wat picked up on the theme with 'They's some strange doins in them stars and like I was saying them stars control some of what we do here and think that we are doin it, but not really.'

'Sal warmed to the idea. 'Who planned to be tucked in this round sea-going fort last year; it sure as shit wasn't this boy. I wanted to marry Katie Sobel and work at DeSoto and sing on the weekends. I figured that the war would be over by the time I got overseas and here I am.'

'All we can do is what we're supposed to do and that is all we can do and there ain't nothing to say about it. Them stars must be God's code machine or something . If we never look up at them, then we never see them and if we are so busy out-thinking God all the time we don't get the message. Like today when that A-20 went up none of those three guys saw a message before take-off because they were so busy checking gas, and loads, and maps and orders and switches and stuff, but we all got the message and loud too and the Skipper shooed us off that rock again and back here. The thing is that we got to stay busy with our work and hope that our mules got sold under the right stars.'

This chat took place one night in July and they were heading to the Marianas for the invasion of Guam. On the 19th, they would clean their weapons, stand calisthenics, crab crawl 'asses and elbows' drill - cleaning the main deck, sun themselves, play cards, fight with each other, invent sexual exploits, and seek assurances of protection from their friends once under fire just as they had every day since the end of May when they boarded LST-448.

On July 20th, they would practice disembarkation stations one last time and go to their designated LVT. Tim, Sal and Wat with their .30 caliber heavy Browning, run-off water can, hoses, spare parts bag and six cans of ammunition would board the starboard side second 22' X 9' ramp-less green Roebling Amphibious Tractor named *'Pa Kettle'* and driven by Sgt. John Kettle of Covington South Carolina and crewed by gunners Pfc.Tarjik Kamil of Toledo, Ohio and Pfc. Boyd Dowler of Red Wing Minnesota – a full-blooded Sioux. All three AmphTrac men had eaten slept and lived with their vehicle for the entire voyage and had only gotten out when tasked to do so at Eniwetok.

The drill was this – Sgt. Jack Howard's squad plus the heavy crew (fifteen men and equipment) would board Pa Kettle at 04:300 hours W-Day tomorrow, after an 0200 hours breakfast of steak and eggs; Company equipment check on the main deck in Full Field Transport Pack; all units going into all beaches would go in wearing coverless helmets – no camouflage covered helmets from W-Day until link-up and Northern Island sweep. Army units of 77th would be going ashore so there would be less distinction obvious to press and photo pools as there was a fire storm of Army/Marine rivalry going on up at Saipan. Marines however would have their distinctive camouflage bedrolls attached to their field transport packs identifying them and no Army Units were going ashore under fire – the bullshit showers down; it do – as Watson Cranthorpe was wont to say- who gives as a lusty shit when the turds hit the fan?

At 6:30 Ships Speakers would command – Land the Landing Forces - All Boats Away! – and the LVTs would grind out of the belly of LST – 449 and into the churning waters off Guam where the vehicles would circle while Naval gunfire elevated away from the beaches and into the far hills above the beaches where the Japs had cut out defenses for the last two years. At about 07:30 AM, General Roy Geiger read the final instructions to the invading forces and play the *Marines Hymn* as troops scaled down the nets of the APAs and into the Higgins LCVP boats and those, like Tim, Sal and Wat, in the LVTs closer to the reef, would snake out of the 360o circles and chug six miles an hour through the waves and over the coral reef onto the beaches and into the fire.

Chapter 30
The Gangs All Here!

Homer kicked off the idea of listing ships in an epic tale of sweep and majesty and this is no *Odyssey* by any means but the boys and men now gone and going who stood watch and stood good for their country deserve to be hailed in group. These ships plowed the waters, fired the support and berthed the men going ashore on Guam in July, 1944:

Battleships
Alabama (BB-60)California (BB-44)Colorado (BB-45)Idaho (BB-42)Indiana (BB-58)Iowa (BB-61)New Jersey (BB-62)New Mexico (BB-40)Pennsylvania (BB-38)Tennessee (BB-43)Washington (BB-56)

Carriers

Bataan (CVL-24), Air Group 50Belleau Wood (CVL-24), Air Group 24Bunker Hill CV- 17), Air Group 8Cabot (CVL-28), Air Group 31Chenango (CVE-28), Air Group

35Coral Sea (CVE-57), Composite Squadron 33Corregidor (CVE-58), Air Group 58Cowpens (CVL-25), Air Group 25Enterprise (CV-6), Air Group 10
Essex (CV-9), Air Group 15Gambier Bay (CVE-73), Composite Sqdrn 10
Hornet (CV-12), Air Group 2Kalinin Bay (CVE-68), Composite Squadron 3
Kilkun Bay (CVE-71), Composite Squadron 5Langley (CVL-27), Air Group 32
Lexington (CV-16), Air Group 16Midway (CVE-63), Composite Squadron 65
Monterey (CVL-26), Air Group 28Nehenta Bay (CVE-74), Composite Sqdrn 11
Princeton (CVL-23), Air Group 27Sangamon (CVE-26), Air Group 37
San Jacinto (CVL-30), Air Group 51Suwonnee (CVE-27), Air Group 60
Wasp (CV-18), Air Group 14Yorktown (CV-10), Air Group 1

Cruisers

Biloxi (CL-80)Birmingham (CL-62)Boston (CA-69)Canberra (CA-70)Cleveland (CL-55)Denver (CL-58)Honolulu (CL-48)Houston (CL-81)Indianapolis (CA-35)Louisville (CA-28)Miami (CL-89)Minneapolis (CA-36)Mobile (CL-63)
Montpelier (CL-57)New Orleans (CA-32)Oakland (CL-95)Reno (CL-96)
St. Louis (CL-49)San Diego (CL-53)San Francisco (CA-38)San Juan (CL-53)
Santa Fe (CL-60)Vincennes (CL-64)Wichita (CA-45)

Destroyers
Abbott (DD-629)Acree (DE-167)Anthony (DD-515)Aulick (DD-569)Charles F. Ausburne (DD-570)Aylwin (DD-

355)Bagley (DD-386)Bangust (DE-739)
Baron (DE-166)Bell (DD-587)Benham (DD-796)Bennett
(DD-473)
Black (DD-666)Boyd (DD-544)Bradford (DD-545)Clarance
K. Bronson (DD-668)
Brown (DD-546)Bullard (DD-660)Burns (DD-588)Cabana
(DE-260)Callaghan (DD-792)Caperton (DD-650)Capps
(DD-550)Case (DD-370)Cassin (DD-372)
Charrette (DD-581)Chauncy (DD-667)Closes (DE-
265)Coggswell (DD-651)
Colahan (DD-668)Conner (DD-582)Converse (DD-
509)Conway (DD-507)
Conyngham (DD-371)Cotten (DD-669)Cowell (DD-
547)Craven (DD-382)
Dale (DD-353)Dashiel (DD-659)Deede (DE-263)Dewey
(DD-349)
Dianne (DE-261)Dortch (DD-670)Dyson (DD-572)Eisele
(DE-34)
Elden (DE-264)Ellet (DD-398)Erben (DD-631)Evans (DD-
552)
Fair (DE-35)Farenholt (DD-491)Farragut (DD-348)Fleming
(DE-32)
Franks (DD-554)Fullan (DD-474)Galling (DD-671)Gridley
(DD-380)
Guest (DD-472)Haggard (DD-555)Hailey (DD-556)Hale
(DD-642)
Halford (DD-480)Paul Hamilton (DD-590)Lewis Honcock
(DD-675)
Harrison (DD-573)Healy (DD-672)Helm (DD-388)John D.
Henley (DD-553)
Hickox (DD-673)Hilbert (DE-742)Hunson (DD-4750Hull
(DD-350)
Hunt (DD-674)Ingersoll (DE-652)Irwin (DD-794)Izard
(DD-589)
Johnston (DD-557)Kidd (DD-651)Knapp (DD-653)Lamons

(DE-743)

Lang (DD-399)Lansdowne (DD-486)Lardner (00-487)Levy (DE-162)

Longshaw (DD-559)MacDonough (DD-351)Manlove (DE-36)Marshall (DD-676)

Maury (DD-401)McCall (DD-400)McCalla (DD-488)McConnell (DE-163)

McDermut (DD-677)McGowan (DD-678)McKee (DD-575)McNair (DD-679)

Meade (DD-602)Melvin (DD-680)Mertz (DD-691)Samuel S. Miles (DE-183)

Miller (DD-535)Mitchell (DE-43)Monaghan (DD-354)Monssen (DD-798)

Mugford (DD-389)Murray (DD-576)G'Flaherty (DE-340)Osterhaus (DE-164)

Owen (DD-536)Parks (DE-165)Patterson (DD-392)Porterfield (DD682)

Stephen Potter (DD-538)Halsey Powell (DD-686)Preston (DD-795)

Prichett (DD-561)Pringle (DD-477)Renshaw (DD-499)Ringgold (DD-500)

Robinson (DD-562)John Rodgers (DD-574)Sauf Icy (DD-465)Schroeder (DD-501)Sederstrom (DE-31)Selfridge (DD-357)Show (DD-373)Sigsbee (DD-502)

Spence (DD-512)Stanly (DD-478)Stembel (DD-644)Sterelt (DD-407)Stevens (DD-479)Stockham (DD-683)The Sullivans (DD-537)Swearer (DE-186)

David W. Taylor (DD-551)Terry (DD-513)Thatcher (DD-514)Tinge (DD-539)

Tisdale (DE-33)Wadsworth (DD-516)Walker (DD-51)7)Waller (00-466)

Waterman (DE-740)Weaver (DE-741)Wedderburn (DE-684)Wesson (DE-184)

Whitman (DE-24)Wileman (DE-22)Williamson (DD-

244)Wilson (DD-408)
Yarnell (DD-541)

Mine Vessels
Caravan (AM-157)Hamilton (DMS-18)Hogan (DMS-6)Hopkins (DMS-13)
Long (DMS-12)Motive (AM-102)Palmer (DMS-5)Perry (DMS-17)Sheldrake (AM-62)Skylark (AM-63)Spear (AM-322)Stansbury (DMS-8)Starling (AM-64)
Terror (CM-5)YMS-136YMS-151YMS-184YMS-195YMS-216YMS-237YMS-241
YMS-242YMS-260YMS-266YMS-270YMS-272YMS-281YMS-291YMS-292YMS-295YMS-296YMS-302YMS-317YMS-321YMS-322YMS-323YMS-396
Zone (DMS-14)

Patrol Vessels
PC-549PC-555PC-581PC-1079PC-1080PC-1125PC-1126PC-1127PC-1136PCS-1396PCS-1457SC-504SC-521SC-667SC-724SC-727SC-1052
SC-1273SC-1319SC-1325SC-1326SC-1328

Submarine
Tarpan (SS-175)

Fleet Auxiliaries

Agenor (ARL-3)Aloe (AN-6)Apache (ATF-67)ARD-16ARD-17Aastabula (AO-51)
Bountiful (AH-9)Cache (AO-67)Cahaba (AO-82)Caliente (AO-53)Chowanoe (ATF-100)Cimarron (AO-22)City of Dalhart (IX-156)Concrete barge 1321
Concrete Barge 1324Enoree (AO-69)Grapple (ARS-7)Guadalupe (AO-32)Holly (AN-19)Hydrographer (AGS-2)Kaskaskia (AO-27)Kennebago (AO-81)

Lackawanna (AO-40)Lipan (ATF-85)Manatee (AO-58)Marias (AO-57)Mascoma (AO-8 3)Monongahela (AO-42)Neosho (AO-48)Neshanic (AO-71)Owklawaha (AO-84)Pakana (ATF-108)Pautuxent (AO-44)Pecis (AO-65)Pennant (Motor Ship)
Platte (AO-24)Sabine (AO-25)Samaritan (AH-10)Saugatuck (AO-75)Schuylkill (AO-76)Sebec (AO-87)Solace (AH-5)Tallulah (AO-50)Tappahannock (AO-43)
Takesta (ATF-93)Tomahawk (AO-88)Tupelo (AN-56)Typhoon (IX-145)Zuni (ATF-95)
Transports and Cargo Vessels
Alcyone (AKA-7)Alkes (AK-110)Almaack (APA-10)Alpine (APA-92)Alshain (AKA-55)APc-46Appalachian (AGC-1)Acquarius (AKA-16)Ara (AK-136)William P. Biddle (APA-8)Bolivar (APA-34)William Ward Burrows (AP-6)Centaurus (AKA-17)Clemson (APA-31)George Clymer (APA-27)Comet (AP-166)Cor Caroli (AK-91)Crescent City (APA-21)Custer (APA-40)Degrass (AP-164)Dickerson (APD-21)Doyen (APA-1)Draco (AK-79)Du Page (APA-42)Elmore (APA-42)Fayette (APA-43)Feland (APA-11)Frederick Funston (APA-89)Golden City (AP-169)
Kane (APD-18)Lamar (AP-47)Harry Lee (APA-10)Leedstown (APA-56)
Libra (AKA-12)Monrovia (APA-31)Noa (APD-24)Ormsby (APA-49)President Adams (APA-19)President Hoyes (AP-20)President Jackson (APA-18)
President Monroe (APA-104)President Polk (APA-103)Rixey (APH-3)
Sheridan (APA-51)Starlight (AP-175)Sterope (AK-96)Titania (AKA-13)
Vega (AK-17)Virgo (AKA-20)Warhawk (AP-168)Warren (APA-53)Waters (APD-8)
Wayne (APA-54)Wharton (AP-7)Windson (APA-55)Zeilin (ALA-3)

Landing Ships and Craft

Carter Hall (LSD-3)Epping Forrest (LSD-4)Gunston Hall (LSD-5)LCI(G)-345LCI(G)-346LCI(G)-348LCI(G)-365LCI(G)-366LCI(G)-437LCI(G)-438 LCI(G)-439LCI(G)-440LCI(G)-441LCI(G)-442LCI(G)-449LCI(G)-450 LCI(G)-451LCI(G)-455LCI(G)-457LCI(G)-464LCI(G)-465LCI(G)-466 LCI(G)-467LCI(G)-468LCI(G)-469LCI(G)-471LCI(G)-472LCI(G)-473 LCI(G)-474LCT(6)-962LCT(6)-964LCT(6)-965LCT(6)-966LCT(6)-968 LCT(6)-982LCT(6)-989LCT(6)-995LCT(6)-1059LCT(6)-1061LCT(6)-1062 LST-24LST-29LST-38LST-41LST-70LST-71LST-78LST-117LST-118 LST-122LST-123LST-125LST-207LST-219LST-220LST-221LST-227 LST-241LST-243LST-244LST-247LST-269LST-270LST-276LST-334 LST-341LST-343LST-398LST-399LST-446LST-447LST-449LST-476 LST-477LST-478LST-479LST-481LST-482LST-488LST-684LST-731 LST-986 Underwater Demolition Teams UDT 3UDT 4UDT 6

These last boys were the Navy Frogmen Underwater Demolition Teams who swept in close to the beach and dived from fast landing craft to swim - wearing only fins and goggle – no breathing tanks - under water holding their breath in order to blow up underwater beach obstacles that would have killed more men going ashore than will die in the pages to come.

If the cataloging device is irritating, skip over it; in fact, why not skip the balance of this narrative. Imagine, if you have patience and heart, the number and quality of the boys who cashed in their wilder years to face the ocean's depths and Man's ability to slaughter his brother. I am awed – of the ships numbered above people the item with a maximum of 3,000 souls and a minimum of twelve. Experts tell us that of the American boys who survived that horrific war, 1,500 more of them die on a daily basis and we give them little or no thought. This is a small opportunity.

I imagined an LST-448 and the careful reader (or the honored veteran searching out his old ship's soul) will note there is no LST-448. This one belongs to my fictive turn of mind and most of the boys who wait for the opening salvos to soften up the beaches. It begins.

CHAPTER 31
PA KETTLE'S LAST RIDE

Not an egg in the hundreds fried was broken, nor was one deemed to be runny. They looked like three huge yellow eyes staring bug-eyed from a nest of hash brown potatoes and they were merely the garnish for the perfectly grilled cut of steak that Chief Marlon York of Shelbyville, Tennessee had hand rubbed with a mixture of garlic salt, fine ground black pepper and a pinch of cayenne and topped with a thick slice of grilled onion. Each Marine going a shore to Guam in a few hours was treated to a meal that only a man aware of the horrors awaiting these men could articulate with his own graces and flourishes. No powdered eggs for these heroes. Marlon's Daddy had fought in the Great War as a doughboy and always bemoaned the fact that the belly-robbers would send men to die on a diet of swill unfit for hogs. Chief York had prepared a similar feast for the dog faces before Attu in the Aleutians and the sea-going bell-hops at Tarawa and had maintained this tradition for five campaigns.

Like the owner of a New York steak house, Chief York table hopped and put a thick hand on each boys shoulder, neck or head and was rewarded with a universal 'Great Chow, Chief! Wish you were coming along!' Chief York and every man on cook's watch worked through two watches to get the breakfast right. Gunny Higgins ordered a 'Three Times Three for Chief York and the Men of 448!' 1st Battalion, Third Marines wildly approved. The entire ship registered to the on-going bombardment that had begun three days prior to the arrival of the Transport Division of the Southern Task Force. The Attack Transports and Landing Ships were elbowing their way into the maelstrom orchestrated by the battleships, cruisers, destroyers and the more distant aircraft carriers that sent relays of fighters, torpedo bombers and dive bombers to churn-up the soil of Guam.

Fed and petted the killers departed the galley in shifts took to their tasks of making final equipment checks and simian-like grooming of their brothers' harnesses, straps, haversacks, knapsacks, ammunition belts, Kay bar knives, entrenching tools, bedrolls, shelter halves, sewing kits, canteens ('two Full; and I mean Full') personal weapons, prayer books, hand rosary decades, photos, mess-gear, medical kits, and tied up their leggings. One last look at the main deck.

Hours before, the three renters of Starboard .20mm Gun Tub #4., Pfc. Tim Cullen, Pvt. Watson Cranthorpe and Pvt. Sal Battaglia said goodbye to their three hosts. Ike Cohen, Tom Brown and Big Al Townsend told them to stake out a great beach area for the party that they'd have once the Japs called it quits. 'Have to kill all the fuckers, Ike; ask Tim, they don't quit.' Tim said they'd do a little better for the Navy once they could get a hold of the real estate and they'd have a real beach party. Sal said that they'd get up a musical night with some of the native girls, because Gunny said that they were all gorgeous. The sailors all exuded affirmative enthusiasm for the date – as each of three men had done for the soldiers at Attu, the Marines of the Second Division at Tarawa and the three other campaigns and never a date was kept.

Now after steak and eggs and gearing up, A Company stood in squad by platoon in front of Capt. Geary Bundeschu. 'Smoking lamp is out until you get the Ok from your drivers out in the surf. Drink water from the scuttlebutt and lay off your canteens. It is expected that temperatures will exceed 95o and 100% humidity today and we have a great deal of ground to cover and most of it up-hill. Go easy on the water. Once ashore find the rally markers and if you hit the wrong area call out for A Company. Sgt, Crandak will mark a pennant at Red 2, Once we form up we head due right through the rice paddies and to the hills. We can expect steep elevation where we hit; once the signal is given keep moving. You are ready Marines – Let's make history.' Less personal was the command to open this dance.

'1st Squad, 1st Platoon starboard hatchway; 1st Squad 2nd Platoon Port hatchway – board the Tractors.'

That was it. No Huzzas. No rebel yells. No Agincourt. Businesslike. All business. The business was deadly and business was good. Taking the Tripod's two legs crooked in his arms and trailing the third leg over his pack and down his back, Cullen led off followed by Wat with the gun barrel with its hose already attached and wrapped around the rubber water proofing cover and the water condenser can and Sal carrying two of the eight ammo cans followed by riflemen who carried the remaining six to the LVTs.

Tim was reminded of going over the side for Bougainville. No jokes. No chat. No noise save the bounce and jingle of equipment. No cowards. No cravens grabbing the legs of officers and begging to stay away from what was waiting. No theatrical heroics or bold words. Business. All Business.

The sounds of the naval gunfire, seemed to get louder as the Marines snaked down the ladder of the hatchway back onto the tank deck where *Pa Kettle* and his thirteen kin folk were idling engines and the atmosphere was thick with noise and diesel despite the sucking force of the already over exerted exhaust fans. Navy wranglers and slingers were making final approach checks on all of the vehicle harnesses that had lashed the amphibious tractors to the deck of 448 for most of two months.

Sgt. John Kettle waved to Tim Cullen who gave him a back head nod salute of recognition and maintained his place until motioned forward by Sgt. Howard who mounted *Pa Kettle's* tracks and straddled his leg over the gunwale of the tractor and hand signaled Cullen to collapse and lock the legs of the tripod and begin hoisting its sixty pounds up to him. Jack Howard pulled up the tripod and Tim boosted himself up to Jack's place repeating the operation with Wat and the gun and water can and Wat the same with Sal and the ammo and so on until all fifteen men and their equipment were mounted in the AmphTrac.

Lt. Buck simultaneously relayed his LVT teams into *Cincinnati Red's* and once loaded took out his flashlight to re-read the letter sent from his father in Giddings, Texas

Dear Jack,

Your Mother is delighted that her confectionary delights have helped win the War. We are both praying for your safe return to us and also for the remarkable young boys that your letters have told us about – what a wonderful thing to witness such skill and determination from youngsters who should be eaten chicken out of a basket with a pretty little thing at a nice pond fill of catfish.

I was in Austin over the weekend sniffing votes for the new Electric Bill that will give lights and power to so many people out in the far reaches of the District. Young fellow named Preston Smith is running out of Lubbock and I went along at Lyndon's suggestion to help him

out in the hustings. He owns a string of movie houses that he bought from a Jap businessman from Spokane, Washington who was interred right after the start of the war. It sure made it easy on us as we could use the movie houses to do our electioneering and we have had a really wet summer for Texas. Preston Smith is a natural and I brought him home to help give Lawndale Sowery a few tickles on my end. Shouldn't worry about such nonsense when you have much more pressing matters to occupy your thoughts, Son. By the way, your mother tells me that you met a perfectly lovely young woman - lawyer just like you - on Guadalcanal of all places. She must be something particularly special and gifted with more than a few handfuls of God's best sand to be taking risks out there in the South Pacific. From what your mother said from your letters the Japs were still bombing Guadalcanal on occasion. Yes, Sir that must be some girl and I can't wait for you to bring her home to our family.

Old Bill Longley's Colt should put you in good stead though it's not been fired in anger since old Bill did his killing in Louisiana. I put flowers on his grave last week. I pray to God that the damned thing stays holstered until it comes home to us in and you can put it away for ever.

Well, Jack it is about time for Lawn Sowery' radios rant against his enemies FDR, The Jews, The Mexicans, The Bucks, the Negroes, Catholics, and all of the sheep that never new the delicate touch of Lawn Sowery –must be nice to have a

rich wife- Hell, I DO!. Be safe and be with Christ and his Holy Mother, Son!
  Your Loving Father,
  Rope

The diesel fumes, the roar of fourteen six cylinder 146 HP Hercules engines idling and waiting for the Navy tank deck officer to get the word to open the bow doors and drop the ramp into the sea. Jack looked at Sgt. Rittenouer who immersed in a pamphlet about accounting that he seemed to have read many times over. 'Karl, you thinking about a new career?' The red faced blond Old Timer nodded with conviction, 'Aye, Sir' and went back to reading.

A Claxon sounded and deadened the noise of the fourteen alligator tractors and an added metallic screech and howling of the bow doors yawned in fresh sea air to mix with the diesel fumes and also the dull BaBOOOMBIMG and OOOOOOWSZZZZZZOOWEEEING of 12, 14, and 16 inch shells arching their way toward Guam. Sea water pooled in when the ramp was lowered and an artificial lake was provided to ease the egress of the amphibious tractors that would soon be lurching into the Pacific waters. The early morning darkness now fighting with the red lights of the tank deck strobed with gun flashes and their shell's impacts on the distant shores.

Still time. Norm Chad puked in his steel helmet – not in its liner mind you -and tossed his steak and eggs over the side of *Pa Kettle* and there would be plenty more boys doing likewise over the next several hours. Most of the boys had done this drill many times before –in training all through the Solomons and many more times again at Kwajelain and even recently a few times at Eniwetok. Tim Cullen counted the number of spare parts for the .30 caliber that he had laid out on a blanket in the Gun Tub so many times over the last two months. BUSHING 3/4", Barrel (spare) M2, WATER COOLED. BUSHING 1/2",

M2, WATER COOLEDSCREW/NUT-ASSEMBLY, M2, WATER COOLED NUT, JAM, M2, LOCK, M2, LOCK-ASSEMBLYVALVE, DRAINBEARING, BEARING, RING, BARRELWRENCH, COMBO, 'BUTTERFLY', M2. Wrench Muzzle Packing Gland Wrench. Plug, Water. CLINOMETER, FLASH HIDER, Back Plate water jacket (spare). Gun was filled to capacity at 8 pints. That's that. Tim carried an M1 carbine, his Smitty Wesson .38, carbine bayonet on his pack and a Kay bar on his utility belt. From his blouse pocket he pulled a round single decade rosary and prayed. Making the sign of the Cross with the cross between his thumb and forefinger he recruited the Apostles Creed and began the rotation of prayers Our Father, Glory Be to the Father & etc. and the five cycles of ten Hail Marys. Equipment and Rosary; Equipment and Rosary.

Watson Cranthorpe hummed. Sal imitated Tim with his own steel rosary, Neil Steinberg slept, Norm Chad threw up, Sgt. Jack Howard played with his last pack of Chesterfields, and Tadeuz Cynopkowitz played with string, Cpl. Dan Miller read about the Cleveland Indians from a pamphlet, PFC. Zeb Carrier whittled a piece of drift wood; Pfc. Frank Dranago wrote a letter, Pfc. Lucius Whitely; looked at pictures; Pfc. Mike Cloud stared at Pvt. Lonnie Newman who cheated in a card game but would not take the pot; Pvt. Henry Clay tried to sleep; Pvt. Leauregard Clavisill grew more yellow and jaundiced by the minute.

'Now hear this! Now hear this! All tractors away from the Boat deck! All Tractors away! God Bless You!' And that was the last time anyone heard Capt. Maurice Higgins, USNR again – that is until Tim Cullen was arrested for drunk driving down Halsted Street at 87th Street in 1961 and taken to Gresham Police Station, where Lt. Mo Higgins, Chicago Police Department had the drunk brought to his office and the citation was lost. It was an August Night, and Tim Cullen was driving home to his Georgian at 99th & Claremont on his way home from

Walter Quinlan & Sons Funeral home where Edward J. 'Spike' O'Donnell was being waked – and a much too along stop at Duffy's Tap at 79th and Carpenter. Watch Commander Higgins remembered the Brig Rat who had caught his best meal while in the Service. Lt. Mo Higgins had Sgt. Paddy Higgins, who had fought in Burma during the war, drive the guy home and keep his car keys. But all of that was way ahead of Tim Cullen – like all of us.

From Portside of the tank deck, the first of the LVTs bearing Capt. Geary Bundeschu crawled into the water and in succession each of the tractors followed suit. Tim bit his tongue slightly when *Pa Kettle* lurched forward and down into the Pacific just as daylight made some headway amid all of the man made noise and fire. Tim sucked on his tongue and guessed that more than that would be bruised before this day catalogued itself. Norm Chad continued to throw up over the side of the tractor as Sgt. Kettle eased his craft into the route behind eight other LVTs making a large 360o circle,

Fire from the Bombardment Task Force increased in fury as LSTs disgorged their reptiles out onto the waves and the dull waiting now two months into the log began to take on a sharper and more immediate impact on each of the men driving, manning and being conveyed in the scores of Amphibious Tractors – some were of the newer armored class with a stern ramp that dropped and still others armed with 75mm cannons in a turret. A Company would hit Red Beach Two from LVT-1s that were used in the Solomons and hit Tarawa. Flocks of Naval aircraft flew over head waiting for the ship bombardment to let up. These birds flew high up over the circling LVTs and would strike positions on Guam just ahead of the landing. Each man maintained his own counsel throughout this sweet monotonous exercise knowing full well that once the circle was broken and the ride into the beach was determined that he would be sole master of his actions – but certainly not the outcomes.

The arching landing craft did five circuits of the orbit at 6mph and the men within kept faith to the tasks assigned them over the months of preparation. The fifteen Marines in *Pa Kettle* concentrated on their expected duties going over each movement and position that had been exercised into them at Guadalcanal and through the map lectures, demonstrations and squad meetings aboard LST-448 now so far in their past these last decades of minutes since the LVT took the steep plunge from the ramp into the Pacific. Spay from the tracks curled back onto their helmets and packs and a few of the men uncoiled and stood to look landward at the beach and high ground beyond still being beaten by naval shelling. It was as if a super heavyweight fighter was being pummeled by a talented fly-weight boxer – shots to the ribs, quick jabs to the ears and nose, but the big bruising opponent stood erect and waiting.

Tim Stood next to Wat and watched the firestorm of heavy shelling and they expertly commented on where 5", 12", '14", and 16" shells were impacting on the ancient soil of the Chamorros. LCI rocket ships were sending up arcs of rockets that landed in playful successions marked by thin fingers of earth. The familiar freight-train *shu, shu, shu, shushing* of big ordinance - Heavy Stuff – careered over-head and landed deep in the island's high grounds. 'Still'pears Big and Mean, Tim. We'll be there a long time. Sal, come up and take a look.' Sal joined his friends and other squad men stood as well to listen to Wat's commentary and witness his report.'

'Look there at the edge of where we're goin'in – See, right of the Cliff a bit and closer to water's edge, but up an in a bit. Them's look like the white stone fence posts for that parking lot at San Diego you know right before we went into Boots at the Depot. Them's American concrete posts. Musta been the same Navy planner that designed the San Diego parking lot and none of our stuff's hit or taken out any of the posts. Ain't that a wonder.'

'Fascinating, Wat.'

'And look at that point - the one making our map Landin' Bitch Front Line – that's one of the devil's horns Col. Hall told us about - Adelup Point. Big house on it still; can make out the house; bet the Japs are dug in there. We goin in further to the right..'

Red Flares shot up and Mine sweepers bolted past the circles of LVTs in order to draw fire from the enemy artillery away from the amphibious/tractor attack boats by offering themselves as more conspicuous targets. Sgt. Jack Howard ordered his men down. "Last look at the beach, clear weapons, check safeties – everybody get the Fuck out of this bathtub the second Kettle yells. Get clear and get cover. Bear a hand with all the gear.'

All talk ceased. *Pa Kettle* took its last curved route and plowed into its linear position like a tubby chorus girl. Sgt. John 'Pa' Kettle went full power in the 12 mph dash of the LVTs to the treacherous razor back of the reef and the craft bumped and ground as the first solid footing the craft had felt since leaving the tank deck, 'Welcome to Guam, Marines!', 'yelled Tarjik Kamil from his position on the big .50 caliber machine gun Port of the driver's seat. 'Looks like a thousand yards to the beach – Japs firing back - Stay Down! Fountains of water were working their way to the approaching boats. *CLANG, CALANG KOW!* Pfc. Tajik's weapon exploded and his fists, forearms, elbows and lower jaw as well. All that remained of the Port .50 was the twisted barrel, some shards of the receiver group and the gun mount welded to the attack boat... Tajik was dying but Doc Brosnan aided his last seconds and he was pillowed by the men of 1st squad and died.

Starboard Gunner Boyd Dowler never looked to see his buddy from Toledo dying in the well eight feet from him but professionally fired short bursts of four at targets of opportunity where he believed enemy fire might come from. More fountains of surf water and shards of coral kicked up by .25mm Japanese dual purpose guns walked over the reef and past *Pa Kettle*. Pfc. Boyd Dowler yelled, 'Straight in there are knocked down palm trees – right where we're going. Pa will get this bitch close to them, Marines.' and continued to deliver arching bursts from his weapon. The boat to the right of *Pa Kettle* took six .25 mm shells and caught fire; men were already going over the side into the three feet of water and getting carved up on the sharp coral. Another LVT moved into its position and the crippled tractor burned. Boyd yelled, 'Beach in thirty seconds. We'll grind on up close to the downed palms. Get Ready.' Heavy explosions rocked and clanged metal off the sides of *Pa Kettle*, but Boyd Dowler stayed erect. 'This beach is hotter than Tarawa!' They have it zeroed in! On the sand!'

Pa Kettle slowed some as its tracks dug deeply into white sand that seemed alive and kicking with ballistics and explosives. Something slammed into the driver's position and exploded and Sgt, John Kettle was erased from Operation Forager's Table of Organization. No flames erupted but all that remained of the driver were his hips, thighs and legs fused to the metal driver's seat. Boyd Dowler's eyes were put out by shards of metal but he commanded, 'OUT!'

Tim Cullen horsed up the tripod and bellied himself over the side of *Pa Kettle* and once placing his burden down on the whitest sand on earth reached up to help ease the blinded Boyd Dowler on to the beach. The horribly wounded Sioux from Red Wing never uttered a sound and remained conscious. *Pa Kettle* was now smoking badly and flames were licking up from the driver's seat. Watson and Sal passed Dowler off to Norm Chad who pulled the blind man behind downed palms away from the LVT that might explode any second. Wat, Sal and Tim grabbed their primary weapon, its parts and secured it behind four downed palms another four feet from Norm and Dowler. Doc Brosnan was with the two men now and aiding Dowler. Every member of the squad was out of the LVT and at least ten yards in advance of it. Jack Howard walked like Quasimodo pointing and ordering each man to his place in this, the Guam Campaign's opening line of battle.

Neil Steinberg and BAR Man Tadeuz Cynopkowicz were echelon left; Cpl. Dan Miller, Mike Cloud, Frank Dranago, and

Henry Clay; then the .30 Caliber team of Cullen, Cranthorpe and Battaglia; Norm Chad and Doc Brosnan who would ease Dowler's pain by pulling shards of metal from his face, but not those in his eye sockets and passing him off to another Corpsman as waves arrived. Norm would stay with Doc; then, Sgt. Jack Howard forward and center and Leauregard Clavisill, Lucius Whitley and card cheat Lonnie Newman. To 1st Squad's right Lt. Buck and Sgt. Rittenouer's LVT was clawing its way in further and miraculously no hits were evident on that tractor. The humming song of hot bullets brought first timers' neck hairs up and reminded those previously under fire at Bougainville that the sound was eternal. No person fired at forgets the sound of bullets ignoring him or her. Every man breathing on this beach was a combat veteran. Fire intensified as more LVTs exploded, burned, burst apart and the men who rode in them screamed when burned, blown up or rendered by explosives.

Twenty yards from the beach, the earth worked its way up as higher ground with a sixty degree incline by what Tim's geometry lessons with Brother Finch could tell him insinuating its neck to the left and rising as Chorito Cliff and from its 500 yards of distance down to the Marines finding protection behind the fallen palm trees and thrown up debris of battle he could make out flashes from machine gun muzzles – had to be at least six from what he could tell. The Laws of Euclidian geometry could not be put into practical uses until the mortar men from the Weapons Company waded ashore, but already Marines were returning fire from the fallen and shattered palm trees. They had not been ashore more than five minutes and already men were taking hits from mortar round shards and high impact 7.5 caliber rounds from Light Type 96 and Heavy Type 92 Nambu machine guns.

An air burst from the 25 mm dual purpose gun - hidden up above the rice paddy they were to cross soon - exploded prematurely and wildly as what was supposed to rifle out to one of the approaching LVTs. Fragments from it went through Jack Howard's ear and tore off the top of his head and also cut Lucius Whitley's femoral artery. Leauregard Clavisill jaundiced but healthy was untouched by the burst's fragments and continued to aim his Garand at the flashing machine guns on Chorito Cliff. Lonnie Newman who had cheated at cards two nights before took a Nambu round through the throat and gurgled up blood shattered membrane.

Lt. Buck ran over to Jack Howard and Sgt. Rittenouer took his dog tags. 'Miller, your squad!' Jack Buck yelled to Cpl. Danny Miller. Move your men up Echelon Left till we can get some fire discipline on those six weapons up there. Go!'

'Steinberg, Go! CZ Covering fire on the Go! Go!' Neil Steinberg did not run like an athlete but he ran up the slope with a grace born of practice for twenty yards and cover and began firing. 'Cullen, Sal and Wat on the GO! CZ Fire on Go. Go! Cullen ran zigzag low up the middle Sal to the left and Wat held the right flank run. When they had reached Neil the four riflemen put up a rapid fire display of marksmanship on the flashing positions above them. Then Miller, Cloud, Dranago and Clay joined them to the right and just above Watson. Now, CZ and his BAR joined them at the middle post next to Tim who scooted left and exchanged places with Neil Steinberg who carried CZ's extra magazine belt.

Lt. Buck and Sgt. Rittenouer relayed their men accordingly and Platoons from Baker and Charlie Companies were working their way up and to the right for a full link up to Chorito Cliff and the ugly ridge that Company A had practiced to attack back on Guadalcanal last April. During these echelon relays of squads in face of the enemy gun nests one hundred and twenty yards up, more men began to fall and roll down the steep cliff's slope. Capt. Geary Bundeschu ordered the assault line to cross the rice paddies and advance up the ever inclining ground to take the nose of ridge that jutted in the face of Able Company's advance. Mortar fire from the ridges and higher plateaus became as intense as the cross-fire from well concealed machine gun positions on the crests of each new ridgeline. Every new high ground proved to be another target of opportunity for enemy fire directed down on the Marines from still higher ground yet to be taken. Here, two hundred yard s from the water's edge, the men of Company A set up a jump off point for that higher ground. Capt. Bundeschu ordered a command down to all squads, 'Drop your packs here! Take all the ammunition you can carry and as many grenades as you can. Go easy on the water!'

In a relay LVT that met Battalion staff's LCVP Higgins boat 1000 yards from the beach Gunny William Wheat Higgins helped Battalion Executive Officer Capt. Maynard Crawford into the bouncing tractor. 'No day to get our linen wet Captain – It is a fine day, Sir. Let me have the map case, Sir. And in you go. That's the last mule in the chute, ferryman; drive this water taxi to New Orleans!'

Gunny wore a huge smile as he watched enemy fire crane to reach his craft. 'Waste them shots! Third Marines are advancing, Major and 1st Battalion boys are out in front. They are crossing the paddies as I can determine and it is now 08:34, Sir. Jap fire coming in hard and all are advancing. Weapons Company is on the beach! '

As the LVT ground across the coral reef, fire from heavy mortars on Fonte Ridge and the dual purpose .25 mm guns hidden on Bundeschu Ridge spouted geysers of water and sent steel fragments and huge chunks of razor sharp coral raining down on the men in the LVT. A boy squatting below Gunny Higgins took a fragment of one of those two elements in his left knee. Gunny yanked a pair of field glasses from the map case he had taken from Capt Crawford and moved next to the starboard machine gunner to get a better view of his boys on the beach and their progress ashore. As he raised the glasses full to his eyes, a flat shard of steel the size of a dinner plate took off his head. Lucas Opley noted that his friend of nearly twenty years was smiling up at him, but that his body was still standing next to the starboard machine gunner. It was a short ride onto Red Beach 2.

PART IV

BUNDESCHU RIDGE & FONTE CLIFF

CHAPTER 32
ABLE COMPANY DECIMATED

Able Company led by Capt...Geary Bundeschu moved out under fire across the rice paddies above the landing beaches and up the steep slopes of the ridge jutting beach ward from Chorito Cliff but still below the fire from enemy positions above on Fonte Plateau. This high ground and the essential Mt. Tenjo road needed to be secured in order to affect the liberation of Agana and to strike out and link up with the 4th Provisional Brigade and the Army's 77th Division sweep north and secure the island of Guam. As of 11:00 all of the 1st Battalion and its support were ashore on Red Beach 2 and fighting its way up Chorito Cliff.

Gunnery Sergeant William Wheat Higgins was killed before he could once again set foot on Guam. His remains stayed in the LVT and later off-loaded and placed along the other dead men on the beach including Sgt. Jack Howard for identification by Graves Registration staff. In his twenty three years of service to the only anchor in his life – The Anchor, the Globe and the Eagle - William Wheat Higgins had committed sins so foul and performed acts of bravery so intense in nature that his name aroused devotion short only of idolatry in all ranks of the Marine Corps. His friend and commander since serving together at Culebra Naval Station Puerto Rico never mentioned his name again.

'I want 60 and 80 mm mortar fire support barrage set to go at 0300 and A Company will take the crest of that ridgeline – Bundeschu Ridge. Tell Lt. Ames to adjust all of his weapons accordingly. Capt. Crawford, send a runner for Capt. Geary. His men are 100 yards short of that crest and I want to know why. Get all stretcher bearers ready to follow-up A Company's assault this afternoon. We are too close in for naval support at this time and we can not get eyes on a target to call in an air-strike. We are still taking heavy fire from those ridges and they are calling accurate fire from their artillery and heavy mortars up on Fonte! That high ground must be canceled out to them and I mean now!'

Regimental Commander Col. William Carvel Hall understood why his 3rd Marines were taking such intense fire but he wanted to know why A Company could not affect the capture of their Final Beachhead Line on the timeline and what would it take to do so! Col. Hall was given the hottest beaches for the Third Marines but this was ridiculous. From Adelup Point to Asan the 3rd Marines found themselves in a triangulated crossfire and every square inch of their sector was pre-sighted by veterans of Chinese Mountain fighting. And was it Hot! Temperatures on Guam reached 96 degrees with 100% humidity and there was no water until it could be brought up to the line by service and depot units, still making the trip in from the fleet.

With six hours on the beach, 1st Platoon, A Company had lost the following men: 1st Squad: Sgt. Jack Howard, Pfc. Lucius Whitely, Pvt. Lonnie Newman, and from 2nd squad Pvt. Bill Kay, Pvt. Gerry Haggerty. Lt. Gallo's platoon was equally down with four men killed outright and two who would die of wounds.

Nearly every man on the beach including Tim Cullen had caught a tiny piece of fragment in the face, the arms, the legs, or the torso and now, that they had dropped their field transport packs, more were taking tiny shards in the back and shoulders. Mortar fire continued unabated from the high grounds. Seven dead men in six hours out of a thirty two man platoon. At this rate they could all be dead by 0700 tonight. But none gave that a thought and the tactics and support of the next few hours would negate most of that possibility.

We watch what happened to these men sixty three years ago and consider the limiting effects of our own insulated lives; especially those of us who have never worn the uniform or gone into harm's way under orders, and can only wonder at the motivation to proceed to where they are going in the next few hours. That is a luxury born of the sacrifices these quiet old men will take to their God shortly. They have work to do.

Lt. Buck, Sgt, Rittenouer, Cpl Miller, and 2nd squad's Sgt. Ed Norris got 'the word' from Major Opley. Ist Platoon would affect a right echelon assault with two light machine gun teams from Weapon's Company: Pvt. Kurt Van Mill Pvt. Louis Coe and Pvt. Dick Raines Pvt. Mitchell Vizier. Van Mill and Coe would go with Dan Miler's 1st Squad and Raines and Mitch Vizier with Ed Norris's. Both light teams would provide flanking fire and once the crest of Bundeschu Ridge was taken Cullen, Battaglia, and Cranthorpe would go back and bring up the heavy machine gun to effect defensive base of fire.

'Sarn't Norris you take right - ten yard intervals at the double on Capt. Bundeschu's whistle; Cpl. Miller take extreme left same intervals I will take the middle with my signal man, Sgt Rittenouer and Doc Brosnan. Weapons is putting down 81mm rounds in fifteen minutes as well as our Company 60mms. Deploy – Go!'

Each leader to his task and Tim Cullen, Sal and Wat knew that once this crown was taken from the Japs that they would need to leg it fast back with the .30 caliber gun. From their positions five hundred yards away the men of A company could hear the distinctive DOOO of 81mm mortar rounds leaving the barrels of the effective weapons. Thinner sounding DOOS went up from the three 60mm mortars. The crest of the hill was a fountain of dirt and debris in seconds and rounds of both calibers were walked back and forth along the top of the ridge where the Japanese veterans of the war in China were waiting.

Capt Bundeschu's already bloodied Company moved on the ridge named for him aboard LST-448 in a practiced and professional manner. The Company came under no direct fire to speak of, save for the sporadic rounds fired from Fonte Plateau on the left but all fell short of the attacking Marines. The grind up the slope was murderously taxing and men needed to crawl most of the way up, grabbing exposed roots to pull themselves more easily and reaching a hand back to men in this struggle with God's Laws of Gravity.

The hill side was blasted away from many days of naval bombardment and men cut their hands on buried shards of spent steel made in Gary, Indiana, Bethlehem, Pennsylvania and Cleveland, Ohio. Just short of the crest, with no rifle or machine gun fire kicking up dirt against them, every man in the Company heard obscene laughter coming from the ridge's crest and shouts of *Kichigaijimata!; Baka yaro! Kuso atama! Koro shite yaru!* but primarily *Kutabare!* Followed by *click, clang pop click clang pop fissssssssss!* At its steepest the exhausted one hundred and eighty men of A Company were treated with a cascade of Type 97 five second fuse fragmentation grenades being rolled down the last fifteen yards of their crawl to the top! Grenades exploded out of the side of the hill and often directly under the man as he clawed his way up the slope, as if the hill were somehow blowing itself out at the Marines - ant-like in their determination to reach the crown of this ridge.

"Mother Fuckers! Jesus ! Christ! Balls! You Cocksuckers! The now rendered Americans cried up at the laughing China veterans who had staked out this piece of real estate with a jeweler's eye for terrain and killing detail. Men rolled dead away only a few feet from the top and others maimed and blinded and frustrated found themselves rolling back down the steep slopes. Into this confusion of the shocked Marines, Japanese Light Machine gunners jumped up from their well concealed spider holes and trenches and poured fire down on the helpless men.

'Return fire on those bastards,' yelled Cpl. Miller who was already firing his Thompson in short bursts while clutching to a very thick and tenacious root. All Marines fired on the – now they were gone and giggling as a thick voiced Japanese – probably their Billy Higgins yelled *Kieuseru!* Which Sgt. Ed Norris knew to mean *Fuck Off!*

Capt. Bundeschu ordered the men down to rally at some pretty effective cover twenty yards lower and as the Company eased its way there firing up at the crest the entire way the Japanese re-emerged from their defensive positions and began sniping and picking off targets of opportunity. A Company was being torn apart. The men not too shattered to do so, burrowed behind any thick tuft of dirt or grass as if it were a mighty buckler.

CHAPTER 33
LIFE WITH FATHER

Edward J. Spike O'Donnell had been home from a prolonged stay at Little Company of Mary Hospital for a little less than two weeks after the return of infection from the gunshot wound and had gotten out to exercise only a few times because his wife Elizabeth, a tough and beautiful girl from a Bohemian Parish in New City had crabbed him into a willingness to avoid risk. Peace in the house meant that Spike should not provoke the peace on the street by taking his usual constitutional up to 79th Street and drinking coffee at the White Castle Hamburger stand on Loomis with all the neighborhood intellectuals, like Buck Weaver and Jack Duffy.

Instead Spike enjoyed his Stewart's Brand coffee from Elizabeth's percolator along with sweet-rolls from Huffkin's Bakery on Halsted that Morry Lanigan brought for him every morning. Morry was a tuck-pointer who had gotten into a jam with cops back in 1939 after a bar fight at a Mick bucket of blood on Halsted. Spike went to bat for the guy who was not a drinker but whose wife had died of cancer at Englewood

Hospital the day before he took a swing at an off-duty cop with a smart mouth.

Spike still had some juice – he had a lot of juice if truth be told – and Spike made good on a good man with three little girls. Lanigan buried his wife out of St. Anne's Church on 55th Street and later moved the girls to an apartment owned by Spike's brother in law at 78th and Hermitage. Lanigan went to work for the County as an in-house tuck-pointer at the Audi Home.

Spike dunked an apricot filled sweet roll into his hot cup of Stewart's and opened the *Herald American* he went directly to the funnies and checked up on the progress of *Maggie and Jigs* who had recently been informed that their son Ethelbert (Sonny) had been declared a 4-F because of his flat feet and Jiggs lamented that 'no son of his would be a copper!' Spike always got a kick out of *Bringing Up Father* that was identified by everyone as *Maggie and Jiggs*. Then he checked the box scores for the White Sox Roy Schalk was still hitting up a storm but had batted into double plays against Detroit three times yesterday and that goof Jimmy Dykes started Ed Lopat, a southpaw, instead of Orval Grove. Guy must have had a snoot full when he made out the damn card.

Finally, to the news of the day. Marines land at Guam – Tim. God watch him.

Chapter 34
Someone to Watch Over Me

God watched Tim Cullen and all of the boys of A Company but He was determined to call in too many of them. As night fell, no one could move because Major Opley had order Captain Bundeschu to hold the ground and prepare to take more. The Skipper had asked Major Opley and Col. Hall directly for permission to withdraw and reform but it was determined that with the success of all other units on W-Day no ground gained should be forfeit. At 11:00 W+1 another assault on the ridge would take place.

During the first night on Guam, Tim Sal and Wat picked tiny pieces of fragments from each other – faces, scalps, neck, back, and took out their own on the legs and thighs. Stretcher bearers were brought up after the assault and the critically wounded needed to be snaked down on a pulley that the riggers of the Field Music section set up just below A Company's defensive position. Company casualties were at 46% - 100% not counting the fact that every man in the Company had received superficial wounds from the scores of Japanese grenades rolled down on the attacking Marines.

'Same things as on Boogan, Tim, them Jap pineapples have too much pyric acid in the mixture and when they blow the steel turns to powder almost on some of them. If them Japs had some of our's we'd all be dead now. Last Chesterfields – here.' Watson gave his friends two of the last good smokes and from now on they'd be content smoking the Luckies.

'I had three of them damn things blow up not two foot from me, Wat and nothing.'

Tim agreed somewhat, 'The Japs overload the mixture on a lot of them – but the ones that worked sure killed a lot of guys today. Ed Carroll from 2nd squad was torn up good and died before the stretcher bearers could take him out. A lot of guys got blinded today. Flanking them is a bitch with those woods to our right and they have that pretty well zeroed in – 2nd Platoon is hitting from there tomorrow –poor bastards. How's the water holding up?'

Both of his friends had a full canteen and a few drops in the other. Water was being brought up in morning but the three machine gunners were going back to beach and bringing up the .30 caliber and they'd fill up then. Star shells burst above the crest of the ridge and gave the night a strange green glow. It still remained oppressively hot and temperatures were expected to exceed 100o tomorrow. Tim Cullen took first watch and his two sweet natured friends coiled up to sleep when they had finished their last good smoke for some time.

Sal woke Tim just before dawn so that they'd have the cover of darkness to make their way down to the beach. They each ate a chocolate bar and swig of water and headed down the steep slope that they had climbed yesterday. "Man I wonder what Chief York is dishing out on Ike and the guys this morning after all those eggs them poor Navy guys are probably getting bird-shit and peppers, noted Sal who was now a blooded and bloodied combat veteran like his buddies. The three Marines squared themselves away to look sharp for the rear echelon commandos making grocery runs and piling up supplies. Blouses were tucked in and leggings tightened before they made their descent.

They arrived at the defensive position that they had secured before noon on W-day and found all of their Field packs and the secured .30 caliber being guarded by guys from the Division Pioneer Battalion. Tim gave the weapon registration card that he had retrieved from the Company clerk and gave it to the Lieutenant on duty and requested that three of Pioneers help them carry ammo cans back up to A Company. Three foul tempered carpenters who were delayed from the tasks of setting up Aid Stations and Operating Theatres joined them for the strain and peril of rejoining Company A.

It took them another thirty minutes to lug the heavy weapon and equipment back up to 1st Platoon and they passed their counterparts from 2nd Platoon taking the same path to beach. 'Early Birds get the Word – War's over! Have a nice Sleep Girls?' cracked Sal. 'Fuck You! Cullen! Hear Gunny's dead? Never got out of the LVT. Fucker was a scream.' Tim stopped and stared – 'Jesus.' Lacy continued, 'Jap shell took his head clean off! Good way to go.' Cullen boiled, 'Kiss my ass, Lacy, he was good guy! Jagoff!' Cullen re-horsed his load and continued his climb up Calvary.

Captain Bundeschu followed the late sleeping Lacey's gun team assessing their slow stroll to the beach. 'Lacy get that weapon to Lt. Gallo before I get backup here or I'll have the three of you at Mast.' He stopped and held a hand up to Cullen, Cranthorpe and Battaglia. 'Leave the weapon where we are set up, until we take that crest. Tell Lt. Buck that I called in for more stretcher bearers and water. Nice work yesterday, Men!' He received a universal 'Aye, Sir!' and went double time past the three machine gunners from 2nd platoon who got the message and sprinted past their Skipper.

"Great Skipper, that guy. Hey, you guys can leave the ammo cans here and head back. Thanks again. We have enough time to come back for them.' And their three helpers from the Pioneers were only too glad to comply. The trio brought the weapon and stored it in a makeshift hole below their protective rise of earth and immediately made their way back for the six ammo cans – fifteen hundred rounds should get them through the day and night. With their morning's chore completed they serviced their rifles and carbine and stretched out for a rest until they would go against the ridge once more.

Capt. Bundeschu returned and met with his platoon commanders and Buck and Gallo relayed the order of attack. At eleven o'clock civilian time, after a fierce bombardment from Weapons Company's 81 mm mortars and 60mm mortars from Company A the Marines assaulted the same ground once more and this time with far fewer men. It was hotter than the day before and the Japanese fire was more intense. Tadeuz Cynopkowicz was killed by a steady stream of machine gun fire that seemed to hold him up in mid air and then toss him like a rag doll from the crest of the ridge. Neil Steinberg immediately picked up his BAR and began firing the weapon and was knocked back with rounds to his shoulders. Tim, Sal and Wat helped push Steinberg down the hill to relative safety after Sal stripped him of the BAR ammo and took over the weapon. All three fired in and to the nearest trench killed its six occupants whom they rolled out and used as make-shift sandbags. To their right they could see that Lt. Gallo's platoon had yet to make it to the crest as they were taking more intense enemy fire from six well-concealed guns. Japs were dug in six feet from Tim Sal and Wat and their shots went into the bodies of their comrades. Wat tossed a fragmentation grenade at them and one man tried to throw it back before it blew... Cpl. Miller and Frank Dranago took their fighting hole but two Jap grenades landed at the same time Frank was able to clear the hole, but Danny Miller took both blasts and died. Capt Bundeschu went over the rise and was not seen again and two of the three men with him died following him -Sgt Karl Rittenouer and his radioman. The third man crawled back up to the crest a bloody rag of a man torn to shreds by grenades. Doc Brosnan pulled him back to the Marines of 2nd Squad. Two groups of Japanese soldiers numbering about twenty charged the crest and Lt. Buck ordered what was left of his platoon back down to the ravine. They took the ridge and now they lost it.

Lt. Buck commanded the tattered Company. He sent a runner to Lt. Jimmy Gallo and they regrouped where they had begun. The two light machine gunners who had joined the platoon from Weapons Company Kurt Van Mill and Louis Coe were killed in this assault and their gun destroyed. Neil Steinberg went back to the beach. Frank Dranago looked crazy. CZ was dead, Norm Chad's two legs were shattered and he would probably lose both. Mike Cloud, Leauregard Clavisill, Henry Clay, Tim Cullen, Sal Battaglia and Wat Cranthorpe were all that remained of 1st Squad. Sgt. Ed Norris now commanded a platoon of ten men and one near crazy man. Lt. Buck commanded a company of forty- four effectives and those men were busy dragging the wounded back to the ravine where they remained pinned down all night.

Major Opley went wild 'They took the Hill . . . but let the Japs throw them off? Send a runner and tell Bundeschu . . .' Capt Crawford interrupted, Bundeschu's dead. Lt. Buck is in command.'

'Here! Written orders! – Take back that Ridge! Runner, you are going to A Company and you will stay with them until that Ridge is taken and then and only then get back to me. Get me artillery, mortars and whatever else we can throw on that hill until we have it back Go!'

The runner did his job and stayed on with 1st Squad his name was Piet Venerman from Holland, Michigan and he died in the next half hour. At 1300 hours the forty-five men under Company Skipper Jack Buck worked their way up the last fifty yards and again Jap grenades were rolled down on them. Piet Venerman three feet above Lt. Buck had one roll under his body which he frantically kicked below him under Jack Buck's hips; when the grenade exploded and blew away his genitalia opened both thighs and ruptured arties. Tim Cullen rolled to the right of his Lieutenant and posted his arms over his shoulders trailing the Lieutenant's body like he had done so many times with his Tripod and with machine gun rounds kicking up dirt and grass hoisted his company commander and hot-legged him down this monstrous ridge. Tim tripped once but Buck was passed out. Cullen and the mutilated Lieutenant passed stretcher bearers and a Navy doctor who signaled four of the stretcher bearers to stop Cullen. 'Was happen a me? 'out of the shock slurred the Texan's awareness. 'Easy, Sir – Aid station . . .' panted the burdened Marine.

'Promise – Ti. .sgun. .take.' and Tim Cullen reached around the undamaged torso and averted his eyes from his friend and commander's blown out crotch and shredded muscles and bones of the hips and thighs. Cullen put on the holster with the mysterious revolver but tucked it inside his shirt. The Navy doctor and two medics applied morphine surrets but it seemed futile to do so; from down Tim's back, ass, and legs had clotted gobs of Buck and pints of blood that the ashen faced Texan had given up for that ridge. 'Tak . . . tha to my . . . Silence! Please Sil.. .' and John A. Buck of Giddings, Texas, son of Texas House Legislator Roper Buck, Notre Dame and Northwestern Law died on a litter in burned grass between Bundeschu Ridge and the Pacific Ocean on July 22, 1944.

The Navy doctor asked where Tim was going with the officer's side arm and he replied – 'To his Mom and Dad' and headed back up to A Company.

He turned and found Sal and Wat with his harness and carbine. 'C and D Companies took the ridge. We got breather,' Sal informed him. And the three boys walked back to the beach area and were joined by what remained of their Company

– Thirteen effectives and twice that number deemed 'walking-wounded' out of the one hundred and eighty men who landed on William Day.

CHAPTER 35
G.K.CHESTERTON

'Miss Cullen, what did Mr. Chesterton mean by 'Nothing is so remote from us as the thing which is not old enough to be history and not new enough to be news.'

'I believe that he meant Faith sister. Something that we might know, but only in our hearts and souls. '

'He did not mean Faith at all, young lady. Think! Faith might seem like a good and pious answer but it is a far cry from that which in fact is. Now think!'

Sister Malachy had been a member of the Sisters of Mercy since 1916 and a teacher at Mercy High School for Girls since 1940. Sister was from a well to do St. Louis Family who had sold crockery to families moving West in the 19th Century. Mae Ellen Corbett jilted a handsome suitor for Christ two months before their wedding and came to Chicago to don the veil. She was tough on the girls who were more accustomed to "Pleasing Sister" for grades than for actually thinking.

Joanie was on the verge of tears as she had read the quite and really wanted to believe that this was actually what the great Catholic writer was talking about.

'Write an essay tonight Miss Cullen – here is your instruction – listen carefully – What are you doing this exact second? Write it down. Go back to the quote and rethink what you have written.'

Joan Cullen spent hours that night at the dining room table after doing theorems for Geometry, and passages from Livy for Sister Eudace working out this conundrum. Tim came home from Mr. O'Donnell's hospital room and explained the whole thing. That was April 1943 and now well over a year later Tim thought about that problem that so plagued his little sister as he, Sal and Wat walked to the beach still packed with Marines and still more wading ashore. They walked to within three thousand yards of Adelup Point and that they had looked at from their LVT on the way to the reef and onto Red Beach 2.

Like a kid seeing the expected stuff under the Christmas tree, Wat ran down to the white stone markers that he had seen from the LVT. 'Look here, boys, them's the posts that look like the ones around the lawns at San Diego Depot!' Wat handed Tim his Garand and got down on his belly to examine the craftsmanship of the concrete post. 'Hell Yes they are! Right here *Allan Masonry Co. S.D., Calif. 1926.* Damn Right, if I didn't see it from way out there!'

'You should go on Major Boles, Wat. Who gives a shit! We just got run off a stupid hill that two other Companies took and lost all those men. Lt. Buck, Jack Howard, Neil's fucked up and probably dead.'

'Sal, this is your first time out and I'll take that - and it was bad - but don't you see what's under that damn smart nose of yours at all? This here means that this place *was* ours and the Japs tried to make it *theirs* and *it ain't*. See?'

Tim agreed with Wat. 'I see it Wat, Sal sees it too and he's just tired that's all.'

Sal walked closer to the waters edge and shots, from the destroyed ranch house out on the point that must have been a beautiful sight to behold before the war, vainly chugged short of the three strolling Marines and kicked up four spouts of water about two hundred feet from the edge of the beach.

This enraged Sal! The big boy roared at them and tore open his shirt popping out all of the buttons into the water – not unlike the futile gunfire from doomed Japanese who would be killed by Marines from 3rd Battalion by dark.

'We are out of range you stupid Fuckers! Oh Jesus! GOOOOOOOOOOOOOODDDDD!' And the giant howled out his misery and little Tim Cullen and skinny Watson Cranthorpe hugged and petted their huge friend and calmed him. Tim Cullen thought of that quote that had so bothered his little sister: 'Nothing is so remote from us as the thing which is not old enough to be history and not new enough to be news.'

That fat old man was so right! What did Tim tell his sister? I am just telling the story.

When Tim and Wat had calmed down Sal the three of them returned to the ravine where they had cowered from sniper shots and mortar rounds for so many hours and serviced the machine gun and moved it up to the new positions on the crest of Bundeschu Ridge that had been taken by Charlie and Dog Companies in a pincer move. Able Company had exacted a heavy toll on the Japanese China veterans who had killed so many of them in the two days of fighting and Capt. Bundeschu's body was recovered in a Jap slit trench with six bodies of his enemies and returned to the beach and Graves Registration. Tim looked out on the ground that they had covered since the landing and he was amazed that any of them were still alive. From his fighting hole, the three of them articulated the machine gunner's knowledge of terrain and target. Wat worked out new range cards and Sal and Tim set the stakes that would limit the traverse of their fire in this new direction. They laid out an extra fifteen fragmentation grenades – five each man to support the four that each carried on their harnesses – around their position. The gun was oiled, sighted and loaded. Very little occurred on the 24th of July. There was, of course, sporadic mortar fire onto their positions below on Chorito and Bundeschu Ridges and the ravines and the stretches of woods between them. All this time Gen. Obata and Gen. Takashima were pulling troops defeated in an attack on the 4th Provisional Brigade to the south of Asan up to their now *essential* positions around Fonte Ridge and deny the Marines use of the Mt. Tenjo Road to Agana.

The next move would be against Fonte Ridge and the full consolidation of the Third Marine Division Beachhead. For now, the decimated Third Marines needed to consolidate the ground taken and shore up Front Line Beachhead Defenses and try to link up with the 21st Marines on their right. There was no reserve forces available to them. For now, the Marines on Guam and their Japanese enemies and the starving Chamorros walking and crawling to Manengon camps were treated with advent of tropical downpours so intense that visibility was reduced to a few feet and hot dusty trails became gully washing floods. Tim Cullen kept Lt. Buck's Colt Hog Leg enclosed in his shirt and it was damn heavy and damn uncomfortable, but it would stay there. Tim vowed to get the damn thing home to his family and he would see that he did. For now, it was range cards, ready boxes, handy spare parts and wide awake eyes. They were not going to back off these hills and they sure as hell were not about to let was keep them. It was coming.

Major Opley made his personal rounds of the Companies and checked on the link up and did not seemed concerned by the huge gaps in his defenses – his boys could take anything thrown at them. Taking this damn ridge had been a disappointment. What had Bundeschu not done? Hell, the man was dead and up for the Navy Cross.

Lucas Opley carried a Garand like any rifleman and he had used it as well. In fact, he had joined Charlie Company for the end-around on Bundeschu and was one of the first men in the Jap trenches. With his new 'First Shirt' Master Sergeant Bob Fitch from Weapons Company Major Opley stopped by the tough guys of 1st squad, 1st Platoon A Company.

'That is one squared away position Cullen. Sal how's the pipes? The Chaplain told me you were sticking your ass out at the Japs on the Point. Laughed my nuts off, Son! Hey, Watson raining like Boogan again.'

Yes, sir! Did you notice them white painted concrete posts down on the beach Major?'

'You know what Wat, I did. What about 'em?'

'Well, sir they was made by the *Allan Masonry Co. SD, Calif. 1926 and it says so right on 'em, Sir!*'

'You don't tell me. Well, Wat, I saw those same posts back in 1940 when I was doing the jungle manual'

'You and Gunny . . .'   the Major walked off like he had been farted out of a phone booth, but turned, ignoring the

Hillbilly bullet sponge, 'Cullen, what happened to Lt. Buck's side-arm?'

Tim worked on the receiver of the .30 caliber Browning and tried to look quizzical like the time Brother Finch had caught him at Top-Notch hamburgers instead of his Latin class. 'I can't say, sir?'

Lucas Opley walked off toward 2nd platoon after giving the three men a politician's smile and regular guy 'see-ya' wave. Wat immediately bubbled like an old woman caught reading *Esquire* 'You see the look he gave me when I mentioned Gunny; damn they was pals. And you got the Lieutenant's Colt Tim and you ought to of give it up to him. Let Maj. Opley send it home to his folks.'

"Wat, I promised Lt. Buck. Lt. Buck would have asked the Major but he thinks the Major wanted to palm the gun, see? Don't mention the damn thing again, until I get it back through Regimental Post and we are not going to be doing that for a few days. Jesus, I wish I did give it up to him.'

CHAPTER 36
THE BOSON TAKES COMMAND

Following the rape and the caning of the Betty, her mother and Kara Tanaka, Boson Otayama was ordered to join Lt. Kato on a sweep of Agana Heights for Chamorro boys and men not yet out of the Governor's designated Defense Zone. Otayama was pleased with his take of loot from both homes; especially the jewelry and the autographed photo of Franchot Tone that he would sell after the war. The dentist was working at the hospital in Agana Heights assisting Japanese military doctors and Chamorro physicians pressed into service.

No need for the dentists to hear about his wife's bruises. Letting the youngsters at the fresh meat was a nice treat and really bucked up the kids against the attacks now getting more intense. Maybe he should have fucked the two older ones but his tastes ran more to the tramps and his lovely Hana. When the American's landed at Asan, Otoyama's force was ordered to serve as a combat reserve for Gen Takashima's Fonte Ridge Defense and stay within hailing distance of that call; Lt. Kato was seconded to Manengon and the supervision of the camps.

At the moment the Yankees were being slaughter from the ridges and cliffs around Asan, but things were going badly around Orote. Oh well.

Otoyama's boys donned the sharp green field uniforms that distinguished them from their Army counterparts and drew weapons for the battles to come. They headed through the streets of Agana on their way up to meet Lt. Kato on their way they encountered two teenagers that were sneaking a wheelbarrow full of rice and cornmeal to a brown driven by 1932 Dodge Pickup truck and bayoneted each boy lightly in the back of his thighs. Rev. Sablan of the Guam Baptist Church got out of the cab of the truck and protested to Otayama that they had been ordered to bring the foodstuffs to a military convoy headed to Manengon. It was a lie but the wily Baptist knew enough Japanese to make it believable and they were allowed to sneak of to a *lancho* near Yiga where refugees from Agana were flocking. Otayama gave the minister a crack across the mouth and tussled the bleeding boys' hair like a tough but fair football coach. He loved this work – and signaled them on their way. Praise Jesus! They looted some homes on the Mt. Tenjo Road and did not find much of anything but they took what they found. Now they needed to report and really get back in this war.

Boson's boys were formed up into the Mixed Brigade and sent to through the Marines into the sea and they were already very, very wet. Several miles from the Boson and his boys were the men that they sweep out into the surf.

The rain was like Bougainville only more so. As the last three day temperatures had exceeded 98 degrees the soaking and the relentless downpour frozen the exhausted teenagers in their holes and slit trenches. The water levels were chest high in some and all fought off the freezing Tropical soaking by pissing in the ever rising waters around them. In this night of July 25th firing from positions down the line from them indicated that Takashima's brave veterans were probing the lines so badly thinned out by the desperate assaults on the ridges.

Naval Illumination rounds – Flare-Star shells were fired from off shore destroyers and cruisers. The sky became a strobe-lit green nightmare of bizarre shapes, rain, lights and noise.

Wat pulled the rubber cover tighter over the ammo box and the belt already locked in the gun's receiver and the rain began to let up some. Sal had his rifle covered as well and as soon as the splashing turned to dink-dink-dinks pulled the cover off and raised it to the ready. Tim pulled back the bolt on the heavy machine gun and began to traverse the weapon as their instincts picked up the sounds of slogging sopping and muted echoes of warning. Sgt. Norris called in an illumination mission over their co-ordinates and within seconds the report and howl of the explosive illumination charge signaled its advent.

Ta-POWWWWWWWWW! And the green lights were on - telling of swarms of troops intruding their way up to the crest of their position and only yards away! 'UP!' was all Sgt. Norris commanded and every weapon went into service on the targets making their away to the remnants of A Company. DrinDinDrin Drin – Drin, Drin,Drin Drin – Drin Drin, Drin Drin reported the powerful Browning machine gun that Tim Cullen punched to redirect the fire every three bursts of four; Pop!Pop!Pop!Pop!Pop!Pop!Pop!PopCLANG! and down Sal dropped to place another clip of eight rounds in the Grand with a dramatic Click Punch as the magazine fed rounds for another octave.

Targets dropped but more and more howled into their place to go down. *Banzai! MALINE -Anata wa dame desu! Kuso shinezo! Shinde kudasai Anata no ketsu wa kusa da oyobi ore wa shibakariki da. Howled* through the explosions, shots, bursts and tossed epithets – Fuck You Slant-eyed Cocksuckers! Come up and Die Motherfuckers! *BANZAI! BANZAI! BANZAI!*

Many of the Japs were singing and continued to sing while being torn apart by American metal. The mud was making their passage through the positions even more terrible for them but waves and waves continued. Leauregard Clavisill, the target of abuse since he contracted yellow jaundice malaria and every other bug born disease in the Tropics on Samoa. Stood above his protective berm firing the same BAR that had gone from CZ to Steinberg to him in as many days. 'Low stay put you're knocking our gun's trav-stake – Fuck it. Stay down –Wat - Belt!' Tim yelled in between his quatrains of lead and opened the breach block for the next 250 rounds. Sgt. Norris yelled, 'Low you have not hit a Fucking one them and even Crazy Mike is popping them – Sal take the BAR and give Low your rife. The guy is so skinny every burst is like anti-aircraft. They've retired for now – Low Give Sal the Browning and the belt.' Leauregard was hurt 'I hit a bunch, Ed! Shit, I *did*! Heavy fucker – *I'm signed on Company paper*, Sal, don't fuck up the Browning – *my name's on it*!' Sal crept from his position to The new one on the right of the .30 caliber – 'Those wedding bells are breaking up that *old* gang of mine,' he sing-songed as the big Italian boy moved away from his buddies for the first time since coming to the Pacific. Though only yards away he was a bit sad but more confident as he no longer needed the assurance of the two young veterans with whom he had tented and foxholed for so long. Leauregard took Sal's hole just to the left of Wat and Tim. 'I can't operate that water-cooler now! Lissey hear; *you* two fuckers stay healthy,' Wat never liked the sickly ghost and replied 'As full of vim, vigor and vitality as you, Low!' 'Fuck you Hillbilly!' Tim had enough ear pounding 'Do any of you red-necks get along?' 'Only when burning bull-whipping Yankees, Tim.' For boys who had been caked with mud, blood and piss fro three day and attacked by fierce waves of veteran troops these last score of minutes the whole line of 1st Platoon laughed at the exchange and tonic of shared love and affection steeled them for a succession of six more attacks. No one died until the seventh.

CHAPTER 37
PIETA CHAMORRITAS

Not a virgin in the three of them. The two older women in their late thirties and equally beautiful with broken noses, split lips and bruised frames; one a red-head dyed black and the other an Asian islander of mixed Chamorro Spanish and somewhere in the genealogy Dutch blood; the other an almond eyed red-head from Minot North Dakota of Hussite Bohemian and French Catholic blood, long of limb and graceful with a dancers ability to falls make them appear beautiful and across the laps lay the limp limbs of a violated girl of fifteen. Betty Cruz, a Chamorro Loretta Young, shivered in the laps on the trunk of shot-up '32 Chevrolet that had belonged to Arturo and Sabrina Torres until an American Hellcat fighter strafed and killed the old couple. Kara tried the car but no luck. Artie and Sabrina were a couple of live-wires and loved to jitterbug to hot platters on the old Jukebox in Casper's soda shop before the war and had helped drive the sailors out of Japanese harm on December 12th, 1941. They took all of them to Barrigarda and Artie's uncle's *lancho*. Kara and Imelda buried the sixty year olds in the jungle and marked their grave with the Chevy's bumper. That was last night. Today they needed to haul ass and find food or this raped little girl was going to die and there was no fucking way Kara Vanecko Tanaka was about to let that happen.

For two days Betty slept for hours only taking time out for nature's call and water and the two women stroked and petted the traumatized child. Imelda was a tough girl. She could handle the fact that her husband and little boy were dragged off by the Japs to fill sand-bags and kill dogs upon Fonte Ridge; she could the beating given her by that pig Otayama and his six goons; she understood that her beautiful home and way of life was stamped out by war; but she could no longer pray the rosary or utter the name of Christ for what was allowed to happen to her beautiful, spirited and sweet little girl. Imelda tore the rosary from her neck and spit on the crucifix and tossed the green beads into the jungle.

Kara slapped her best friend in the world. 'Look you! I do not give a fat rat's ass if you spit or shit or smile, but you had better not toss something to anchor you. Now go out there and get that damn rosary – Move!'

Imelda cried no end by complied. "Yesterday, I would have gouged out your eyes Kara! I'm better today. Hell with this God who does nothing!'

'Immy, I'm no St.Teresa – in fact, I play paint by numbers in Church, sexy Teddy is all Cardinal Manning enough for our family, but I do not want you to lose anything else! Don't let the Japs take your Faith, Honey. We are out of it now and that is always good enough. Maybe tomorrow we'll be up to our pretty little eyelashes in shit again but we have a breather today. Hang on! Nothing else! I'm sorry I slapped you; I'd rather slap Teddy and that ain't in the cards. That tough little guy is probably fixing his cousins from Yokohama without gas – I hope. How's the baby?'

Imelda now understood. She would take care of the now and let God or whatever take the rest. She put the rosary around her neck again, but she did not kiss the crucifix – not yet.

CHAPTER 38
SEVEN BANZAI ONE NIGHT

After six assaults and the end to the rain, Tim and Wat surveyed the ammunition and discovered that they were down to 500 rounds – one belt locked in and one more can. Ed Norris crawled over. "Called in for ammunition you guys Ok?'

'Belt and a box – got a Chesterfield Sergeant? Asked Tim.

'Thought you weren't a smoker Tim– here– and he butted up a couple from the brown and tan pack. Light up low the Japs know we're here but why task it. Sal's a natural on the cutter. Takes his time, Poor old Low was like nuts on an Archbishop with that weapon... Look - we'll get hit again, there they're already chattering up and singing. I think most of them are loaded on some kind of Jap booze. I smelled three of the louses outside my hole and they smell like me on a good liberty. Just stay frosty for a while more. I had Maj. Opley on the line and he said the 21st and 9th Marines are really getting it and a bunch broke through on the last two and got to the Division Field Hospital. Pioneers, Corpsmen and wounded finished them all off. This next one will be a doozy but it will be light soon. Stay frosty.'

When Norris had gone Wat asked Tim about his sisters and brothers and the schools they went to – 'How far they got to go to school, Tim?'

'My older sisters all went to Mercy High School an all girls high school run by the nuns, like I went to Leo run by the Irish Christian Brothers and the little guys – there's three in St. Sabina's and its only about half a mile from our house. The Protestant and Jewish kids and a few of the Catholic kids in my neighborhood go to public schools. Joanie is a sophomore at Mercy and she is pretty as my mother. The older girls work at Ford's B-29 plant not too far away.'

'What's it like being in a big city Tim. Man is it all night clubs and slums like the movies?'

'No it's like a bunch of little villages all tied together. Last year I worked at the Post Office and hauled mailbags. In order to get there, I had to go through Irish, Polish, Lithuanian, Colored, Bohemian, Russian Jews and Swedes to get to work. My area is mostly Irish but a lot of Swedes, Germans, and Russian Jews too. We all get along pretty much but they have their own clubs that I can't join – like the Eagles – you have to be 100% American which means Protestant and we can't go to the YMCA and stuff like that. But like I said we all get along. Two of my best Pals Dave McDonald and Marsh Nelson are Presbyterians and went to Calumet High. They were Eagles but are going out with two girls from Mercy. How about your high school, Wat?'

'Well, sir, we had a long way to go as we lived in the Holler near the mines but went by bus to Huntington High. I played football one year but I was too skinny and joined the UMW basketball team and played for the Union against my own high school and the Civics teacher there was the coach and did not take too kindly to that fact and had it in for me until quit and joined the Corps before the War. I lied about my age and my mom signed me up cause she thought I'd be safer on a ship guarding an Admiral like in those Wallace Beery movies. I never had a sweetheart in high school cause I was always working and such. and ...

Sal interrupted 'You fuckin' rambling Hillbilly you are boring the fucking Japs out of the fight – Start a Story and PLEASE – conclude it!' and the entire exhausted line of Marines laughed up a storm and then came the sound of a Japanese voice about thirty yards away –"Yes, *Thank You!*' followed by more laughter from both sides of the world conflict.

'Any way they was this girl that worked at the IGA that I sorta had a crush on and after Boots, I came home in my dress blues and talked to her and she was . . . ZIIIIIP!

A Japanese 7.7 round went through Wat's left eye and out the back of his head. Tim erupted in a rage that he had not felt since seeing MacArthur's bulldozers bury 3rd Marine ammunition on Tulagi and was only stopped from assaulting the New McClellan by Gunny's thick fingers – Tim let loose a steady steam of fire on the open ground now filling with attacking Japanese, while screaming open mouthed with rage and impotence and he nudged his dead mate out of the way. The water in the cooling jacket boiled furiously as the weapon's barrel was challenged by Cullen's need to exact execution on the killers of the finest man Tim had ever known.

Sal ten yards away with the Browning Automatic Rifle popped out well aimed bursts and dropped the targets he chose. All along the decimated line of Company A, men repeated the calculated and deadly exercises repeated these many months in the Corps. A great flash and its equally loud report highlighted Sal's fighting hole and impacted upon Tim Cullen who was loading the last belt in his weapon. He understood that Sal was harmed and continued to fire until the barrel over heated and jets of scalding water and steam burst through the cooling jacket – the weapon was done. Cullen grabbed the Carbine and popped out rounds at targets and the enemy breached their line.

Tim Cullen emerged from his gun pit to engage a fat helmet - less young soldier who appeared to be drunk and Tim Smashed in his face with the butt of the Carbine and then shot him.

Two more Japanese soldiers, without rifles grabbed Tim who, according to the rules of engagement in hand-to-hand combat swung out to keep both of his opponents flanked and assault the man he kept closest to him. Using the carbine without bayonet, Cullen jabbed that man in the teeth with barrel followed by an upper-cut with the rifle's butt and doing the same with the next one. Once down Cullen fired three rounds into each of his attackers and looked for new targets which brought him to Sal's smoking hole, where he found his huge pal's mutilated body - smoking from a 50mm mortar round. Cullen picked up Sal's Browning and took the spare magazine belt lying within easy reach of the dead singer's hand. Armed with the BAR and carbine Tim Cullen went after Sal's killers below in a patch of trees thirty yards down the slope and to the right with Sgt Ed Norris yelling 'Back on the line!' and his friends now dead.

My First General Order: *To take charge of this post and all government property in view.* Nevertheless, Tim Cullen swept down from the slope that had been the last place on earth clutched by so many of his friends. All of his closest friends at any rate. There were no attacking Japanese to his left and those before him were covered in the woods below. He heard the distinctive snap and pop of the Jap knee mortar about twenty feet from the trees. Tim applied the lessons taught to him by Bob Foster, Lt. McWatt, and Jack Howard on Bougainville – without making a sound and in the evaporating darkness of one very long night, Tim Cullen moved through the trees and jungle growth on the left flank of four Japanese soldiers operating two 50mm knee mortars. They were in an exposed clearing that afforded them enough arc above this grove on to the Company lines. With a full magazine and on full automatic the Browning cut down the mortar men beginning with the couple farthest to those nearest him. And Tim heard three more Japanese —probably ammunition bearers - in the growth to the right of the clearing making their way out of the woods to higher ground. Once firing rounds into the four, the anguished and talented mechanic went after the fleeing Japs. Daylight broke on the 26th of July and Pfc. Timothy Cullen was listed as Missing in Action on the Company roster. All that night of July 25 to the morning of July 26th when he found himself cut off from Able Company, Tim Cullen was convulsed in the crushing complexity of human frailty – his duty, training, physical condition, natural talents and intelligence conflicted with his fear, frustration, physical limitations as to height, weight, agility and his sense of duty. We can only imagine the condition of environment in which he found himself, unless we are combat veterans who have faced an overwhelming assault. Imagine - a landscaped disco of hallucinating lights and blaring sounds – a disco where the doors are locked, the heat turned up to it's limit and packed to the limit with two well-armed and vicious gangs of men or women bent upon one another's annihilation. Survival instincts might only be one part of the equation.

Stephen Crane's Henry Fleming fled from the field of battle when he saw his fellows skedaddle. Henry found sanctuary in the natural environment where birds chirped and trees vaulted cathedral-like to God's empyrean. The Youth could sort out his imagined or real cowardice and confront the reality of returning to his fellows or leading a life of self-imposed exile as a craven, but he was saved *Deus ex Machina* by a fellow Yankee skedaddler who clubbed the youth on the noggin and gave Fleming *The Red Badge of Courage* that would grant him the passport to human fellowship with comrades he deserted and reclaim his honor as a fighting man.

Tim Cullen was a little more tightly wound and far less cerebral than Crane's antagonist. He was numbed cold with hypothermia from sitting for many hours in freezing rain water into which he'd piss to gain some warmth in a Tropical heat exceeding 100 degrees. He had been in almost non-stop combat for over seventy two hours- having lugged along with his own equipment, a 53 lb tripod up Chorito Cliff and Bundeschu ridge under constant fire. He had lugged down the grenade mutilated and castrated body of his dying Platoon commander and friend to whom he had vowed to protect and return the Chorito Hog Leg Colt revolver, still strapped to this own chest and shoulder over his green t-shirt and buttoned up under his sage green herringbone Marine Corps Utility shirt, from the carnage of Bundeschu Ridge to a Battalion Aid Station. Tim Cullen had returned to his post and fought off seven Banzai charges from General Takashima's troops operating the reliable and well-maintained .30 caliber Browning machine gun. He had pushed the body of his best friend Watson Cranthorpe away from him without a valediction or hug in order to maintain his rate of fire. He witnessed the death of his next best friend still rendered and smoking in his fighting hole. Cullen's weapon was no longer operable due to an over-heated barrel and the gun's water cooling jacket had burst and the barrel warped and was nearly out of ammunition. He had emerged from his position to fight with his carbine and fought two attackers to their deaths – both men were obviously drunk, but the combat ballet had moved Tim further to the right of his position and he took Sal's BAR and ammo and pursued the destruction of the men who were yet raining fire down on A Company.

Rage, Fear, Instinct, Motivation to Duty, Revenge, Desperation, Exhaustion, and Esprite D'Corps, all worked to move the Youth away from his fellows and await his own personal deus ex machina.

CHAPTER 39
JAUNDICED -BUT NOT YELLOW

When light broke over the hills beneath Fonte Plateau and above the Asan region of Guam on July 26th 1944, hundreds of mostly Japanese bodies began the process of putrefication, which in this Pacific climate meant that the threshold for burial was hours. By this afternoon the American bodies including Watson Cranthorpe and Salvatore Battaglia would be carried back to the beaches where the men of Graves Registration would identify and report their deaths up the chain and home and inter their bones on the soil of their sacrifice. Later their bodies would be returned to America or possibly buried at sea. But the Japanese bodies that had housed heroic souls only hours before would bloat and burst under the soaring and blistering Guam sun and would be removed when the Service Companies got around to pouring them into mass unmarked graves.

Already the heroic stretcher bearers of the Field Music section who had withstood snipers fire and incessant mortar barrages since W-Day had taken the badly wounded and the dead back to Battalion Aid, Division Hospital and Graves Registration.

Sgt. Ed Norris took in new men from the replacement pool and catalogued his losses with the new Company clerk and Skipper a JASCO Officer sent up by Major Opley when Capt. Bundeschu was killed.

After seven Banzai charges with the most fierce occurring between 0400 and dawn, Ed Norris surveyed his Platoon. Frank Dranago was still unbalanced but had stayed in the fight and he needed to be pulled off the line. All morning long he openly masturbated and laughed like a six year old in the bathtub. Sal was in three pieces. Wat had taken a round through his left eye and the back of his head was like a smashed gourd. Sitting behind the useless .30 caliber, twenty rounds left, barrel warped cooling jacket destroyed, sight destroyed and breach block damaged was the sad and hideous figure of the jaundiced Leauregard Clavisill.

Sal's M1 Garand with bayonet attached clutched in his hands. His eyes fixed on the terrain and sighted past the many, many, many dead attackers who had tried seven times to breakthrough. 'Jesus Low you Ok?' asked the tall, tough and sweet-natured sergeant.

'I'm fine Sarge, but them Japs ain't doin so hot. Some fight we gave them last night. Where's Cullen? Last I saw - he was dancing with two Japs and I thought that he put them down and went for the Browning when Sal got smeared.' Leauregard no longer looked any where near as yellow or orange as he had for the last seven months. In fact he looked fully robust and undisturbed.

'Cullen's missing? Jesus, I wonder if the Japs snatched him. Come with me.'

The two Leathernecks carefully surveyed the slopes nearest their area and occasionally put a round into a wounded or possum playing body. All the dead Americans - and there were sure as shit enough of them - were being carted down the reverse slope. Eventually the two men carefully made their way into the woods where Tim Cullen had ventured only a couple of hours before. They found four dead Japanese, their weapons and ammo, including the 50mm knee mortars that had killed Sal and so many other Able Company men.

'These clowns are sho'nuff shot up – wonder if the .30 Cal you were manning took them out. The range is just about right but they'd be four lucky shots through these tree.'

Leauregard lied 'Well I did fire about a belt and a half this way after no Japs jumped me from my side.'

Ed Norris was a bit doubtful, 'You did. - Thought you never wanted to handle the heavy.'

'Tim was up fighting those two Japs that jumped him and so I sat in.' Once a lie begins it always requires more and more mascara and Leauregard Clavisill, a good man who had done his duty as much as every other Jarhead on that hill was entitled to credit where credit was due. Tim was probably dead. 'Maybe Tim got shit in his blood after Wat and Sal got killed.' Lies always get uglier with the added cosmetics, but - that is fashion, after all.

'Hey, look shithead; take credit for the shoot; shit I'll write you up myself, but say something like that again, you ignorant Louisiana fucker and I'll boot your raisin like nuts up through the roof of your fucking big mouth!'

'Hey, look Sarge, all I meant. . .'

'Explain to me what the fuck you mean and you will rot here with these fuckin' Nips, So help me God! Get the fuck back up that hill! Say nothing. Have no fucking thought.'

When the two of them, a good guy who told a lie and a solid good man, returned to the position, Major Opley and his staff were checking on the positions and noting the number of attacking troops killed in the seven attempts on A Company. Major. Opley still carried his M1, butt on his right hip and sling at open loop. "Sgt. Norris, your platoon's defense of this section of the line is in the finest tradition of our Corps. Sound tactical command like yours is needed. I am putting you in for a bar. I want you to turn over the Platoon to 2nd Lt. Ames here and report to Battalion. I am giving you to Weapons Company and you'll take over the mortar section. Lt. Ames and Sgt. Joyce will be Platoon Sgt... Fill Joyce in on the roster. Let's hear the bad news.'

'I have six dead and twelve badly wounded and one man missing, Cullen, Sir.'

'Sweet Jesus what happened to him?'

'Clavisill said that he got out of the machine gun position when Cranthorpe was killed and engaged two Japs and then when Sal was killed he took up the BAR. And no one has seen him since –think maybe the drunk bastards dragged him off.'

'Was the .30 out of commission?'

'Not sure exactly when that happened, this morning. Pfc. Clavisill was behind the gun and he said that he took over the weapon from Cullen when Cullen engaged those two Japs –one on the right got his teeth knocked out. Pfc. Clavisill said that he fired a belt and half into those woods on the right and if he did, Major, he killed the Jap mortar teams that were giving us such hell, last night,' deadpanned Lt. Norris.

'Clavisill, 4-O gunning, son! You are from Louisiana, are you not? Bayou man or city Cajun?'

'North Bayou Teche, Major.'

'These your Japs, as well?'

'One's on the right and center.'

'How'd the gun get disabled and when?'

'Not sure, Major. Not my usual weapon, Cullen's specialty'

'So how did Cullen get killed? He must have been killed and where is he? Did he have Lt. Buck's side-arm? I hope not. At least I hope it's not on some Jap Warrant Officer.'

'Clavisill you get down to Battalion and tell your story to Capt. Crawford – I want to put you in for the Silver Star.'

'Aye, aye, Sir and thank you!'

'Don't thank me, Marine. You did more than what was expected of you. I thank you! Lt. Ames, these are the men of iron that you getting. I expect you will live up to their heroism. Lt. Norris, I am proud of you and good sailing with your new command. Clavisill are you still here? Shove off to Battalion!'

'Aye, Sir!' and a new American hero was minted and would have his story printed in *Stars and Stripes, Leatherneck, Life and Look.* He would wear the Silver Star at every event held at the VFW of North Bayou Teche- named for him - until he was laid out in a coffin at Beauclair & Sons Funeral Home in 1978.

Major Opley and newly minted Lt. Ed Norris went back down to the woods on the right to take a closer look at the men killed by Silver Star designate Leauregard Clavisill of North Bayou Teche, Louisiana.

Major Opley assessed the wounds taken by the Jap mortar men. Thirty caliber rounds alright, but the distance to Cullen's gun position and the close proximity of the protective trees defied the imagination. 'These Nips are hacked up pretty good and from close range. Look at the density evident in these impacts – lot of broken bones and bleeding out and it appears that these two were thrown back from the mortar pretty good. Cullen grabbed the Browning automatic, right?'

'Yes, sir.'

'Seems that our missing Brig Rat tore up these Japs on his own. There is a mighty slim possibility that that career shit- bird up there killed them with the heavy but that shit-bird is alive and Cullen is more than likely dead: tough little kid. Shame. Ok, Lieutenant, go to Battalion before you check in with Weapons Company and get that moron's story straight for Capt. Crawford, please. Officially, Pfc. Leauregard Clavisill is the hero of Able Company on this one. Command is a bitch, Lieutenant.'

'Aye, Aye, Sir.'

The fabric of history includes weaves that seem to have been made by any number of craftsmen, but credit is given to the one whom history believes to be that craftsman; thus, the Sistine Chapel had many hands dipping brushes in pots of pigment, but we only remember Michelangelo. For our story's purpose we remember Leauregard Clavisill – the hero of Bundeschu Ridge.

Chapter 40
Dr. Tanaka Takes a Jaw

Ted Tanaka was working at the Japanese Field Hospital now that the town of Agana had been smashed by American naval and air bombardment. His Packard had been commandeered and take to a lancho two miles north of the Japanese Army airfield.

Ted helped Japanese doctors and nurses dress head wounds and conducted hundreds of oral surgeries in a quick and efficient manner. He had no seen or heard from his baby-cakes since a week before the landings and now that the Americans were breaking out of the beachhead at Orote and close to consolidating the beachhead above Asan near Fonte Ridge he hoped that his smart and tough wife would figure some way to get to the Americans. She was headstrong and clever and knew this island as well as the natives.

He would need to keep focused on healing these wounded Japanese kids and bid his time until he could get himself captured by the Marines. There was blood and teeth and spilled antiseptic everywhere in this operating theatre and these poor teenagers who had survived the desperate fighting in North China mountains, Allied strafing at sea and here on Guam and now were in the skilled but dispassionate hands of their kinsman and enemy.

Ted removed a boy's jaw that morning and the kid was still alive and gauzed up, but staring at him. Was he assessing Ted's skills, thanking him with his eyes, or waiting for an opportunity to kill the man who had disfigured him for life. Ted smoked a Japanese cigarette and stared back at the kid. *You clowns have taken away my paradise. You have taken my exile from me. I hope to Christ that you are hurting as bad as you look, Kiddo!* He thought while considering the nasty after taste that Japanese cigarettes really seemed to have.

Ted had seen Juan Cruz and his son on their dog killing tasks and little Tog a ten year old had the look of a fifty year old man. Ted's father had departed Dai Nippon to become an obscenely wealthy American businessman. But, the old man retained that racial purity ethic that these kids all seemed to buy into – no different from the bigots who shunned him and his wife back in the States. "I'll give you call soon Teddy Boy and we can talk about an RCA contract for your boys. You and Cookie can join me and Dixie and the boys for good old California wine guzzle over some sizzlers at the Derby. Leave the number with my boy Morgan and Bob and I will give you a jingle!' Sure, Bing. Those nickels are tough to throw down a slot. And that fat assed bully McLaglen coming off the Clipper with 'OOFFF- oooffff-ooofff –oofff! If Ain' Mr. & Mrs. Moto, Thim-sels- the Island Castaways!' Thought Kara would kick him in the balls. Mostly, America was damn good to Ted and Ted would be good back. These kids were like the one with his jaw shot off were nuts with hate of everyone but their own – they treated the Chamorros worse than any KKKer would to an uppity field hand. Miserable pricks the bunch. Especially that Commie sneak Kato. Where was he?

CHAPTER 41
CAPT. LOU WILSON'S PATROL

In the late morning of 26th Captain Louis Hugh Wilson led a patrol of seventeen men from his company along the Mt. Tenjo Road through Mt. Mangan and the back way onto Fonte Plateau where the Japanese had rained down artillery and heavy mortar fire onto the 3rd Division since the 21st of July, 1944.

The Fonte Plateau was the key to taking Fonte Ridge and had been to the prize sought by Col. Hall's 3rd Marines who had been ground up by a steady stream of pre-sighted machinegun, artillery and mortar fire, as well as the 60o slopes of Chorito Cliff and Bundeschu Ridge, from which the Japanese defenders rolled hundreds of grenades. Col. Hall's time table for conquest was set back by geography, gravity, and grenades. His 3rd Marines lost over 600 men since W-Day and had yet to take Fonte Ridge. Col. Hall was relieved of command. A fierce and thoughtful commander was rewarded with reassignment. Military and Justice.

One of Col. Hall's boys armed with a Browning Automatic Rifle, a carbine and his dead platoon commander's Colt

Revolver had reached Fonte Plateau's back door after chasing three ammunition bearers from a woods to the right of his Company position. Tim Cullen had killed four mortar men and was pursuing their ammo carriers up a trail that curved north from those woods. As he fired on the three, he noticed a group of Marines along the ridgeline just west of his position. Cullen fired off a burst of four rounds that caused the three to scatter and they were a good sixty yards up and ahead of him. He looked again at the trail of Marines and noticed one using the standard infantry hand signals for 'rally to me.' A tall Marine faced Tim and held up his right arm -palm toward Tim - and made fast circular movements with his arm.

Tim Cullen had not thought about his singular state in the last forty minutes of pursuit of these three. Now he responded to his training and moved up the slope toward the line of Marines. It was about three hundred feet uphill to them and Tim watched the officer signal his men take defensive position where they were until this lost lamb could join them.

Pulling roots to help him up, which had been the common practice for A Company since William Day, Tim made the crest of the hill with an assist from two Marines. 'Easy does it Mac, we got you.'

Tim collapsed like a vertical rope and the man who assisted him a fattish thirty year old sergeant with a very heavy beard dumped a canteen of water in Tim's lap and snatched the Browning out of the exhausted kid's hands. 'Cool off, tough guy. Personal? Is it? Them three take your wallet?'

'Fu –ck you.'

'Simmer down. Hear take that gear off.' And the other man unharnessed Tim and laid down his carbine. 'This guy is Gary Cooper. What's with the Hog-leg?' and tried to remove the holster inside Tim's shirt as well.

'Take your fuckin' hands off. My Lieutenant's. Dead - Home to his dad.'

"Ease up kid. We'll let the Skipper get your story when he gets back from the look see. Calvin take Quinlan and set up a BAR position near that draw on the right. It seems clear to there. Go! I'm Ernie Dobbs kid. You 21st?'

'3rd Marines.'

'Deserter?'

'Fuck You.'

'Kid, you had a tough run get some water down you and over that hot fuckin' head of yours before I gives you a crack. Ease up. We're 9th Marines surprised to see the 3rd this far out of course after last night's hoo-ha everything is ass over tit. The Skipper is Capt. Wilson and he never let's no one do nothing. So you ca loosen your leggings. You stay with us for this patrol or until Big Lou let's you skip home. What's your name kid?'

'Pfc. Tim Cullen A-1-3-3'

'You boys got well and truly fucked on this one. My old pal Billy Higgins got clobbered coming over the reef. We were here in 1940. Good Nookie Garrison.' Rest up, Junior.'

Tim laid back and tried to regain some of his wind and found that once on his back he could not get back up. He not taken a drink of water since about 0200 that morning and had been madly chasing the guys who helped kill his friends. His stomach cramped and all of his leg muscles tightened. Sgt. Ernie dumped more water over Tim's forehead like he was own sweet baby boy. Ernie tossed Tim a packet of biscuits. 'No pogey bait until that water works its way through you, Kid, nibble on these and get some strength back, when you feel up to it.'

After about twenty minutes, their Skipper returned. He was tall, blond, red-faced, serious eyed, and jug-eared, This man was the chart for 'Command Presence.' He carried a carbine and a .45 automatic in a shoulder holster and had three fragmentation and two WP grenades hooked to his harness. His shirt was buttoned to the neck and soaked with blood and sweat. He had a bullet wound that had taken out about an inch of fat from just above his right hip bone and had a huge gash that had been bandaged badly on his left thigh. There was also a thick gauze pad clotted with blood below is right ear. "How you farin' Ernie?'

'Hot work for a fat man Skipper.'

'Ernie we have the back door wide open to us on that Plateau and we are taking it. I got all the way up there and we can call in an air strike on three ridgelines tha Japs hold just below the position we will hold. Bring Casper up with the JASCO team and have that kid looked after, must have twenty fragments in him. We'll get started leave Polecki and Kotel to bring them up to us. Once the JASCO team gets here call Battalion and have Col. Cushman detailed on our progress. Who's the kid?'

'A foul tempered killer by his demeanor and the cut of him. Cullen, 3rd Marine, A Company of the 1st. Lucas Opley's boys. Kid's exhausted and dehydrated by the looks of him. Give him ten Skipper.'

'BAR good to have. The Japs have no flank men or patrols out this way. Must think that the 3rd is beaten down there or too weak to advance. The 21st is moving on the beach side of Fonte with the 3rd and we can back door these clowns and shut it slam hard on them. Tanks won't be worth a damn up here until we can clear out those positions. Once we have that back porch taken and held we can call in all kinds of hate on them with the JASCO team. This thing might close shop sooner tha we thought, Ernie.'

Tim woke up to more cascades of cool water from Gunnery Sergeant Dobbs' canteen. Eat them biscuits, boy; time to earn your rating. Chow down and go see the Skipper.'

The sweet fortified biscuits tasted like a steak dinner and washed down with cool water, Tim felt better than he had since leaving the LVT. His muscles relaxed and he was breathing normally. He buttoned up his shirt, but the Colt was still obvious and led to opening gambit of Capt. Lou Wilson's interview. 'Who's sidearm you steal, Cullen?'

'This was my Platoon Lt's Colt, Sir. He made me vow to return it to his folks in Texas first chance that I could. He got killed on W+2 taking the ridge we got tossed. I have not used it sir.'

'Why not his Skipper?'

'Skipper's dead too and he asked me personally, Sir; we got along, Sir.'

'What's your story? BAR man?

And Tim explained how he came to possess the Browning and the Colt as well as his carbine and the night that he had experienced and the fouled machine gun, Wat's death, Sal's death, and the Jap mortars. How that morning he had chased the three Jap mortar ammunition bearers through the edge of woods and up into the hills. He also recounted the devastation suffered by the 3rd Marines in taking Chorito Cliff and later Bundeschu Ridge and the Jap grenades and that was why he was all pin-cushioned with fragments. 'They're all tiny and only hurts when I get brushed up on something and some them are probably coral chips from the reef.'

'Fascinating. The rest we will save for *Esquire*. Nevertheless, you are with me until we finish this patrol and maybe then some. Draw another bandolier for the BAR; fill up your canteens, button up your utilities and protect that hog-leg and make yourself useful – stick with Ernie. Back into the war, Men.'

Part V
Secured – End of
July and Despair

CHAPTER 42
BUCK JONES & THE BIRTH OF THE GUAM COMBAT PATROL – TIYAN AIRFIELD

Prior to the American bombardment which began on July 8th, Chamorros were impressed into Japanese service. Men and boys swept the island killing dogs, others filled craters on runways at Orote or North on the island at Barrigarda or Dededo. The civilian population of the towns of Piti, Santa Rita, Tamuning, Agat and the Capital of Agana were forced westward, south and north to Manengon, Yona, Tai, and Yigo.

By 1944, most people on Guam depended upon the thrift of family elders who ordered that families stockpile and hoard canned goods. The Japanese had ordered the planting of rice paddies in the south and some in the Asan region, but flour was almost nonexistent/ island women made flour from fruit and taro roots. The American Navy and Army Air Forces bombed warehouses and often the rice paddies to deny their enemies a food source, but they also succeeded in starving the people of Guam.

Juan Cruz and his son Tomas- "Tog" from the time he was three and could only make that sound audible to the delight of his father - were put to work in the Fonte Plateau region filling sand bags and killing dogs. Juan realized that his little boy was becoming more and more surly with their captors and received a cut on the mouth from a civilian Japanese overseer on regular basis. Defiance at this stage in their relations with the occupiers meant death and Juan exercised as much paternal control over his son's willful desire to fight back.

On the night of July 25th, Juan, Tog, Ernesto Lujan, the taxi cab owner and his sons Jorge, Nardo, and Esteban and eighty other island men were assigned to loading eight Toyota flat-bed trucks with sandbags that would be hauled up to positions on Fonte Plateau. While loading the sandbags in the torrential downpour, hundreds of Japanese infantry men, disciplined, cheerful, and proud men marched by the work party and several soldiers treated Tog with pats n the head and gifts of candy, tea, sugar, water, and one soldier gave him soft cloth cap. These troops were nothing like the abusive naval troops under Otayama or the conscripts drawn from Japanese civilians and Japanese Saipanese. They were busy being soldiers and not interested in exercising authority over poor and starving islanders. These men were preparing to throw the Americans back into the Pacific and they were proud.

That night, deep in their protective caves after a meal of rice gruel and water, the Guam men and boys listened to fighting and the endless shelling and small arms fire. On the morning of the 26th none of their civilian guards could be found and all of the food supplies and the Toyotas were gone. Juan and Tog and the Lujan men as well as the Gutierrez's, Chupenases, Goliads, Torres men and the others held fast to their position all morning. At night they would take a look around and see who had decided Guam's future, but for now in this deep dark wet cold protective rock fathers and sons who had endured two and half years of abuse and now outrage would try to gain strength with a long day's troubled sleep. Juan Cruz tried to snuggle his baby but the hardened little man squirmed from his father.

'I am tired of our war, Poppi. I want to find Momma and Betty.'

'Look little man you have been a lion! I am so proud of you that even those Jap soldiers could see what a strong and brave boy you are. You take too many risks with the *sensei* and their goons – be quiet from now on with them and maybe they will ignore you. I'm sure your mother and Betty are fine and that they are safe with the neighbors in one of the camps the Japs have built. The Americans will win, but we need to stay smart and tough but mostly smart. You be a good boy and don't sass the Japs anymore. You here me Tog? Hug me baby and sleep tight with your old man. I'll bet they will bring some new movies for you – more Buck Jones would be ok Huh Buckaroo? Wish Old Buck were here with us now and get us back on the trail, again pardner. We'll take look see tonight. ' But the ten year 'old' man who had seen so many boys his age killed outright or accidentally was well beyond the quick justice of good men like his Poppi or Buck Jones.

Other men of Guam were taking their chances around the island and breaking away from their captors as well as they could and a number of the young men were already at work setting tarps and ambushes for cut-off or isolated Japanese soldiers and sailors and also outright murdering occupying Japanese civilians who had dreamed being colonizers; just as so many Americans had succeeded in doing since the last century. When we climb toward a dream of good living over the backs of another man's disadvantage that is the chance – the gamble – the risk and the thrill of doing what we know to be wrong. How many of us had so when we decided to take another man's job, cross the picket line as a scab, sell a relative on a broader level of a Ponzi scam, outsource a whole town's industry to save some stock, move the local factory to the Third World are we to expect anything different than the poor Japanese slob who arrived on Guam in 1942-43 ready to make bundle on the Gooks?

Hector Torres was doing that up at Tiyan and the first man he killed was an engineer who drove a Packard, not as nice as Dr. Tanaka, but that had belonged to the America pharmacist now in a prison camp in Kobe. That was Al Balawender a retired Navy Corpsman who married Marguerite Lose of an old Chamorro family when he set up shop in 1935. Marguerita died in May of this year of jaw cancer. Balawender probably had no idea of her death and might even have died himself. Hector knew the Packard. The Japanese engineer waved to Hector and his five friends over to help him push the car into a jungle clearing and keep it safe from the Hellcats that strafed every vehicle visible. After, every plane had been destroyed on Guam; Hector continued to work under the gray-haired engineer and his Army over-seers. After the Marines landed, troops from the airfield were moved south by Gen. Obata to help in the planned counter attack by Gen Takashima. With fewer soldiers around it was simpler for Hector and his pals form Washington High School in Agana to escape and slip off into the jungle.

The engineer spoke English pretty well and had tried to impress the guards with his ability to get work out of the boys by appealing to their better angels. They would work more efficiently if they understood that Japan was here to Liberate them from the white colonizers and would turn their island into an Asiatic paradise. 'We are brothers young men and the Emperor is your long lost father. You have been made to believe that you are destined to serve as wood choppers and fruit pickers, but you are a warrior people! With our help we will take back what is rightfully ours as Asians.'

Those pep talks were well-received because Hector had told the boys to go along with this guy. The engineer, like Luke Long, Ward Bond's sweet talking villain in the *Crimson Trail*, was intent on stealing whatever he could including Kitty – he meant Betty – the love of his life whose father thought Hector – he meant Buck Jones to be a rustler. Hector waited until this moment when he and Joaquin S. Aguon, Vicente L. Borja, Jose

307

S. Bukikosa, Francisco J. Cruz, George G. Flores, Roman N. Ignacio, Antonio P. Pangelinan, Agapito S. Perez, Pedro A. Perez, Ignacio R. Rivera, Jose P. Salas, Pedro R. San Nicolas, Jose S. Tenorio and Felix C. Wusstig would exact a revenge on these varmints.

Once the Packard was pushed deep into the jungle about eighty-five feet in and the tracks covered, Hector followed the engineer's instructions and camouflaged the car with cane and brush after throwing a netting over the vehicle.

The engineer was pleased. 'We will recover the car when we can. Now we will find the military unit near Tamuning and you boys will be well treated as heroes of the new world.'

Hector, smiled broadly and put a thick hand on the gray haired man's neck. 'Not so, Pard. We'll come back for the Packard alright, but after we turn you over to the Marines with all your maps and charters, Bub.'

The panic-ed man tried to pull a Nambu pistol from his holster but his thin wrists were cobra-ed in the thick fingers of Buck Jones's biggest fan on Guam. Felix Wusstig handed Hector the eight pound hammer and Hector caved in the man's head... The boys dragged the engineer off deeper in the jungle and off to higher ground and buried the best field designer in the Japanese Corps of Engineers so he would not stink up their camp.

Hector could not make heads nor tails of the engineer's charts and maps but he knew that they would be of help to the American's He distributed the cases and satchels to Joachim and two of the smaller boys. Joachim Aguon had been a hammer thrower on the Washington track team and had shoulders almost as broad as Hector's. 'Hwa – you are the squad leader make sure that these stay safe. You three guys should stay in the middle of the pack when we hit the trail. We need to get this stuff to the Cavalry, boys. Now, let's get some shut eye.'

Once away from the airfield, the boys posted three guards in order to allow the other twenty some time to sleep. American planes continued to strafe and bomb the roads and the airfield itself, but up in the hills the boys realized that they could become targets of opportunity for the Hellcats and Avengers that swept in low looking for Japanese soldiers. They chose to stick to the jungle where creeks gave them water and the heavy over growth cover, but near enough to the roads to maintain a sense of direction – they needed to keep a heading of southeast toward Tumon Bay and then Tamuning. Hector maintained his leadership by being the first up and the last to sit down and always taking the risk. It was his idea to form five groups for the walk away giving each group a separate path and a fixed destination. It was Hector who rationed the food and Hector who assigned the weapons – clubs, pieces of sharp steel pole, hammers and sling shots. They killed wild pig, gathered oranges and limes, and dug out roots. After three days, of cutting jungle scouting and resting they had only gone about three miles. They could hear the artillery up in the Fonte region, but knew that between them and then Americans were hundreds of Japanese. They'd get some weapons soon and then they could really make some mischief, but the charts and maps were what really needed to be taken care of first of all. Hector and his soldiers need to find the Americans. 'Sam, Sam, My dearest Uncle Sam won't you please come back to Guam – Won't you please come back to Guam!'

CHAPTER 43
LOU WILSON'S FONTE REDOUBT

'Cullen, put down some fire the minute you see my hand go up. I want them to pour every thing they have at you and Ernie. Let 'em think that you two are the show. When you re-load and Ernie lets go with the grenades, We will have them flattened, fucked, and fixed for fair. They'll rush you two here. And we will have three groups of five triangulating them. Got it.?'

Deep in the fighting hole with two bandoliers of BAR magazines and eight grenades a piece, Tim Cullen knew that targeting him and Ernie was a brilliant lure to the frustrated Japs who had been pushed from their own assault on the Asan beachhead line back up here. He and Gunny Dobbs would have their own personal banzai position. 'Aye, aye, Skipper.'

'I ain't your Skipper – you are on loan is all. Stay deep. Not too deep – you had better hit something. From what I saw this morning you couldn't hit a bull in the ass with a bass fiddle. Machine gunner my broad manly ass! Ernie, keep the 3rd Marine score card?'

'If this kid worked for Billy Higgins, he'll do Ok.'

The link up between the three regiments of Marines – 9th, 21st, & 3rd was going to happen and this night's action was the pivot point – like Babe Baranowski's left hand in the 1941 City Championship Game, Tim remembered, the squat running sensation of Leo High School evaded Tilden High tacklers by running with his torso almost parallel to the ground and throwing down his hand to pivot off and away from tacklers. Lou Wilson's patrol of seventeen men from E Company, 2nd battalion, 9th Marines and Tim Cullen lost lamb 3rd Marines would be the lynch pin.

Just as the night before had been a nightmare of green, orange and gold flashes, this night was as thick black as a Republican's love of the working man. Tim maintained his practice of concentration and mechanical manipulation –focus. Dug deep on the northwest side of the Fonte Plateau, Capt. Wilson's patrol spilt into three fire teams – the one on the highest ground with a light .30 caliber machine gun and the other two around a BAR team each, as well as the pigeon team of Tim Cullen and Gunnery Sergeant Ernie Dobbs. It was Capt. Wilson's plan to suck in as many Japs to this vortex as possible, by having Cullen and Dobbs engage them and appear to be an isolated pocket of Marines. Once the attackers could be drawn into the cross fire they could eliminate as many Fonte troops, while buying time until Co; Cushman could arrive with the 2nd Battalion – they needed about a solid forty minute's time.

At 2300 hours on the night of July 27th, seven Japanese soldiers moved toward Cullen's position to rest up from the day's fighting. When they got to within twenty of Cullen's BAR Ernie Dobbs punched the back of Tim's helmet upon seeing his Skipper give the open fire signal from the left. Tim chopped out a burst of four rounds that killed two of seven and caused the remaining five to hit ground and begin firing on the flash of the BAR's muzzle. Ernie popped out three shots that killed another and the four began to withdraw. Tim ceased fire and checked his magazine – about ten round and pulled another close to him from the edge of their well rampart-ed fighting hole.

Shots continued to spray in from the east of the flat ground for the next five minutes. A mortar round like the one that killed Sal the night before blasted earth and steel down onto the bait-Marines. Ernie slapped his left hand and quickly pulled a long smoking splinter from the fat between his thumb and under finger. 'I must have picked up enough of this shit since Friday to build a Buick.'

'Hear them? They're jabbering like the other night. Not as peppy though. Let's let them get close enough for a couple of grenades before I open up again.'

'Nix, Junior. The Skipper masterminded this one! *You* open up and let *them* see us. *That's* the plan. Your bright idea to go after them three fuckers last night landed you here in my bosom; now, do as your told and don't alter the script.' whispered the less salty but no less business-like Gunny. 'They'll come at us from two sides – bull horn us. Then the knock out punch. Keep focused right with your fire; I'll pop at the left. They should be about ready.'

Banzai! Baka yaro! Namen nayo! Nametonka! MALINE Kuso yarou! The hoarse and now familiar battle-oaths from the twenty or more Japanese veterans accompanied by wild shots from bayoneted Arisakas and Nambu light machine guns hurled westward at Cullen and Dobbs. Tim methodically let out bursts of four rounds and deftly replaced empty for full magazines. Another group of fifteen soldiers orchestrated the second note of this tactical chord from the left and Ernie Dodd fired on them. It was unclear, given the darkness and the flash how many of the attackers were knocked down but the bulk of men in each group hurtled forward to within thirty yards of the two Marines. At this distance the final note of about thirty Japanese soldiers emerged up the center lane of this flat ground and Tim increased his rate of fire proportionate to the proximity of the advancing targets. About ten feet from their hole Ernie tossed out a White Phosphorous grenade that flashed and burned those closest to him and pulled the pins on two fragmentation grenades with the wooden clothes pin that he had inserted in their loops and tossed both at Tim's most immediate attackers.

Now! All of Lou Wilson's well concealed ambushers opened fire on the trapped attackers and slaughtered the desperate men as they tried to bull their way into Cullen's hole and KILL SOMEBODY!? ? Bodies flap-jacked and bounced as well placed American fire destroyed another concerted Japanese exercise in *Bushido!* Wilson's killers methodically shot down targets. Not one of the seventy Japanese soldiers survived the ambush; but, now, aware that there were more than a few isolated pockets of Americans to their rear, Japanese officers began to turn the heavier guns on the western side of the Fonte Plateau. Mortar rounds rained down on the Marines again and several rounds from 70mm. mountain guns exploded in the mix. As this barrage lifted another ground assault came head on to the Marine positions.

Tim and Ernie kept up the same tactical imperatives and wordlessly operated their weapons. Ernie tossed grenades into the thicker packs of attackers and Tim Cullen returned to the proper rate of fire for this effective weapon of his.

Three more barrages attempted to find Americans to kill and three more frontal assaults were aimed at throwing the Americans off the vital Plateau. Capt. Wilson took a large fragment in his left pectoral muscle but stayed on his feet. It was his third good sized wound of the day. His Corpsman was called to his aid by his communicator but told to go fuck himself. The sailor laughed at his genuinely pissed off Alabama Skipper, but knew enough to skulk away when told and was rewarded with 'I am genuinely sorry, Doc. No Shit!'

At 0245 of July 28th, Pfc. Casmir Polecki and Cpl. Tommy Kotel brought up the JASCO team along with the balance of Easy Company and two heavy machine gun squads from weapons Company. 'Capt. Wilson this Lt. Zbierski and Sgt. Prendergast JASCO.'

'Lou Wilson. We can now rain down some harm.'

'Tom Zbierski, Lou. Good men those two (nodding to Kotel and Polecki) you have real trail hands. Where can I get my team going? Oh, This is Sgt. Prendergast. Sergeant., Follow Cpl. Kotel to where they want us.'

'Aye, aye, Sir.' Sgt. Dick Prendergast was a classmate of Tim Cullen and they had shared cans of fruit with the now convalesced and honorably discharged Dick Burke who was clobbered at Eniwetok, while driving a truck. A 70mm. shell blew the truck off the trail while it was hauling water up to the lines early in the battle. Burke, a neighborhood kid who went to Calumet High School or 'Our Lady of Calumet' as it was known due to the fact that so many Catholic kids attended, was now an out patient at Hines Veterans Hospital in Maywood. Dick Prendergast, Tim Cullen and Dick Burke got together on Guadalcanal before Dick shipped out for Eniwetok.

Dick Prendergast and Tim Cullen went into Boot Camp at the same time and then Prendergast went to communications school at Camp Elliot. Now they were about twenty yards from one another but they would not cross paths. Years after the war at a Leo Reunion at the Sherman House in downtown Chicago, they would discover that they had fought almost side by side in the taking of Fonte Plateau, but Tim Cullen was busy with Gunny Dobbs shooting the bodies of fallen Japanese soldiers of the 48th Independent Mixed Brigade.

'Pretty nice job of it last night, Sonny. This old fat man is all the way tired. Here – that one. . 'Tim, using his carbine and allowing the BAR to cool, fired into the back of very tall man in what appeared to be officer's clothing. 'Yep – he was possum. Hey! Kotel! Tommy, get some boys to police up these Jap weapons. Watch for grenades. Shoot or stick every body within reach. Anyway, nice cool work son. Know Billy?'

Tim never looked up. 'No. Heard about him.' Ernie got real expansive. 'We served in China with the 6th Marines in Shanghai from '37 to '38. This Jap officer crossed into the International Settlement with about twelve men and we stopped them. The Jap officer, Captain I think, spit in Billy's face and tried to step through and Billy punched him in the throat – flat-heeled like – and the Jap was dead before he hit the flagstones. The others got shit in their blood and returned from whence they came. Dutch Red Cross saw the whole incident and when the *ichi ban* Jap tried to turn up the heat Billy was cleared – told them the man died of a heart attack and he was merely trying to ease the man down to the pavement. He was a caution. Good men die and that's a sad fact of the trade. Pretty gabby for a Marine – ain't you? Oh well, '

By the time that they cleared the corpses taken down that morning, the balance of the Battalion under Col. Cushman arrived. Lt. Col. Bob Cushman was 29 years old and had already established himself as leader of men. An Annapolis graduate, Cushman had served in Shanghai with the 4th Marines at the same time Billy Higgins murdered the Jap Officer. When Pearl Harbor was attacked Cushman commanded the Marine Detachment aboard *U.S.S.Pennsylvannia* and he had hiked the 9th Marines from San Diego to Camp Pendleton in 1942. Cushman made things happen on Guam – when Tim's Company was being wiped out at Bundeschu Ridge, Cushman sent his Fox Company to help fill in. Now Cushman was leading the assault to end this important phase in the campaign.

'Gunny Dobbs, who's your artillery? '

'One of Billy's boys – Pfc. Timothy Cullen A-1-3-3. He was chasing three Japs on his lonesome when the Skipper snared this tough pup. Me and Tim serviced these fine human specimens, Colonel.'

'Good to have you aboard Cullen. Shame about Billy; Tough men die.'

'Weak sisters stay home Colonel – these stinkers had no end of balls Colonel. None of them drunk last night either. Pure Balls. Good men.'

'Ernie how does man who works so hard stay so fat? You should by God be as skinny as your chatty pal here.'

'Kid says plenty when provoked Colonel – tried to kill me when I tried to take his Lieutenant's hog-leg off him. Show the Colonel, boy.'

Tim reluctantly opened his shirt and displayed the Colt and the tale that goes with his possession of the pistol and of the banzai and of the deaths of Wat and Sal and of how he came to fight with the 9th. It was too much and too soon and Cullen collapsed in a fit of tears. Col. Cushman and Ernie walked the boy out of an audience and calmed him down. "We are taking the top of that ridge this morning and making the link-up that will end this campaign. You have been a big part of this and you'll stay with Capt. Wilson until this task is done, Cullen. Ernie once we take E Company off the line get this Marine back to his Company. Good to have a man like you in the 9th, Cullen. Ernie, get your boys ready to move.'

'Aye, aye, Colonel. More hot work for a fat man. Let's go Tim, you can carry my umbrella. BAR signed out to A?'

'Yes, Gunny. Changed a lot of hands since last Friday.'

'Hang on to that weapon. You are an artist with it; especially for a feather merchant.'

CHAPTER 44
THE DORMITION OF THE THEOTOKOS

Joanie Cullen was asked by Sister Malachy to write a paper on the Feast of the Assumption of Our Blessed Virgin Mary at the end of May for a competition of the Catholic Interscholastic Catholic Action group of Mercy High School. The task of the paper was to explain the devotion of Catholics to Our Lady and explain in practical terms to non-Catholics. The paper would be read by C.I.S.C.A. moderators throughout the Archdiocese of Chicago and passed on to a final board of readers headed by Bishop Bernard Sheil himself. He would recommend that the winning paper would be read at the High Mass celebrating The Feast of the Assumption on August 15th by Cardinal Samuel Stritch himself.

Prizes included a $200 War Bond purchased by the Knights of Columbus Joint Chicago Councils and holy medal celebration Our Lady's Assumption into heaven and blessed by Pope Pius XII. The winner's family photo would be featured in *The New World* and private mass and confession from the Cardinal himself.

319

Joanie worked on the essay every night for weeks and typed, duplicated and presented a 500 – 550 word composition that follows –

Joan Anne Cullen, Sophomore
Mercy High School, Chicago, Illinois

To die,--to sleep,--
No more; and by a sleep to say we end
The heartache, and the thousand natural shocks
That flesh is heir to,--'tis a consummation
Devoutly to be wish'd. To die,--to sleep;--
To sleep! perchance to dream:--ay, there's the rub;
For in that sleep of death what dreams may come,

The Bard only tries to say what sleep might mean, because he, like all of us, never fully appreciates what sleep's truth tells us. Animals hibernate; a debt lies dormant; a patient slips into a coma; and a field lies fallow. But what is going on?

A bear or any other hibernating animal slows down its metabolism in order to fight off starvation in winter; a debt owed to a bank stays alive until such time as the debtor can pay, but with an added cost; a patient who has had a severe injury regenerates damaged tissues; and a field that has been cut into seeded and bears fruit must restore its growth agents. So do we all.

People are active every day and some of our activities might do us some harm – we need rest and recovery, sometimes our activities deeply hurt us and others and we Catholics call that sin. We all sin and we all need to recover.

Grace is what gives us the rest to recover. Grace is Sleep. Grace is from the Latin word for gift – *gratia! Gratia Plena Full of Grace!* Catholics believe that Mary Mother of God is free from sin and therefore Full of Grace. From her womb the Author of All Grace, Jesus Christ, The Son of God, came to save Man from Sin. To give Us Grace – God the Father Created the Woman Free from Sin.

Grace is Sleep and in that Sleep we restore our powers, we use time to absolve our debts, to fight the starvation of the World's chill, to generate the soil that is our earthly flesh to bear fruit in God's Will.

Our friends in the Eastern Rite Church celebrate the Dormition of the Theokotos or the Sleep of the Mother of God. We Western rite Catholics call this the Assumption of Mary. Because she was not born of sin she could not dies of the consequences of sin – the Wages of Sin is Death. Mary the Mother of God was freed of Death through the Assumption into Heaven. As we avoid harm, starvation and debt through sleep, hibernation, coma, So did Our Mother Mary sleep into the Hands of God.

The Voice of The Risen Christ asked Mary Magdalene when she came into the Tomb. 'Do you seek the Living Among the Dead?' Mary's Assumption or the Dormition of the Theotokos affirms our Restoration.

America was asleep and awakened by Pearl Harbor. Our Boys went away from us – like being asleep. My Big Brother was on an island in the South Pacific that had a dormant volcano. He wrote to me that he was asleep in a hammock and he was rocked out of that sleep when the volcano awoke! My Brother like our Nation is wide awake and he prays to Our Lady that her Sleep will awaken the Will of Her Son and bring him home. His return and their return to us all will come from our devotion to the Sleep – to the assumption of Our Lady!

On July 30th, 1944 Sister Malachy, English Professor, at Mercy High School received a notice from the Chancellor of the Archdiocese of Chicago Rt. Rev. Bernard Sheil, Auxiliary Bishop of Chicago, that Joan Agnes Cullen, Sophomore Mercy High School was the winner of the CISCA Essay Competition. Sister Malachy received permission to take the 79th Street Trolley, accompanied by Sister Doralese, RSM, and hand deliver the announcement to the Cullen family.

Sister Malachy was more excited than she had been when she received the call to Christ and needed to turn down the hand of Brice May in marriage. The odd thing was that Brice May never married. A good and gentle man; he lived out his bachelorhood in St. Louis doing great acts of charity for the poor, especially the Negroes. The May family had been slave owners until the Civil War. May opened All Hallow's Colored Orphanage for Boys in 1927, run by the Josephite Priests of New Orleans.

Sister Malachy and Sister Doralese used a nickel at Steinways Drug store on Ashland and did the Cullen's courtesy of a call before appearing on their doorstep. They also decided to treat themselves to a Green River at the soda fountain. Seated at the end of the counter was Mr. Edward O'Donnell, taking a coffee break from his phone calls and Ashland Heating & Oil; Highland Asphalt Consulting, and Lord Only Knows What Else (the man was a Scamp!) and stood erect but gave the Brides of Christ an overly formal bow,

'Good afternoon, Ladies! It is hotter than Moses' toes out on that pavement today. May I treat you Sisters to a pop?'

'No!' spat Sister Doralese, a twenty year old who had just made her Simple Vows as a Religious Sister of Mercy and a simpleton to boot. Born to a Galway rock farmer and sent to 'live with the Sisters' at ten years of age, Emma Redmond was as hard as Joyce Country itself, in the wilds of Galway. Now, Sister Doralese cast her sour gimlet-eyed view on the world and its inhabitants with her own brand of sanctified malice.

'We would be delighted Mr. O'Donnell and it so good to see you up and about. How's the back? More importantly how are your beautiful daughters?'

'Sister, if I had only spent more time in St. Louis, the good lord would be shy of one great Nun. That and the fact that the most beautiful Bohemian girl in God's garden allowed me to marry her.' And turning to the puckered face within the white wimple 'And . . . Who is the sorcerers apprentice? Sister, how do you find America? To your liking - no? Well, we, Yanks, tend to keep the piggies in a big pen up around 45ᵗʰ and Halsted.'

Without bursting into laughter, Sister Malachy continued for her subordinate, 'Mr. O'Donnell, this is Sister Doralese and she has recently come to Mercy as a Proctor, while she continues her studies.'

'Getting the grammar school certificate, Sister are you? I hear that you have some big news Sister.' O'Donnell teased the smart pretty woman.

'Mr. O'Donnell, I should have known that I would be one of the last to know and I won't pretend to affect surprise. Bishop Sheil must have put the bite on you – getting a new gymnasium is he?'

'Sister, I swear before God and Man that that - if there ever comes the day when Ladies are made priests - that - you'll be the Greatest Pope this Church has had since old Pete went yellow in the garden!'

As the two nuns finished their Green Rivers the soda jerk, a fourteen year old freshman at Leo named Bill Koloseike tried to pick up the nuns' nickels from the marble counter, Mr. O' Donnell exercised his rights as the landlord for this business. 'Billy, these Dames don't pull change while Edward J. is around, get me, Pal? Here's deuce for yourself, kiddo, and have Pete from Crete burn me a couple of hamburgers around three and send them up to the office.'

'Thanks Mr. O'Donnell! Sorry Sisters – please take back the nickels.

Sister Doralese only got fouler with Mr. O'Donnell's gallantry but Sister Malachy howled with laughter which only added to her intrinsic beauty. God, O'Donnell thought, she must have been murder on the simps down in St. Looey – Suicides soared when this peach took the veil.

'Sister Malachy, it is always a pleasure to meet with a beautiful and brilliant woman in the service of Holy Mother the Church – Oh and you too Sister. Sr. Doralese, you in the right line of work!' and the dapper retired beer runner, tough guy, and businessman pushed through the glass doors leading into the Highland Theatre.

The two nuns would double back to Bishop Street and walk south to the Cullen two-flat at 8134 S. Bishop Street. Mrs. Cullen acted non-chalant but suspected that Sr. Malachy's phone call and subsequent visit was a harbinger of big news. Mary Hannah Cullen dusted imaginary dust and shooed the three little guys out to Foster Park. The older three girls would be at the Ford Plant until at least four o'clock and would not get home until near half-six. Joanie was at cutting the small lawn in front of the flat and Larry was downtown at Local 12 for a Dance Committee Meeting and would need to go straight into the Highland for tonight's show and monitor the new air-conditioning apparatus that to him, simple man that is, was akin to conducting the Chicago Symphony Orchestra.. 'I pull this switch and feed this line and watch this gauge – For Christ Jesus Almighty I do not know how the air gets cold, Woman! It Does so! That's Enough, So?' Larry, the poor thing, knew how to exercise a policeman's Billy alright enough, but now he was operating huge boilers in the winter and this air-conditioning thing all summer and not knowing the how or why of it. Talk a laugh. Tim knew the devil's own business of any contraption that man could make, but Larry shunned the poor boy's help. There was a great frost between the two of them, so.

Mary could hear Joanie greet the sisters. 'Oh, Sister! You are pulling my leg! Please, come in and let's tell Mother – Oh, sister thank you for this opportunity!'

Joanie in tan shorts, white blouse and tennis shoes was a sight. She had thick curly brown hair, long athletic legs, elegant fingers, huge green eyes highlighted by long dark eyelashes and the same see-through Irish pallor as her brother now stomping across Fonte Ridge with Capt Lou Wilson and Ernie Dobbs. Tim was dormant. Far away.

The kettle was poured into the teapot with a silver tea capsule with a long chain. The capsule was tightly packed with Barry's tea from home – Ireland. There were cookies on the plate as the yanks called them – Lorna Doone's which were like Jacob's shortbread biscuits, back home. Sisters will you have a sup of tea?

The four women, three delightful and one an atrocity, sat down and had tea while Sister Malachy explained the honors to be bestowed up the Cullen Clan by the Cardinal himself. She read the commentary by Bishop Sheil and his recommendation that such a talented young student should give 'careful consideration to Holy Orders herself.' And that from Bishop Sheil!

Twenty minutes into the tea party, The hall buzzer to the two flat keened! Joanie went down to find a Western Union messenger and signed for the telegram and bounded back up the stairs to get a quarter's tip for the man from her Mother's purse. She tipped the uniformed twenty year old with green teeth, who ogled the beauty in tennis shorts and was shown his way back out the doors by Joanie's shove and heard her mother's cry 'Immaculate Heart of Mary! My Baby! Jesus!'

Sister Malachy was easing Mrs. Cullen back into the chair from which she had sprung in reaction to the news, 'Joanie, Tim is Missing in action and presumed dead.' Missing. Sleeping, perchance? Most Holy Mother!

Death Notice in Giddings, Texas
Buck, John A.

1ˢᵗ Lt. John A. Buck, USMCR, Son of Texas Representative. Roper Christian Buck (Dem.) and Angelina Dolores Romea Y Madura Buck, Graduate University of Notre Dame 1940 Northwestern Law is reported killed in action on Guam.

CHAPTER 45
HECTOR AND JOACHIM

The Japanese were flooding away from the now consolidated beachhead and General Takashima had been killed in the attempt to throw the Third Marine Division into the Philippine Sea. Hundreds of shattered men with whatever they could carry were headed north and passing the hidden bands of young Chamorro conscripts from the work parties – in the jungles above the beachhead and north of Agana – once beautiful Americanized city a smoking ruin.

After killing the Japanese engineer and hiding his stolen Packard deep in the brush south of Tiyan, Hector Torres, sixteen, a bull-like and toothy Buck Jones aficionado and his athletic hammer throwing pal Joachim took their group of twenty teenagers toward Tumon Bay after they noticed that all of the Jap stragglers and unified troops were heading northwest of the island. It made sense that the Americans would bring more troops in at Tumon Bay and General Obata was trying to effect a solid defense and avoid annihilation. Hector decided to move their troop to Tumon and wait for the first American that they could hand over the maps and the charts.

'Hwa, this makes sense doesn't it? I mean the Japs are moving their troops toward Yigo it seems. Let's take a look at some of the maps Mr.Moto gave us.'

The two high school boys who should have been going into their Junior year tried to make sense of the maps and noticed on three that were obviously plans of the airfield and the fields and woods around it. On these next to a legend with Japanese calligraphy but also standard notations for elevations creeks and utilities also had strange marks ^ * and a few others that highlighted patterns on the terrain around the edge of the runways and also on access roads and certain hills and clearings.

'These seem to be important so lets get them to the first American we meet. I think that we will have some luck near Two Lovers Point above Tumon Bay.' The Torres/Aguon patrol made better time now that they had open grass fields to cross and sighted no Japs whatsoever. They were pulling back fast now. At Two Lovers Point they watched a Navy patrol boat cruise the edge of the point and waved shirts at the navy men aboard. Soon the boat made a return and was followed by three LCVP's that landed on the beach below them and armed sailors took up positions deep from the water's edge and an officer waved the boys down indicating that they should have their hands up. Hector took the map cases and laid them next to two rocks for easy recovery.

On the beach the boys were checked out and affirmed to be Chamorros. Hector asked to speak to the officer in charge and three sailors walked him to a tall helmeted man holding a carbine. 'I am Ensign Campbell. You boys look like you have had a rough time of it. Chief, signal the boat to send get some quartermaster requisitions for clothing and food – yesterday. We will have some rations for you boys in an hour and some new clothes. Now, who are you, son?'

I am Hector Torres. I am from Agana – most of us here are. We were made to work on the airfield at Tiyan up –up on the Point, sir I have some Jap maps we took from the engineer we worked for – we killed that Jap.'

'Hector did Ensign. He's our leader.' Chimed in Joachim.

'Slow down fellows. Hector take me up with you – Barnes and Noble come along should be something. How's it look for Japs around here?

'We have not seen any but the troops and they all seem to be moving toward Yigo, but I would guess that they will fan out and make a fight of it around the airfield.'

'What makes you say so, Hector?'

'Just the way – we watched them set up from the jungle after we took off – they were moving in north of the field but so many are pulling back that way.'

'That's plenty for now, Hector. Great full report. Barnes – Noble let's follow Hector up the cliff.'

After about twenty minutes, Hector and Campbell returned leaving Barnes and Noble above to scout out the fields beyond the point. Barnes had a field radio as well as his carbine and would keep in touch on what they saw. Ensign Campbell went to one of the LCVP's and had the radioman contact the fleet intelligence officers. Before the clothes and the rations arrived on the beach at Tumon Bay, a YIP boat was taking the maps and documents back to the Naval Intelligence Staff. It turned out the maps indicated most of the minefields and gun emplacements for the defense of the Jap airfields on the north of Guam there were two one near Yigo as well as one between Dededo and Barrigarda. Hector and the boys did handsome work.

When the food and clothing arrived Hector and his troop were decked out with Navy dungarees, boondockers and blue baseball caps. Each boy was give two sets of clothing as well as helmets and rations for 5-days. Hector broached the subject of weapons.

'We all know how to fire rifles and shot-guns. We can help you find the Japs from where we were and we already know how to kill them. We even have a Packard hidden up near Dededo – one that the Jap stole from Mr. & Mrs. Losa'

It made sense to Ensign Campbell and he received permission to draw shotguns and carbines webbing gear and ammunition for the Chamorro Scouts attached to Naval Engineering Company 321. Buck Jones was heeled.

Pearl Harbor was bombed in a sneak attack. From the luxury and ease of our age, bought with the precious blood and sacrifice of a generation that is dying at too great a rate, we can sit on our fat asses and fire out opinions about the "Roosevelt Conspiracies" and argue about America's propensity for war-mongering and racism and corporate slavery and religious hypocrisy that tries to sanctify the actions of millions of America boys and girls during the 1940's. We can worry about whether skank-superstars are really misunderstood, or which NBA star needs more street cred, or which video game to buy our already chubby zombie-eyed teenagers and completely ignore the eighty year old man who still gets off his ass and sweeps the snow off his sidewalk in 20-below zero weather. That same old man was up to his hips in snow in January 1944 fighting off the huge German counter attack in the Ardennes Forrest, when he was 17 years old and vowed that if he lived through that 'he would never complain about the cold – ever. And he never did.

This same old man never cheated on his wife even when she developed a drinking and a gambling problem in her seventies and died in the garage with the Crown Victoria running, while he was sitting *Shiva* in Skokie, Il for Manny Gannet, who had carried him to safety when a tree branch went through his neck after a barrage. This same old guy walked his girl through AA and GA and joined Gam-anon to help her out. Their kids were grown and had families of their own out in Phoenix and Anaheim. Babe could never get Al to open up even after all these years and never ever talked about War, except to say that it was behind. Babe slipped in the last few months – bought Lotto tickets, scratched off a $ 600 winner and took it to Bettendorf, IA where she disappeared for three days and maxed out four new credit cards, as well as this months pension dividends. Al was still trying to pay-off the second mortgage that Babe took out on a home that was paid off in 1974.

We have the luxury not to give a thought to the silly old geezer sweeping snow with an extra-long stiff brushed broom, because he was up to his hips in snow a long time ago. Likewise, we do not need a sense of history because cheese-eaters like Bill Maher or Rush Limbaugh or Sean Hannity can tell us what to think and we do not mind taking a sip of the "Kool-Aid" now and then and we really do not mind being pigeon holed or locked into a demographic. We won't do what that old guy did. We are too smart and secure in our place on this planet for that. We live in a global village.

The villages on Guam were shattered by the Americans and the Japanese. The people of Guam were exiled to Yona or points south on that small island in the Marianas But, things were about to get a little better for those heroic and long- suffering loyal Americans. More Guamanians were about to die to be sure but things were getting better. The Ist Provisional Marine Brigade and the 77th Army Division were fully linked up after fighting of fierce Japanese counterattacks around the Orote Peninsula and they were pushing north. Navy CBs were landed to begin refitting the blasted away Japanese Naval Air Field and soon Hellcats and Corsairs would be flying missions from there. Later, in the fall, VT-99 would land and fly anti-submarine missions and a radio/gunner by the name of Paul Newman would swim on Guam's beaches in between missions. Things were going to get better.

Juan Cruz and his son Tog and about eighty other Guam men survived the assault of the linked up regiments of the 3rd Marine Division in the Fonte sector. The night after their captors and guards left them to participate in the Takashima counter-attacks the men stayed put deep in caves and stayed put for another whole day. When parties of Marines were blasting Japs out of their caves, the men determined to signal the Americans to let them know that they were friendlies.

Tog offered 'Let's all sing 'Mister Sam, Mister Sam!' With that strategy all of the Chamorro men and boys were saved from TNT and Napalm. Things were getting better. Juan Cruz and his son and their neighbors told the story of how the Japs had moved everyone else west and south to concentration camps and that 'let the troops know that our people are starving there.' The men of the 77th Army Infantry Division were well on their way. Things were getting better.

CHAPTER 46
WHAT'S THE HIPSTER TO THE SLAMMER?

Dr. Ted Tanaka had spent the husky side of a month with a Japanese Medical Unit but had managed to slip away when the disastrous counterattacks forced the move north. Looking busy was something that Ted learned to do during the summers between sessions at Gonzaga University while he worked on the loading docks of one of the canning factories that his Dad an old shrimper and crab fisher thought would toughen Ted up. Like hell. Well there's tough and then there's smart tough. Ted could handle himself – use his dukes – and he was very good company. But, when mind-numbing hard work came up the pike, Ted developed methods for looking busier that the eight other guys around him and applied himself accordingly and avoided an excess of tasks and chores.

Now, those skills came to life-saving use and Ted horsed an already expired head wound case into his operating chair and continued to do Oscar winning work on the head of a corpse while American naval gunfire erupted all around the operating theatre and other lesser souls were packing gear and patients off to the north. The heroic Dr. Tanaka stayed with his man and waved off the others. Soon he was all alone, except for the rigid open jawed Sgt Koshi Yomura of the 38th Mixed Brigade – Koshi didn't make it. Now it was time to skedaddle!

Ted took off the make-shift Japanese military wear that he was ordered to don under his operating gown. He threw on his bloodied grey worsteds and light blue polo shirt and on his steppers he eased into the two-tone bucks that took forever for May's Department Store in San Francisco to send to him back in '41. They still felt better than sex – well they felt pretty damn sweet – a treat on the feet! Back to natty in a bombed out island city – city by Guam standards, Ted hoped to lay low and not get killed by either side.

Stragglers and isolated units of Japanese infantry and some sailors were hiding in the ruins of Agana. Ted needed to find just the right place for his own personal refuge while the larger forces in the world butchered one another. SOLID! Stay cool, Teddy boy! What's the Hipster to the slammer? What's the Hipster to the Slammer?

The Hipster is the key
That opens up the Slammer
To the chicken fricassee

'Reet!' The firing slowed and the American CRACK! Won out with also and occasional blast. Ted heard steps on the street; careful steps; they were the steps of guys who had been fired on steady for over a week saw many of their pals die and get maimed and were not about to get knocked off or crippled this late in the game – No Sir!

Ted sang Minnie the Moocher in his best and most authentic Cab – Solid, Jackson!

Nice and slow! Here Goes
Folks, now here's the story 'bout Minnie the Moocher,
She was a red-hot hootchie-cootcher,

She was the roughest, toughest frail,
But Minnie had a heart as big as a whale.

[Call and response scat chorus differs every time. The
following is simplified:]
Hi-de-hi-de-hi-di-hi!
Ho-de-ho-de-ho-de-ho!
He-de-he-de-he-de-he!
Ho-de-ho-de-ho!

Now, she messed around with a bloke named Smoky,
She loved him though he was cokie,
He took her down to Chinatown,
He showed her how to kick the gong around.

Now, she had a dream about the king of Sweden,
He gave her things that she was needin',
He gave her a home built of gold and steel,
A diamond car with a platinum wheel.

Now, he gave her his townhouse and his racing horses,
Each meal she ate was a dozen courses;
She had a million dollars worth of nickels and dimes,
And she sat around and counted them all a billion times.

Poor Min, poor Min, poor Min.
Four Marines from 3rd Battalion of Third Marines appaluded
and howled to 'Whoever'thefucksdownthere – Swell Show! Talk
fast or we drop Willie Pete in' Ted yelled up. 'I'm an American
dentist – I 'm a Jap too, if that makes a difference'
'It do!' Laughter – Good laughter
'I'm a Gonzaga grad, basketball star and married to a red-
head who will kick the living shit out each and every one of you
if you harm one of my manly gray hairs! Honor Bright Boys!

Okay!' All four Marines laughed and they had not laughed since the LST opened its big wide doors.

'Okay with us Doc – You know the drill! Come out with your hands Up!'

'On my way Boys!' Ted was Okay!

CHAPTER 47
BANDAGES AND SOCKS

Ernie Dobbs took the kid to see Doc Reynuad, best Corpsman in the service and Col. Cushman's shadow. This Navy man had been with Cushman from the time that he joined the 9th at San Diego and hiked with him on the long march to Pendleton. Albert Reynaud was the son of Vermont maple sugar harvester who had hit it big during the Great Depression by getting a federal contract to sell maple syrup to the Navy. While others lost land and savings Hercule Reynaud was flush and sent his boy Albert to prep schools and hoped to send him to medical school, but Albert was a brawler and succeeded in getting tossed from three exclusive eastern boys prep schools before finishing at Canterbury School for Boys in Connecticut.

In the fall of 1935, Albert missed the appointment interview secured by his old man for Holy Cross, got drunk with some sailors in Boston and joined the U.S. Navy. That was it. His old man wrote to him. 'You have chosen your life. Live it. God Bless you and good luck to you.'

Al never regretted that drunk. He shipped in and shipped over in 1939 and went to medics training at New London. After having served in the Caribbean Squadron of destroyers, Albert decided to make his niche as a corpsman and possibly go on to medical school on his own motor. In 1940 he was assigned to the Marine Detachment of the *U.S.S. Nevada* and was aboard when that mighty and gallant ship when it was attacked on December 7th and beached itself and avoided blocking the harbor channel; thus keeping what was left of the Pacific Fleet in the war. In January of 1942, he was reassigned to the 9th Marines at San Diego and was with Bob Cushman from that point on.

Ernie and Tim had shared a great few hours together and the portly Gunny saw much of what Billy Higgins had seen in the feather merchant – quiet honor, mind set to task, and fierce loyalty. The kid was the goods and Ernie was going to miss him.

Since coming ashore, Tim Cullen and nearly every man in the 3rd Division had their flesh encrusted with fragments of steel, coral, rock, wood and dirt. He had fragments in his back, face, forearms, thighs, buttocks, and an inch and a half hole above his right ankle. The sweat, dirt, battle-grime and grease acted as a coagulant, but he needed to be picked over by a pro and Ernie took him to Doc Reynaud. ' Frog-eater, I have a personal friend of mine who needs your artist's skills in shedding some steel. Albert, meet Tim Cullen, one of Billy Higgins' boys from the 3rd.'

'Strip, sonny and let me have a look at the harvest report. Billy was a caution. Off with the – where'd you get the hog-leg?'

'Later, Al.'

'When was the last time you changed you socks? These are fucked, son. Here put on these – you had better get some formaldehyde on them dogs of yours; they are soured. Should have put on some new ones after the soaking we got the other night – Yeah, I know you were busy – save it for the stiff-collar. Hold the fuck still.'

With his powerful hands the corpsman manipulated steel shards from Tim's flesh without much agony and swabbed the wounds with iodine and alcohol and applied battle dressing only to the large hole above the right ankle. 'I have no idea what the fuck hit you here, kid, but it bounced out and there are no fragments in the wound – that's a weird one for my memoirs – change this dressing every six hours and have your Doc look at it when you get back with the 3rd.' While Tim put back on his ragged and foul smelling clothes and the holster containing the hog-leg, Ernie entertained Albert with tales of the young man's derring-do over the last three days. When the Colonel's Doc had finished with the kid he went to work on Ernie. 'The Colonel has ordered your Skipper back to Battalion Aid – he lost a lot of blood and that last hit in his tit did him proud. Ernie your lard must act like a magnet you look like a god damn pin cushion. Here this is gonna hurt you a lot more than anyone else. Hold the fuck still you god dam Nancy. You have more steel wedged way back in the hand here. You won't be able to make much of a fist for while.'

'I make love with my right hand anyway, Al; cut away.'

While the medic probed and pulled long thin pieces of steel from Ernie's left hand he interrogated Tim. 'Where you from again?'

'Chicago.'

'Spent a week there, one day. The *most* dog-shit town I ever had liberty in. Nothing to do there. The whole town is foreigners and groceries.'

'Nice lake.'

'Yeah, water is big seller to a sailor. I stayed at the LaSalle Hotel and saw more rats there than when I served on the *Salt Lake City*, for Chrissakes. Hell Boston and Philly and New York are towns. You a school boy? Course you are. Any plans for after the War? I mean any thoughts?'

'I was looking into air-conditioning business of some sort. I like that stuff.'

'Sound policy. You'll never bring your work home to your wife and kids. Fix it and fuck with it and forget it.'

' I should have gone into the Navy maybe and got a jump on things.'

'You *are where* you are supposed to be, sonny-boy. If you were not, you would be somewhere else and never forget that. Regrets, or second guesses, are for the clowns that never do a Goddam thing with their lives to begin with – hold the fuck still Ernie you squirming pussy – what this cry-baby tells me, you operated like a man possessed with God's own Grace, boy. Remember, keep your plans and do what you are supposed to do. I am doing just that and so is Ernie. That is why we will triumph. Keep your mind on your business and your dreams will follow. There, last one – about 5/16s I'd say. I am gauzing this mitt up proper, Betty Davis; now do not get this hook infected.'

Ernie was in agony. 'Feels like new, Doc, you work like a Shanghai whore with a kid's Holy Communion money. What's the fee?'

'Try not to get gangrene, asshole. Give me your beer ration when this waltz is done. Tim it was a pleasure and now I will let Ernie escort you back to a real fighting outfit. Remember what I said. Never second guess what you have chosen to do. Take him home James.'

Ernie and Tim covered much of the ground that had brought him to his service with E Company but when they had reached the place where Sal and Wat and so many others had been killed, where hundreds of Japanese soldiers had, drunk or sober, attacked, Able Company had been replaced by members of the 3rd Defense Battalion who were mounting and sighting in twin 40mm guns on Bundeschu Ridge.

A sergeant with the gun crew told them that A Company had moved up to the Agana –Pago Road and was getting refitted and re-supplied for a push against Barrigarda and that the 3rd Battalion was already moving through Agana itself. Ernie told the sergeant what the deal was and the sergeant arranged for the two of them to hitch a ride on a DUKW amphibious truck that was hauling ammo up to 1st Battalion area.

The entire foreword area had been pushed several miles westward and all of the hills and caves that just hours ago had teemed with Japanese soldiers were smoking from the napalm and TNT that had roasted so many of them or sealed them in the cliffs above Guam's beaches for eternity.

Ernie and Tim waited for the arrival of an amphibious truck and marveled at the eastern expanses of the Philippine Sea and the hundreds of ships and boats anchored or moving about the lagoons and bays. The old beachhead was dotted with makeshift buildings, and shops and hospitals and supplies were stacked forty feet high in some places Cranes operated and vehicles of every size and capability snaked their way up new roads dug out of the low hills and cliffs. In less than nine days, America had returned to Guam –for Keeps.

After about fifteen minutes, the huge green steel truck-boat roared up to the two bandaged combat infantrymen – one in his thirties and portly with his left hand wrapped in think battle dress and the younger one a skinny eighteen year old with a Browning Automatic Rifle slung on his right shoulder, a carbine looped on his left and a rugged looking condition to both. The driver of the DUKW was a Negro and so were the three men in clean utilities – 'Jitney to the frontlines, Marines!'

'Hiya, fellows, Well - you are the very first Colored Marines that I have ever laid eyes on! Read about you men! Montford Point – that is one shit-hole that they stuck you kids in.'

'Is it not, Gunny? We are proud to serve! Taylor help these fighting men aboard. What's the matter, killer? Can't stomach the sight of Colored Marines!'

Tim was in a state of shock. He had not heard that Negroes were in the forward area with the Marines but he had met plenty of Army men on Bougainville and Guadalcanal. 'Naw. Nothing. Just tired. What's the big deal anyway?'

'The Big Deal is that not only did these men endure the same shit that you had to in boots, but they also were given the worst place to learn the trade. I was in Montford Point years ago; it was shit then and probably made a bit worse to welcome these boys. Am I not correct driver?'

' You are exactly correct, Gunny. Tough but Fair, Tough but Fair! Yes sir. Tough but fair. How's things up here? We unloaded yesterday - 298ᵗʰ Depot Company. White officers are good men. Our Skipper was on the 'Canal, got clobbered and sent to make sure us coloreds don't steal too much. Looks like you men seen plenty of action. Bad as they say?'

'Depends on who's talking Corporal. Pussies say a slap is rugged. This quiet Mick eats pain like its filet mignon. He don't say much but works like he was born to it. Me, I'm as gabby as a maiden aunt that sneaked out for a night with the fellas. Japs still sighting in on the beachhead?'

'We took only a couple of rounds when we came ashore from that LST back there, yesterday. You should have seen all the crackers watching to see if colored Gyrenes hit the deck before they did. Disappointed the lot of them! We are on our third run up this way of the day.'

All the while Ernie Dobbs chatted with the first Black Marines to come ashore on Guam, he marveled at their salty and good-natured understanding of the fire coming their way. Tim grew up believing that colored were strike-breakers and that was all. Never heard anything else. More and more blacks had moved to Chicago's south side since the beginning of the war and Mayor Kelly was going out his way to accommodate these new Democratic voters and taking no end of heat from the whites in the south side Wards over fair housing –'Fuck 'em! Kelly they take our jobs and homes.'

That was the extent of Cullen's understandings on race relations. He was at war. The Corporal driving the DUKW was a thick voiced man and a solid driver. The roads cut into the hills were narrow, but the Corporal drove them like it was a two lane interstate.

'End of the line, Gentlemen!' roared the Corporal. God Bless you Marines!' The DUKW roared to a stop and the three ammunition carriers helped the two walking wounded men down from the tub of the truck. Tim waved the three men goodbye. Ernie shot the shit with the Corporal some more and tagged up to Tim after a few seconds. ' Good man, that Corporal. All four of them must have balls like King Kong himself to join a service that hates them with every fiber of its being. From Gen. Holcomb on down those men are unwelcome. Big injustice – those men are Marines. Hey I sound like Old Eleanor herself! Tim, I'm going in with you. Capt. Wilson already gave a heads up to your platoon commander, Lt. Ames and a former JASCO Officer Capt. Bob Patterson is still the Company Skipper.'

2nd Lt. Forrest Ames 1st Platoon Leader
Platoon Sgt. Mike Joyce
1st squad
Cpl. Leauregard Clavisill
Pvt. Monty Adams
Pvt. Patrick Collins
Pvt. Mrodig Blagonovich
Pvt. Nick Novich
Pvt. Stanley Paul
Pvt. Onarga Roberts
Pvt. Odell Peotone
Pvt. Souther Willingham
Pfc. Tim Cullen
Pfc. Henry Clay
Pfc. Seymour Tessler
Pfc. Lester Hatfield
PhnM1st Class Henry Brosnan

Harry Brosnan, Hank Clay and Leauregard Clavisill were the only men left from the 1st Squad who landed on W-Day. All the others were buried or evacuate. Jesus. Nine new guys. Snowflakes – pretty clean all working parts and then – nothing – vanished! All in fresh utilities and camouflaged helmet covers – Hollywood Marines – were faceless to Tim Cullen. Doc Brosnan ran up and pumped Tim's hand and arm and pulled the Browning off his shoulder. 'Jesus, man, we went nuts when the Lt. gave us the word that you were Ok, Tim!' Henry Clay just smiled and Low Regard smiled like he had rifled through Tim's sea bag and had just been caught.

Tim could only manage a heads-back nod to one and all and averted his eyes from the new men who were curious and ready to ingratiate themselves with this now legendary phantom member of the squad. 'So, *this* is the Brig Rat.' Declaimed a six foot five inch youngster from Chicago, Patrick Collins. 'I hear you went to Leo. I played at St. Phillip. And I . . . '

Tim and Ernie stared at the big mouth like he had just announced that he had sex with a pet pig and was waiting for applause. 'Where the fuck, did Gen. Turnage go to find a stack of horse-shit this tall to fill the sights of a good man with a Nambu, Tim?' asked Gunny Dobbs 'Who's the he-bull of this sewing circle?'

'Low Clavisill, Gunny. I'm an old shipmate of Cullen's me and Doc and Henry Clay here – the ones with the tired wardrobes.'

'Ernie Dobbs. Well, shipmate it was a short cruise but one with a couple laughs. Good sailing Tim!'

'You too, Ernie. First beer call's on me.'

'Until God farts recall, Tim!'

With that Tim Cullen's career with Capt. Lou Wilson and Gunny Dobbs came to a close and it was time to get re-acclimated to A Company. Tim was starting over. Lt. Buck's shoulder holster containing the Colt .45 Revolver the hog leg boosted the curiosity of the new men and piqued the three survivors as well.

'Major Opley asked me about that Tim and I had no idea that you still had it.'

'Leauregard's a Silver Star winner, Tim. Knocked off three hundred Nips with the .30 caliber, folks say.' Dead-panned Doc Brosnan.

'No shit – way to go Low! Where'd you get the .30?'

'He manned your's Cullen.'

'Honor bright?'

'Honor bright'

'Good to know that you are handy on that weapon. I'm carrying the BAR from now on. Signed out to Neil still? Low?'

'Uh, Yeah. Tim, you left a belt and half.'

'Damn it, Low. Who's Company clerk, now? I'll check with Ed Norris.'

'Ed Norris is a 2nd Lieutenant with Weapons now. Mike Joyce is Platoon Sergeant. Good guy,'

'Who asked you Low?'

'What's your problem Tim I'm just trying to . . . ?'

'No sweat Low - just tired's all. Who's Company clerk?

'Sgt. Masterson.'

'I'm heading over to check in with the Skipper.'

Mind if I tag along, Tim?' Doc Brosnan joined his new pal. Tim was about the last of the Mohicans. Low couldn't find his ass with both hands and Henry was barely maintaining. Frank Dranago and Mike Cloud were both Section 8'd to the beach and probably to a hospital ship. Frank was really off his peach and Mike could not stop pissing himself and barking like a dog. Henry was going the way of the two of them and was one sheet shy of a Section 8. 'Have Masterson sign you to some new utilities and boondockers, your's are about shot.' They followed the road another one hundred feet and came to a cul de sac on the right side where a tent was set up with desk typewriter and filing cabinet, where Sgt Masterson and his clerks took in reports of damaged weapons, fouled 782 gear, and manpower updates.

'Heard you were back, Cullen. Here fill out this on your Browning Heavy – how it was damaged – be specific and not 'battle damage' S'That Steinberg's BAR? Here, set her down. That's your carbine.'

'I want to turn it in, Sarge, and draw the Browning back.'

'Fair enough.'

'You off the .30 cal? Well Weapons is going to handle all that now, anyway. Here sign here and initial here, here, and here. Good to have you back Cullen. The work is plenty and good men are scarce.'

'Capt. Patterson, this Pfc. Tim Cullen who was listed MIA on the 26th.'

'Heard good things about you at your wake, Cullen. Glad you are alright. Capt. Wilson said you did good work for him while you were with the 9th. Pretty rough couple of days. Brosnan here put you in for the Navy Cross for your actions on the 23rd. That was some act of courage.'

'I'm sorry sir. What d you mean?'

'When Lt. Buck was hit, you strapped him on like a tripod and carried him several hundred yards under heavy fire to a Battalion Aid Station according to Brosnan. The papers were sent up the great chain. They are with Major Opley and Col. Stuart now.'

'Col. Stuart? Sir?'

'Col. Hall was relieved and Col. Stuart is 3rd Marines CO. Many changes in nine days, Cullen. I was a JASCO officer and now I'm A Company Skipper. Semper Fi, I got mine. Welcome back, Cullen.'

'Thank you, Sir!'

Down the road Brosnan noticed that Cullen was fuming. 'Hey Tim what's the beef?' Cullen stopped and started again 'Nothing. What did you put me in for, anyway? What the fuck? I got to him because you were down the slope. Shit - fuck that.'

'Look, if hound-fucker Low can merit the Silver Star for sitting behind your weapon . . .'

'Who gives a shit? Look Low stood up all night like every man on our line. He deserves it as much as any one does. Don't make a federal case out of this will you Broz. It's not worth it.'

'Sure, but I just hope that the papers go through.'

'Fuck it.'

You are really becoming the foul-mouthed Catholic youth. A few more years in this man's Corps and you'll be limited to that word.'

'You – Broz – are a sailor. What's with the string bean big-mouth?'

'Oh, Collins? The guy has not given his gums a rest since they came up this hill. I thought Henry was going to put a round in him after five minutes but he just tossed his ration box at him and that kept him quiet for five minutes. Not a bad bunch – typical Marine squad – hillbillies and foreigners.'

In a matter of hours, A Company would be moving north and taking the Jap airfield and then into the jungle. The Army 77th Division was moving up and would partner with the 3rd Division on the northern sweep of Guam. Nine new men joined 1st Squad of 1st Platoon Able Company and they would be veterans by this afternoon. They too would know the sound of shots and shells being fired at them. They too would be combat veterans, but they would never really make friends with the men who had live through landing, Chorito Cliff, Bundeschu Ride, the night of Banzai and Fonte Ridge – they had come aboard too late to be friends. There was no rule. That's the way it was.

CHAPTER 48
RED SON SETTING

After beheading Father Duenas and his nephew and several other groveling Chamorros who crossed his path, Lieutenant Ryugo Kato fought with the Mixed Brigade that included the sailors under his command. It was a foolish and drunken mistake on the part of the overall commanders, who should have continued to pound the Marines from the heights above Asan, or lure them into the jungles of the north and tear them up for many months.

This was the folly of the old ways and all Kato needed to do was survive this war and continue the work of the world with its temporary victors. After making a great show of his personal courage and bravado by running out in front of his crazed troops, Kato went down and waited between assaults and then stole his way back to Agana where he had spent the last three days barking at stragglers and stealing as much food and water as he could.

He chose the first battered bungalow on the way into Agana from the Agana Heights Road right near Fort Santa Agueda.

The home had been a shoe repair shop and still retained the stench of many leathers despite the cordite and offal. Kato figured to evade the American's grasp for as long as possible and wait until the battle lust cooled in them as well because they were as rigidly fixated on their moral sensibilities, as the Emperor's troops now rotting all over Asan. Only once a true classless society could be effected world-wide there would be no peace – no brotherhood of man.

He picked up the commands in the distance and sporadic shots at the idiots who needed to loot one more shop before fleeing into the jungles. Kato eased himself into a wardrobe in the center bedroom behind the shop and remained calm and motionless. The Americans would seek out their enemies – like me only deeper into the town or at least this street. Only an idiot or a very wise man would choose this one. And Mr. Kato made first honors at Oberlin and U of C. No dope he. He made out three American voices that got more clear.

'Yo, Tenny! Looka Here - a cobbler's shop! Damn we could a used this old boy a couple days ago before we got the new boondockers. Don't touch nothin' whole town's prolly rigged.'

He heard footsteps – stop – something touched the door. Kato fingered the samurai sword which he would offer as surrender - hilt first and his head bowed – the noise was obviously the barrel of a rifle. The door to the wardrobe opened – A tall Marine in camouflaged helmet leveled an automatic rifle at Kato. Kato bowed his head slightly holding the sword point down - hilt up. The Marine closed the closet door. What was this – a pass? 'Jap Officer. Fuckin' Coward!' were the last words Kato heard before the Browning automatic tore up the pink painted wooden wardrobe and the most devout Communist in the Imperial Japanese Navy.

CHAPTER 49
'I WANT THAT MAN'S GUN, SON!'

Major Lucas Opley deployed two companies around the back of Bundeschu Ridge when Geary Bundeschu's men failed to seize and hold the objective on W-Day, W+ 1 and the husky side of W+ 2. Objective secured. He masterminded a superb defense of 1st Battalion ground though down to less than half strength. Lucas Opley had gotten the boys into the Jap caves and gun positions all around Fonte Ridge and still he felt some cold eyes on the back of his neck.

Col. W. Carvel Hall was relieved of 3rd Marines in an act of monstrous injustice to the man and his leadership. Who else needed to have his head roll for losing most of the men in the Regiment. Hell, Marines are shock troops and supposed to take casualties but after Tarawa all the sob-sisters got out their cry-towels and whined to SecNAV about the slaughter of American boys. Shit they are supposed to get slaughtered. The Japs are using guns.

Well now it was down to the kind of war that Lucas Opley had fought all of his life – a jungle war was coming and he knew

351

every trail and creek in the north part of this island. Shit, he should be commanding this regiment. Well, maybe Jim Stuart will fuck the pup in the next few hours. It was hot and he Lucas Opley loved the tropics. Navy meteorological reports indicated that it would get to up over 110 degrees in the next few days. The Japs were high-tailing it and getting popped at by Navy fighters and bombers as well as naval gunfire. Hot work and they would be out of water until they hit the streams around Dededo Tiyan and Barrigarda. The dog-faces of the 305th Infantry of the 77th Division would be on our right and take Barrigarda. We would hit Tiyan Airfield and the little town of San Antonio and sweep north. My God this place is beautiful!

Cullen had Buck's Colt. No use to that feather-merchant; where did he pick it up? Back on the line before the counterattacks he had told me 'Can't say.' Did he pick up the gun later or was the little fucker lying and had it all this time? Well, I'll just take a see so for myself. I want that damn Colt.

Major Opley, Capt. Crawford , Chaplain Krieg, and the rest of the Battalion staff made a water inspection of the three line companies and the Weapons Company. Water had been a bitch and a half for the first three days of the invasion and getting it up those cliffs nothing short of a miracle. Now, Major Opley had secured several trucks to carry fresh water and had folded Service troops into this operation. Gunga Din all over. In Inja's sunny Clime, where I used to spend me time! Lot's of new men. Opley was expansive and salty!

'Afternoon, men! Two canteens and get plenty into you before we push off. How's your killer's, Bob? Ready to make some Nip widows? Yeah me too! Loosen those leggings, Boot, you got nothing but time right now. *Hey,* I do *not* want to see any of those *new men* making Havelocks with the camo covers. We're *Marines* not the god damn Foreign Legion! *You,* Private, front and center! What's your name?

The tall big mouth from St. Phillip High School in Chicago who had gotten wise with Cullen earlier had cut the extra cloth

on the helmet cover so that it would cover the back of his neck
– not so much because the sun beat down on him but because he
had seen a photo of a Marine in *Look*- sitting on a dud 16" shell
and cleaning his boondockers and thought that *this is the image I
want to project to the world!* The fact of matter -notwithstanding-
that he had not heard a shot fired in anger and that every
survivor of the slaughters at Asan, Chorito, Bundeschu & etc.
had bowed to the will of the Corps Commander General Roy
Geiger and had gone into this combat without the distinctive
helmet covers and continued to do so.

'*You* a *Hollywood Marine*. Private? Your Name again!'

'Pvt. Patrick Collins 5649864, Sir.'

'How tall are you?'

'6'5" Major!'

' Well, son, I can tell - from way down here - that your eyes
are brown.'

'They're Blue Sir, begging the Major's pardon, Sir!'

'They are deep *asshole brown* because YOU are full of shit,
Son! Square away that cover, pronto! I do not want to see *any
replacement* remove those covers, Keep them on new men - nor
do I want to see any alterations to the helmet cover whatsoever!
The men who waded into fire while you wear taking fashion
tips from *Look* over on Saipan or aboard ship 'til today, shall be
distinguished by coverless helmets. That is your badge of honor
Marines. Any replacement – Officer or Enlisted man found
with coverless helmets will stand tall before ME – prior to HIS
summary execution. Got that Brown eyes? *Comprende?*'

'Aye, aye Sir!'

'Disappear Brown eyes. Now here are Marines. If you
new men want to get through this war stay close to Cullen,
Clavisill and Henry Clay, here. Doc Brosnan good thorough
recommendation. I want to see you, Doc. Cullen, how's the
9th?'

'They ain't the 3rd Major but they'll do.'

'I want to speak with you when I finish my tour here, Don't disappear –again. Hey, Montgomery . . .' and on he greeted the Battalion for the next half hour.'

Tim changed into new utilities and drew his chit for possession of the BAR from the Company Clerk. He took a quick whore's bath using his helmet and had Doc Brosnan change the dressing on his leg wound. It felt good to toss the ragged and bloody mess that had been his uniform and standard dress since leaving LST-448. His helmet, still chalked with his 782 numbers was dented but usable and the new utilities were stiff, but clean – new skivvies on underneath as well for the exacting reader.

Cullen laced up his leggings loosely and tossed his old webbing gear into the heap with his old utilities. He lit up a Chesterfield and sat back to take in the activities of the new men grab-ass-ing and joshing with the bean-pole big mouth who had yet to square away the Havelock look of his helmet. Didn't this clown think that Maj. Opley would land on him? Should be a great second act.

Tim took his cleaning kit from the musset bag on his new harness and went to work on the Browning. First he pulled out his blanket and folded it in thirds leaving about ten full inches of green cloth as a service area and the thick padding as a rest for the weapon. Then he placed his swabs, ramrods and oils on the service area and began the process of taking the weapon apart as he had done so many times with Lt. Buck giving the standard lecture while standing over Tim during the demonstrations. Tim moved no less quickly through the process as he had aboard ship and the formerly kid-like replacements snapped to at his example to them.

Soon he had an audience of every one but Patrick Collins who was disconcerted at losing his audience for his mockery of Maj. Opley. The new men began to ask questions about servicing the weapon in combat and Tim told them about the best method for un-jamming rounds and clearing the action.

Soon the bean-pole blocked Cullen's sunlight. 'How do you get the cam to get back in there without losing a thumb?' It was a good question as the spring on the Browning was notoriously unforgiving.

'Take this –cam and sort of drop it in here.'

The bean-pole reached down and picked up the cam piece without being asked. 'Just drop it in you say?

'Yes.'

'Like this?' and Standing to his fullest height and holding the tiny steel piece above his eyes, Collins dropped the cam and it bounced off the weapon and into the dirt. No one laughed but Collins who was killing himself with laughter. Tim Cullen grabbed the tall boy by his entire male reproductive package and squeezed while pulling the giant boy down to the work space.

'That is exactly what you do. You drop it. Then you *work* the mechanism to see if it will not *obstruct* the bolt, spring and receiver – like *this*.' And Cullen continued the torturous yanking and twisting of the vulnerable funnyman for what seemed an eternity and much to the delight of Collins' fickle audience and ultimately twisted and shoved the boy into a puking heap.

'Get that cover squared away,' quietly suggested Tim who continued to clean the Browning after he found, cleaned, oiled and DROPPED the cam piece into its proper place and worked the receiver and bolt as he had instructed.

Pat Collins finished vomiting and immediately began to roll the excess cloth of the helmet cover and attached it according to regulations. Henry Clay sat next to Tim when the other 'snowflakes' disappeared. 'Smart and smart ass. There is a big difference. Tim, I am sorry about Wat and Sal. I am so lonely now, because Wat was the best string musician we had and I miss singing with him. Can I be your assistant BAR man, Tim?'

'No, I'd rather you did not Henry. I like you too much and I want some old friends around - like you. Besides, you are one of the best marksmen in the Company. We need you at the trail position to cover our backs going into the jungle and all, Henry. Really, I'll pick one of the new boys. But we're Pals, Henry, don't ever not believe that. Here, want some gum?'

'Cullen gave Henry a pack of Black Jack licorice flavored gum that Tim's sisters sent to him. He always kept the Black Jack for himself but gave away the Wrigley's and his chocolate bars – Tim was partial to some candy from Chicago called Mary Janes. Henry had the look of the lost - 'the thousand yard stare' they called it and needed to be gentled along. Low was pretty busy with his new found rank and notoriety and steered clear of Tim. Cullen didn't care about the credit and Low was on the line all night firing away – he laughed when he remembered just how Sal had been given the BAR by Ed Norris when poor Dead-eye Low couldn't hit anything with the heavy automatic rifle – Low Regard killer machine gunner of Guam! Well God Bless Him. Really.

'Cullen, glad to have you back, Brig Rat! Come with me.'

Major Opley, sans his retinue of staff officers, returned to A Company staging area like a ghost on his own property. Pvt. Collins stupidly pointed to his helmet and the Major nodded faux approval.

'Cullen, I asked you for the whereabouts of Lt. Buck's personal property and you said that you did not know, is that right?'

'No, Sir. I said that I couldn't say. I had the gun under my utility shirt the whole time, sir.'

'Well that's the truth – I guess. Here's another truth. I want you to hand that weapon over to me. I want that man's gun, son. It does no other mortal good to you or anyone else. Here I'll take the piece.'

'No, Sir. I made a vow to Lt. Buck that I would return the gun to his folks back in Texas and I will do that, Sir.'

'You are not real clear about some things. You have not accounted for leaving your post while it was under attack. Cpl. Clavisill needed to take over the operation of your heavy weapon and for that action above the call of his duty he is awarded the Silver Star for knocking out Jap mortars. Where you were at that time is uncertain.'

'Sir, my weapon was out of commission – the cooling jacket was shot up and the barrel overheated and could not be fired. I picked by the BAR after killing two Japs. I attacked the mortar position with the Browning.'

'Now, that is just sad. You trying to grab credit away from a brave man?'

No, sir. I do not want any credit.'

'You are not getting any. Brosnan wrote you up for the Navy Cross *but no officer confirmed* some action of yours that Brosnan described. Lt. Gallo was evacuated and all other officers in A Company are dead. Now, turnover the Colt and we can start all over again. Look we jump off soon Cullen and I want that Colt for the push you understand? I want that man's gun.'

'Sir, bring me up on charges. I will turn over the weapon to Col. Stuart at regiment which is SOP, after this operation. I do not want the damn thing, but I give it to no one and I turn it over to no one else, Sir.'

'Anything *can* and *does* happen in combat. Dismiss-ed.'

CHAPTER 50
THE DENTIST SWINGS SOUTH

When he emerged from the cellar near Plaza de Espana – about a quarter of mile south of where Lieutenant Kato took half a magazine from a BAR – Ted made enough hip patter to convince the four Marines from the 3rd Battalion, 3rd Marines that not only was He a Hep Cat but good American and he accompanied the boys on the patrol and pointed out where Japanese critically wounded might be housed and where Korean and forced labor Chamorros might be and saved several dozen lives.

In the one hour it took for the Battalion to liberate Guam's capitol, Ted Tanaka had a fan club of about one hundred Marines who would just as gladly have pumped him full of holes two hours before. Ted was taken to Major Royal Bastian who led the liberation and succeeded in command of 3rd Battalion on the death of Lt. Col Houser on July 24th. Ted was offered a set of Marine Utilities that at first he demurred, but was convinced to wear them. 'I just stripped of the enemy uniform, Major, I feel safer in civvies.'

The Major shook his - 'Your heritage is going to do you no end of grief until we sort things out better on this island. Doctor, I insist that you don the Snuffy garb until that time and I will post two Marines – Thompson and Perner – as your escorts.' Pfc. Ray Thompson and Pfc. Judge Perner had been with Major Bastian since Bougainville and he trusted both men to take good care of the long suffering dentist.

'You men will need to hike it back to regiment with my orders re-assigning you both to help Dr. Tanaka find his wife and friends. Doctor, you have performed a wonderful service to your country today and I will make note of your contribution to the Battalion in today's liberation. Quite frankly Doctor, I don't know how you and your people managed.'

'The people of this beautiful place I call home, major, are the most loyal and brave Americans you will find. Please, make sure your boys afford them every courtesy and kindness. You have no idea what these wonderful and kind people have endured. Keep an eye out for a Japanese naval office by the name of Kato. He is a monster. Keep him alive. He needs to answer for many crimes done to these people Major. God bless you!'

'Let's roll Doc!'

'I am at your command, Your Honor!'

'It's my name Doc not my title – my name is Judge.'

'If it please the court. . '

'Another smart ass! You have a cousin name of Bob Keegan? Andale!'

The Dr. Tanaka patrol would return these men to the Asan landing beaches where Ray Thompson hitched a ride with and Army Supply Company heading in the direction of Santa Rita and from there the three man patrol would follow the men of the U.S.Army 77th Division as it swept north. His two marching companions gave him a little time to himself in between what seemed to Ted interminable questions about Hollywood the stars and his wife and what roles she played and with whom. Neither, young man had any idea of who Cookie Vanecko had

360

been as she was one of countless pretty and talented girls who flocked to Hollywood.

Ted thought back to the day that they met in an Oyster bar outside of San Francisco where Kara was auditioning for a radio role on one of KQW's dramas - the local CBS station. Kara had scooped the role of Dottie Manfred a teenager who helped break spy-rings and smash rackets in Frisco. She was fumbling with an unshucked oyster and the nimble fingers of the bow tied Brooks Brothers knock-out handsome Oriental plucked the thick sea-freak from her place at the bar and delicately opened its shell with his pen-knife. 'They have a shucker but he's powdering his nose or something, allow me.' Kara was hooked.

'You are pretty slick with the digits my friend. I have never eaten one of these before. What do I do - spear it?'

'Slurp it. Terrible word to use on a first meeting, please forgive me but that is the only appropriate measure,'

'Do a Here's How for me, while you?'

Ted delicately added hot sauce a squeeze of lemon and just the tip of a shrimp fork of house horseradish and held the natural plate of flesh and juice to this exquisite girl's red lips and tipped the contents on to her delicate tongue and watched her eyes close to the sensation of cold sea matter and earth's condiments splashing her palate. Ted was hooked. He melted into the girl's mouth with the shucked oyster meat and all the spice that he applied to his first overture to the woman of his soul . . . and his hiking pal Ray shattered the reverie with . . .

' Hey Doc what's Errol Flynn like is he as big a snatch hound as the papers make out? He a souse? How about Orson Welles? Judge says he's a fairy.'

'Okay again, one last time. When I came to Guam, you guys were ten or eleven years old, remember? So - let's see . . . No, never met Orson Welles or heard of him until he pulled that stunt back in '41 and then the Japs – rather my cousins came. Errol Flynn you will be sad to hear is not, nor was he as much of the hot button as you guys think he is. The guy I knew was a pretty conventional and very nice guy. He was never a pig and never talked up any conquests that he might have had; you see Hollywood's like anywhere else in the world. The studio made him an Irishman – he's not. In fact he can't stand the Irish and only plays at it – ever see him do a movie with Cagney, Tracey, or O'Brien? See - feelings mutual. Spencer Tracey can put it away, Cagney's a tea totaler – almost - and Pat O'Brien can handle his booze. Bing Crosby is a sponge but only periodic. He and I are from the same town and school and we used to be pals. He got invisible when Kara and I hooked up. I was his pet Jap I guess. Great guy though; he helped Kara get in films and he and I partnered on some jazz recordings. I was the dough and he was 'the Know.' His brother, Bob, is a wonderful guy – the band leader. That's enough boys. The next guy to ask a Movie Star question for next two hours gets his brown rotting choppers looked at.'

The three new pals, two eighteen year old kids from Hamburg, Kentucky and Persimmon , Wyoming and a Japanese American dentist/record producer/beachcomber/Hep-cat sat down on crates of rations and waited for the truck to take them down to Santa Rita and from there northwest to Manengon.

The problem was that Kara, Imelda and Betty were already in Santa Rita and this would not become evident until Doc got all the way up to Manengon and was appalled to witness the suffering and starvation of his friends and neighbors. Kara, Imelda and the still pole-axed little girl ducked and dodged Japanese troop movements and blended in with the Chamorros being routed to the camps at Yona, but during a strafing by an American Hellcat that made a pass too soon and killed about fourteen women, old men and babies before realizing that they were not a troop concentration, fled into the jungle at a creek crossing. From there the three women worked their way south and due east and found shelter in an abandoned house that had been hit by a bomb. Though unlivable by normal standards the shelter was more than adequate for people who had slept in the jungle for days.

Betty was beginning to come out of her stupor after a week of exhausting travel and near death encounters with escaping Japanese forces. On the morning of July 29th, Betty woke up and made her way into the bushes for a bowel movement. While completing that call, she heard men moving from the east and the sound of vehicles further off. She froze with terror believing it to be more Japanese. The girl stayed put.

Imelda and Kara also heard the sounds and shocked themselves awake to find the damaged girl missing. 'Stay Immy. She might have gone to the John is all, I'll take a look for her, but for God's sake stay put.'

Kara crawled through the tall grass that had shot up from what had once been a well manicured lawn and crept like a Comanche to the edge of the cover, There she found the immobilized girl who had both hands up making ready to surrender to whoever was making their way toward them. Kara strained her senses and listened with every fiber of her being. Americans! Kara sang 'God Bless America . . . Land that I Love . . . Stand beside her and guide her to.

'Do *not* move! We will come to you. We are American Army!'

'I am Mrs. Ta . . . Vanecko! I am a redhead! Do not shoot us there is a mother in the bombed out house. I am with a fifteen year old girl was raped by Jap sailors. Do not frighten this little , , ,

'Shut the fuck up lady and wait until we come to you! Make no move. '

A Line of ready olive-drab tall and tanned soldiers of the 305th Infantry Regiment had been ordered by General Geiger to sweep all of the areas south of the island and clean out any pockets – and there were plenty – of organized resistance. This group had just slaughtered eight Japanese in Chamorro garb only a half a mile east of this former home. Ten of these soldiers who had fought along side of the 4th Marines for the past week were on their own in the Patrol Zone, as the southern districts of Guam were now designated.

A tall staff sergeant and a radio man approached the brush where Betty, still with her hands raised in submission and Kara crouched. 'Come up slowly ladies. Relax. I'm Jack Hurley - Dog Company 1st Battalion 305th Infantry, United States Army we will take good care of you. Lady, call out your friend while my men set up around the building. Gimme the phone, Saattoff! Bridger 9 er; Bridger 9er; this is Pattycake 5. we are at grid 90 Fox Tango two miles south of Santa Rita – Over.' As the phone was jammed to Hurley's ear the reply was inaudible – 'That is correct. We need medics and a stretcher bearer - path clear and no mines. Follow grid pattern Mike – Over.'

'Coleman, Burnet, Zell and Capriotti stay with the ladies and stay sharp.' Hurley motioned his line of men forward to the north and disappeared. Imelda slowly made her way and clutched her daughter who was *finally* safe and kissed her tough beautiful friend who kept her from despair. ' In Nomine Patris, et Filius , et Spirit Sanctus . . ., Imelda intoned like she had done so many times many, many ,many, - well, it seemed like a long time ago.

CHAPTER 51
IT WOULD GO INTO THE FORGE
AND BACK TO WILD BILL

Gov. Cole Stevenson had Rope Buck on his mind all summer long. The U.S. Supreme Court decided *Smith vs. Allwright* in April 'that the exclusion of Negroes from voting in a Democratic primary to select nominees for a general election -- although, by resolution of a state convention of the party, its membership was limited to white citizens -- was State action in violation of the Fifteenth Amendment.' Well Buuuuuulllshit! Calculating Coke knew that the primary elections with Negro votes going toward FDR's fourth term was going to ensure that the crippled Knickerbocker and his Commie wife would be applying even more pressure on the Republic of Texas than they had already gotten away with since the Japs attacked. It was nothing short of a dictatorship and a sharp Texian like Rope Buck needed to be steered away from his New Deal pal Lyndon.

Gas rationing was an affront of the Texas economy – but the big threat lay in the stink organized labor will make after this war. Getting State Reps like Rope Buck to see their way to keeping the lid on labor was the key. The strain on the State, when millions of boys came home would be heartache on a daily basis and those boys would want work. Gov. Stevenson put in a call to Rope.

No answer. Roper Buck was still numb from the telegram and the thoughtful letter from Lyndon. His boy was dead. No Buck would carry on the name. Roper Buck waited and stalled before he would return the Governor's call. Once the Old family Colt could be returned from Guam and melted down by a huge fire and beaten into a blue steel plate and placed on the Grave of Wild Bill Longley then and only then could Roper Buck come to grips with battle for the soul for Texas.

CHAPTER 52
THE AGANA PAGO – ROAD"
'ORDERS, MAJOR!'

The reconstituted 3dr Marines were assigned to take the strategic Agana Pago Road and Tiyan Airfield. The road ran north and southwest and would be vital to the Army 77th Division on its march to Yiga, while the 3rd Marine Division would sweep northeast of the island to Ritidian Point. They took Ordot and smoothly moved up their timetable.

Hector Cruz and his Chamorro Combat Patrol working with the Navy engineers at Tumon Bay had turned over a vital cache of maps and charts that outlined the minefields of the Japanese Airfield at Tiyan – the navy intelligence teams were still translating the Charts when the 3rd Marines stepped off.

After his rather disturbing encounter with Major Opley, Tim Cullen tried to understand why the man who had been so good to him since Bougainville was now so frightening and over the stupid pistol of a dead man. When they had spoken Tim felt that if the circumstances presented themselves, Major Lucas Opley would not be above seeing Tim dead.

Gangsters back home killed over tiny slights, like Spats Grogan – Spat was a homicidal moron who worked briefly for Mr. O'Donnell and was now on Death Row in Joliet for stabbing to death a painter on his lunch break in the Point in Bar at Canal and Archer for not knowing the exact date of Mother's Day. Spats tried to use O'Donnell's name as drag with the cops who grabbed him and a call was placed to O'Donnell to see if he knew the guy – he said he knew a Spats. When the details of the murder were relayed to Spike he replied, 'No – Nope. Wrong Spats Grogan. I know a Spats Grogan who loves his mother. This guy is not that man. See that he cooks. Make sure that our *revered and learned* Cook County States Attorney knows that this would be a capital offense. Glad to help, Tubbo!'

Right and wrong had nothing to do with life and death. Tim was here because he joined to fight the Japs. As a result, he came to make a promise to a man he respected and liked. Another man that Tim *had* respected and liked wanted to see that Tim's word would be no good. And, he would have Japs shooting at him as well.

The Colt was strapped over his new green undershirt and buttoned inside his new utilities. The temperatures were exceeding 110o but at least they were getting water. The ground here was a bit more level and the Piper Cub artillery spotter planes flying out of Orote were giving them good fixes on Jap movements and fixed positions. They needed to secure the Agana-Pago Road for the Army units and give the engineers the ability to widen the lanes and get more tanks and trucks up that road to the north. As it stood prior to jumping off the 77th Division's 307th would move up and to the right of the 3rd Marines and to their right the 305th now completing its sweep of the south with the 1st Marine Provisional Brigade would take the mountains around Barrigarda. They were well short of water and it was up to the 3rd Marines to secure the road to get the water and supplies to the 77th Division. All they needed to do was keep the retreating Japanese on the run.

105 and 155 millimeter artillery were tearing up the woods and the hills before them; naval aircraft had been flying sorties deep into the North of the island. It was hot and noisy and Tim Cullen tried to untangle the net of Major Opley's demands upon him to turn over the Colt. Lt Ames was out in front with Sgt. Joyce, a thick-set middle-weight boxer with a scar on his upper lip and ten years of service to Corps. Joyce had joined the 3rd after Bougainville, but had served with the Raiders on Midway and on Guadalcanal.

Joyce was chewing out the new radioman about some tubes that were corroded and called up on the radio but found that it was dead. The new man was sent to the rear with the set and the look of a man who knew that his days as Pfc. were to be numbered. 'You fuck up! Stay with the clerks. Clavisill, Paul, Roberts! You two twenty yards apart on my go! Willingham – you're platoon runner! Radio's FUCKED UP! Then it's Cullen, Clay, Collins – twenty yards; Novich, Adams, Blagonovich, You fuckers cousins? Peotone, Tessler, Hatfield – Doc Brosnan twenty behind center and then 2nd squad. Check Magazines and clear actions. Lieutenant?'

Lt. Ames looked at his watch – held up both arms – lowered both slowly – pointing forward. After two hundred yards, the line paused as instructed and crouched. Willingham ran to the rear and reported to Company – Dashed back and the process began again. They passed many dead Japanese but never without a jab or a solid kick at their wounds even though some were bloated and in the advanced stages of decay. They passed destroyed Toyota trucks and light tanks two hundred yards to their left was the Tiyan airfield and the smoking remnants of scores of Japanese planes hollowed out buildings and blasted revetments. 2nd Battalion was approaching the right side of the field when six explosions went off almost simultaneously stopping the progress on the left. Another one hundred yards beyond the point men, Leauregard Clavisill, Onarga Roberts and Stanley Paul, was the edge of the Agana-Pago Road. Able Company would cross the roads and take to the woods on its far side. Nothing. Not a round fired on them. To their left, 2nd Battalion was halted by the minefield planned and laid by the Japanese engineer whom Hector Torres executed in his capacity as Chamorro Combat Patrol Leader. Leauregard Halted the Advance and pulled his bayonet from his field pack and began probing the ground with it while his two flank men stood at the ready. For new boys they looked sharp and salty. Leau had dug around something and was marking his buried treasure with a stake. He waved up an advance to the road itself. Nothing.

Leauregard – the butt of so many jokes due to the persistent jaundice contracted on Efate and further yellowed by malaria at Bougainville was now like Gary Cooper. He exuded a combat confidence born of withstanding punishment understood by only Tim, Henry, Doc, and Mike Joyce. Leauregard had also dispatched some of the punishers to the afterlife. Now he was the tip of the spear and in command of the moment. Mike Joyce tapped Cullen on the back of the helmet. "Let's take a stroll. The Browning is just the ticket. Come on, Collins learn the trade.'

The three men joined Low and his two scouts on the road itself and set up a defensive posture on both sides of it. When Tim had refused Henry Clay as his assistant, Cullen tapped Pat Collins; he was big and he could carry an extra bandolier of magazines. Tim and Joyce moved to the north side of the road and checked the tree line and brush, nothing. To their rear left more Marines were setting off mines and they could hear cries for Corpsmen and stretcher bearers. Ist Battalion should be getting some as well but where? And how? Where and How Much?

The Agana - Pago Road cut northwest from Tiyan Airfield to the village of San Antonio and then North to Barrigada. The 3rd Marines were to hold the road for the 307th who now moving up for the link with 3ʳᵈ Marine Division. 1ˢᵗ Battalion would leave San Antonio to the dog-faces to liberate. Thus far the 1st Battalion had not so much as liberated lean-to let alone a village or town, Willingham crossed to the road and Mike Joyce waved up the balance of 1ˢᵗ Platoon.

'Sarge, orders from Division. Hold and secure road; no vehicles should be allowed on or near the road. We are to challenge and then fire on any and all vehicles. Japs have cars and trucks hid for a breakout north. Only tanks are to be sent up this way, From General Turnage. We move off to the north at 0830. Til then we effect night defenses. No vehicles. On the road or the approaches. '

'Cullen you and Collins drop back to where Low stacked that mine until the engineers get up here. I'll have you relieved in two hours and then you can get in some sack drill –that's Cullen, numb nuts, you draw post for another four three, until relieved. Low set up your defenses for the first round and 2nd squad the rest 'til daybreak. Lt. Ames, Sir all points taken and defenses effected. Shove off Cullen.'

The two Chicagoans carefully retraced their steps back two hundred yards and stood watch. Cullen watched his perimeter south and Collins to the east toward the airfield. Collins put a Camel in his mouth and pulled his Zippo, Cullen signaled – No. 'You are working.'

"How did I do today, Tim?

'Cullen, Jagoff, and keep your eyes open.'

'I mean did I do Okay?'

'You walked like you were born to it.'

'I'm sorry if we got off on the wrong foot. . .'

'What's with we? Just do your job.'

As darkness elbowed its way onto the end of July, the sound of a fast moving vehicle put Cullen at the ready. It was a jeep with four men. Major Opley was driving. When the jeep approached to within one hundred feet, Tim signaled an emphatic HALT with hand signals. When the jeep slowed but still maintained its route, Cullen fired a burst of four into the ground well ahead of the jeep.

The startled vehicle bolted to a full stop but not, it seemed, before the Battalion commander leapt from it with his carbine. 'You Shit Stuffed Asshole!'

Tim leveled the weapon menacingly and shouted ' Halt !'

'Cullen You are well and truly fucked now! I'll have you shot for mutiny!'

' Sir, I am following the orders of the Divisional Commander – Halt and fire on any approaching vehicle.'

'Sir, those were our orders give . . .'

'Shut that hatch, Private. You are correct. Crawford drive the jeep back to Battalion and return. '

'Aye, aye, sir! And the jeep sped back from whence it came. Major Opley peeled off to the left of Cullen towards A company command. No more was said of the matter.

Maj. Opley understood. He would recommend that tomorrow's sweep of the jungle to the immediate right of the north folk of the road be preceded by a good BAR man and his assistant. The Japs ARE there and that is no shit for certain.

Chapter 53
The Guam Combat Patrol's First Ambush

Able Company Skipper Bob Patterson was well pleased with the fact that his men – most of them replacements from the pool on Saipan – had executed the advance like veterans. Without losing a man, the Company had secured the vital road that would effect the link up between the 3rd Division and the Army 77th Division. The rod ran north through the village of San Antonio and on to the larger town of Barrigada but there was a good quarter mile deep of jungle to the right of the road threatening the half mile into San Antonio and Major Lucas Opley had stomped through most of it four years before with Billy Higgins and twenty other peace-time Marines in order to develop a handbook for fighting in the tropics.

There were tiny creeks, varieties of fruit trees and tall thick undergrowth tailor made for ambush. A good man with a Browning Automatic Rifle and his assistant would be an effective means of rousing such an ambush well-before a more numerous body of scouts could find themselves enfiladed. Bob

Patterson was skeptical, but Major Opley commanded and he had written the manual on these jungle sweeps. 'I want Cullen from 1st Platoon to do the job he was an outstanding breaker of trails on Bougainville and we will be sure that his weapon won't jam. The kid walks like a ballerina as thick as he is – Bob, keep the next fire team back about twenty yards with intervals of about ten feet. Noise discipline is a must so keep each member within sight for hand signals. I want your 1st Platoon out wide before 2nd Platoon makes their move from the road. Baker and Charley Companies will maintain the road and the left. We need this patch cleaned out Bob. Keep your communications team on the edge with you. I will have Weapons form the pivot at the crotch of the road going into San Antonio with the mortar teams set up for any necessary fire. Use runners from the squads to the communicators. No noise in the salad. Got it Bob? These maps and grids are very accurate for this sector. Up north it will be a little more dicey; so, if you need to call in 60 & 80s from the mortar section you can make book on where they'll drop. Call in your platoon and squad leaders and give them the word.'

Major Opley did his 'touch of Harry in the night' for the boys at breakfast – the night had been brutally hot and humid, but there had been no probing or raids by the Japanese. Some of the men got in a restful few minutes here and there, but most did not.

'Steak and eggs – better yet Marines. Ever have caribou? Caribou calf is about as tasty a cut of meat as you'll ever set your choppers to. When this sweep is over I will personally butcher a couple of fat little critters and we'll have a good meal. Corporal Clavisill, wonder if they're any things akin to mud-bugs here abouts. With all the rice paddies we've crossed it stands to reason. Crawdad boil son! Cullen, you steel eye-eyed assassin. Boys, follow this man's steps in the salad. He knows how to cut trail. Doc, no business yesterday; Let's keep it that way. Henry

Clay – how's University of Kentucky lookin' this fall? Don't answer that! Henry Clay, yes sir.'

He stood among the boys who trusted and admired his understanding of the ground pounder. He had been a Snuffy. This was no ring-knocker. This was a Marine of legend.

'Marines, do not take any chances in there. Stop! Peel them eyes before you move on. It is thicker in there than a Notre Dame transfer student at Purdue. I am imagine that it's thicker than it was four years ago. The Japs are not the best jungle fighters. They do not understand noise discipline. They are tired and starving and beat to shit, but do not for minute think that they will throw their hands up. Do not give them targets. Use cover. Use Quiet and Use a lot of lead. Toss grenades in there – easy tosses. Don't try to pitch like Orval Grove or you'll have it back in your laps. See, some Japs – gently toss it into them. Go clear them trees. Jump off in twenty.'

Tim Cullen had cleaned and manipulated the action of the Browning twice this morning. He was down to sixteen round in the magazine he used yesterday and replaced it handing the magazine to Collins.

'Take *every round* out and add *four more* and reload this mag – *don't* fuck around. Do as I say. Stay back and right of me. Do not let me catch you looking left – I'll have that covered. Keep your left eye on my hand at all times and if twitches – you stop and squat behind what ever cover there is. Collins, I have done this before. Do not think. Do *not alter the script.* Let's go.'

Waiting two hundred yards into the thick jungle were ten Japanese survivors of the Fonte Ridge battles, including three mortar men – ammunition bearers. These three men helped kill Sal and were pursued by A Company's point man. They now were armed with Arisaka rifles and one assisted a Nambu light machine gunner, loading the banana shaped clips of 7.6 ammunition. They were ragged and starving and well concealed. They were the first line of general Obata's defense

375

of the north of Guam and poised to kill Americans trying to secure the road to San Antonio.

They had heard the Americans the night before and remained in their positions dug-in deep one and two man fighting holes and covered with branches and fronds of palm. They could feel the approach of the Americans in their shrunken bellies and thorough the thick coatings of hunger and thirst that layered their tongues, but more so they could smell the Hershey's cocoa that Collins had spilled over the front of his blouse and the wad of minty Wrigley's gum that he played with over and over with his well-nutritioned tongue. Where were they?

Finally, a soft stepping short man eased between the narrow gap of the two wild lemon trees. The assistant gunner started when he recognized the squatty Marine who had chased him and his two comrades from the woods below Bundeschu Ridge. The gunner's helper signaled his two friends noiselessly – 'See HIM? That's HIM! KILL THE FUCKER!' The Nambu gunner slowly applied pressure to the trigger with his right forefinger when it exploded into bloody shards of bone and tissue and felt the pounding of seven other hammer-like blows from his buttocks to his head. Jungle ground and timber and human flesh souped up into the humid and thick atmosphere as .30 caliber, .45 caliber and 12 gauge rounds eviscerated the bodies of the survivors of Fonte Ridge from the Imperial Japanese Army's 48th Mixed Brigade – China veterans and the first line of General Obata's northern defensive line. Cullen and Collins never fired a round. But they heard an Asaiatic voice 'Yippee! Buck Jones to the rescue! Not a Jap left Marines!' And then a distinctly New England voice, 'Ensign Campbell, Navy Engineers with Guam Fighters, These boys saved your asses, Gyrenes.

Tim's heart was still where his Adam's apple should have been and he quietly cursed himself for being so slow on the draw. The navy ensign was outfitted like a Marine in the same herringbone twill but USN and no service emblem stenciled on the left breast pocket. He was wearing one of the new Raider caps that would soon become standard under helmet covers. Thanks be to God. Tim hated the helmet except when mortar rounds were popping.

'Pfc. Cullen, A 1st of the 3rd, Sir. Jesus, we were right on them. This is Pvt. Collins.' Tim turned and noticed that the over tall boy was white as ghost, but he had not pissed himself nor had he left Tim's side. Good man!

'Company's sweeping this section, Sir!'

'These boys have done just that. This is Hector Torres – Leader of the Guam Patrol.'

'Hector, you saved my life! How did you boys get in here?'

'We live here and they don't.'

'Who yelled the Buck Jones?'

'That was me.'

'I loved Buck Jones. You know about him?'

'The greatest cowboy in the movies! He died saving people in Boston! Ensign Campbell told me.'

'Here, have a Chesterfield.'

'I don't smoke and neither do my boys. Got any gum?'

'Here's a pack of Black Jack.'

By now all of A Company had come through the jungle to scene of the massacred Japanese ambushers. Ensign Campbell filled in Capt. Paterson in on the activities of the Guam Combat Patrol and their coup in turning over the maps of the minefields round Tiyan Airfield. A Company had secured this jungle without firing a shot thanks to Hector Torres, who sat on the ground with Tim Cullen and Pat Collins and telling them about the occupation and their escapes and adventures. All of the Guam Patrolmen were decked out in Navy issue dungarees and Raider caps, but a couple of the younger boys wore steel helmets. All of the Patrol got familiar with the 3rd Marines and swapped tales of combat with Leauregard and Henry Clay. To their credit, none of the replacements offered so much as a raised upper lip about combat. Pat Collins was the only one who came close to being a combat veteran and each man knew the tale of the slaughter endured by their *four* betters.

It took only four hours to clear this jungle and Able Company enjoyed some ass in the grass with the Patrol. At 1500 hours the first elements of the Army's 307th Infantry arrived and relieved the 1st Battalion, 3rd Marines of their duties on the Agana – Pago Road. Able Company joined the other three Companies of the 1st Battalion for their next operation to the north. It would be no cake-walk and the Guam Combat Patrol was headed to Manengon to look up family and then hunt down the men who made them suffer in the south of the island.

Chapter 54
Back From Manengon

Ted Tanaka was ecstatic with joy at learning that his love and meaning, Kara, was safe and returned to Agana with Juan's girls. Juan and little Tog had not been heard from since before the landings – God keep them safe. His two body guards, Judge Perner and Ray Thompson had extracted every lurid and hot Hollywood yarn in Ted's memory and he treated the boys with a few fabricated tales of spurned overtures from Jean Harlow, Gloria Swanson, and Billie Burke prior to his meeting with Kara Vanecko the only woman on this unhappy planet that would ever mean anything to him.

The delighted teenagers had a trove of tales to tell their girlfriends back Stateside and would bore their children and grandchildren rigid with their repetitions well into the 21st Century. As both good men survived this war, and went on to build America's standard of living when mustered out of the service in two years time. The three men hitched a ride back to Asan beachhead with an Army DUKW returning to Orote and from there they would hike and hitch their way back to 3ʳᵈ Marine Division area at Asan.

The suffering of the Chamorros at Manengon and the surrounding concentration camps was beyond Ted Tanaka's understanding. He was of their blood, but not of the will that could operate so coldly and brutally upon a generous and loving people. The lines of brutalized friends and neighbors, who bore him no ill-will, welcomed his sight once again. The Japanese woman who had married the Navy man Mrs. Estherhausy and operated the drug store in Agana had been beheaded by a Japanese Naval Officer for objecting to his execution of three women and two little - little girls ages three and four for hiding fruit? My God what code do they live by? Teenagers were discovered by troops of 305ᵗʰ Infantry murdered at Fena Cave with hand grenades by Japanese soldiers and not mention the scores and scores of elderly people who would die in the next few days due to starvation and exposure. Their poor old limbs shaking uncontrollably as they gasped out their last minutes in loving words to their children and grandchildren.

The sharing and the defiance of these generous people, who lived by the act of giving to others! Christ's Cross could not seem anywhere near as passionate in its will as the heart of the most mean spirited of these Chamorros. Ted was overcome with shame and pride. Shame —that these were his kinsmen who committed these atrocities goaded by a tyrannical military dictatorship elevated to a spiritual cult that launched brutality to virtue and pride in a culture and political creed that helped make a man or woman choose the better path in living. America was flawed, still a psychological teenager, like these kids Thompson and Perner, but it will grow better and nobler than it ever dreamed, because America invited the generous instincts and softer impulses of people as its strengths.

' Hey, Doc, you ever slip the high hard one past Joan Blondell?'

'Judge, as a matter of fact I did . . .it was right after Crosby made *Mississippi* and he and I were . . .' This 'noble' exchange made the trip back to Asan go more quickly and without doubt helped to shape the American republic, in some small way, in years to come. These kids were not about to make women and old people and babes suffer in order to exercise control of power, or terror. Not this generation. They could take a punch and return in kind. Ted was proud of boys like Judge Perner and Ray Thompson; he saw how they reacted to the gummy wrinkled old woman laying beside the road out side of Manengon 'HOM GLA YO HEE SAHM! HOM GLA YO HEEE SAHM!' I'm glad you're here Sam! And Ray Thompson scooped her up as smelly and festering as she was and gave her a kiss and carried her to the camp, like she had been his Granny. Joan Blondell my ass. I'd tell them that I had sheeted Carole Lombard after that. What good boys. Ted was going to see Kara today and he vowed to never let her out of sight – come what may. He had never been happier in his life.

As the DUKW ground down to the beach area, Ted was awed with the build-up of American forces and especially the endless vista of ships in the bays and harbors of his home. An endless stream of vehicles - that trotted out into the surf and crossed the coral, or bounced from the gaping mouths of LSTs right onto the beaches. From the heights, the dentist and his two star-struck bodyguards witnessed the transformation of the isolated American postcard stop on the Clipper Orient run into strategic and tactical hub of this Pacific theater of war.

Ted had been on the receiving end of America's munitions in his role as blotter surgeon and dentist to the maimed Japanese soldiers and had cringed, shuddered and convulsed under the pounding of bombs and artillery shells, but nothing stunned him as this vision of raw corporate power – bulldozers leveled cliffs that had endured thousands of years of Typhoons and cities of Quonset huts and tents were swelling the landscape.

But, the panorama of naval vessels extending to the eastern horizon is what really bowled him over.

'My word, boys, in my wildest dreams I could never imagine such power. Have you boys seen this before?'

'Hell, Doc we were aboard ship in the middle of that for the better side of month and that is only what's here. You oughta see Eniwetok and Saipan and Guadalcanal. This ain't the half of it. It's only Guam. Doc. You got to get out more.'

Half a mile from the approaching amphibious truck carrying the sexy and soft Japanese boy that she had flirted with in the San Francisco oyster bar – God he was cute –skin like a teenage boy and muscled like a Colt and those eyes so coppery brown with flecks of green and thick black hair cut close and lips that knew how to break a girl's heart with a slight twist of self-irony that said 'I'll share what I have. I don't take too much stock in its worth but if you'll be interested -the store is yours.' Ted knew how to dress and picked out a look that belied his age and dropped him back a decade. No glitter or show or jewelry, but cloth that wrapped a package worth opening. From the moment Kara teased the oyster over her delicate and talented tongue she could not wait to invite this soft sexy man's own into her mouth and roll it around in its new home – for starters - and then – slowly work her delicate fingers up to the bone behind his right ear and gently pull that intelligent face and skull deeper to her own. For hours together in the quiet night's retreat to dawn, when the touch and caress awakened the balance of love, Kara had more than grounded the charge and current that would course their lives. Teasing and measuring his naked trunk and muscles with billows of her red hair and milky white flesh that would invite no other's matter to such intimacy. And when, time and experimentation had worked the magic of motion into the knotted chord of their beings in the discharge of their passion, no song or sound could match their mutual understandings but more and softer sweeps of their flesh would mange. They knew exactly what God had done in placing order to matter in that

Prime Motion. Teddy called it the billiard shot of God – let's see where this one goes. All of the force and management of the cue to cup and the rattle and snap and roll and drop of the ordered chaos of the stoke, finding satisfaction in going where the player intended – sometimes soft brush that clicked the motion to its home or the impact of a real crasher that punched its target in the patterned geometry of play. Lord!

This poor little beauty denied that soft force joined by sight, sound and smell – God Teddy's Pinaud Clubman Bay Rum and talcs – his scent – of the boy who could give Betty the same understanding of God's animal - joy and find its balance and company –by those idiotic brats and that monstrosity Otayama – Otis. God I hope he lives through this.

Betty had not smiled and by rote ate and slept and moved herself – functioned. Kara recalled how Shirley Gaskell had been raped by Turner Somerville the Yale boy producer at RKO and had gone on to make several short features and then went to bed - after months of showing the world that she could take – with a quart of Sunnybrook and a handful of sleeping pills. Somerville went to work for Paramount and married the grand daughter of Florado Helios Muybridge, whose father, Eadweard, invented movies for Leland Stanford and murdered his wife in a fit of jealousy – Old Floddie was nutty as they come. Maybe it's the movies that's a curse – that or a warning – hell, she's a baby – that's nuts.

Kara wrapped her arms around the beautiful girl, whose bruises and cuts were disappearing, as she stood staring at the vast show of might investing Guam. Kara nuzzled and petted the baby woman outside of their tent fixed by Marine Pioneers in the Cemetery outside of Agana. ' Eat your eggs, Honey?' the teenager nodded. 'Your Mommy is up at the hospital with your Daddy helping clean up some of the neighbors and she wanted me to make sure that you ate, baby. Tog is with his new pal Mike Quinlan of the 3rd Pioneers and wants to go into the construction business. Quinlan has a willing pawn in Tog's schemes to capture the Guam real estate market and Tog worships the man. My God, Quinlan has a head on him like a boulder in a Gene Autry movie. Talk to me.'

'About what?'

'Sweetie my friend was raped by a creep – one creeep - and she took pills and booze and died before she had a chance to live. Look Baby. What those bastards did to you was not your fault and not your choice and not your fight. It happened. Please, let me help you get it out. It is like a bug or a thorn and you need to pull it out before the poison gets deeper.'

'You don't know.'

'No I don't. But my friend did and she is not with me anymore and I needed her. We were not through yet. You are alive and that is the only thing that matters and what happened can't be undone.'

'Why didn't they do it to you? Why not Mommy . I'm ugly. Shit-nose."

'No baby you are as beautiful as God made you to be. This happened. That is all. It does not mean anything else *but* was *done to* you. These Marines will kill those bastards. We'll do this slow and I will be here to hold you sweetie all day all night and everyday.'

'You are *not* my Mom.'

'I am your Mommy's friend and your Daddy's friend and you mean more to me than time itself, Baby. From the second I laid eyes on you, you became mine too.' Kara petted the stunning girl's long black hair and watched her.

It was dicey. Betty was going to be a full time job but now, things would get better.

'*That* is the most gorgeous woman in size 12s, Boys!'

Teddy!

Flanked by two teenagers and wearing Marine utilities and a Raider cap in between two slack-jawed kids in helmets and slinging Garands was the oyster feeder. Kara bounced out of her heart! 'Where in hell have you been Mister? Did you two find this crumb near the Sumay hooker shops?' She shouted up to the approaching trio picking up their pace to the water's edge and two beautiful females.

'No Ma'am, he was hiding in the Agana geisha house!'

'Why *you crumb*, Perner. Do *you* know Bob Keegan?'

'Well, you just made my day sweetheart. Sit down and take a load off.' Kara brushed the man in the middle through his flankers and passionately kissed and coiled her long legs around the now weeping dentist.

Betty smiled. Not big – a start.

CHAPTER 55
GUAM SECURED & THE COLT
REVOLVER – THAT'S WAR

Col. Stuart's 3rd Marines with the Doggies of the 307th on their right were gaining about four miles of Guam a day. Now shifted to the Division's left flank with elements of the 1st Provisional Marine Brigade taking the east coast roads north shattered the Japanese at Finegayan and finally liberated a town – huts, pigs a chapel and gas station and plenty of desperate Japs. Guys from the 21st Marines discovered about 30 Chamorros mostly teenagers and old men, beheaded with their arms tied behind their backs. Everywhere the Marines found abused and terrified people – real boon dock dwellers and as unfamiliar with English as they were with Japanese. The Marines and G.I.s showered the people with boxes of rations and in turn the liberators were kissed and housemaided! Many people tried to follow the Marines up to the combat and needed to be gently but sternly kept back. At night Marines heard howling through the jungle and thought that some small animals were signaling their presence until they learned that they were Chamorro children in final stages of starvation.

Lt. Ames - over Sgt. Mike Joyce's strident 'Are you fuckin' nuts? Table of Organization, Sir!'- demanded to take point two miles past Finegayan and was decorated with a sniper round that made a clean hole through his forehead – he walked three paces before he fell over. Pat Collins killed the sniper.

Stanley Paul and little Onarga Roberts were killed at the road block defended by twenty Japanese soldiers and a light tank. Henry Clay killed the crew of the tank when he noticed that one of the hatches was opened slightly; tossed a white phosphorous grenade down into the turret. Henry was still talking to himself and his act of valor might have been an attempted suicide, but he was awarded the Bronze Star (V) and picked up a Purple Heart to boot because he had not closed the hatch and a white hot smoking fragment went into his left cheekbone. Never uttered a squeak. Maybe he was nuts.

Tim Cullen made great use of the Browning in this fire fight and damaged the barrel so badly that he needed to have the weapon surveyed with Sgt. Masterson and drew a new Browning when they were pulled off the line.

On August 10th, the 3rd Marines reached the northern shore of Guam and the 4th Marines of the 1st Brigade made Ritidian Point. General Bruce's 77th (MARINE) Division had conquered Mount Santa Rosa and Yiga in the northwest of the island and organized Japanese Operations ceased.

General Roy Geiger declared Guam secured. That was nice, true and all, but more than 10,000 armed Japanese needed to be flushed from the jungles of America's most important forward Base of Operations in the Pacific. A Company of 1st Battalion, 3rd Marines was relieved of duties and marched back to Agana. Chorito Cliff had been worth the sacrifice and now Tim Cullen could honor his debt. He needed to stay as public as possible. Though he genuinely liked Pat Collins now, Tim Cullen would use his nearness; not so much for companionship but to have some witness to whatever Major Opley planned in the way of getting the Chorito Hog Leg. Tim could not wait to have Regiment clerks prepare shipping manifests and Col. Stuart's signature and get rid of this fucking Colt! He marched south carrying the Browning now out of action and Lieutenant John A. Buck's Colt Revolver buttoned up under his utilities.

The long line of the A Company men passed their two brother Companies and the Headquarters Company of 1st Battalion and Major Lucas Opley. The Major caught Pfc. Cullen's stare and returned it in kind and but snapped a twitch when the BAR man patted the covered shoulder holster and Colt in an open act of defiance. 1st Battalion had work to do in the north and would be back in Agana and Third Division Camp in a day or two. This contest was far from over. Guam was secured but Lieutenant Buck's Colt was still on Guam. Opley would have it. Cullen would return it to Buck's family. Guam was secured, but 10,000 Japanese disagreed and would until 1972. That is war.

The End of Book I of *The Chorito Hog Leg*

ACKNOWLEDGMENTS: THE CHORITO HOG LEG

I thank the great people who operate the U.S. Nation Parks Service, U.S. Department of the Interior: War in the Pacific Park on Guam – this from their wonderful website:

War in the Pacific National Historical Park is located on the tropical island of Guam, approximately 13 degrees north of the equator and about 3,300 miles southwest of Hawaii. On Guam there is an embracing "hafa adai" attitude that welcomes visitors and makes the island a friendly travel destination and a unique place to live in the United States.

I especially wish to thank Ms. Tammy Duschene of the War in the Pacific Park who helped me in my study of the fascinating Guam Campaign and the more fascinating Chamorros of that beautiful and heroic American island. ALL PHOTOS USED IN THIS BOOK CAME FROM THE WAR IN THE PACIFIC SITE.

I wish to thank the men of Leo High School; particularly the Class of 1943 and especially, Mr. Richard F. Prendergast (USMCR); My father, Mr. Patrick Eugene Hickey (USMCR) a member of Able Company, 1ˢᵗ Battalion, Third Marines, Third Marine Division in World War II; Ms. Rose Keefe celebrated historian and biographer; Richard Lindberg, historian, journalist and patron; Dr. J. Sean Callan, M.D. biographer of James J. Shields; Eileen McMahon for her brilliant study of St. Sabina Parish in Chicago, *What Parish Are You From;* Mr. Kevin Baker, the best historical novelist in America, Mr. Larry Raeder, Chicago's best local historian and archivist; Chicago Fire Commissioner James T. Joyce, CFD (ret.); Mr. Robert W. Foster, President Leo High School and my great friend; Ms Rochelle Crump, Asst. Illinois Director of Veterans Affairs; Mr. Mike McQuade of San Francisco , CA Vietnam Veteran, Patriot and writer; Mr. Frank Nofsinger of Connecticut; the Late Brother Francis Rupert Finch, CFC; Brother John Stephan O'Keefe, CFC; Det. Martin J. Tully(Vietnam Green Beret Decorations too numerous to log), Chicago Police Department (ret.) and Det. William Higgins Chicago Police Department – the two best Homicide men in Chicago; Mr. Bernard Callaghan, County Armagh one of 'the best read' Irish scholars and union men; Virginia C. Hickey my mother, Joan Demateo, my sister and Kevin J. Hickey, my brother; my late wife Mary's family Alice and Chuck Holm and the late Patrick Cleary; Mike , Jim and Gail Cleary and my best friends in the world Charles E. Olson and cousin Willie J. Winters.

I wish to thank my children, Nora, Conor and Clare for putting up with their goofy father's noise at 4 AM – typing and cursing his stubby fingers. Honor the past, so that you may become honorable.

As yellow as a duck's foot and never having served my country in the military, my poor knowledge of the depth and height of commitment our women and men in the military give their country came from books and these wonderful internet website sources.

THE THIRD MARINE DIVISION, 1st Lt Robert A. Arthur USMCR and 1stLt Kenneth Cohlmia USMCR,

Infantry Journal Press, Washington DC, 1948. VG-. First Edition.

THIRD MARINE DIVISION'S: TWO SCORE AND TEN HISTORY Turner Editorial Staff NEW copy. Turner Publishing Company, 1992.

EDSON'S RAIDERS: THE 1ST MARINE RAIDER BATTALION IN WORLD WAR II, by Joseph H. Alexander Annapolis: Naval Institute Press, 2001.

SEMPER FIDELIS: THE HISTORY OF THE UNITED STATES MARINE CORPS by Allan Reed Millet Publisher: New York: Macmillan Pub. Co., ©1980.

THE LIBERATION OF GUAM, 21 JULY - 10 AUGUST 1944, by Harry Gailey Presidio, 1988. VG/VG. First Edition.

THE LONG AND THE SHORT AND THE TALL by Alvin M Josephy, Publisher: Short Hills, NJ: Buford Books, [2000].

THE RECAPTURE OF GUAM by Major O.R. Lodge, USMC. Battery Press, Nashville, 1991. Reprinted from the 1954 edition.

Of the entire internet sources concerning the Guam Campaign available, none was more important than Dr. Cyril O'Brien's reconstruction of the battle and aftermath on the Hyperwar website.

For the life of the average enlisted Marine, Mark Flowers' WWII Gyrene website was crucial.

Lastly, *Hafa Adai website* gives us, continental bound Americans a glimpse into the most loyal and loving American people and the rich soil that nurtured them – Guam

http://www.nps.gov/wapa/

http://www.bayonetstrength.150m.com/UnitedStates/united%20states%20marines%20F&G%20battalion.htm

http://www.nps.gov/archive/wapa/indepth/extContent/Lib/liberation26.htm

http://www.nps.gov/archive/wapa/indepth/extContent/usmc/pcn-190-003126-00/sec1.htm
http://www.ww2gyrene.org/index.htm
http://en.wikipedia.org/wiki/LST
http://www.uslst.org/
http://www.lstmemorial.org/
http://www.xlsite.com/lst660/basiclstinfo.htm
http://www.geocities.com/Pentagon/5791/WWII.html
http://www.geocities.com/nubiansong/montford.htm
http://www.network54.com/Forum/135069/viewall-page-77
http://www.au.af.mil/au/awc/awcgate/usmchist/3rdMar.txt
http://www.offisland.com/

ABOUT THE AUTHOR

Pat Hickey is proud to have been of some service to Leo High School for many years. As Development Director for Chicago's Leo High School, Hickey developed his first book and the main character of The Chorito Hog Leg, Books 1-2, Tim Cullen. A graduate of Loyola University of Chicago Undergraduate (Bachelor of Arts –English) and Graduate (Master of Arts – English) Schools, Pat Hickey has spent most of his life as a high school English teacher .

A native Chicagoan and a career educator, Hickey taught at Bishop McNamara High School, in Kankakee, IL and La Lumiere School, LaPorte, IN. In 1990, he began doing fundraising work which he continues at Leo High School. Hickey is a free-lance writer for GAR Media, Capitol Fax Blog and is a member of the Society of Professional Journalists. His first book Every Heart and Hand: A Leo High School Story has been a Chicago favorite.

In the Fall of 2007, the second book of The Chorito Hog Leg story will follow the adventures of Tim Cullen through the mopping-up actions on Guam, the Iwo Jima Campaign, the sinking of U.S.S. Indianapolis, the Atomic Bombings of Japan, the beginning of the War Crimes Trials on Guam and return Cullen, through the great Pacific Typhoon of 1945, to Chicago. Again, the author will employ the 'intrusive narrator' technique used by William Makepeace Thackeray in his 19th Century historical fictions.

Pat Hickey, widowed (Mary) in 1998, is the father of Nora, Conor and Clare Hickey. The Hickey's live in St. Cajetan's Parish in the Morgan Park neighborhood of Chicago.

Printed in the United States
81003LV00004B/49